I WILL
FIND YOU

Harlan Coben

I WILL FIND YOU

CENTURY

1 3 5 7 9 10 8 6 4 2

Century
20 Vauxhall Bridge Road
London SW1V 2SA

Century is part of the Penguin Random House group of companies
whose addresses can be found at global.penguinrandomhouse.com.

Copyright © Harlan Coben 2023

Harlan Coben has asserted his right to be identified as the author of this Work in
accordance with the Copyright, Designs and Patents Act 1988.

First published in the US by Grand Central Publishing in 2023
First published in the UK by Century in 2023

www.penguin.co.uk

A CIP catalogue record for this book is available from the British Library.

ISBN 978-1-529-13550-3 (hardback)
ISBN 978-1-529-13551-0 (trade paperback)

Typeset in 12.25/17.5 pt Fairfield LT Std by Jouve (UK), Milton Keynes
Printed and bound in Great Britain by Clays Ltd, Elcograf S.p.A.

The authorised representative in the EEA is Penguin Random House Ireland,
Morrison Chambers, 32 Nassau Street, Dublin D02 YH68

For
my nephews and nieces
Thomas, Katharine, McCallum, Reilly, Dovey,
Alek, Genevieve, Maja,
Allana, Ana, Mary, Mei,
Sam, Caleb, Finn,
Annie, Ruby, Delia,
Henry, and Molly

With love,
Uncle Harlan

I WILL
FIND YOU

PART 1

1

I am serving the fifth year of a life sentence for murdering my own child.

Spoiler alert: I didn't do it.

My son Matthew was three years old at the time of his brutal murder. He was the best thing in my life, and then he was gone, and I've been serving a life sentence ever since. Not metaphorically. Or should I say, not *just* metaphorically. This would be a life sentence no matter what, even if I hadn't been arrested and tried and convicted.

But in my case, in *this* case, my life sentence is both metaphorical and literal.

How, you wonder, can I possibly be innocent?

I just am.

But didn't I fight and protest my innocence with every fiber of my being?

No, not really. This goes back, I guess, to the metaphorical sentence. I didn't really care that much about being found guilty. I know that sounds shocking, but it's not. My son is dead. That's the lede here. That's the lede and the headline and the all-caps. My son is dead and gone, and that fact would not have changed had the jury forewoman declared me guilty or not guilty. Guilty or not guilty, I had failed my son. Either way. Matthew wouldn't be less dead had the jury been able to see the truth and free me. A father's job is to protect his son. That's his number-one priority. So even if I didn't wield the weapon that smashed my son's beautiful being into the mangled mess I found on that awful night five years ago, I didn't stop it either. I didn't do my job as his father. I didn't protect him.

Guilty or not guilty of the actual murder, it is my fault and thus my sentence to serve.

So I barely reacted when the jury forewoman read the verdict. Observers concluded, of course, that I must be sociopathic or psychopathic or deranged or damaged. I couldn't *feel*, the media claimed. I lacked an empathy gene, I couldn't experience remorse, I had dead eyes, whatever other terminology would land me in the killer camp. None of that was true. I just didn't see the point. I had been on the receiving end of a devastating blow when I found my son, Matthew, in his Marvel-Hero-themed pajamas that night. That blow had knocked me to my knees, and I couldn't get up. Not then. Not now. Not ever.

The metaphorical life sentence had begun.

If you think this will be a tale about a wronged man proving his innocence, it is not. Because that would not be much of a story. In the end, it would make no difference. Being released from this hellhole of a cell would not lead to redemption. My son would still be dead.

Redemption isn't possible in this case.

Or at least, that was what I believed right up until the moment that the guard, a particularly eccentric case we call Curly, comes to my cell and says, "Visitor."

I don't move because I don't think he is talking to me. I have been here for almost five years, and I have had no visitors in all that time. During the first year, my father tried to visit. So had Aunt Sophie and a handful of close friends and relatives who believed me innocent or at least not *really* guilty. I wouldn't let them in. Matthew's mother, Cheryl, my then-wife (she is now, not surprisingly, my *ex*-wife) had tried too, albeit half-heartedly, but I wouldn't let her see me. I made it clear: No visitors. I was not being self-pitying or any kind of pitying. Visiting helps neither the visitor nor the *visitee*. I didn't and don't see the point.

A year passed. Then two. Then everyone stopped trying to visit. Not that anyone, other than maybe Adam, had been clamoring to make the schlep up to Maine, but you get my point. Now, for the first time in a long time, someone is here at Briggs Penitentiary to see me.

"Burroughs," Curly snaps, "let's go. You have a visitor."

I make a face. "Who?"

"Do I look like your social secretary?"

"Good one."

"What?"

5

"The social-secretary line. It was very funny."

"Are you being a wiseass with me?"

"I have no interest in visitors," I tell him. "Please send them away."

Curly sighs. "Burroughs."

"What?"

"Get your ass up. You didn't fill out the forms."

"What forms?"

"There are forms to fill out," Curly says, "if you don't want visitors."

"I thought people had to be on my guest list."

"Guest list," Curly repeated with a shake of his head. "This look like a hotel to you?"

"Hotels have guest lists?" I counter. "Either way, I did fill out something that I don't want any visitors."

"When you first got here."

"Right."

Curly sighs again. "You got to renew that every year."

"What?"

"Did you fill out a form this year saying you wanted no visitors?"

"No."

Curly spread his hands. "There you go. Now get up."

"Can't you just tell the visitor to go home?"

"No, Burroughs, I can't, and I'll tell you why. That would be more work for me than dragging your ass down to Visitors. See, if I do that, I'll have to explain why you're not there and your visitor might ask me questions and then I'll probably have to fill out a form myself and I hate that and then you'll have to fill out a form and I'll have to walk back and forth and, look, I don't need the hassle, you don't need the hassle. So here's what'll happen: You'll go with me now and you can just sit there and say nothing for all I care and then you can fill out the correct forms and neither of us will have to go through this again. Do you feel me?"

I have been here long enough to know that too much resistance is not only futile but harmful. I am also, truth be told, curious. "I feel you," I say.

"Cool. Let's go."

I know the drill, of course. I let Curly put on the handcuffs, followed by the belly chain so that my hands can be shackled to my waist. He skips the leg cuffs, mostly because they are a pain to get on and off. The walk is fairly long from the PC (protective custody, for those not in the know) unit of Briggs Penitentiary to the visiting area. Eighteen of us are currently housed in PC—seven child molesters, four rapists, two cannibal serial killers, two "regular" serial killers, two cop killers, and of course, one filicidal maniac (yours truly). Quite the coterie.

Curly gives me a hard glare, which is unusual. Most of the guards are bored cop wannabees and/or muscleheads who look upon us inmates with staggering apathy. I want to ask him what gives, but I know when to keep quiet. You learn that in here. I feel my legs quake a bit as I walk. I'm oddly nervous. The truth is, I've settled in here. It's awful—worse than you imagine—but still I've grown accustomed to this particular brand of awful. This visitor, whoever it is after all the time, is here to deliver rock-my-world news.

I don't welcome that.

I flash back to the blood from that night. I think about the blood a lot. I dream about it too. I don't know how often. In the beginning, it was every night. Now I would say it's more a once-a-week thing, but I don't keep track. Time doesn't pass normally in prison. It stops and starts and sputters and zig-zags. I remember blinking myself awake in the bed I shared with my wife Cheryl that night. I didn't check a clock, but for those keeping score at home, it was four in the morning. The house was silent, still, and yet somehow I sensed something was wrong. Or maybe that is what I believe—incorrectly—now. Memory is often our most imaginative storyteller. So maybe, probably, I didn't "sense" anything at all. I don't know anymore. It's not like I bolted upright in my bed and leapt to my feet. It took time for me to get up. I stayed in my bed for several minutes, my brain stuck in that weird cusp between sleep and awake, floating ever upward toward consciousness.

At some point, I did finally sit up. I started down the corridor to Matthew's room.

And that was when I noticed the blood.

It was redder than I imagined—fresh, bright Crayola-crayon red, garish and mocking as a clown's lipstick against the white sheet.

Panic gripped me then. I called out Matthew's name. I clumsily ran to his room, bumping hard into the doorframe.

I called out his name again. No answer. I ran into his bedroom and found . . . something unrecognizable.

I'm told I started screaming.

That was how the police found me. Still screaming. The screams became shards of glass careening through every part of me. I stopped screaming at some point, I guess. I don't remember that either. Maybe my vocal cords snapped, I don't know. But the echo of those screams has never left me. Those shards still rip and shred and maul.

"Hurry up, Burroughs," Curly says. "She's waiting for you."

She.

He'd said "she." For a moment I imagine that it is Cheryl, and my heart picks up a beat. But no, she won't come, and I wouldn't want her to. We were married for eight years. Happily, I thought, for most of them. It hadn't been so good at the end. New stresses had formed cracks, and the cracks were turning into fissures. Would Cheryl and I have made it? I don't know. I sometimes think Matthew would have made us work harder, that he would have kept us together, but that sounds a lot like wishful thinking.

Not long after my conviction, I signed some paperwork granting her a divorce. We never spoke again. That was more my choice than hers. So that's all I know of her life. I have no idea where Cheryl is now, if she's still wounded and in mourning or if she's managed to make a new life for herself. I think it's best that I don't know.

Why didn't I pay more attention to Matthew that night?

I'm not saying I was a bad father. I don't think I was. But

that night, I simply wasn't in the mood. Three-year-olds can be tough. And boring. We all know this. Parents try to pretend that every moment with their child is bliss. It's not. Or at least that's what I thought that night. I didn't read a bedtime story to Matthew because I just couldn't be bothered. Awful, right? I just sent my child to bed because I was distracted by my own meaningless issues and insecurities. Stupid. So stupid. We are all so luxuriously stupid when things are good in our life.

Cheryl, who had just finished her residency in general surgery, had a night shift in the transplant ward at Boston General. I was alone with Matthew. I started drinking. I'm not a big drinker and don't handle spirits well, but in the past few months, with the strain on Cheryl and my marriage, I had found some, if not comfort, numbness there. So I partook and I guess the drinks hit me hard and fast. In short, I drank too much and passed out, so instead of watching my child, instead of protecting my son, instead of making sure the doors were locked (they weren't) or listening for an intruder or heck, instead of hearing a child scream in terror and/or agony, I was in a state the prosecutor at the trail mockingly called "snooze from booze."

I don't remember anything else until, of course, that smell.

I know what you're thinking: Maybe he (meaning "I") did do it. After all, the evidence against me was pretty overwhelming. I get that. It's fair. I sometimes wonder about that too. You'd have to be truly blind or delusional not to consider that possibility, so let me tell you a quick story that I think relates to this: I once kicked Cheryl hard while we slept. I'd been having a nightmare that a giant raccoon was attacking our little dog, Laszlo, so in a sleep panic, I kicked the raccoon as hard as I could and ended up kicking Cheryl in the shin. It was oddly funny in hindsight, watching Cheryl try to keep a straight face as I defended my actions (*"Would you have wanted me to let Laszlo get eaten by a raccoon?"*), but my wonderful surgeon wife, a woman who loved Laszlo and all dogs, still seethed.

"Maybe," Cheryl said to me, "subconsciously, you wanted to hurt me."

She said that with a smile, so I didn't think she meant it. But maybe she did. We forgot about it immediately and had a great day together. But I think about that a lot now. I was asleep and dreaming that night too. One kick isn't a murder, but who knows, right? The murder weapon was a baseball bat. Mrs. Winslow, who had lived in the house behind our woods for forty years, saw me bury it. That was the kicker, though I wondered about that, about me being stupid enough to bury it so close to the scene, what with my fingerprints all over it. I wonder about a lot of things like that. For example, I had fallen asleep after a drink or two too many once or twice before—who hasn't?—but never like this. Perhaps I'd been drugged, but by the time I was a viable suspect, it was too late to test for that. The local police, many of whom revered my father, were supportive at first. They looked into some bad people he'd put away, but that never felt right, not even to me. Dad had made enemies, sure, but that was a long time ago. Why would any of them kill a three-year-old boy for that kind of revenge? It didn't add up. There were no signs of sexual assault or any other motive either, so really, when you add it all up, there was only one true viable suspect.

Me.

So maybe something like my raccoon-kick dream happened here. It's not impossible. My attorney, Tom Florio, wanted to make an argument like that. My family, some of them anyway, believed that I should take that route too. Diminished capacity or some such defense. I had a history of sleepwalking and some of what could have been described as mental health issues, if you pushed the definition. I could use that, they reminded me.

But nah, I wouldn't confess because, despite these rationales, I didn't do it. I didn't kill my son. I know I didn't. I *know*. And yes, I *know* every perp says that.

Curly and I make the final turn. Briggs Penitentiary is done up in Early American Asphalt. Everything was a washed-out gray, a faded road after a rainstorm. I had gone from a three-bedroom, two-and-a-half-bath Colonial, splashed in sunshine yellow with green shutters, decorated in earth tones and pine antiques, nicely situated on a three-quarter-acre lot in a cul-de-sac, to this. Doesn't matter. Surroundings are irrelevant. Exteriors, you learn, are temporal and illusionary and thus meaningless.

There is a buzzing sound, and then Curly opens the door. Many prisons have updated visiting areas. Lower-risk inmates can sit at a table with their visitor or visitors with no partitions or barriers. I cannot. Here at Briggs we still have the bulletproof plexiglass. I sit on a metal stool bolted into the floor. My belly chain is loosened so that I can grab hold of the telephone. That is how visitors in the supermax communicate—via telephone and plexiglass.

The visitor isn't my ex-wife Cheryl, though she looks like Cheryl.

It's her sister, Rachel.

Rachel sits on the other side of the plexiglass, but I see her eyes widen when she takes me in. I almost smile at her reaction. I, her once beloved brother-in-law, the man with the offbeat sense of humor and the devil-may-care smile, have certainly changed in the past five years. I wonder what she notices first. The weight loss perhaps. Or more likely, the shattered facial bones that had not healed properly. It could be my ashen complexion, the slump from the once-athletic shoulders, the thinning and graying of my hair.

I sit down and peer at her through the plexiglass. I take hold of the phone and gesture that she should do the same. When Rachel lifts the phone to her ear, I speak.

"Why are you here?"

Rachel almost manages a smile. We were always close, Rachel and I. I liked spending time with her. She liked spending time with me. "Not much on pleasantries, I see."

"Are you here to exchange pleasantries, Rachel?"

Whatever hint of a smile there was fades away. She shakes her head. "No."

I wait. Rachel looks worn yet still beautiful. Her hair was still the same ash blonde as Cheryl's, her eyes the same dark green. I shift on my stool and face her at an angle because it hurts to look directly at her.

Rachel blinks back tears and shakes her head. "This is too crazy."

She lowers her gaze and for a moment I see the eighteen-year-old girl I'd met when Cheryl first brought me to her New Jersey home from Amherst College during our junior year. Cheryl and Rachel's parents hadn't really approved of me. I was a little blue-collar for them, what with the beat-cop father and row-house upbringing. Rachel, on the other hand, had taken to me right away, and I grew to love her as the closest thing I would have to a little sister. I cared about her. I felt protective of her. A year later, I drove her up and helped her move in at Lemhall University as an undergrad and later to Columbia University, where she studied journalism.

"It's been a long time," Rachel says.

I nod. I want her to go away. It hurts to look at her. I wait. She doesn't speak. I finally say something because Rachel looks like she needs a lifeline and so I can't help myself.

"How's Sam?" I ask.

"Fine," Rachel says. "He works for Merton Pharmaceuticals now. In sales. He made manager, travels a lot." Then she shrugs and adds, "We're divorced."

"Oh," I say. "I'm sorry."

She shakes that off. I'm not really sorry to hear it. I never thought Sam was good enough for her, but I felt that way about most of her boyfriends.

"Are you still writing for the *Globe*?" I ask.

"No," she says in a voice that slams the door on that subject. We sit in silence for a few more seconds. Then I try again.

"Is this about Cheryl?"

"No. Not really."

I swallow. "How is she?"

Rachel starts wringing her hands. She looks everywhere but at me. "She's remarried."

The words hit me like a gut punch, but I take it without so much as flinching. This, I think to myself. This is why I don't want visitors.

"She never blamed you, you know. None of us did."

"Rachel?"

"What?"

"Why the hell are you here?"

We fall back into silence. Behind her, I see another guard, one I don't know, staring at us. There are three other inmates in here right now. I don't know any of them. Briggs is a big place, and I try to keep to myself. I am tempted to stand up and leave, when Rachel finally speaks.

"Sam has a friend," she says.

I wait.

"Not really a friend. A co-worker. He's on the marketing side. In management too. At Merton Pharmaceuticals. His name is Tom Longley. He has a wife and two boys. Nice family. We used to get together sometimes. For company barbecues, stuff like that. His wife's name is Irene. I like her. Irene is pretty funny."

Rachel stops and shakes her head.

"I'm not telling this right."

"No, no," I say. "It's a great story so far."

Rachel smiles, actually smiles, at my sarcasm. "A hint of the old David," she says.

We go quiet again. When Rachel starts speaking, her words come out slower, more measured.

"The Longleys went on a company trip two months ago to an amusement park in Springfield. Six Flags, I think it's called. Took their two boys. Irene and I have stayed friends, so she invited me over to lunch the other day. She talked about the trip—a little gossipy because I guess Sam brought his new girlfriend. Like I'd care. But that's not important."

I bite back the sarcastic rejoinder and look at her. She holds my gaze.

"And then Irene showed me a bunch of photos."

Rachel stops here. I don't have the slightest idea where she is going with this, but I can almost hear some kind of foreboding soundtrack in my head. Rachel takes out a manila envelope. Eight-by-ten size, I guess. She puts it down on the ledge in front of her. She stares at it a beat too long, as though debating her next step. Then in one fell swoop she reaches into the envelope, plucks something out, and presses it against the glass.

It is, as advertised, a photo.

I don't know what to make of it. The photograph does indeed appear to have been taken at an amusement park. A woman—I wonder whether this is pretty-funny Irene— smiles shyly at the camera. Two boys, probably the Longleys, are on either hip, neither looking at the camera. Someone in a Bugs Bunny costume is on the right; someone dressed like Batman is on the left. Irene looks a little put out—but in a fun way. I can almost imagine the scene. Good ol' Pharmaceutical Marketing Tom cheerily goading Pretty-Funny Irene to pose, Pretty-Funny Irene not really in the mood but being a good sport, the two boys having none of it, we've all been there. There is a giant red roller coaster in the background. The sun is shining in the faces of the Longley family, which explains why they are squinting and slightly turning away.

Rachel has her eyes on me.

I lift my eyes toward hers. She keeps pressing the photograph up to the glass.

"Look closer, David."

I stare at her another second or two and then I let my gaze wander back to the photograph. This time I see it immediately. A steel claw reaches into my chest and squeezes my heart. I can't breathe.

There is a boy.

He is in the background, on the right edge of the frame, almost out of the picture. His face is in perfect profile, like he's posing to be on a coin. The boy appears to be about eight years old. Someone, an adult male perhaps, holds the boy's hand. The boy looks up at what I assume is the back of the man, but the man is out of frame.

I feel the tears push into my eyes and reach out with tentative fingers. I caress the boy's image through the glass. It is impossible, of course. A desperate man sees what he wants to see, and let's face it—no thirsty, heat-crazed, starved desert-dweller who ever conjured up a mirage has ever been this desperate. Matthew had not yet reached the age of three when he was murdered. No one, not even a loving parent, could guess what he would look like some five years later. Not for certain. There is a resemblance, that's all. The boy looks like Matthew. Looks like. It's a resemblance. Nothing more. A resemblance.

A sob rips through me. I put my fist into my mouth and bite down. It takes a few seconds before I am able to speak. When I do, my words are simple.

"It's Matthew."

2

Rachel keeps the photograph pressed against the plexiglass. "You know that's not possible," she says.

I don't reply.

"It looks like Matthew," Rachel says, her voice a forced monotone. "I'll admit it looks like him. A lot like him. But Matthew was a toddler when he . . ." She stops, gathers herself, starts again. "And even if you judge by the port stain on his cheek—this one is smaller than Matthew's."

"It's supposed to be," I say.

The medical term for the enormous port-stain birthmark that had cloaked the right side of my son's face was congenital hemangioma. The boy in the photograph had one too—smaller, more faded in hue, but pretty much on the exact spot.

"The doctors said that would happen," I continue. "Eventually it goes away entirely."

Rachel shakes her head. "David, we both know this can't be."

I don't reply.

"It's just a bizarre coincidence. A strong resemblance with the desire to see what we want—what we *need*—to see. And don't forget the forensics and DNA—"

"Stop," I say.

"What?"

"You didn't bring it to me because you thought it just looked like Matthew."

Rachel squeezes her eyes shut. "I went to a tech guy I know who works for the Boston PD. I gave him an old photo of Matthew."

"Which photo?"

"He's wearing the Amherst sweatshirt."

I nod. Cheryl and I had bought it for him during our tenth reunion. We had used that photo for our Christmas card.

"Anyway, this tech guy has age-progression software. The most up-to-date kind. The cops use it for missing people. I asked him to age the boy in the photo up five years and . . ."

"It matched," I finish for her.

"Close enough. It isn't conclusive. You get that, right? Even my friend said that—and he doesn't know why I was asking. Just so you know. I haven't told anyone about this."

That surprises me. "You didn't show this picture to Cheryl?"

"No."

"Why not?"

Rachel squirms on the uncomfortable stool. "It's crazy, David."

"What is?"

"This whole thing. It can't be Matthew. We are both letting our want cloud our judgment."

"Rachel," I say.

She meets my eye.

"Why didn't you show this to your sister?" I press.

Rachel twists the rings on her fingers. Her eyes leave mine, dart about the room like startled birds, settle back down. "You have to understand," she says. "Cheryl is trying to move on. She's trying to put this all behind her."

I can feel my heart going *thump-thump* in my chest.

"If I tell her, it'll be like ripping her life out by the roots again. That kind of false hope—it would devastate her."

"Yet you're telling me."

"Because you have nothing, David. If I rip your life out by the roots, so what? You have no life. You gave up living a long time ago."

Her words may sound harsh, but there is no anger or menace in the tone. She is right, of course. It's a fair observation. I have nothing to lose here. If we are wrong about this photograph—and when I try to be objective, I realize that the odds are pretty strong that we are wrong—it will change nothing for me. I will still be in this place, eroding and decaying with no desire to slow that process down.

"She remarried," Rachel says.

"So you said."

"And she's pregnant."

Straight left jab to the chin followed by a powerful blindside right hook. I stagger back and take the eight-count.

"I wasn't going to tell you—" Rachel says.

"It's fine—"

"—and if we try to do something with this—"

"I get it," I say.

"Good, because I don't know what to do," Rachel says. "It's not like this is evidence that would convince a reasonable person. Unless you want me to try that. I mean, I could take it to an attorney or the police."

"They'd laugh you out of the room."

"Right. We could go to the press maybe."

"No."

"Or . . . or Cheryl. If you think that's right. Maybe we can get permission to exhume the body. A new autopsy or DNA test could prove it one way or another. You'd get a new trial maybe—"

"No."

"What, why?"

"Not yet anyway," I say. "We can't let anyone know."

Rachel looks confused. "I don't understand."

"You're a journalist."

"So?"

"So you know," I say. I lean in a little. "If this gets out, it will be a big news story. The press will be all over us again."

"Us? Or do you mean you?"

For the first time, I hear an edge in her voice. I wait. She's wrong. She will get that in a moment. When Matthew was first found, the media coverage was kind and sympathetic. They played up the whole human tragedy angle, ladling it with fear that the killer was still out there so you, dear public, must remain wary. Social media wasn't quite so enamored. *"It's a family member,"* an early tweeter stated. *"Dollars to donuts, it's the loser stay-at-home father,"* another, who received many likes, claimed. *"Probably pissed off by his wife's success."* And so it went.

When no one was arrested—when the story started to die down—the media got frustrated and impatient. Pundits started to wonder how I could have slept through the carnage. Then the small leaks began to turn into a pour: The murder weapon, a baseball bat that I had purchased four years earlier, had been unearthed near our home. A witness, our neighbor Mrs. Winslow, claimed to have seen me bury it the night of the murder. Forensics confirmed that my fingerprints and only my fingerprints were on the bat.

The media loved this new angle, mostly because it gave a dying story new life and thus eyeballs. They swarmed in. A psychiatrist who had treated me in the past leaked my history of night terrors and sleepwalking. Cheryl and I had been having serious marital issues. She may have been having an affair. You get the picture. Editorials demanded that I be arrested and prosecuted. I was getting preferential treatment, they said, because my father was a cop. What else had been covered up? If I weren't a white man, I'd be behind bars already. This was racism, this was privilege, there was clearly a double standard at work.

A lot of that was probably true.

"Do you think I care about bad press?" I ask her.

"No," she says softly. "But I don't understand. What harm can the press do us now?"

"They'll report it."

"Yeah, I get that. So?"

Her eyes latch onto mine. "Everyone will hear about it," I say. "Including"—I point now to the adult hand wrapped around Matthew's in the photograph—"this guy."

Silence.

I wait for her to say something. When she doesn't, I say, "Don't you see? If he finds out, if he knows we're onto him or whatever, who knows how he'll react? Maybe he'll run away. Go underground so that we never find him. Or maybe he will figure that he can't risk it. He thought he was in the clear and now he's not and so maybe this time he gets rid of the evidence for good."

"But the police," Rachel says. "They can investigate quietly."

"No way. It'll leak. And they won't take it seriously anyway. Not with just this photo. You know this."

Rachel shakes her head. "So what do you want to do?"

"You're a respected investigative journalist," I say.

"Not anymore."

"Why, what happened?"

She shakes her head again. "It's a long story."

"We have to find out more," I say.

"We?"

I nod. "I have to get out of here."

"What the hell are you talking about?"

She looks at me with concern. I get that. I can hear it in my tone too. Some of the old timbre is back. When Matthew was murdered, I crawled up into a fetal ball and waited to die. My son was dead. Nothing else mattered.

But now . . .

The buzzer sounds. Guards step into the room. Curly puts his hand on my shoulder.

"Time's up."

Rachel quickly slides the photograph back into the manila envelope. I feel a longing when she does, a thirst to keep staring at the photograph, a fear that it was all an apparition, and now that I couldn't see it, even for a few seconds, it all felt wispy, as though I were trying to hold on to smoke. I try to sear the image of my boy into my brain, but his face is already beginning to ebb away, like the final vision of a dream.

Rachel stands. "I'm staying at the motor lodge down the road."

I nod.

"I'll be back tomorrow."

I manage another nod.

"And for what it's worth, I think it's him too."

I open my mouth to thank her, but the words won't come out. It doesn't matter. She turns and leaves. Curly gives my shoulder a squeeze.

"What was all that about?" he asks me.

"Tell the warden I want to see him," I say.

Curly smiles with teeth that resemble small mints. "The warden doesn't see prisoners."

I stand. I meet his eye. And for the first time in years, I smile. I really smile. The sight makes Curly take a step back.

"He'll see me," I say. "Tell him."

3

"What do you want, David?"

Warden Philip Mackenzie does not appear pleased by my visit. His office is institutionally sparse. There is an American flag on a pole in one corner along with a photograph of the current governor. His desk is gray and metal and functional and reminds me of the ones my teachers had when I was in elementary school. A brass pen-pencil-clock set you'd find in the gift area at TJ Maxx sits off to the right. Two tall matching gray metal file cabinets stand behind him like watchtowers.

"Well?"

I have rehearsed what I would say, but I don't stick to the script. I try to keep my voice even, flat, monotone, professional even. My words would, I know, sound crazy, so I need my tone to do the opposite. To his credit, the warden sits back and listens, and for a little while he does not look too stunned. When I finish speaking, he leans back and looks off. He takes a few deep breaths. Philip Mackenzie is north of seventy years old, but he still looks powerful enough to raze one of those steel-reinforced concrete walls that surround this place. His chest is burly, his bald head jammed between two bowling-ball shoulders with no apparent need for a neck. His hands are huge and gnarled. They sit on his desk now like two battering rams.

He finally turns toward me with weathered blue eyes capped by bushy white eyebrows.

"You can't be serious," he says.

I sit up straight. "It's Matthew."

He dismisses my words with a wave of a giant hand. "Ah, come off it, David. What are you trying to pull here?"

I just stare at him.

"You're looking for a way out. Every inmate is."

"You think this is some ploy to get released?" I struggle to keep my voice from breaking. "You think I give a rat's ass if I ever get out of this hellhole?"

Philip Mackenzie sighs and shakes his head.

"Philip," I say, "my son is out there somewhere."

"Your son is dead."

"No."

"You killed him."

"No. I can show you the photograph."

"The one your sister-in-law brought you?"

"Yes."

"Okay, sure. I'm supposed to know that some boy in the background is your son Matthew who died when he was, what, three?"

I say nothing.

"And let's say, I don't know, that I did. I can't. I mean, it's impossible, even you admit that. But let's say it's somehow the spitting image of Matthew. You said Rachel checked it with age-progression technology, right?"

"Right."

"So how do you know she didn't just photoshop his age-progressed face into the picture?"

"What?"

"Do you know how easy it is to doctor photographs?"

"You're kidding, right?" I frown. "Why would she do that?"

Philip Mackenzie stopped. "Wait. Of course."

"What?"

"You don't know what happened to Rachel."

"What are you talking about?"

"Her career as a journalist. It's over."

I say nothing.

"You didn't know that, did you?"

"It doesn't matter," I say. But of course, it does. I lean forward and pin the man I've known my whole life as Uncle Philip with my eyes. "I've been in here for five years now," I say in my most measured tone. "How many times have I come to you for help?"

"Zero," he says. "But that doesn't mean I haven't given it to you. You think it's a coincidence that you ended up in *my* prison? Or that you got so much extra time in the isolation wing? They wanted you back in regular population, even after that beating."

It was three weeks after the start of my incarceration. I was in general pop, not here in the isolation wing. Four men whose bulk was only outsized by their depravity cornered me in the shower. The shower. Oldest trick in the book. No rape. Nothing sexual. They just wanted to beat the hell out of someone to feel some sort of primitive high—and who better than prison's new celebrity baby-killer? They broke my nose. They shattered my cheekbone. My cracked jaw flapped like a door missing a hinge. Four broken ribs. A concussion. Internal bleeding. My right eye only sees fuzzy images now.

I spent two months in the infirmary.

I pull the ace out of my deck. "You owe me, Philip."

"Correction: I owe your father."

"Same thing now."

"You think his marker passes down to his son?"

"What would Dad say?"

Philip Mackenzie looks pained and suddenly weary.

"I didn't kill Matthew," I say.

"An inmate telling me he's innocent," he says with an almost amused shake of the head. "This has to be a first."

Philip Mackenzie rises from his chair and turns toward the window. He looks out into the woods past the fence. "When your father first heard about Matthew . . . and even worse, when he found out you were arrested . . ." His voice trails off. "Tell me, David. Why didn't you plead temporary insanity?"

"You think I was interested in finding a legal loophole?"

"It wasn't a loophole," Philip says, and I hear sympathy in his tone now. He turns back to me. "You blacked out.

Something inside of you snapped. There had to be an explanation. We would have all stuck by you."

My head begins to throb—another product of that beating, or perhaps his words are the cause. I close my eyes and draw a deep breath. "Please listen to me. It wasn't Matthew. And whatever happened, I didn't do it."

"You were set up, huh?"

"I don't know."

"So whose body did you find?"

"I don't know."

"How do you explain your fingerprints on the weapon?"

"It was my bat. I kept it in the garage."

"And what about that old lady who saw you burying it?"

"I don't know. I only know what I saw in the photograph."

The older man sighs again. "Do you realize how delusional you sound?"

I stand now too. To my surprise, Philip takes a step back as though he's afraid of me. "You have to get me out of here," I whisper. "For a few days anyway."

"Are you out of your mind?"

"Get me a bereavement leave or something."

"We don't offer those to your class of felon. You know that."

"Then find a way to help me break out."

He laughs at that. "Oh sure, no problem. And let's say hypothetically I could do that, they'll come after you with everything they got. Brutally. You're a baby-killer, David. They'll gun you down without a second thought."

"Not your problem."

"Like hell it's not."

"Suppose this happened to you," I say.

"What?"

"Suppose you were in my place. Suppose the murdered boy was Adam. What would you do to find him?"

Philip Mackenzie shakes his head and collapses back into his chair. He puts both hands on his face and rubs vigorously. Then he hits the intercom and calls for a guard.

"Goodbye, David."

"Please, Philip."

"I'm sorry. I really am."

————

Philip Mackenzie diverted his gaze so he wouldn't see his correctional officer enter and escort David out. He didn't say goodbye to his godson. After he left, Philip sat in his office alone. The air felt heavy around him. He had hoped that David's request to see him—the first one David had made in the nearly five years he'd been incarcerated here—would be some sort of positive sign. Perhaps David finally wanted to get help from a mental health professional. Perhaps David wanted to take a deeper dive into what he'd done that awful night or at the very least, try to scratch out some kind of productive life, even here, even after what he'd done.

Philip opened his desk drawer and took out a photograph from 1973 of two men—correction: dumb kids—decked out in military fatigues in Khe San. Philip Mackenzie and Lenny

Burroughs, David's father. They'd both gone to Revere High School before being drafted. Philip grew up on the top floor of a three-family row house on Centennial Avenue. Lenny lived a block away on Dehon Street. Best friends. War buddies. Cops patrolling Revere Beach. Philip had stood as David's godfather. Lenny had been Philip's son Adam's. Adam and David had gone to school together. The two had been best friends at Revere High School. The cycle had started anew.

Philip stared at the image of his old friend. Lenny was lying on his deathbed now. There was nothing anyone could do to help him. It was just a matter of time. The Lenny in the old photo was smiling that Lenny Burroughs smile, the one that made hearts melt, but his eyes seemed to bore right now into Philip's.

"Nothing I can do, Lenny," he said out loud.

The photo Lenny just smiled and stared.

Philip took a few deep breaths. It was getting late. His office would be closing soon. He reached out and hit the intercom button on his desk again.

His receptionist said, "Yes, Warden?"

"Get me on the first flight to Boston in the morning."

4

There is never silence in a prison.

My "experimental" wing is circular with eighteen individual cells on the perimeter. The entrance still has old-school see-through bars. In one of the oddest moves, the stainless-steel toilet and sink—yes, they are combined into one—are right by the bars. Our cells, unlike general pop, each have a small private shower in the back corner. The guards have shutoff valves if you take too long. There is a poured-concrete bed with a mattress so thin it's almost transparent. Handles are built into the bed's corners for attaching four-point restraints. So far, that has not been necessary for me. There is also a poured-concrete desk and poured-concrete stool. I have a television and a radio that only broadcast religious or educational programming. A single narrow window slot is angled up, so I can only teasingly see the sky.

I lay on said concrete bed and stare up at the ceiling. I know this ceiling intimately. I close my eyes and try to sort through the facts. I go through the day again—*that* horrible day—and search for something I may have missed. I had taken Matthew out, first to the local playground by a duck pond and then to the supermarket on Oak Street. Had I noticed anybody suspicious at either? I hadn't, of course, but I reach back now and comb my memory for new details. None are forthcoming. You'd think I would remember this day better, that every moment would still be vivid in my mind, but it all grows fuzzier day by day.

I had sat on a playground bench next to a young mother with an aggressively progressive baby stroller. The young mother had a daughter Matthew's age. Had she told me her child's name? Probably, but I don't remember. She wore yoga clothing. What had we talked about? I don't remember. What exactly am I searching for here? I don't know that either. The owner of that hand, I guess—the adult man's hand holding Matthew's in Rachel's photograph. Had he been watching us at the playground? Had he followed us?

I have no idea.

I go through the rest of it. Coming home. Putting Matthew to bed. Grabbing a drink. Flipping channels on the television. When had I fallen asleep? I don't know that either. I only remember waking up to the smell of blood. I remember heading down the hallway . . .

The prison lights come on with a loud snap. I shoot up in bed, my face coated with sweat. It is morning. My heart thumps in my chest. I swallow down some breaths, trying to calm myself.

What I saw in those Marvel-themed pajamas, that awful misshapen bloody form . . . it was *not* Matthew. That was the key here. It was *not* my son.

Was it?

Doubt starts to worm its way into my brain. How could it not? But for now, I won't let the doubt in. There is nothing to gain from doubting. If I'm wrong, I will eventually find out and then I'll be back to where I am now. Nothing ventured, nothing gained. So for now: No doubts. Just questions about how this could possibly be. Perhaps, I surmise, the brutality had been to cover up the victim's—yes, good, think of him as a victim, not Matthew—identity. The victim was male, of course. He was Matthew's size and general shape and skin tone. But they hadn't run a DNA test or anything like that. Why would they? No one doubted the victim's identity, right?

Right?

My fellow inmates began their daily rituals. We don't have roommates in our twelve-feet-by-seven-feet cells, but we can look in on almost every other inmate. This is supposed to be "healthier" than the older ones where there was no social interaction and too much isolation. I wish they hadn't bothered, because the less interaction the better. Earl Clemmons, a serial rapist, starts his day by offering the rest of us a play-by-play of his morning constitutional. He includes sound effects like cheering crowds and full sportscasting, mimicking one voice for the straight play-by-play and another offering color commentary. Ricky Krause, a serial killer who cut off his victims' thumbs with pruning shears, likes to begin his day with a song parody of sorts. He twists lyrics, taking old classics and giving them his own perverse spin. Right now, Ricky is repeatedly belting out, *"Someone's in the kitchen, getting vagina,"* and cracking up harder and harder as those around him shout for him to shut up.

We get in line for breakfast. In the past, those of us housed in this wing had our meals delivered, which makes it sound like we used DoorDash or something. No more. One of our fellow inmates protested that forcing a man to eat by himself in his cell was unconstitutional. He sued. Inmates love lawsuits. In this case, however, the prison system happily exploited the opening. Serving prisoners in their cells was expensive and labor-intensive.

The small cafeteria has four tables, each with metal stools, all bolted to the ground. I like to meander and wait until everyone else is seated, so that I can find the stool that will put me as far away from the more animated of my fellow inmates as possible. Not that the conversations aren't stimulating. The other day, several inmates got into a heated one-upmanship over who had raped the oldest woman. Earl "bettered" his opponents with his claim of sodomizing an eighty-seven-year-old after he broke into her apartment via the fire escape. Other inmates questioned the veracity of Earl's claim—they thought that he might be exaggerating just to impress them—but the next day Earl came back with saved newspaper clippings.

This morning I get lucky. One table is totally open. After scooping up some powdered eggs and bacon and toast—I'll skip the obvious comment about how awful prison food is—I take a stool in the farthest corner and begin to eat. For the first time in forever, I have an appetite. I realize that my mind has stopped going back to that night or even that photograph and has started to focus on something ridiculous and fantastical.

How to escape from Briggs.

I have been here long enough to know the routines, the guards, the layout, the schedule, the personnel, whatever. Conclusion: There is no way to escape. None. I had to think outside the box.

A tray slamming down on the table startles me. A hand is stuck into my face for me to shake. I look up and into the man's face. People say that the eyes are the windows to the soul. If that's true, this man's eyes flash NO VACANCY.

"David Burroughs, am I right?"

His name, I know, is Ross Sumner. He'd transferred in last week, purportedly waiting on an appeal that would never happen, but I am surprised they'd let him out of his cell at all. Sumner's case made headlines, the stuff of streaming-service documentaries and true crime podcasts. He was a superrich prep—do they still use that term?—who'd gone psychotically bad. Ross, who was handsome in a Ralph Lauren–ad way, had murdered at least seventeen people—men, women, children of all ages—and eaten their intestinal tracts. That was it. Just the intestinal tract. Body parts were found in a top-of-the-line Sub-Zero freezer in the basement of his family estate. None of these facts are in dispute. Sumner's appeal is based on the jury's conclusion that he is sane.

Ross Sumner still holds his hand out and waits for me to

take it. There is a smile on his face. I would rather French-kiss a live rodent than shake the man's hand, but in prison, you do what you have to. I reluctantly shake the hand as fast as possible. His hand is surprisingly small, dainty. As I pull mine back, I can't help it—I wonder what that hand has touched. Supposedly, he slit his victims open while they were still alive and used his hands—including *that* hand—to rip open the slit and reach inside the abdomen and grab hold of the intestine.

So much for having an appetite.

Ross Sumner smiles as though he can read my thoughts. He is about thirty years old with jet-black hair and delicate features. He takes the stool directly across from me. Lucky me.

"I'm Ross Sumner," he says.

"Yeah, I know."

"I hope you don't mind me sitting with you."

I say nothing.

"It's just that the other men in here"—Ross shakes his head—"I find them rather coarse. Unrefined, if you will. Do you know that you and I are the only college graduates?"

"That so?"

I nod. I keep my eyes on my plate.

"You went to Amherst, am I right?"

He pronounced Amherst correctly, keeping the H silent.

"Fine school," he continues. "I liked it better when they called themselves the Lord Jeffs. The Amherst Lord Jeffs. Such a majestic name. But of course, the woke crowd didn't like that, did they? They have to hate on a man who died in the eighteenth century. Ridiculous, don't you think?"

I play with my powdered eggs.

"I mean, now they call themselves the Amherst Mammoths. Mammoths. Please. That's so pathetically PC, don't you think? But here's something you'll enjoy knowing. I went to Williams College. The Ephs. That makes us rivals. Funny, no?"

Sumner gives me a boyish grin.

"Yeah," I say. "Hilarious."

Then he says, "I hear you had a visitor yesterday."

I go stiff. Ross Sumner sees it.

"Oh, don't look so surprised, David."

He still wears the boyish grin. That grin had probably gotten him far. On a purely physical level, it was a nice grin, charming, the kind that opens doors and lowers inhibitions. It was also probably the last sight his victims saw.

"It's a small prison. A man hears things."

That is true. Rumor has it that the Sumner family is not afraid to use their money to influence his treatment. I believe those rumors.

"I try to make it a point of staying informed."

"Uh-huh," I say, keeping my eyes on the eggs.

"So how did it go?" he asks.

"How did what go?"

"Your visit. With your . . . sister-in-law, was it?"

I say nothing.

"It must have been something, right? Your first visitor after all this time. You seemed distracted before I came over."

I look up. "Look, Ross, I'm trying to eat here, okay?"

Ross throws up his hands in mock surrender. "Oh, pardon

me, David. I didn't mean to pry. I wanted us to be friends. I have been starving for any sort of intellectual stimulation. I imagine you must feel the same. Both of us being graduates of the Small Ivies, I thought we would have a bond. A rapport, if you will. But I see now that I've caught you at a bad time. Please forgive me."

"It's fine," I mutter. I take another bite. I can feel Sumner's eyes on me.

Then he whispers, "Are you thinking about your son?"

The chill starts at the base of my skull and scurries down my spine. "What?"

"How did it feel, David?" His eyes are ablaze. "I am talking on a purely intellectual level. A proper discussion between educated men. I consider myself a student of the human condition. So I want to know. Be analytical or emotional, that's up to you. But when you lifted that baseball bat above your head and smashed it down on your own child's skull, what went through your mind? Was it a release? I mean, did you feel you had to do it? Or were you trying to quiet voices in your head? Or was the feeling more euphoric—"

"Go fuck yourself, Ross."

Sumner frowned. "Go fuck myself? Seriously? That's the best you can come up with? Really, David, I'm disappointed. I came here for a serious philosophical discussion. We know things others don't. I want to understand what could possess a man to do something so barbaric. To kill his own son. The flesh of your own flesh. I know that might make me sound like a hypocrite—"

"Lunatic," I correct.

"—but you see, I kill strangers. Strangers are life's props, don't you think? Stage dressing. Deep background for our worlds—the inner world we create. We are all that matter in the end, don't you think? Think about it. We cry harder when a beloved pet dies than when a tsunami kills hundreds of thousands of humans. Do you see my point?"

I see no reason to open my mouth. That will just encourage him.

Ross Sumner leans toward me. "I killed strangers. Props. Scenery. Window dressing. But to kill your own child, your own flesh and blood . . ."

He shakes his head as though mystified. I seethe but stay silent. What's the point? I don't need to win favor with this psychopath. I look for another seat, but it isn't as though another table companion would be less disturbing.

Ross Sumner daintily unfolds his paper napkin and lays it on his lap. He takes a tiny bite of the eggs and makes a face. "This food is simply awful," he says. "Absolutely tasteless."

I can't help myself. "As opposed to, say, human intestines?"

Sumner stares at me for a moment. I stare back. You never show fear in here. Not ever. Not for a second. It is, in part, why I made the wisecrack in the first place. Much as you might want to wallow in silence, you can never take shit in here because the shit will just grow exponentially.

Ross Sumner keeps up the eye contact for another second or two before throwing his head back and bursting out in laughter. Everyone turns toward us.

"Now *that*," he exclaims when he catches his breath, "was funny! No, really, David, that's what I was talking about. That's why I sat here. For that kind of give-n-take. For that kind of mental stimulation. Thank you. Thank you, David."

I don't reply.

He is still laughing as he rises and says, "I'm going to grab some toast. May I get you something while I'm up?"

"I'm good."

I close my eyes for a moment and rub my temples. A headache is crashing through me like a freight train. They started after that first beating, the remnants of a concussion and cracked skull. The prison doctor called them "cluster" headaches. I am still massaging my temples, stupidly letting my guard down, when an arm snakes around my neck. Before I can react, the arm snaps back hard, crushing my windpipe. My throat feels as though it's about to spurt out the back of my neck. My eyes bulge, my hand clawing impotently at his forearm.

Ross Sumner tightens his grip. He pulls back harder now. My legs shoot up, my shins smacking the table. The utensils jump. I start falling backward. Sumner releases his iron grip as the back of my head slams against the floor.

I see stars.

I blink. When I look up, Ross Sumner is leaping high in the air. That boyish grin is way north of maniacal now. I try to roll away. I try to raise my hands to ward him off. But I'm too late. Ross lands on me with his full weight, both knees pulverizing my rib cage.

I see more stars now.

I try to call out, try to scramble away, but Sumner straddles me. I wait for him to start throwing punches, wondering what I can do to stop him. But that's not what he does. Instead, he opens his mouth wide and lowers his head toward my chest.

Even through my prison jumpsuit, the bite breaks my skin.

I howl. Ross sinks his teeth deeper into the fleshy area right below my nipple. The pain is excruciating. The other inmates quickly surround us and lock arms, a fairly common prison technique to keep the guards away. But somewhere in the deep recesses of my brain, I know that no guards will step in. Not yet anyway. Not until one of us is unconscious. It's safer for them. Guards don't like risking injury.

I am on my own.

Still on my back, his teeth drawing blood, I draw on whatever reserves are left in my empty tank. I lift my hands up, palms facing each other, and with all my limited strength, I box Ross Sumner's ears. The blows do not land flush, but Sumner's jaw still unclenches. That's all I could have hoped for. I roll hard, trying to get him off me. He goes with my momentum. When his feet hit the ground, he pounces on my back. He threads the arm back around my windpipe.

His grip tightens.

I can't get air.

I twist back and forth. Ross holds on. I try to buck and flail. Ross's grip does not slacken. Pressure is building in my head. My lungs are crying out for air. The stars are back, swirling, but what I mostly see now is night. I struggle for one breath, just one, but that's a no-go.

I can't breathe.

My eyes start to close. My fellow inmates' cheers are one indistinct blur. Ross Sumner lowers his head closer to me.

"That ear looks tasty."

He is about to bite down on my ear. I barely care. I try again to buck, but there is nothing behind it. All I can think about is being able to breathe. Just one breath. That's all. His lips are right up against my ear now. I struggle like a dying fish on the line.

Where the hell are the guards?

By now, they should be stepping in. They don't want a dead inmate. That's not good for anyone. But then I remember Ross Sumner's wealth, his family's proclivity for payoffs, and again I realize that no one is going to save me.

If I lose consciousness—and I'm about to—I die.

And if I die, where would that leave Matthew?

Seconds now from passing out, capillaries bursting in my closed eyes, I lower my chin and let myself go limp. This isn't easy. It goes against every instinct. But I pull it off. There is only one thing left to do. Fight fire with fire.

I open my mouth and bite down on Ross Sumner's arm.

Hard.

His cry of pain is the most satisfying sound I have heard in a long time.

The grip on my windpipe immediately eases as he tries to pull his arm away. I greedily gulp air through flaring lips. But my teeth don't let go. He screams again. My jaw clenches down even stronger. He shakes his arm. I hang on like a bulldog. I feel the hairs of his arm against my face. I bite down even harder.

His blood trickles into my mouth. I don't care.

Ross has managed to stand. I am on my knees. He throws a punch. I think it hits the top of my head, but I don't feel it. He tries to gather enough leverage to pull his arm free, but I'm ready. The crowd is on my side now. I throw an elbow at his groin. Ross Sumner collapses like a folding chair. His weight tears his arm free from my teeth, but some flesh stays behind.

I spit it out.

I jump on him, straddle his chest, and start throwing punches.

I flatten his nose. I can actually feel the cartilage spread under my knuckles. I grab his collar and pull him up. Then I cock my fist again, take my time, and throw hard at his face. Splat. I do it again. Then again. Sumner's head lolls now as though his neck is a weak spring. I'm almost giddy now. My eyes are wide. I pull back again to hit him, but this time, someone hooks my arm. Then someone tackles me from behind.

The guards are on me now, pinning me to the ground. I don't resist. I keep my eyes on the bloody mess of a man lying on the floor in front of me.

And for a brief moment, I actually smile.

5

Warden Philip Mackenzie's plane touched down at Boston's Logan Airport without incident. He had grown up a stone's throw away from Logan in nearby Revere. Back in those days, Logan Airport's main landing route had flown the noisiest of jets over his house. To a little boy, the sound had been deafening, earth-shattering. His two older brothers, who shared the bedroom with him, would somehow sleep through it, but Little Philip would grasp the railing of his top bunk as the planes passed, the bed shaking so hard he feared falling off. Some nights, the planes seemed to be swooping so low they'd rip the fraying roof right off the house.

Back then, Revere Beach had been a blue-collar community right outside of Boston. It still was in most respects. Philip's father had been a house painter, his mom stayed home (no married women worked in those days—single women could be teachers, nurses, or secretaries) with the six Mackenzie kids—three boys sharing one bedroom, three girls sharing another, one bathroom for all of them.

The taxi dropped Philip off in front of a familiar four-family home on Dehon Street. The dwelling was decaying brick. The front door was shedding faded-green paint. The large stoop, the stoop where Philip had spent countless childhood hours with his buddies, especially Lenny Burroughs, was made up of chipped concrete. For thirty years, the Burroughs family had taken up all four apartments. Lenny's family was on the first floor on the right. His cousin Selma, who had been widowed young, had the apartment above with her daughter Deborah. Aunt Sadie and Uncle Hymie were on the first floor left. Other relatives—a churning potpourri of aunts, uncles, cousins, who-knows-what—took turns in the fourth apartment above Hymie and Sadie's. That was how this neighborhood was in those days. Immigrant families—Philip's being Irish, Lenny's Jewish—had poured in from across the Atlantic over a three-decade period. Those already here—they took in family. Always. They helped the newcomers find jobs. Some relatives slept on a couch or a floor for weeks, months, whatever. There was no privacy, and that was okay. These homes were breathing entities, in constant motion. Friends and family members constantly flowed through the corridors and stairwells like lifeblood through veins. No one locked their doors, not because it was super safe—it wasn't— but because family members never knocked or were denied access. Privacy was an alien concept. Everybody minded every-body else's business. You celebrated one another's victories and mourned their defeats. You were one.

You were family.

That world was gone with so-called progress. Most of the Burroughses and Mackenzies had moved on. They now lived in quasi-mansions in wealthier suburbs like Brookline or Newton with shrubs and fences and fancy marble bathrooms and swimming pools and where the very idea of living with non-nuclear family was nightmarish and incomprehensible. Other family members had moved to gated communities in warmer states like Florida or Arizona, sporting leathery tans and gold chains. Newer immigrant families—Cambodians, Vietnamese, whatever—had taken over a lot of the old homes. They, too, worked hard and took in all manner of extended family members, starting the cycle anew.

Philip paid the cabdriver and stepped onto the cracked sidewalk. He could still get a faint whiff of the salty Atlantic Ocean two blocks away. Revere Beach had never been a glamour spot. Even in his youth, the threadbare mini-golf and rusty roller coaster and worn Skee-Ball machines and assorted boardwalk arcades had been on their last legs. That didn't bother him and Lenny and their friends though. They hung out behind Sal's Pizzeria and smoked and drank Old Milwaukee because it was the cheapest and rolled dice. The guys they hung out with—Carl, Ricky, Heshy, Mitch—all became doctors and lawyers and moved out. Lenny and Philip stayed in town as local cops. Philip debated taking a quick walk down to Shirley Avenue to see the house where he and Ruth had raised their five children. But he decided against it. The memories were pleasant enough, but he was not in the mood to be distracted.

Memories always sting, don't they? The good ones most of all.

The concrete steps were too damn high. As a kid, as a teen, as a young man, Philip took them two at a time, with a skip and a jump. Now he winced through the creak in his knees. Only one of the four apartments still housed Burroughses. Lenny, his oldest friend, his former partner in the Revere Police Department, was back in the same first-floor apartment on the right that his family had called home seventy years ago. He lived here now with his sister Sophie. For some reason, Sophie had never moved on, almost as though someone had to stay behind to watch the old homestead.

He thought about Lenny's son serving a life sentence at Briggs. The whole incident was beyond heartbreaking. David wasn't well. That was obvious. Philip was David's godfather, though they managed to keep that secret so that they could conspire to get David into Briggs. David had no siblings (Lenny's wife, Maddy, had a "condition" of some sort—in those days, you never talked about such things), but Philip's oldest son, Adam, was David's best friend and nearly a brother, their relationship not unlike Philip's with Lenny. Adam too had spent hours here, in this four-family dwelling, just as Philip had. The Burroughs household had been a strange and wonderful place in those days. Back when Philip was young—and even when his son was young—this was a house of warmth and color and texture. The Burroughses lived life out loud, like a radio always set on high. Every emotion was felt intensely. When you argued—and you argued a lot in here—you did it with passion.

Then David's mother, Maddy, died and everything changed.

Now the building stood silent, joyless, a withering apparition. For a moment, Philip couldn't move. He just stood there on the stoop, staring at the door. He was about to knock when that faded-green door opened. Philip froze. If he had been disoriented before, he felt completely lost now. Being in the old neighborhood had brought on a bout of nostalgia, but seeing Sophie's face again, still beautiful despite the years, plunged him back. She too was closing in on seventy, but all Philip could see was the breathy teen who'd answered the door for him on this very spot the night of senior prom. A lifetime ago, Philip and Sophie had dated. They had fallen in love, he guessed. But they were young. Something happened—who remembered what anymore? The military, the police academy. Whatever. Fifty years ago. Sophie had married an army guy from Lowell named Frank. He died in some kind of training exercise in Ramstein, making Sophie a widow before her twenty-fifth birthday. She'd moved in with Lenny after Maddy's death to help raise David and never remarried. Philip had been betrothed to Ruth for over forty years, but some nights he still thought about Sophie more than he cared to admit. The sliding door. The road not taken. The big what-if. The good one he'd let get away.

Was that a crime?

He stared at Sophie now, his mind still traveling through some alternate universe where he hadn't let her go.

Sophie put her hands on her hips. "I got something stuck in my teeth, Philip?"

He shook his head.

"Then why are you staring?"

"No reason," he said. Then he added, "You look good, Sophie."

She rolled her eyes. "Come on in, Silver-Tongue. Your charm is making me woozy."

Philip stepped inside. Little if anything had changed. He could feel the ghosts surround him.

"He's resting," Sophie said, heading down the corridor. Philip followed. "He should be awake soon. Want some coffee?"

"Sure."

They reached the kitchen. It had been updated. Sophie used one of those new coffee pod machines everyone seems to have. She handed him the thick mug, not asking how he took it. She knew.

"So why are you here, Philip?"

He forced up a smile over the brim of the mug. "What, can't a man visit an old friend and his beautiful sister?"

"Remember what I said about your charm making me woozy?"

"I do."

"I was joking."

"Yeah, I figured." He put down the mug. "I need to talk to him, Sophie."

"This about David?"

"It is."

"He's sick, you know. Lenny, I mean."

"I know."

"Almost completely paralyzed. He can't talk anymore. I don't even know if he knows who I am."

"I'm sorry, Sophie."

"Is this going to upset him?"

Philip thought about that. "I don't know."

"Not sure I see the need."

"There probably isn't one."

"But this is what you two do," Sophie said.

"Yes."

Sophie turned her head toward the window. "Lenny wouldn't want to be spared. So go ahead. You know the way."

He put down the mug and rose. Philip wanted to say something, but no words came to him. She didn't look at him as he left the kitchen. He made the right and headed toward the bedroom in the back. The grandfather clock still stood in the hallway. Maddy had bought it at an estate sale in Everett a hundred years ago. Lenny and Philip had picked it up in Philip's old pickup truck. The thing weighed over two hundred pounds. It took them forever to disassemble it and move it. They had to wrap the pendulum and the main spring and the cable and the chains and the weights and the chime rods and Lord knows what else in heavy blankets and bubble wrap. They used masking tape to affix cardboard over the beveled glass door and then something still chipped off the toe molding. But Maddy loved it and Lenny would do anything for her and hey, when you add up the pros and cons, there was no doubt Philip got the better end of the deal on the friendship. Not that either would ever keep track.

Philip stopped when he reached the bedroom. He took a deep breath and plastered on a smile. When he entered, he fought hard to keep that smile locked in place and hoped his eyes didn't betray the sadness and shock. For a moment he stayed near the doorway and just stared at what had been his best friend. He remembered how powerful Lenny had been. Lenny had been all coiled muscle, built like a bantamweight fighter. He had been a health nut before it was in fashion, a careful eater in the days before that became so mainstream. Lenny did a hundred push-ups every morning. Exactly. Without break. His forearms had been steel cords, his veins thick and ropey. Now those powerful arms looked like milky reeds. Lenny's filmy eyes had the thousand-yard stare of the guys who had seen too much action in Nam. His lips were color-less. His skin resembled parchment paper.

"Lenny," Philip said.

No reaction. Philip forced himself to take a step closer to the bed. "Lenny, what the hell is going on with our Celtics? Huh? What happened to them?"

Still nothing.

"And the Pats. I mean, they were so good for so long so we can't complain, but come on." Philip smiled and inched closer. "Hey, remember when we met Yaz after that Orioles game? That was something. Such a good guy. But you said it early on. Free agency. It's going to kill the teams, just like you predicted."

Nothing.

From the doorway behind, he heard Sophie's voice. "Sit next to him and take his hand. Sometimes he'll squeeze it."

53

She left them alone. Philip took the seat next to Lenny. He didn't take his hand. That's not what they were about. All that touchy-feely stuff. Maybe David and Adam were into that, but not him and Lenny. Philip had never told Lenny he loved him. And vice versa. They didn't have to. And despite what David had said, Lenny had never told him that Philip owed him one. That wasn't their way.

"I got to talk to you, Lenny."

Philip dove in. He told Lenny about David's visit to his office. The whole story. Everything he could remember. Lenny, of course, did not respond. His eyes kept that same stare. His expression may have grown grimmer, but Philip chalked that up to his own imagination. It was like talking to a bed frame. After some time passed—when Philip was getting closer to the end of the story—he did indeed slide his hand over his old friend's. The hand didn't feel like a hand either. It felt like some distant inanimate object, a frail object, like a dead baby bird or something.

"Not sure what to do here," Philip said, as he started to wind down. "It's why I came to you. We've both seen perps try every which way to claim innocence or justify what they did. Hell, we spent our careers listening to that psychobabble. That's not what this is. I truly believe that. Your son wouldn't do that. David believes it. He's wrong, of course. I wish it was true—God, do I wish it—but Matthew is dead. David did it in some kind of fugue state. That's what I think. You and I talked about this already. He doesn't remember and hell, I don't know about guilt or blame. Neither of us were big fans of insanity defenses, but we also both know David is a good kid. Always has been."

He looked at Lenny. Still nothing. Only the rising and falling of his chest told Philip that he wasn't talking to a corpse.

"Here's the thing." Philip leaned a little closer and, for some reason, lowered his voice. "David wants me to help him break out. I mean, that's nuts. You know that. I know that. I don't have that kind of power. And even if I did, I mean, where would he go? There'd be a massive manhunt. He'd probably end up being gunned down. We don't want that for him. I still wish he'd tried to get help, maybe a new trial, something. That's his best chance, you know what I mean?"

A radiator pipe started banging. Philip shook his head and smiled. That damn pipe. It had been banging for, what, forty, fifty years? He remembered trying to bleed the radiators with Lenny, but they could never figure out what caused the banging. Trapped air or something. They'd go down and fix it and it would be okay for a few weeks and then—bang, bang—it would come back.

"We're old men, Lenny. Too old for this crap. I'm retiring in another year. Double pension. I could lose it all if I mess up. You know what I'm saying? I can't risk that. It wouldn't be fair to Ruth. She's got her sights set on some gated community in South Carolina. Nice weather year-round. But you know I'll always look out for David. No matter what. Like I promised. He's your boy. I understand that. So I want you to know. I'll look out for him . . ."

He stopped talking. His chest started to heave. Right now,

today, this moment—this was probably the last time he'd ever see Lenny. The thought hit him out of nowhere. Like a punch he didn't see coming. He felt tears start to come to his eyes, but he bit them back. He blinked hard, turned away. He stood and put his hand on his friend's shoulder. There was no flesh there, no muscle. It felt like he was touching naked bone.

"I better go, Lenny. You take care of yourself, okay? See you soon."

He walked toward the door. Sophie met up with him at the threshold.

"You okay, Philip?" she asked.

He nodded, not trusting his own voice.

Sophie met his eye. It was almost too much for him to bear. Then she looked over at her bedridden brother. She gestured for Philip to turn around. He slowly followed her gaze. Lenny had not moved. His face was still that skeletal death mask. His eyes still stared out, lifeless, the mouth still slightly open in some awful silent scream. But he saw what Sophie was trying to show him.

A single tear track glistening off Lenny's ashen skin.

Philip turned back toward her. "I have to go."

She led him back down the corridor, past the grandfather clock and the piano. She opened the door. He stepped out onto the stoop. The fresh air felt good. The sun shone in his eyes. He shielded them for a moment and smiled weakly at her.

"It was good seeing you, Sophie."

Her smile was tight.

"What?" he said.

"Lenny always told me you were the strongest man he ever knew."

"*Were*," he repeated. "Past tense."

"And now?"

"Now I'm just old."

Sophie shook her head. "You're not old, Philip," she said. "You're just scared."

"I'm not sure there's any difference."

He turned away. He did not look back as he descended the concrete steps, but he could feel her eyes on him, heavy and perhaps, after all these years, unforgiving.

6

I'm too fired up to sleep.

I pace back and forth in my tiny cell. Two steps, turn, two steps, turn. The adrenaline from my altercation with Ross Sumner pumps through my veins. Sleep didn't come last night. I'm not sure when it will again.

"Visitor."

It's Curly again. I'm surprised. "I'm still allowed visitors?"

"Until someone tells me otherwise."

Every part of me aches, but it is a good ache. After the guards jumped in, both of us were taken to the infirmary. I was able to walk there. Ross had to be carried on a stretcher. Them's the breaks. The nurse dabbed some peroxide on the bite marks and scrapes before sending me back to my cell. Ross Sumner, alas, was not so lucky. He was, as far as I know, still in the infirmary. I should be above feeling good about this. I should recognize that my private glee-filled gloating comes from a primitive place that this harsh prison has nurtured in me, but too bad.

I am taking great satisfaction in Ross's pain.

Curly leads me down the same route to the visiting area in total silence. Today I strut more than walk.

"Same visitor?" I ask, just to see what I'll get in return.

I get nothing.

I sit on the very same stool. Rachel does not bother hiding her horror this time.

"My God, what the hell happened to you?"

I smile and deliver a line I never thought I would: "You should see the other guy."

Rachel openly studies my face for a few long moments. Yesterday she tried to be more circumspect. All of that pretense is over now. She points at me with her chin. "How did you get all those scars?"

"How do you think?"

"Your eye—"

"I can't see much out of it. But it's okay. We have bigger concerns."

She keeps staring.

"Come on, Rachel. I need you to focus. Forget my face, okay?"

Her eyes trace over the scars for another few seconds. I stay still, let her get on with it. Then she asks the obvious question: "So what do we do?"

"I got to get out of here," I say.

"You have a plan?"

I shake my head. "For mental exercise, to keep myself semi-sane, I used to dream up ways of getting out of here.

You know, escape plans. Nothing I'd ever act on. Just for the hell of it."

"And?"

"And using my investigative skills, not to mention my innate wiles, I came up with"—I shrug—"nada. It's impossible."

Rachel nods. "No one has broken out of Briggs since 1983—and that guy was caught in three days."

"You did your homework."

"Old habit. So what are you going to do?"

"Let's put that aside. I need you to research a few things for me."

When Rachel whips out her reporter's notebook, the familiar four-by-eight-inch kind with the wire spiral on the top, I can't help but smile. She'd used them for years, even before getting the job at the *Globe*, and it always made it look like she was cosplaying a reporter, like she was going to don a fedora with a card reading PRESS jammed into the rim.

"Go ahead," Rachel says.

"First off," I say, "we need to figure out who the real murder victim was."

"Because now we know it wasn't Matthew."

"*Know* may be an optimistic word, but yes."

"Okay, I'll start with the National Center for Missing and Exploited Children."

"But don't stop there. Go to any websites you can think of, social media pages, old newspapers, whatever. Let's start by making a list of any Caucasian male children between the ages of two and, say, four years old who were reported missing within a two-month span of the murder. Try to keep the search within a two-hundred-mile radius. Spread out after that. Go a little younger, a little older, farther away, you know the deal."

Rachel jots it down. "I may have a few sources I haven't burned in the FBI," she says. "Maybe one of them can help."

"Sources you haven't burned?"

She shakes it off. "What else?"

"Hilde Winslow," I say.

We both go silent for a moment.

Then Rachel asks, "What about her?"

My throat closes. It is hard for me to speak.

"David?"

I signal that I'm okay. I put myself together one piece at a time. When I trust my voice again, I ask, "Do you remember her testimony?"

"Of course."

Hilde Winslow, an elderly widow with twenty-twenty vision, testified that she saw me burying something in the woods between our homes. The police dug at that spot and uncovered the murder weapon covered with my fingerprints.

I feel Rachel's eyes on me, waiting.

"I could never explain that," I manage to say, trying to give myself some distance, pretending that I'm talking about someone else, not me. "At first, I thought that maybe she saw someone who looked like me. A case of mistaken identity. It was dark. It was four in the morning. I was pretty far away from her back window."

"That was what Florio said on cross-examination."

Tom Florio was my attorney.

"Right," I say. "But he didn't make much headway."

"Mrs. Winslow was a strong witness," Rachel confesses.

I nod, feeling the emotions start to rise up and overwhelm me again. "She seemed to be just a sweet little old lady with a steel-trap mind. She had no reason to lie. Her testimony sunk me. That was when those closest to me started having serious doubts." I look up. "Even you, Rachel."

"And even you, David."

She meets my glare without the slightest flinch. I'm the one who turns away.

"We need to find her."

"Why? If she was mistaken—"

"She wasn't mistaken," I say.

"I'm not following."

"Hilde Winslow lied. It's the only explanation. She lied on the stand, and we need to know why."

Rachel says nothing. A young woman, still a teen, I would bet, walks behind Rachel and takes a seat on the stool next to her. A beefy inmate I don't recognize, blanked in razor-scratch tattoos, comes in and sits across from her. Without preamble he starts cursing at her in a language I can't make out, gesturing wildly. The girl hangs her head and says nothing.

"Okay," Rachel says. "What else?"

"Prepare."

"Meaning?"

"If you have any affairs to get in order, do it now. Max out your ATM card every day. Same with your bank. Get out as much cash as you can, keeping it below ten grand a day so it doesn't signal anything to the government. Start today. We need as much cash as possible, just in case."

"Just in case what?"

"I find a way out of here." I lean forward. I know that my eyes are bloodshot, and judging by the look on her face, I look . . . off. Scary even. "Look," I whisper, "I know I should give you the big speech now—about how if I manage to escape—I know, I know, but just hear me out—if I manage to escape, you'll be aiding and abetting a federal inmate, which is a felony. If I were a better man, I would hand you a line about how this is my fight, not yours, but the truth is, I can't do that. I have zero chance without you."

"He's my nephew," she replies, sitting up a little straighter.

He's. She said "he's." Present tense. Not "he was." She believes it. God help us both, we really believe that Matthew is still alive.

"So what else, David?"

I don't reply. I've gone quiet. My eyes wander off, my thumb and forefinger plucking at my lower lip.

"David."

"Matthew is out there," I say. "He's been out there all this time."

My words linger in the still, stilted, prison air.

"The last five years have been hell for me, but I'm his father.

I can take it." My gaze locks on to her. "What have they been like for my son?"

"I don't know," Rachel says. "But we have to find him."

———

Ted Weston liked using the nickname Curly at work.

No one called him that at home. Only here. In Briggs. It gave him distance from the scum he had to work with every day. He didn't like these guys using or even knowing his real name. When Ted finished work, he showered in the correctional officers' locker room. Always. He never wore his uniform home. He showered with very hot water and scrubbed this place off him, these horrible men and their horrible breath that may still linger on his clothes and in his hair, their sweat and DNA, their evil which feels to him like a living, breathing parasite that attaches itself to any decent microcosm and eats away at it. Ted showers all that away, scrubs it off with scalding water and industrial soap and a harsh-bristled brush, and then he carefully puts on his civilian clothes, his real clothes, before he goes home to Edna and their two daughters, Jade and Izzy. Even then, when he first gets home, Ted showers again and changes clothes, just to be sure, just to be certain that nothing from this place contaminates his home and his family.

Jade is eight and in the third grade. Izzy is six and autistic or on the spectrum or whatever damn term the so-called specialists use to describe the sweetest daughter God ever created.

Ted loved both of them with all his heart, loved them both so much that sometimes at the kitchen table, he would look across and just stare at them and the love would pump into his veins so hard, so fast, that he feared he would burst from it.

But right now, as he stood in the prison infirmary by the bedside of a particularly evil inmate named Ross Sumner, Ted scolded himself for even thinking about his daughters, for letting that kind of purity enter his mind while he was in the presence of a monster like Ross Sumner.

"Fifty grand," Sumner said.

Ross Sumner was in the infirmary. Good. David Burroughs had put a beating on the guy. Who knew Burroughs had it in him? Not that either guy was what Ted would call "hardened," as opposed to simply awful. Still, Sumner's pretty-boy face had been busted open. His nose was broken. His eyes had swollen mostly shut. It looked like he was in pain and Ted was happy about that.

"Did you hear me, Theodore?"

Sumner, of course, knew his real name. Ted didn't like that. "I heard you."

"And?"

"And the answer is no."

"Fifty grand. Think about it."

"No."

Sumner tried to sit up a bit. "The man murdered his own child."

Ted Weston shook his head. "You're the killer, not me."

"Killer? Oh, Ted, you have it all wrong. You wouldn't be a

killer. You'd be a hero. An avenging angel. With fifty thousand dollars in his pocket."

"Why do you want him dead so badly anyway?"

"Look at my face. Just look at what Burroughs did to my face."

Ted Weston did. But he wasn't buying it. There was something more going on here.

"A hundred grand," Sumner said.

Ted swallowed. A hundred grand. He thought about Izzy and the price of all those specialists. "I can't."

"Of course you can. You already tipped us off about Burroughs's visitor with the photograph."

"That was . . . That was just a little favor."

Sumner smiled through the bruises.

"So think of this as another favor. A larger one perhaps, but I have a plan. An utterly flawless plan."

"Right," Ted scoffed. "Never heard that one in here before."

"How about I tell you what I'm thinking? Just theoretically. Just listen, okay? For fun."

Ted didn't say no or tell him to shut up. Ted didn't walk away or even shake his head. He just stood there.

"Let's say a correctional officer—someone like you, Ted— brought me a blade of some sort. A prison shiv, as they say. As you know, there are plenty around in a place like this. Let's say, just hypothetically, that I clutch the shiv in my hand to make sure my fingerprints are on the weapon. Then, again hypothetically, let's say the correctional officer dons gloves. Like, for example, the ones here in the infirmary." Ross smiled through the pain from the beating. "I then take the blame. I then confess, freely, easily—after all, what do I have to lose? If anything, this will help me get free."

Ted Weston frowned. "Help you how?"

"My appeal is based on my mental sanity. Killing Burroughs will make me appear to be even more loony. Don't you see? They'll have the murder weapon with my fingerprints on it. They'll have my confession. Dozens of witnesses just saw our altercation, a fight nearly to the death, which will thus add in motive for me." He turned both palms to the ceiling. "Case closed."

Ted Weston couldn't help but squirm. A hundred grand. That was more than a year's salary. Plus it would be cash, no taxes taken out, so it was closer to two years' worth. He thought about what he and Edna could do with that kind of cash. They were drowning in bills. That kind of money wouldn't just be throwing them a life preserver. It would be throwing them a damn yacht. And he knew Sumner was good for it. Everybody knew that. He had already transferred two K into his and Bob's account to look the other way in the cafeteria, which they'd done until it went south.

Looking away for two grand was one thing. Getting $500 a month to report on what Burroughs was up to, as Ted had for years now, that was nice too. But one hundred grand—man oh man, the number staggered Ted. And all he had to do was stab a worthless baby-killer who should have gotten the chair anyway, a man who, if Sumner wanted him dead, would end up dead no matter what. So what was the harm? What was the big deal?

Sumner was right. Nobody would finger Ted. Even if it went wrong, Ted was liked in here. His colleagues would back him.

It would be so easy.

"Theodore?"

Ted shook his head. "I can't."

"If you're trying to negotiate for more money—"

"I'm not. This isn't who I am."

Sumner laughed. "Oh, you're above it, is that what you think?"

"I need to be right with my family," Ted said. "With my God."

"Your God?" Sumner laughed again. "That superstitious nonsense? Your God who lets thousands of children starve every day but lets me live to murder and rape? Do you ever think about that, Theodore? Did your God watch me torture people? Was your God too weak to stop me—or did he choose to watch my victims suffer horrible deaths?"

Ted didn't bother replying. He stared down at the floor, his face reddening.

"You don't have a choice, Theodore."

Ted looked up. "What's that supposed to mean?"

"It means I need you to do this. You've already taken money from us. I can let your bosses know—not to mention local law enforcement, the press, your family. I don't want to do that. I like you. You're a good man. But we are desperate. You don't seem to appreciate that. We want Burroughs dead."

"You keep saying 'we.' Who is we?"

Sumner looked him dead in the eye. "You don't want to know. We need him dead. And we need him dead tonight."

"Tonight?" Ted couldn't believe what he was hearing. "Even if I—"

"I can make further threats if you'd like. I can remind you of our wealth. I can remind you that we still have resources on the outside. I can remind you that we know all about you, that we know where your family—"

Ted's hand shot out for Ross Sumner's throat. Sumner didn't so much as flinch as Ted's fingers closed around his neck. It didn't last, of course. Ted let go almost immediately.

"We can make things bad for you, Theodore. You have no idea how bad."

Ted felt lost, adrift.

"But let's dispense with such unpleasantries, shall we? We are friends. Friends don't make idle threats. We are on the same side. The best relationships are not zero-sum, Theodore. The best relationships are win-win. And I feel as though I've behaved poorly here. Please accept my apology. Plus a ten-thousand-dollar bonus." Sumner licked his lips. "One hundred and ten thousand dollars. Think about all that money."

Ted felt sick. Idle threats. Guys like Ross Sumner don't make idle threats.

Like the man said, Ted had no choice. He was about to be pushed across a line from which there was, he knew, no coming back.

"Tell me your plan again," Ted said.

7

Back in her room, Rachel stared at the maybe-Matthew photograph, picked up her phone, and debated calling her sister Cheryl and blowing up her world.

It was odd that David didn't ask her to show him the photograph again. She had been prepared for that. Doubt burrows in when the photograph isn't front and center. When you're staring right at it, you somehow know that it has to be Matthew. When you put it away, when you rely on your imagination instead of something as concrete as the actual image, you realize how ridiculous your supposition is, that your belief that a distant view of a young child is somehow evidence that a toddler murdered five years earlier is, in fact, still alive is beyond ludicrous.

She shouldn't call Cheryl. She should keep this from her.

But did Rachel have the right to make that decision?

Rachel was staying at the Briggs Motor Lodge of Maine, famed, she imagined, for having walls made of some kind of gauze or cotton mesh. Right now, she could hear her neighbors fervently and lustily enjoying their stay as though they were sharing this bed with her. The woman kept yelling out "Oh, Kevin," and "Go, Kevin," and "Yes, Kevin," and even— oh, how Rachel hoped this was something the woman shouted lost in the throes of passion rather than trying to be cute or funny—"Take me to Heaven, Kevin."

A little afternoon delight, Rachel mused somewhat bitterly. *It must be nice.*

When was the last time she'd had an afternoon like that?

It wasn't worth thinking about. Rachel was still coming down from a full-fledged panic attack brought on, she assumed, by the combination of seeing David and going off her antianxiety medicine. The medicine didn't work for her. Not really. She took the Xanax or whatever, hoping to deaden the pain of being responsible for another human being's death, but while it may have put some of the guilt at a distance—made it feel more elusive—the guilt clung on.

She blinked her eyes and tried to focus on doing the right thing here.

She should call her sister and tell her. That was what Rachel would want if their roles were reversed and Cheryl was the one holding this photo. Rachel picked up her mobile. Service was spotty up here in rural Maine. This was a prison town. Everyone staying at this motor lodge was somehow connected to Briggs Penitentiary—visitors, vendors, suppliers, deliverers, that kind of thing.

She had enough bars to make the call. Her fingers clicked

the Contacts icon and scrolled to Cheryl's name. Her finger hovered above the call button.

Don't do it.

She'd promised herself that she would keep this from Cheryl—protect her sister—until she knew for certain. Right now, when you stripped out the emotion, she still knew nothing. She had a photograph of a boy who resembled her dead nephew. Period. The end. David's enthusiasm notwithstanding, they had diddly-squat.

She flicked on the motor lodge's television. On the sign outside, the Briggs Motor Lodge of Maine actually boasted that all rooms had a COLOR TV, spelling out each letter in a different color—the C was in orange, the O in green, the L in blue—to emphasize that fact, though Rachel figured that the real draw would be if the motor lodge still had black-and-white televisions. She flicked through the stations. Mostly daytime talk shows and bad-take cable news. The commercials—buy gold, get a second mortgage, consolidate your debt, invest in crypto—all seemed like legal versions of Ponzi schemes to her.

The American economy relies more on the con than we like to think.

The festivities next door reached a crescendo when Kevin repeatedly announced with great gusto that he was nearing the finish line. A few seconds later, the symbolic cymbals crashed and then all went quiet. Rachel was tempted to applaud. David had asked her about her journalism career, and she'd balked at answering. There was no reason to get into how she'd messed up and destroyed herself, how she'd been fired and humiliated and how, in truth, a story like this might be the only chance to resurrect her career. It wasn't worth discussing. It was a distraction. She would be here anyway. That was what she told herself, and it was probably true.

Her phone was on the bed.

The hell with it.

She picked it up and before she could talk herself out of it, Rachel hit her sister's number, the top one in her favorites. She put the phone to her ear. No ring yet. Still time to hang up. She closed her eyes as the first ring sounded. Still time. On the second ring, Rachel heard the phone being answered. A clipped voice, not her sister's, said, "Hello?"

It was Ronald, Cheryl's new husband.

"Hello, Ronald," Rachel said. And then, even though the phone undoubtedly had caller ID, she added, "It's Rachel."

"Good afternoon, Rachel. How are you?"

"Fine," she said. Then: "Isn't this Cheryl's phone?"

"It is," Ronald said. He was always Ronald, never Ron or Ronny or the Ronster, which told you everything you need to know about his diction and affect. "Your sister is just getting out of the shower, so I took the liberty of answering for her."

Silence.

"If you'd like to hold a moment," Ronald continued, "she will be with you soon."

"I'll hold."

She could hear him put the phone down. Rachel's skull had a touch of the alcohol swirls going on, but she felt pretty firmly in control. There were mumbled voices before Cheryl got on the line sounding a little frazzled.

"Hey, Rach."

Rachel realized that some might view her distaste for Ronald Dreason as either overblown or unfair. That was probably accurate, of course. Cheryl's fault. Her introducing this new man into her life had been poorly timed.

"Hi," Rachel managed to say.

She could almost see her sister's frown. "You okay?"

"Fine."

"You been drinking?"

Silence.

"What's wrong?"

Rachel had been rehearsing her words in her head since she got back to her room, but that all flew out of her head now that the time had come. "Just checking in. How are you feeling?"

"Pretty good. The morning sickness stopped. We have an ultrasound on Thursday."

"Terrific. Will you learn the sex?"

"Yes, but don't worry—no reveal party."

Thank God for small favors, she thought. Out loud she said, "That all sounds great."

"Yeah, Rach, terrific, great, whatever. Do you want to stop stalling and tell me what's wrong?"

Rachel lifted the photograph again. Irene and Bugs Bunny and that boy's profile. She thought about David's scarred face through the plexiglass, the way his head had tenderly tilted to the side as he lifted his finger up to the image, the naked, haunting pain in his hollow eyes. She had been right before. David had nothing. Cheryl had a life. She had suffered immeasurably, losing her child and then finding out the cause was her own husband. It was not fair to uproot her over what was probably nothing.

"Yo," Cheryl said. "Earth to Rachel."

She swallowed. "Not over the phone."

"What?"

"I need to see you. As soon as possible."

"You're scaring me, Rach."

"I don't mean to."

"Fine, come over now."

"I can't."

"Why not?" Cheryl asked.

"I'm not home."

"Where are you?"

"In Maine. Briggs County."

The silence was suffocating. Rachel gripped the phone and closed her eyes and waited. When Cheryl finally did speak, her voice was an anguished whisper. "What the hell are you trying to do to me?"

"I'm leaving tomorrow. Meet me at my place. Eight p.m. And don't bring Ronald."

———

There is a fine line between day and night in Briggs.

We have "lights out" at ten p.m., but that just means

dimming them. It never gets dark in here. Perhaps that's a good thing, I don't know. We are all in our own cells, so it isn't as though we could walk around and bother one another. I have a lamp in my cell so I can read late into the night. You would think that I would do a lot of that in here—read and write—but I have trouble focusing due in part to my eye trouble from the first assault. I get headaches after more than an hour at either task. Or maybe it isn't just physical. Maybe it's more psychosomatic or something. I don't know.

But tonight, I put my hands behind my head and lay back on the flimsy pillow. I open the mental floodgates and for the first time since I entered this place, I let Matthew in. I don't stop the images. I don't put a block on them or filter them. I let them flow in and surround me. I practically bathe in them. I think about my father, no doubt dying in that same bedroom he shared with my mother. I think about my mother who died when I was eight years old and yes, I realize that I never quite moved past that. I can't see her face anymore, haven't been able to conjure up her image in many years, relying on those photos we had on the piano more than anything from my memory banks. I picture Aunt Sophie, my wonderful Sophie, the kind and generous woman who raised me after Mom died, the celestial being whom I love unconditionally, still trapped in that house, caring no doubt for my father until his final breath.

A sound by my cell door makes me cock my head.

Night sounds are not uncommon here. They are awful sounds, sounds that chill a man's blood, unescapable, constant. This wing is not full of men who sleep soundly. Many cry out in their sleep. Others like to stay up at all hours and chat through the bars, reversing their internal clocks, staying awake all night vampire-like and sleeping during the day. Why not? There is no day or night in here. Not really.

And of course, there are men who openly masturbate with far more lusty pride than discretion.

But this sound, the one that makes me cock my head, is different. It is not coming from another cell or the guard booth or anything involving the general population blocks. It is coming from the door to my cell.

"Hello?"

A flashlight lands on my face, momentarily blinding me. I don't like that. I don't like that at all. I block it with a cupped hand and squint.

"Hello."

"Stay still, Burroughs."

"Curly?"

"I said stay still."

I don't know what's going on, so I do as he asks. We don't have traditional locks and keys in Briggs. My cell door works off what's called a "slam lock," an electromechanical system that automatically deadlocks. It is all controlled by levers in the guardroom. The doors only work on keys as a backup.

Which Curly was using now.

I have never seen the key used before.

"What's going on?" I ask.

"I'm taking you to the infirmary."

"No need," I say. "I feel fine."

"Not your call," Curly says in a near whisper.

"Whose call it is?"

"Ross Sumner has filled out an official complaint."

"So?"

"So the doctor needs to catalogue your injuries."

"Now?"

"Why, you busy?"

His words are typically sarcastic, but his voice is tight.

"It's late," I say.

"You'll get your beauty sleep later. Get your ass up."

Not sure what else to do, I stand. "You mind taking the light out of my eyes?"

"Just move."

"Why are you whispering?"

"You and Sumner got this place riled up. You think I want to do that again?"

That makes sense, I guess, but again the words ring hollow. Still, what choice do I have? I have to go. I don't like it, but really, what's the big deal? I'll go. I'll see the doctor. Maybe I'll smirk at Sumner lying in the bed.

We leave our block and start down the corridor. Distant shouts from the general population bounce off the concrete walls like rubber balls. The lights are dimmed. My footwear is prison-issue canvas slip-ons, but Curly's shoes are black and echo off the floor. He slows his step. I do the same.

"Keep walking, Burroughs."

"What?"

"Just keep going."

He stays half a step behind me. We are alone in this corridor. I sneak a glance behind me. Curly's face is ashen. His eyes glisten. His bottom lip is quivering. He looks as though he might cry.

"You okay, Curly?"

He doesn't reply. We pass a checkpoint, but there is no guard here. That's odd. Curly unlocks the gate with some kind of fob. When we reach the T-intersection, he puts his hand on my elbow and steers me to the right.

"The infirmary is the other way," I say.

"You have to fill out some forms first."

We move down another corridor. The sounds of the prison have gone from faint to nonexistent. It is so quiet I can hear Curly's labored breaths. I don't know this section of the prison. I've never been here before. There are no cells. The doors here are pebble-glassed like shower doors. Philip's office had a door like this. I assume I'm in some kind of executive area where we will meet up with someone who will help me fill out the paperwork. But there are no lights coming through the pebbled glass. It feels very much as though we are alone.

I notice something else now that I hadn't before.

Curly is wearing gloves.

They are black latex. Guards rarely wear them. So why now? Why tonight? I am not one who believes you always go with your gut or follow your primitive instincts. They often lead you in the wrong direction. But when you add it up—the gut, the instincts, the hour, the excuse, the gloves, the route, Curly's attitude, his demeanor—something is definitely off.

A few days ago, I wouldn't have cared much. But everything has changed now.

"Up ahead," Curly says. "It's the last door on the left."

My heart is thumping in my chest. I look up ahead, at the last door on the left. That too has a pebble-glass door. That one too has no light coming through it.

Not good.

I freeze. Curly stays behind me. He isn't moving either. I hear a small sound coming from him. I slowly turn. Tears are flowing down his face.

"Are you okay?" I ask.

Then I see the glint of steel.

A blade is heading straight toward my stomach.

There is no time for thought or anything beyond a reaction. I lean my body to one side while hammering down toward the blade with my forearm. The blade veers off course just enough—it misses my right side by no more than an inch. Curly pulls the blade back hard toward him, slicing through the flesh of my forearm. Blood spills, but I don't feel pain. Not yet anyway.

I leap back. Curly and I are a few feet apart now, both in fight crouches.

Curly is crying. He holds the blade in front of him, like a scene from a poor man's *West Side Story*. Sweat coats his face, mixing in with the tears.

"I'm sorry, Burroughs."

"What are you doing?"

"So sorry."

He regrips the knife. I'm holding my forearm, trying to stem the blood that's seeping now through my fingers.

"You don't have to do this," I say.

But Curly isn't listening. He lunges at me. I jump back. There is a rushing sound in my ears. I don't know what to do. I know nothing about knife fighting.

So I do the simplest thing I can.

"Help!" I scream as loud as I can. "Somebody, help me!"

I don't rely on that, of course. This is a prison. I'm a prisoner. People are yelling crazy shit in here twenty-four seven. Still, the suddenness of my scream makes Curly pull up. I use that. I turn and sprint down the corridor, back toward where we came from. He chases me.

"Help! He's trying to kill me! Help!"

I don't turn around. I don't know if he's closing in on me or not. I can't risk it. I just keep pumping my legs and screaming. But now I'm reaching the end of the corridor, that same checkpoint we had gone through earlier. No one is there.

I ram the gate. Nothing. I try to pull it open.

No go. It's locked.

Now what?

"Help!"

I glance back over my shoulder now. Curly is closing in. I'm trapped. I turn to face him. I keep screaming for help. He stops. I try to read his face. Confusion, anguish, rage, fear—it is all there. Fear, I know, is always the overwhelming emotion.

He is scared. And the only way to not be scared anymore is to silence me.

Whatever led him to this, whatever doubts he may have had, they are no match for his need to survive, to save himself, to worry about his self-interest above all else.

And that means killing me.

I am backed up against the gate with nowhere to go. He is about to lunge for me when a voice from behind me says, "What the fuck is going on here?"

Relief courses through my veins. I am about to turn and explain that Curly here is trying to kill me when I feel something hard smack the back of my head. My knees buckle. Blackness closes in around me.

And then there is nothing.

8

Cheryl grabbed a cup of coffee and a section of the morning paper and sat in the breakfast nook across from her husband Ronald. It was six a.m., and this had become her blessed morning routine. She and Ronald wore matching one hundred percent cotton spa robes with thick shawl collars and cuffed sleeves; Ronald had ordered them during a luxurious stay at the Fairmont Princess Hotel in Scottsdale.

Most people had moved on to online papers, but Ronald insisted on going old-school with an actual daily newspaper delivery. He started with the front section while Cheryl preferred reading the business section first. She didn't know why. She didn't know much about business, but something about the dynamic read to her like a great soap opera. Today, no matter how hard she tried to focus, there was zero comprehension. The words swam by in meaningless waves. Ronald, who normally offered a running commentary on whatever he was reading—an act she found endearing and annoying in equal measure—was quiet. He was, she knew, studying her. She had not slept well after her sister's call. He wanted to ask what was wrong, but he would not ask. One of Ronald's strengths was his wonderful sense of when to pry and when to let it be.

"What time is your first patient?" he asked.

"Nine a.m."

Cheryl's practice saw patients three days a week starting promptly at nine a.m. The other two weekdays were saved for surgery. Cheryl was a transplant surgeon. It was, without a doubt, the most interesting field of medicine. She mostly worked on kidney and liver transplants, which was both high-stakes and challenging, but her patients, unlike other surgeons', always needed a great deal of follow-up, often years' worth, so she could see the results of her labor. In order to become a transplant surgeon, you start with general surgery (six years in her case at Boston General) plus one year of research plus another two years of a fellowship in transplant surgery. It had been staggeringly difficult, but after the disasters, after the tragedy and the fallout, the medical center—her education, her occupation, her calling, her patients—had sustained her.

Her work. And Ronald, of course.

She met her husband's eye and smiled. He smiled back. She could see the concern etched on his handsome face. She gave her head the smallest of shakes as if to say all was fine. But it was not fine.

Why was Rachel at Briggs Penitentiary?

The answer was obvious, of course. She was visiting David. On one level, okay, fine, do your thing. David and Rachel had always been close. He'd been up there for nearly five years now. Maybe Rachel felt that was enough time. Maybe she felt she should reach out, that he deserved some level of, if not support, sustenance. Maybe, with all the professional and personal heartache in Rachel's life over the past year, Rachel would find—what?—comfort in visiting a man who had always believed in her and her dreams.

No.

It had to be something else. In the same way Cheryl loved being a surgeon, Rachel had loved her job as an investigative journalist. She had lost it all in a snap, fair or not, and now she wasn't the same. Simple as that. Her sister had been wounded. The experience had changed her, and not for the better. Rachel used to be reliable. Now her judgment was something Cheryl constantly questioned.

But why would she be at Briggs?

Perhaps she saw David as an opportunity. David had not spoken to the press. Not ever. He had never told his side of the story, as though there was one, or tried to elaborate on his own theory about what had happened that awful night. So maybe that was Rachel's game. Her sister was still an investigative journalist at heart, so maybe she went to visit David on the pretense of caring about him. She was good at being a sympathetic ear, at getting people to open up. Perhaps Rachel could get a story out of David, a huge headline-making, true-crime-podcast type of story, and maybe, just maybe, Rachel could use that to regain her professional standing and get "uncanceled."

But would Rachel really do that?

Would Cheryl's own sister dredge all this horror up again, rip apart Cheryl's sutures (to use a surgical analogy) just to get back in the game? Could Rachel be so cold?

"How are you feeling?" Ronald asked.

"Great."

He smiled at her. "Is it corny or romantic to say my wife looks extra-hot pregnant?"

"Neither," she said. "More like you're horny and trying to get some."

Ronald faked a gasp and put a hand to his chest. "Moi?"

She shook her head. "Men."

"We are a predictable lot."

She was pregnant. Such an all-consuming marvel. And it had happened so easily this time. Ronald was watching her again, so she forced up a smile. They had redone the kitchen last year, knocking down a wall, expanding the space by fifteen feet, adding a mudroom (for when they had muddied little feet traipsing through the backyard), putting in floor-to-ceiling windows, and topping it off with a six-burner Viking stove and oversized Northland Master Series refrigerator and freezer. Ronald had designed the kitchen. He liked to cook.

Maybe, Cheryl thought, it was simpler. Maybe Rachel had figured that it was finally time to reach out to her ex-brother-in-law. Cheryl could sympathize with that. Hadn't she wanted to stand by her then-husband too? Hadn't Cheryl stayed by David's side, even when the investigation began to circle back to him? The idea of David hurting Matthew was preposterous. At the time, she would have believed space aliens had been responsible for the brutal murder over her husband.

But as the evidence mounted, doubt started to burrow its way under her skin and fester. The two of them hadn't been good for months, their marriage a plane on nosedive though Cheryl told herself they'd gain control of the aircraft in time and pull out of the plunge. They had been together a long time—since their junior year at Revere High. Good times, bad times, they always stayed together. They'd have made it.

But would they have?

Maybe not this time. That's the thing with trust. Once David lost it in her, nothing was the same. And once she lost it in him . . .

As the suspicion started to circle in, Cheryl tried to maintain a supportive facade, but David saw through it. He reacted by pushing her away. The strain of it became an unbearable weight. By the time the trial rolled around, by the time the courtroom surprises came to light, the marriage was over.

In the end, David had murdered their son. And Cheryl was a big part of the reason.

Ronald took too loud a slurp of his coffee, jarring her back into the sunlit breakfast nook. She looked up, startled. He put down the mug.

"I got an idea," he said.

She plastered on the fake smile. "I think you already made your idea pretty clear."

"How about tonight we go out to Albert's Café for dinner? Just the two of us."

"I can't," she said.

"Oh?"

"Didn't I tell you? I'm meeting Rachel."

"No," he said slowly. "You didn't tell me."

"It's not a big deal."

"Is she okay?"

"I think so, yes. She just asked me to come over. It's been a while since we've seen each other."

"It has," he agreed.

"So I thought I'd stop by after rounds. I hope that's all right with you."

"Of course it's all right with me," Ronald said with a little too much bravado. He found his newspaper, snapped it open, started reading again. "Have a nice time."

Cheryl felt the anger start to boil up inside her. Why? Why the hell would Rachel do this to her? If her sister wanted to forgive David, fine and dandy, go for it. But why drag Cheryl in? Why now, when she was rebuilding and pregnant? Rachel had to know what a strain a call like that would be. Why would she do that?

That was the question that really troubled Cheryl. Rachel was a good sister. The best. They were there for each other, always and forever, good times and bad, all that. And even though Cheryl was the older sister by two years, Rachel had—until recently anyway—been the more prudent and overprotective of the two. She knew how hard Cheryl had worked just to get herself out of bed after Matthew's murder. David, well, not to put too fine a point on it, but Cheryl had cut him from her life, from her thoughts. In order to move on, as far as she was concerned, David had never existed. But Matthew . . .

Oh, that was another matter.

She would never forget her beautiful little boy. Never. No matter what. Not for a second. That was what she realized. You don't move past something like that—you learn to live with it. No matter how much pain you are in. You don't fight that pain. You don't push it away. You embrace it and let it become a part of you. It's the only way.

The only thing more painful than remembering Matthew was the idea she might actually forget him.

A groan escaped her lips. She quickly smothered it with the heel of her palm. This wasn't the first time. Grief rarely attacks from the front. It prefers to sneak up on you when you least expect it. Ronald shifted in his seat, but he did not look up or ask. She was grateful for that.

So again the question rose up in her: *What does Rachel want to tell me?*

Her sister was not one for melodrama, so whatever it was, it had to be important. Very important. Something concerning David maybe.

But more likely: Something concerning Matthew.

9

"Good morning, Staaaaaar-shine! The earth says hello . . ."
I must be dead, I think. I am dead in hell, where I sit in blackness and hear Ross Sumner mangle the soundtrack from the musical *Hair* for all eternity. My head pounds as though someone is driving a stake through my forehead with a mallet. I start to see light through the darkness. I blink.

Ross Sumner: *"You twinkle above us, we twinkle below . . ."*

"Pipe down," someone tells him.

I swim up to consciousness. My eyes open, and I stare into the overhead fluorescent light fixture. I try to sit up, but I can't. It isn't exhaustion or pain or injury that is stopping me. I look to my left. My wrist is cuffed to the bedrail. Same with the right and both ankles. Classic four-point restraint.

Ross Sumner whoops with maniacal laughter. "Oh, how I love this! What joy this brings me!"

My vision is still blurred. I take calm breaths and absorb my surroundings. Green-gray concrete walls. Lots of cots, all empty except mine and Ross's. Ross's face is still a pulpy mess, a strip across the broken nose. The infirmary. I'm in the infirmary. Okay, good. I know where I am, at least. I turn the other way and see not one, not two, but *three* prison guards by my bedside. Two are seated next to me like visiting relatives. One is patrolling behind them.

All three are giving me their most menacing glares.

"You are truly screwed now, old boy," Ross Sumner says. "Truly, *truly* screwed."

My mouth feels as though I've been chewing sand, but I still manage to croak out, "Hey, Ross?"

"Yes, David."

"Nice nose, asshole."

Sumner stops laughing.

Never show an inmate fear.

I turn my gaze back toward the guards now. Same thing here. Never show fear—not even to the guards. I meet all of their gazes one at a time. The rage I see in theirs does not sit well with me. They are righteously pissed off at something, and apparently that something is me.

Where, I wonder, is Curly?

A woman I assume is the doctor approaches my bed. "How are you feeling?" she asks in a tone that isn't even pretending to care about the answer.

"Groggy."

"That's to be expected."

"What happened to me?"

She glances over at my glaring guards. "We are still piecing that together."

"Can you at least untie me?"

The doctor gestures toward the glaring guards. "That's not my call."

I look at the three unyielding faces and see no love. The doctor leaves the room. I am not sure what to do or say here so opt for silence. There is an old black-hands white-face clock on the wall. It reminds me of the kind I would stare at, hoping those hands would move a little faster, back in the day at Garfield Elementary School in Revere.

It's a little after eight. I suspect it's a.m. rather than p.m., but with no windows in here, I can't know for sure. My head hurts. I try to piece together what I assume was last night, right up until the time I heard a voice I thought might rescue me. I mostly remember Curly's face, the fear, the panic.

So what happened?

The pacing guard is tall and thin with an overly prominent Adam's apple. His real name is Hal, but everyone calls him Hitch because he's constantly hitching up his pants because, as one of the inmates put it, "Hal got no ass." Hitch rushes toward me, still glaring, and leans so close that our noses are practically touching. I push my head back in the pillow to get a little space. Nothing doing. His breath is awful, like a small gerbil climbed into his mouth, died, and is now decaying.

"You're a dead man, Burroughs," he hisses in my face.

I nearly choke on the stink. I am about to make a rejoinder

about his breath, but a fly-through of sanity stops me. One of the other two guards, a somewhat decent guy named Carlos, says, "Hal."

Hitch Hal ignores him. "Dead," he repeats.

Anything I say right now would either be superfluous or harmful, so I stay quiet.

Hal starts pacing again. Carlos and a third guard, a man named Lester, stay in their seats. I lay my head back on the pillow and close my eyes.

I'm clearly unarmed yet I'm being held by a four-point restraint and watched closely by three guards. Three guards. At the same time.

That seems like overkill to me.

What the hell was going on here? And where was Curly?

Did I hurt him?

I think I remember everything, but based on my history, could I be sure of that? Maybe I blacked out. Maybe that other guard, whoever heard me yell, didn't unlock the gate fast enough. Maybe, instead of Curly getting the better of me, I grabbed the shiv from him and . . .

Oh damn.

And while all these theories are swirling in my head, the big tornado keeps ripping through, throwing everything else out of the way: Is my son still alive?

The back of my head pressed down on the pillow, I try to pull my arms and legs free, but they are shackled. I feel help-less. Time passes. I don't know how much. I am plotting, and I'm coming up with nothing.

The wall phone rings. Carlos stands, walks toward it, picks it up. He turns so his back is to me and speaks low. I can't make out what he's saying. After a few seconds, he hangs the receiver back on the wall. Lester and Hal both turn to Carlos. Carlos nods.

"It's time," Carlos says.

Hal takes out a small key. He unlocks my ankles first, then my wrists. Carlos and Lester stand over me as though they expect me to break for it. I obviously don't. I massage my wrists.

"Get up," Hitch Hal snaps.

I feel woozy. I sit up slowly—too slowly for Hitch. He reaches down and grabs me by the hair and pulls me up. Blood rushes south. My head reels in protest.

"I said," Hitch spits out between clenched teeth, "get up."

Hitch rips the blankets off me. I hear Sumner start laughing again. Then Hitch picks up my feet and throws them to the side. I swing with them so that they land on the floor. I manage to get myself to a standing position. My legs are rubber. I take a step and stumble like a marionette before I'm able to get my footing.

Ross Sumner is enjoying this. He sings, "*Nah nah nah, nah nah nah, hey hey hey . . .*"

My skull aches. "Where are we going?" I ask.

Carlos puts a hand on my back and gives me a gentle shove. I almost trip and fall.

"Let's go," Carlos says.

Hitch and Lester stand on either side of me. They take hold of my arms, making sure they grip that pressure point beneath both elbows hard. They half escort, half drag me out of the infirmary.

"Where are you taking me?"

But the only reply is Ross Sumner finishing up his repeat of the opening stanza and waving, ". . . *Goodbye!*"

I try to clear my head, but the cobwebs cling stubbornly to the corners. Carlos leads the way. Lester is on my right arm, Hitch on my left. Hitch's stare is palpable, a beating thing of hate. My pulse picks up. What now? Where the hell are we going? And a reminder:

A guard tried to kill me last night.

That's the headline here, right? Curly had taken me into an abandoned corridor in the hospital and tried to stick me with a shiv. The wound on my forearm from that blade is wrapped now in thick gauze, but I can feel it pulsating.

The four of us trudge down a corridor and through a tunnel lined with light bulbs protected by metal cages. The walk is doing me some good. My head clears. Not completely. But enough. At the end of the tunnel, we head up a flight of stairs. I see daylight through a window. Okay, so the clock was at eight a.m., not p.m. Made sense. A sign lets me know we are now in the ADMINISTRATIVE WING. It is quiet, but office hours don't start, I know, until nine a.m.

So what are we doing here now?

I debate trying to make a move of some kind, just to make sure someone would know where I am. But what good would that do? Like I said, it's just after eight in the morning. No one is even here yet.

Carlos stops in front of a closed door. He knocks and a muffled voice tells him to come in. Carlos turns the knob. The door opens. I peer inside.

Curly is standing there.

My stomach drops. I try to backpedal, but Hal and Lester have both my arms. They shove me forward.

Curly sneers at me. "You son of a bitch."

Our eyes lock. He is trying yet again to look so tough, but I can see that once again, Curly is scared and close to tears. I am about to protest, to ask him why he tried to kill me, but again, what's the point? What's the play here?

Then I hear a familiar voice say, "Okay, Ted, that's enough."

Relief floods my veins.

I lean into the room and turn to the right. It's Uncle Philip. I'm safe. I think.

I try to catch the old man's eye, but he does not so much as glance in my direction. He is dressed in a blue suit and red tie. He stands by the window for another second before crossing the room and shaking Curly Ted's hand.

"Thank you for your cooperation, Ted."

"Of course, Warden."

Philip Mackenzie's gaze sweeps past me and finds the three guards who escorted me here. "I'll handle the prisoner now," he says. "You all go back to your regular duties."

Carlos says, "Yes, Warden."

I hadn't really thought about this before, but I am still clad only in my flimsy hospital smock, which opens in the back. I wear socks that I assume are hospital issue. I don't have my canvas shoes anymore. I feel suddenly exposed and near naked, but to them, all of them, I must also appear like no threat.

Curly heads toward either me or the door, it is hard to know which. He slows as he gets closer to me and tries again to give me his toughest gaze, but there is nothing behind it. It's for show.

The man is terrified.

As Curly reaches the door, Philip Mackenzie says, "Ted?"

He turns back toward the warden.

"The prisoner will be with me for the rest of the day. Who is working your block?"

"I am," Ted said. "I'm on until three."

"You've been up all night."

"I feel fine."

"Are you sure? You can take this shift off. No one would blame you."

"I'd rather work, Warden, if that's okay."

"Very well then. I doubt we'll be done with him before your shift is through. Just as well. Tell your replacement."

"Yes, Warden."

Curly steps out of the room. Hitch Hal greets him with a buddy-clap on the back. Philip has still not so much as glanced my way. Curly and Hal start down the corridor. Lester follows. Carlos leans his head in and says, "You need me, Warden?"

"Not right now, Carlos. I'll contact you if I need a statement."

Carlos looked over at me, then back to Philip. "Okay then."

"Carlos?"

"Yes?"

"Please close the door on your way out."

"You sure, Warden?"

"Yeah, I'm sure."

Carlos nods and closes the door. Philip and I are alone. Before I can say anything, Philip signals me to take a seat. I do so. He stays standing.

"Ted Weston says you tried to kill him last night."

Label me surprised.

Philip folds his arms and leans across the front of his desk. "He claims you faked an illness to get him to take you to the infirmary. Because of your earlier altercation with an inmate named Ross Sumner where you sustained injuries, he took you at your word."

Philip turns his head to the right and points to the shiv—I assume it's the one Curly used last night—on his desk. The blade is sealed in a plastic crime-scene bag. "He further claims that once you were alone, you pulled this on him and tried to stab him. You two fought. He wrestled the weapon away from you, slicing your arm in the process. Then you ran down the corridor. Another correctional officer heard the commotion and subdued you."

"It's a lie, Philip."

He says nothing.

"What motive would I have?"

"Oh, I don't know. Didn't you come to see me yesterday for the first time and beg me to get you out?"

"So . . . ?"

"So maybe you became desperate. You get in a fight with a high-profile inmate—"

"That psycho jumped me—"

"And that gets you to the infirmary. Maybe that's part of your escape plan, I don't know. Or maybe you get the weapon from Ross Sumner once you're there. Maybe you're working together."

"Philip, Curly is lying."

"Curly?"

"That's what we call him. I didn't do this. He woke me up. He walked me to that corridor. He tried to kill me. I got injured trying to defend myself."

"Right, sure, and I guess you expect me—and the world at large—to take the word of a convicted baby-killer over the word of a fifteen-year correctional officer with a spotless record."

For the moment, I say nothing.

"I saw your father yesterday."

"What?"

"Your aunt Sophie too."

He looks off.

"How are they?"

"Your father can't talk. He's dying."

I shake my head. "Why did you go see him?"

He doesn't reply.

"Yesterday of all days. Why did you go to Revere, Philip?"

He starts toward the door. "Come with me."

I don't bother asking where we are going. I stand and follow him. We start down the corridor and down the steps. We walk side by side. Philip keeps his spine ramrod straight, his eyes straight ahead. Without turning to me, he says, "You're lucky the correctional officer who subdued you was Carlos."

"What?"

"Because Carlos called me right away. To report the incident. I immediately ordered three correctional officers, including Carlos, to watch you around the clock."

I stop and take hold of Philip's sleeve. "So no one could finish the job," I say. "You were afraid someone would kill me."

Philip stares down at my hand on his sleeve. I slowly let him go.

"You're still in danger," he says. "Even if I put you in solitary. Even if I get you an immediate transfer. A correctional officer who is now claiming a vendetta wants you dead, plus you still have Ross Sumner and the Sumner fortune on your back—all of that is not conducive to a healthy outcome."

"So what do I do?" I ask.

Philip replies by opening the door to his office, the one I had visited just yesterday. When I see Philip's son Adam standing there in his full police uniform, my heart soars for the first time in I don't know how long. For a moment, I just stare at my best friend. He smiles and nods as if to tell me that this is real, he is there, right in front of me. I let my mind fall back to another era, to the locker room before basketball practice at Revere High or double-dating with the Hancock sisters at Friendly's or hanging out in the last row of the Fenway Park bleachers and razzing the opposing team's right fielder.

Adam spreads his arms and steps forward and I fall into his bear hug. I squeeze my eyes shut because I'm afraid I'll cry. I feel my legs give way, but Adam holds me up. How long has it been since I've experienced any physical affection? Almost five years. The last person to hug me with any genuine feeling or caring? My father, who now lay dying, on the day the jury read the guilty verdict. But even with him, even with the father I loved like no other man, I had sensed some hesitancy in the embrace. My father loved me. But—and perhaps this is me projecting—there had been some doubt, as though he wasn't sure whether he was embracing his son or a monster.

There is no doubt in Adam's hug.

Adam doesn't release me until I finally let go of him. I step back, not sure I can even speak. Philip has already closed the door. He stands next to his son.

"We have a plan," Philip says.

10

"What plan?" I ask.

Philip Mackenzie nods at his son. Adam smiles and starts unbuttoning his shirt.

"You're about to become me," Adam says.

"Say again?"

"I would have liked more time to plan," Philip says, "but I meant what I said. If you stay here, no matter how hard I try to protect you, it won't end well. We got to do this now."

Adam takes off his uniform shirt and hands it to me. "I'm wearing the smallest size I have, but it'll still be loose." I take hold of the shirt. Adam undoes his belt.

"Here's the plan in a nutshell," Philip continues. "You set us up, David."

"I did?"

"You came to me yesterday for the first time—that meeting is on file—and you said that you wanted to be rehabilitated for your crimes. Gave me a whole big sob story of how you wanted to make amends and confess and get real help."

I slip off my hospital gown and throw Adam's white T-shirt over my head. Then I shrug into the uniform. "Go on."

"You begged me to bring your old pal Adam in to see you. That's where you wanted to start—with someone who'd listen and still accept you. Because of my loyalty to my old friend— your father—I fell for it. It made sense to me. If anybody could pull you back from the abyss and get you to confess the truth, it was Adam."

Adam hands me his pants. He is grinning.

"So I arranged a long visit today—just like I told the correctional officers out there. You and Adam were going to spend the day together."

The pants are too long. I roll them up and create cuffs.

"What I didn't know was that you had a gun."

I frown. "A gun?"

"Yes. You pulled it on us. You made Adam undress and then you tied him up and locked him in the closet."

Adam smiles. "And me being afraid of the dark."

I return the smile, though now I remember that as a child Adam had a Snoopy night-light near his bed. It kept me up sometimes when I slept over. I would stare at Snoopy and not be able to close my eyes.

Funny the memories that stay with you.

"Then," Philip continues, "you put on Adam's uniform, including his trench coat and cap. You forced me at gunpoint to take you out of here."

"How the hell did I get a gun?" I ask.

Philip shrugs. "It's a prison. People smuggle in a lot of things."

"Not guns, Philip. And I just spent the night in the infirmary surrounded by three guards. No one is going to buy that."

"Good point," Philip says. "Wait, hold up." He opens his desk drawer and pulls out a Glock 19. "You took mine."

"What?"

Philip opens his suit jacket to reveal an empty holster. "I had the gun on me. We were reminiscing. You started to cry. I foolishly moved to comfort you. You caught me off guard and grabbed my gun."

"Is it loaded?"

"No, but . . ." Philip Mackenzie reaches into his drawer and draws out a box of ammunition. "It is now."

This plan is insane. There are a dozen holes. Big holes. But I am being swept out to sea in the riptide. There is no time for second-guessing. This is my chance. I have to get out of here. If Philip and Adam end up facing consequences or making sacrifices, so be it. My son is alive and out there somewhere. Selfish or not, that trumps all.

"Okay, so what's next?" I ask.

Adam is down to his underwear. I take a seat and slip on his socks and start on the shoes. Adam is two inches taller and while we used to be around the same weight, he probably has twenty or thirty pounds on me now. I tighten the belt to keep my pants from falling down. I throw on the trench coat, which helps.

"I had Adam wear his cap on the way in," Philip says,

tossing me the police hat. "That'll cover your hair. Walk fast and keep your head down. We only pass one checkpoint on the way out to the parking lot. When we get to my car, you will order me—at gunpoint, of course—to drive to my house. Stupid me, I went to the bank yesterday and took out five thousand dollars in cash. I would have taken more but that would be too obvious."

Adam tosses me his wallet. "I have a thousand dollars in there. And maybe I'll forget to cancel one of my credit cards. That Mastercard maybe. I never use it anyway."

I nod and try not to get too emotional. I need to focus, stay in the moment, think it through while still moving. The Mastercard, for example. Could I use it? Or would that make it too easy to track me?

Later, I tell myself. Think about it later. Concentrate. "So when do we head to your car?"

Philip checks his watch. "Right now. We should get to my house before nine. You'll tie me up, and I'll escape at, say, six tonight. That should give you a decent head start. I'll be panicked when I finally get free, especially because you tied up my son and left him in the closet. I'll rush back here to let him out before I tell anyone what's going on. Then I'll sound the alarm. Probably around seven tonight. That should give you a solid ten-hour head start."

I tighten the laces of Adam's shoes so they don't slip off. I have the cap's brim tilted down over my eyes. Adam thinks about putting on the hospital gown, but there's no point in that.

"Get in the closet," Philip tells his son.

Adam turns to me. We hug deep and hard.

"Find him," Adam says to me. "Find my godson."

Philip tosses him a few candy bars along with restraints I might have used to tie him up. I don't know if someone will buy that or not, but with luck, he won't be found until later tonight—and by his father. Philip closes the closet door and locks it with his key. He picks up the Glock and presses the button on the hand grip, ejecting the magazine. I know that this Glock can hold fifteen rounds, but without an autoloader, arming it is slow. You have to insert ammunition one bullet at a time into the top of the magazine, making sure the rounded side is forward. Philip throws in six or seven bullets and then slams the magazine back into the handle.

He hands me the weapon.

"Don't use it," he says, "especially not on me."

I manage a smile.

"You ready?" he asks.

I feel the adrenaline kick in. "Let's do this."

———

Philip Mackenzie is one of those guys who exude confidence and strength. When he walks, he walks big and with purpose. His strides are long. His head is high. I try to keep up with him, the brim of Adam's cap pulled low enough to provide a modicum of disguise but not so low as to be conspicuous. We stop at an elevator.

"Press the down button," Philip tells me.

I do as he asks.

"There's a camera in the elevator. Flash the gun a little in there. Threaten me with it. Be subtle, but make sure the gun is visible."

"Okay."

"When I get back here, there will be questions. The more they can see I felt in mortal danger, the easier it'll be."

The elevator dings and the doors slide open. Empty.

"Got it," I say as we step in. I have the gun in the pocket of the trench coat. It feels so playact-y, as though I'm threatening him with my finger. I take the gun out and keep it close to my side but in line with the camera overhead. I clear my throat and mutter something about not making any false moves. I sound like a bad episode of TV. Philip doesn't react. He doesn't throw his hands up or panic, which, I agree, adds to the realism of my "threat."

When the elevator stops on the ground level, I put the gun back in my pocket. Philip hurries out of the elevator. I rush to keep up with him.

"Just keep walking," Philip says to me in a low voice. "Don't stop, don't make eye contact. Stay a little bit behind me and on the right. I'll block security's line of vision."

I nod. Up ahead I see a metal detector. I almost freeze, but then I realize it is only checking people incoming, not outgoing. No one is really paying attention to who is exiting except in the most cursory way, but then again this is the administrative branch. Inmates are never in here. There is only one guard. From a distance he looks young and bored and reminds me of a stoned hall monitor in a high school.

We are ten yards away. Philip steps on without hesitation. I try to slow down or speed up, gauging what angle would keep my face blocked by Philip's big shoulders. As we get closer, as the young guard spots the warden barreling toward him, he throws his feet down and stands. He looks first at the warden, then at me.

Something crosses his face.

We are so close to that damn door.

I realize with something approaching dread that I still have the gun in my hand. My hand is in my pocket. Without conscious thought, my grip on the weapon tightens. I slide my finger onto the trigger.

Would I shoot? Would I really shoot this guy to escape?

Philip nods to the guard as we pass him, his face firm. I manage to make a nodding motion too, figuring that Adam might do that.

"Have a good day, Warden," the guard says.

"You too, son."

We are at the exit now. Philip presses hard against the bar, pushing the doors open.

Two seconds later, we are out of the building and on our way to his car.

———

Ted "Curly" Weston sat in the break room with his head in his hands. He couldn't stop shaking.

Oh God, what had he done?

Messed up. Messed up big-time. He'd known better, hadn't he? He'd tried to live his life on the straight and narrow. "A solid day's work for a solid day's pay." That's what his father had always said. His father worked as a butcher in a huge meatpacking plant. He woke up at three in the morning and spent his day in refrigeration and dragged himself home in time to eat dinner and go to sleep because he had to wake up the next day at three in the morning to get to work. That was his life until he keeled over and died at the age of fifty-nine of a heart attack.

Still, Ted had lived on the up-and-up for the most part. Did he take some graft in here? Sure. Everyone did. Everything in life is graft when you think about it. That's life, man. We are all scamming one another. Ted had been better about it. He wasn't a pig, but with the crap wages they pay you, you're expected to skim to make up the difference. To supplement your earnings. That's the American way. You can't live on what Walmart pays you. Walmart knows that. But they also know the government will make up the difference with food stamps and Medicare or whatever. So yeah, maybe this is all self-justification, but when someone asks him to keep an eye on a prisoner, like he'd done over the years with Burroughs, or when a family wants to give him a tip—that was how Teddy viewed it, like a gratuity—to sneak a relative some sort of comfort item, well, why the hell not? If he said no, the next guy would say yes. It was expected. Everyone does it. It makes the world go round. You don't rock the boat.

But Ted had never hurt anybody.

That was important to note here. He may have turned his back when these animals wanted to clobber one another. Why the hell not? They'd find a way to clobber one another anyway. One time Ted had gotten in the middle of one of those scrums and an inmate who looked like a walking venereal disease had scratched him deeply with his fingernail. His fingernail! Damn wound got infected. Ted had to take antibiotics for like two months.

He should have stayed away from Ross Sumner.

Yeah, the money had been big and real. Yeah, he didn't so much need a "better life"—he had a pretty great one, really—but man, to just get above that pile of bills that were smothering him, drowning him, just to be able to float above those bills, just to go through a few days and not worry about money, maybe have enough to take Edna out to a nice dinner—was that too much to ask? Really?

Ted searched for a donut on the table, but there were none. Damn. Some jackass had brought croissants instead. Croissants. Ever try to eat a croissant and not get the crumbs all over you? Impossible. Yet that was the thing now. They were French, someone said. They were cultured and classy.

Are you kidding me?

Two of his fellow correctional officers, Moronski and O'Reilly, stuffed croissants in their pie holes, the flakes sputtering out of their mouths like out of a wood chipper, as they argued over best bosom point-of-view on Instagram. Moronski favored "deep cleavage" while O'Reilly was waxing poetic on the "side boob" shot.

Oh yeah, Ted thought. *The croissants add a touch of class.*

"Hey, Ted, you got an opinion on this?"

Ted ignored them. He stared down at the pastry and debated taking a bite. He started to reach out for one, but his hands were shaking.

"You okay?" O'Reilly asked.

"Yeah, I'm fine."

"We heard about what happened," Moronski said. "Can't believe Burroughs would try something like that. You do something to piss him off?"

"Don't think so."

"Not sure why you'd take him to the infirmary without letting Kelsey know."

"I buzzed him," Ted lied, "but he didn't reply."

"Still. Why not wait?"

"Burroughs looked bad to me," Ted said. "I didn't want him dying on us."

Moronski said, "Leave him alone, O'Reilly."

"What? I was just asking."

Enough, Ted thought. The big question: What was Burroughs telling the warden right now? Probably his version of the truth—that Ted had been the one with the shiv, not him. But so what? Who'd believe a baby-killer like Burroughs over Ted Weston? And O'Reilly's questions notwithstanding, his fellow guards would back him. Even Carlos, who seemed pretty shook up when he came upon the scene last night, would fall into line. No one in here makes waves. No one in here is going to buck the system or side with an inmate.

So why didn't Ted feel safe?

He had to think about his next move. The first thing was, put it behind him. Get to work. Act like it was no big deal.

But my God, what had Ted *almost* done?

True, Sumner had backed him into a corner, had really blackmailed him into it, but suppose if Ted had been "successful," he would have killed a man. Murdered a fellow human being. That's the part he still couldn't get over. He, Ted Weston, had tried to kill a man. Part of him wondered whether he had subconsciously sabotaged himself, that it wasn't so much that Burroughs had been quick or good at self-defense, but rather that Ted, no matter what else was true, knew that he could not go through with it. He thought about that now. Suppose the blade had hit home. Suppose he had punctured Burroughs's heart and watched the man's life leave his body.

Ted was in a panic now. But if he had gone through with it, if he had succeeded, would he be any better off?

He grabbed a cup of coffee and scarfed it down like an aardvark on an anthill. He checked the clock. Time to start his shift. He headed out of the break room.

Ted Weston was starting up the stairwell, fear still coursing through every vein in his body, when something outside the caged window caught his eye. He stopped short and hard, as if some giant hand had grabbed him by the shoulder and yanked him back.

What the . . . ?

The window looked out over the executive parking lot. The

bigwigs parked there. The correctional officers, like Ted, had to park way out back and take a shuttle to their respective wings. But that wasn't what bothered him right now. Ted squinted and looked again. The warden had been pretty specific: He was going to spend hours, if not the entire day, with Burroughs.

Yeah, okay, whatever.

So why was the warden getting into his car?

And who was the guy with him?

Ted felt something cold slide down his spine. He couldn't say why. In many ways, this was no big deal. Ted watched the warden get in on the driver's side. The guy with him—some guy in a hat and trench coat—got in on the passenger side.

So if the warden was heading out, where the hell was David Burroughs? Ted had his radio. There had been no call about a prisoner pickup. So maybe the warden had put him in solitary. No, if that had been done, they would have been informed. So maybe the warden left Burroughs with someone else, an underling, to interrogate him further.

But Ted knew it was none of those things. He felt it in his bones. Something was wrong here. Something big.

He hurried over to the wall phone and lifted it.

"It's Weston, sector four. I think we got a problem."

11

I can't believe I'm in Philip's car.

I look through the front windshield. It's a gray morning. Rain will be coming soon—I can feel that in my face. I have heard of arthritis sufferers who can predict rainstorms by the pain in their joints. I can feel it, strange as this sounds, in my cheek and jaw. Both had been shattered in that first prison beating. Now, whenever a rainstorm is on the horizon, the bones ache like an infected wisdom tooth.

Philip starts the car up, puts it in reverse, and pulls out. I look out the window at the fortresslike edifice and I shudder. I won't be back, I tell myself. No matter what. I won't ever let myself come back here.

I turn to Philip. His big bushy eyebrows are lowered in concentration. His thick hands grip the steering wheel as though he's preparing to rip it off.

"People are going to wonder how I got your gun," I say.

He shrugs.

"You're taking a big risk."

"Don't worry about it."

"Are you doing this because of what happened last night," I ask, "or because you believe me about Matthew being alive?"

The older man chews on that for a moment. "Does it matter?"

"I guess not."

We fall into silence as Philip makes the turn into the circle. Up ahead, I can see the guard tower and exit gates we will soon be driving through. Less than a hundred yards away now. I sit back and try to stay calm.

It won't be long now.

———

Sitting on the floor of the dark closet, Adam Mackenzie tried to make himself somewhat comfortable. If all goes well, he should be stuck in this dark closet for ten or eleven hours. He sat up against the back of the closet. He'd left his phone in his father's car because there'd be no way "Crazed David Burroughs" would have let him keep it with him. Still. Ten or eleven hours sitting in the dark in this closet? Adam shook his head. He should have brought a flashlight and something to read.

He closed his eyes. Adam was exhausted. His father had called him after midnight to tell him about David's incident with the guards and his bizarre claim about Matthew being alive. It was nonsense, of course. It had to be. He remembered when David asked him to be Matthew's godfather, just as David's father had once asked Adam's father to do the same. It had been one of the proudest moments of Adam's life. He'd always felt that way about his relationship with David. Proud, that is. David was special. He was *that* guy. Men wanted to be him, women fell for him, but there were demons there. It was why, when Adam first heard the speculation about David being the killer, sure, on the outside, Adam refused to believe it, but there was a small part of him, a little gnawing in the back of the brain, that couldn't help but have doubts. David had a temper. There had been that fight during their senior year of high school. Adam had been the team's leading scorer and rebounder, but still it was David, the role player, the guy who hustled, the gritty defender, who'd been voted captain by their teammates. It has always been that way. Adam the finesse player, David his more popular enforcer. Anyway, during their senior year, Revere High had lost to their rivals from Brookside, 78–77, when Adam, who'd scored 24 points, missed a layup with four seconds left to play. That missed layup haunted Adam. Still. Today. But it was later that night, when several guys from Brookside mocked Adam for the big miss, that David took matters into his own hands. He beat the shit out of two guys in an attack so filled with fury that Adam had to pull David away and get him in a car.

More than that, there was David's father, Lenny. Lenny and Adam's own father—what was he saying?

The sins of the father shall be visited upon the sons.

He should have been visiting his old friend all along. So why hadn't he? At first, David refused any visitors. Yeah, okay, but Adam could have tried harder. He just gave up. He didn't have the strength. That was what he told himself. The man incarcerated in this hellhole wasn't his best friend. His best friend was gone. He had been bludgeoned to death and left for dead with his son.

Adam was about to shift his legs when he heard the door to his father's office swing open.

A gruff voice said, "What the hell is going on?"

Oh shit.

Adam grabbed the ropes and began to wind them around his legs. He lifted the handkerchief up to his mouth so that it would appear to be a gag. The plan was simple. If anyone found him before his father got back, Adam was supposed to make it look like he was in the midst of escaping.

Another voice said, "I told you. He's gone."

Gruff Voice: "How the hell can he be gone?"

"What do you mean?"

"Where's the inmate?"

"You mean he didn't return him before he left?"

"No."

"You sure?"

"I work in that wing. I think I'd know if the inmate who tried to murder me was back in his cell."

Adam stayed very still.

"Maybe another guy escorted Burroughs back."

"No, that would be my job."

"But you just said you were on break, right? Maybe the warden was in a rush, you know? Maybe he got one of the other guys to do it."

"Maybe." But Gruff Voice sounded dubious.

"I'll call and check. I don't know what you're worried about."

"I just saw him with somebody. The warden, I mean. In the parking lot."

"That was probably his kid."

"His kid?"

"Yeah, he's a cop."

"He brought his kid today?"

"Yep."

"Why?"

"How the hell am I supposed to know?"

"I don't get it. The warden gets a call one of his correctional officers was nearly killed by a prisoner—and he decides it's Bring Your Son to Work Day?"

"I don't know. Maybe."

Gruff Voice says, "Think we should sound the alarm?"

"For what? We don't even know if Burroughs is missing. Let's call your cell block and solitary. See if he's there first."

"And if he's not?"

"Then we sound the alarm."

There was a short pause. Then Gruff Voice said, "Yeah, all right. Let's make the call."

"We can use my phone. It's next door."

Adam heard the two men leave. He stood. The closet was suddenly stifling. Adam felt trapped, claustrophobic. He tried the knob. Locked. Of course. His father had locked him in to make it all look good.

Christ, so now what?

Things were unraveling fast. It wouldn't be long now. They'd make the call. They'd find out there was no David. The alarm would sound. Damn. He tried the knob again, turning it harder. No go.

No choice now.

He had to break down the door. The shoulder wouldn't work as well. Trying to break a door down with your shoulder only leads to dislocation. With his back pressed against the back of the closet, Adam lifted his foot. He checked to see which way the hinges were facing. If the door opens toward you, there is little chance for success. But that wasn't the case here. Very few closets open to the inside. Not enough space. Second thing, you always kick to the side where the lock is mounted. That's the weakest part. Using the back of the closet as leverage, Adam drove his heel hard into the area just below the knob. It took three tries, but eventually the door gave way. Adam blinked into the light and stumbled toward his father's desk.

He picked up the landline. It took him a few seconds to remember his father's number—like most people, Adam hadn't seen a need to memorize it—but it came to him.

Adam dialed and heard the phone ring.

———

When Philip's car glides to a stop behind a large white truck, a guard comes toward us with a handheld device.

"Just keep your brim down," Philip says.

The guard circles the car, staring at the device in his hand. He pauses by the trunk before continuing his sweep.

"What is that?" I ask.

"A heartbeat monitor," Philip replies. "It can actually sense a beating heart through walls."

"So if anybody is hiding in the back or in the trunk . . ."

Philip nods. "We find them."

"Thorough," I say.

"There hasn't been an escape at Briggs since I've been warden."

I keep my face turned away until the guard is back in his booth. He nods at Philip. Philip gives him a friendly wave. I wait for the electronic gates to slide open. It seems to be taking an inordinately long time, but I imagine that's more in my head than reality. I stare out at the twelve-foot-high fence of chain-link, topped with coiling circles of barbed wire. The grass along the perimeter is surprisingly lush and green, like something you might see on a golf course. On the other side of the grass, not far past the fence, the landscape becomes thick with trees.

I start breathing faster. I'm not sure why. I feel as though I'm hyperventilating and maybe I am.

I have to get out of here.

"Steady," Philip says.

Then the phone rings.

It's hooked up to the car, so the sound is jarringly loud. I look at the screen and it reads NO CALLER ID. I turn to Philip. His face registers confusion. He takes the phone off the cradle and puts it to his ear.

"Hello?"

Sounds like Adam. I can't make out his words, but I hear panic in his tone. I close my eyes and will myself to stay calm. The gates start to slide open with a grunt, as though reluctant to move. The white truck is still in front of us.

"Damn," Philip says to the person on the phone.

"What?" I ask.

Philip ignores me. "How much time do we have before—?"

The prison's escape siren shatters the still air.

———

The siren is deafening. I look at Philip. His expression is understandably grim. The gate, which had been almost fully open, stops and reverses course. I can see the tower guard on the phone. He drops the receiver and picks up a rifle.

"Philip?"

"Point the gun at me, David."

I don't ask for clarification. I do as he says. Philip hits the accelerator. He swerves to the right and then speeds in front of the white truck. He is headed toward the closing gate. He tries to drive through the opening. No go. The gate is no longer open enough for us to get through. Philip noses the car in. He stomps the accelerator to the floor. Our tires spin. He doesn't let up on the gas pedal. The gate gives way, just a little. Not enough.

The guard with the rifle bursts out of the tower.

"Keep the gun on me!" Philip shouts.

I do.

The guard with the rifle suddenly stops and points the weapon at the car.

Philip shifts the car into reverse. He backs up, the gates scraping the sides of his car. He puts it back in drive and rams the gates again. They budge, but not by much. Two more guards are rushing at us now, both armed with handguns. I watch them close in. The gun feels heavy in my hand.

The guards are almost on top of us. The siren continues to blare.

I look at the gun in my hand. "Philip?"

"Hang on."

The car leaps forward. There is a crunching sound. The gates open a bit more, the nose of the car jammed between them. Philip hits the gas pedal, stops, hits it again. The engine thuds and whirs.

The guards are yelling at us, but I can't hear them over the siren.

The car begins to squeeze through the opening now. We are almost out, almost in the clear, but the gates are still closing, squeezing the car. It reminds me of that trash compactor scene in *Star Wars* and all the old TV shows where the heroes are trapped in a room with the walls closing in to crush them.

The first guard is at my car window. He's shouting—I don't know or care what. Our eyes actually meet. He starts to raise the weapon. I don't see how I have a choice. I can't go back. I can't give up. My gun is pointed at Philip, but now I spin toward the guard.

Aim for the legs, I think.

Philip shouts. "Don't!"

The guard has the gun in his hand, pointing it at me. Him or me. That's how it is. I hesitate, but I really have no choice. I am about to fire when the car suddenly lunges forward, snapping my head back. The gates hold on to the car for another second, no more than that, and with one last scrape, we break free.

The guards run after us, but Philip keeps his foot on the gas. The car accelerates to full speed, hurling us down the road. I turn around. The guards stand there. They, along with Briggs Correctional Facility, grow smaller and dimmer until I can no longer see a trace of either.

But even then, I can still hear the siren.

12

Rachel heard the siren too.

She was having breakfast at the Nesbitt Station Diner, an eatery inside two converted railcars with a menu only slightly shorter in word count than your average novel. Her favorite listing on the menu, listed under forty different ways of having a burger (beef, bison, chicken, turkey, elk, portobello mushroom, wild salmon, cod, black bean, veggie, plant-based, lamb, pork, olive, etc.) was the "My Wife Doesn't Want Anything," which was their way of supersizing your French fries order and throwing in two mozzarella sticks. The diner had a sign at the door saying OPEN 24 HOURS BUT NOT IN A ROW before stating their working hours, which went from five a.m. until two a.m. Monday through Saturday. Another sign read: BYOB BUT WE ENCOURAGE YOU TO SHARE WITH YOUR SERVER.

The Air Fryer Cheeseburger last night had been pretty good, but the draw of this place for Rachel was the excellent Wi-Fi.

The Briggs Motor Lodge's Wi-Fi was so bad she thought she heard a phone-modem shriek when she tried to access it. The Lodge, a word with too many meanings, also didn't have a bar or restaurant, just a foyer by the front desk that featured free "Continental" breakfast, a truly upmarket term for a stale roll and a half-melted margarine packet.

The diner's clock had all number 5s on it, with the words NO DRINKING UNTIL AFTER FIVE across the face. Still an hour until visiting hours—enough time to continue her research. That was why she had camped out here last night and again this morning, nursing coffee and ordering enough so as not to draw eye daggers for taking up a booth.

Her laptop had been humming all night, unearthing a mixed bag of information. On the negative side, she had not been able to find one Caucasian male between the ages of two and three anywhere in the country who had disappeared—and *remained* missing some five years later—that would fit the timeline of Matthew's murder. Not one. Some boys that age had died. Some had even been kidnapped, usually in custody battles, and eventually found. Three had even vanished for as long as eight months before their bodies were located.

But so far, not one child who could fit the criteria remained unaccounted for, thus raising the most troublesome question: If the body wasn't Matthew's, whose was it?

Of course, it was still early. She would widen the search, try more months, farther away from the area, check other databases. Maybe the dead boy in Matthew's bed—God, that sounded so crazy—had been younger or older or light-skinned

Black or Eurasian or something else entirely. Rachel would be thorough. Before her scandal, she had been known as a ruthless researcher. Still, there was no other way to spin it: This "no body" news was a blow to any theory about Matthew being alive.

Matthew alive. Seriously, how crazy pants was that theory anyway?

The more positive news, if you could call any of this positive, involved the main witness against David, the "sweet old lady" (as the media had naturally dubbed her) Hilde Winslow. Locating the elderly widow should, in theory, have been no problem. When it first proved difficult, Rachel wondered whether the woman had passed away in the last five years. But there was no record of her dying. In fact, Rachel had only been able to find two people with that name. One of the Hildes was thirty years old and lived in Portland, Oregon. The other was a fourth grader in Crystal River, Florida.

Nope and double nope.

The name Hilde was derived from the more common name Hilda. No surprise there. The court documents from David's case and all the pursuant media listed her as Hilde, but just to cover all the bases, Rachel tried Hilda Winslow. There were only two of them as well and neither fit the profile. Then she tried Hilde Winslow's maiden name—women often go back to using that—but that too bore no fruit.

A dead end.

The siren—Rachel assumed that it was some sort of fire alarm—kept screeching.

Her phone buzzed. She checked the number and saw it was Tim Doherty, her old friend from her days at the *Globe*, calling her back. Tim had been one of the few to stick with her when the shit hit the fan. Not publicly, of course. That would have been career suicide. She didn't want that for him or anyone else.

"I got it," Tim said to her.

"The entire murder file?"

"The court documents and transcripts. There's no way the cops are going to let me look at their murder book."

"Did you get Hilde Winslow's Social Security number?"

"Yes. Can I ask why you wanted it?"

"I need to find her."

"Yeah, I figured that. Why not go the regular routes?"

"I did."

"And you got nothing," he said.

She could hear the lilt in Tim's voice. "That's right. Why? What did you get?"

"I took the liberty of running the Social Security number."

"And?"

"Two months after your brother-in-law's trial, Hilde Winslow changed her name to Harriet Winchester."

Pay dirt, Rachel thought. "Whoa."

"Yes," he said. "She also sold her house and moved to an apartment on Twelfth Street in Manhattan." He rattled off the address. "By the way, she turns eighty-one this week."

"So why would a woman of her age change her name and move?" Rachel asked.

"Post-trial press?"

"Come again?"

"This murder was a big story," Tim said.

"Yeah, but come on. Once her part was over there was no more scrutiny on her."

The press was like the worst womanizer. Once it metaphorically bedded someone, it quickly grew bored and moved on to something new. A name change, while perhaps explainable, was extreme and curious.

"Fair," he said. "Do you think she lied about your brother-in-law?"

"I don't know."

"Rachel?"

"Yes?"

"You got something big here, don't you?"

"I think so."

"Normally I would ask for a taste," he said. "But you need it more than I do. You deserve another chance, and this world doesn't like to give that to people anymore, so if you need anything else from me, you let me know, okay?"

She felt tears come to her eyes. "You're the best, Tim."

"I know, right? Talk soon."

Tim hung up. Rachel wiped her eyes. She stared out the diner window, into the crowded parking lot, the siren still blaring in the distance. The world may eventually give Rachel another chance, but she wasn't sure she deserved it. It had been two years since Catherine Tullo's death at Rachel's hands.

Catherine wouldn't get another chance. Why should Rachel?

It had been the most important story of Rachel's career. After an exhaustive eight-month investigation, the *Globe*'s Sunday magazine was going to feature her exposé of Lemhall University's beloved president Spencer Shane for not only turning a blind eye over the past two decades to sexual assault, abuse, and misconduct by certain male professors but participating in a pattern of systemic abuse and cover-ups at one of the country's elite institutions. It was a case so egregious yet so frustrating and slippery that Rachel grew obsessed in a way no journalist should. She lost perspective, not on the outrageousness of the crime and culture—there was no way you couldn't be outraged about that—but on the frailty and decency of the victims.

Lemhall University, her alma mater, managed to get a lot of NDAs signed, so no one could or would go on record. While Rachel kept it from her editors, she herself had been pressured to sign one her freshman year after a disturbing incident at a Halloween party. She refused. The school mishandled her case.

Maybe that was where it started. She lost then. She wouldn't lose again.

So she went too far.

In the end, the charges were too loaded for the *Globe* to publish because no one could slip past the NDAs. Rachel couldn't believe it. She went to the local DA, but he didn't have the appetite to take on such a popular figure and institution.

So she went back to her former classmate Catherine Tullo and begged her to break her NDA. Catherine wanted to, that's what she told Rachel, but she was afraid. She wouldn't budge. So that was it. That was what was going to kill the entire story and allow an institution—an institution that had let Rachel's own attacker skate—to remain unblemished.

Rachel could not allow that.

With no other alternatives available, Rachel went harder at Catherine Tullo: Do the right thing or get exposed anyway. If Catherine couldn't put other victims first, then Rachel saw no reason to protect her. She would take the story online herself and reveal her sources. Catherine started to cry. Rachel didn't budge. Half an hour later, Catherine saw the light. She didn't need the money from the settlement. She didn't care about the NDA. She would do the right thing. Catherine Tullo hugged her friend and sorority sister and told her that tomorrow she would give Rachel a longer interview and go on the record, and then that night, after Rachel left her apartment, Catherine Tullo filled a bath full of water and slit her wrists.

Now Catherine haunted her. She was here right now, sitting across the diner booth from her, smiling in that unsure way she always did, blinking as though awaiting a blow, until Rachel heard her waitress, a blue-haired diner special if ever she'd seen one, say to the customer at the table next to Rachel, "I haven't heard that go off in, how long, Cal?"

The man she assumed was Cal said, "Oh, years now."

"You think—?"

"Nah," Cal said. "Briggs is probably just running a drill. I'm sure it's nothing."

Rachel froze.

"You say so," the waitress said, but judging by the expression on her face, she wasn't fully buying it.

Rachel leaned over and said, "Excuse me, I don't mean to pry, but is that siren coming from Briggs Penitentiary?"

Cal and the waitress exchanged a glance. Then Cal nodded and gave her his most condescending smile. "I wouldn't worry your pretty head over it. It's probably just a drill."

"A drill for what?" Rachel asked.

"An escape," the waitress said. "They only blow that whistle when an inmate escapes."

Her cell phone buzzed. Rachel stepped away and put the phone to her ear. "Hello?"

"I need your help," David said.

13

Three cop cars, all with flashing lights atop them, are on us now.

I feel numb. I am out of Briggs for the first time in five years. If they catch me, I will never get out again. Never. I know that. There is no second chance here. My fingers curl around the gun. The metal feels oddly warm and comforting.

The police cruisers spread out in a V formation.

I turn to Philip. "It's over, isn't it?"

"You willing to risk your life?"

"What life?"

He nods. "Point the damn gun at me, David. Keep it up where they can see it."

I do so. The gun feels heavy now. My hand shakes. The adrenaline—from the fight with Sumner, from Curly's attack, from this makeshift escape plan—seems to be ebbing away. Philip hits the accelerator. The police cruisers stay right with us.

"What now?" I ask.

"Wait."

"For what?"

As though on cue, the car phone rings again. Philip's face is a stern mask. Before he answers it, he says, "Remember you're a desperate man. Act it."

I nod.

Philip picks up the phone and says a shaky hello. A voice immediately says, "Your son is safe, Warden. He managed to untie himself and break the door down."

"Who the hell am I talking to?" Philip asks. His voice is brusque and hostile.

There is a moment of hesitation on the other line. "I'm, uh . . . this is—"

Again Philip's voice booms. "I asked who the hell this is."

"I'm Detective Wayne Semsey—"

"Semsey, how old are you?"

"Sir?"

"I mean, have you always been an incompetent moron or is this a relatively new thing?"

"I don't understand—"

Philip glances over at me. "I have a desperate inmate holding a gun against my ear. Can you appreciate that, Semsey?"

I press the gun against his ear.

"Uh, yes, sir."

"So tell me, Semsey. Do you think the wisest course of action is to upset the inmate?"

"No—"

"Then why the hell are those cruisers riding up my ass?"

Philip gives me the smallest of nods. I take my cue. "Give me that!" I shout, grabbing the phone from him. I try to sound crazed, on edge. It doesn't take much for me to get there. "I'm not in a chatty mood," I scream, spitting out the words, trying to sound as menacing as possible, "so listen up. I'll give you ten seconds. I won't even count. Ten seconds. If I see a cop anywhere near us after that, I'm going to put a bullet in the warden's head and drive myself. Do you hear what I'm saying?"

Philip adds, "Jesus, David, for God's sake, you don't want to do that."

I worry he's overselling it, but he's not.

On the phone, I hear Semsey say, "Whoa whoa, David, let's all slow down here a minute, okay?"

"Semsey?"

"What?"

"I'm serving a life sentence. I kill the warden, I become the most popular guy in Briggs. You understand me?"

"Of course, David. Of course. They're dropping back right now. Look."

I do. The squad cars are giving us distance.

"I don't want them dropping back. I want them all the way gone."

Semsey gives me the soothing voice. "Listen, David. Can I call you David? That's okay, right?"

I fire the gun through the back window. Philip raises a surprised eyebrow. "The next one goes between the warden's eyes."

Philip gets fully into character: "Jesus, no. Semsey, listen to him!"

Semsey's words turn into a panic sputter. "Okay, okay, hold up, David. They're stopping. See? I promise. Look out the back window. Take a look. We can still make this right, David. No one has gotten hurt yet. Let's talk it out, okay?"

"What's your phone number?" I ask.

"What?"

"It says NO CALLER ID. I'm going to hang up now. I'll call you back in five minutes with my demands. What's your number?"

Semsey gives it to me.

"Okay, get paper and pen ready. I'll call back."

"I already have paper and pen, David. Why don't you just tell me now? I'm sure we can work—"

"Keep back and nobody gets hurt," I say. "If I even sense a cop car, this ends with a bullet in his brain."

I hang up the phone and look over at Philip. "How long will that buy us?" I ask.

"No more than five minutes. They're probably getting a copter airborne now. They'll be able to keep surveillance on us from the air."

"Any ideas?" I ask.

Philip thinks about it a moment. "There's a big factory outlet center up ahead in a few miles. It has an underground garage. We'll be out of sight for maybe ten seconds. You can jump out then without them seeing you. There's a Hyatt attached to it. They used to have a taxi stand, but I don't know if it's still there with Ubers or whatever. From there, well, you're on your own. It's the best I can do. There's a train and bus station a mile away, if you want to try that."

I don't like it. "When they see us go underground, won't they know what's up?"

"I don't know, to be honest."

I look behind me. I don't see any cop cars, but that doesn't mean there aren't any. I open the window and stick my head out. No sign of any helicopter. No copter sound yet either. I could call Semsey back and make more threats about staying away so that maybe they won't see us going into the mall. But would that work? I don't know. Police aren't magicians. We think that when we watch them on TV, but we do have time. The helicopter isn't in the air yet. If they were using long-range surveillance—telescopes, cameras, whatever—they take time to set up. The same with getting some kind of location lock on either Adam's or Philip's mobile phone.

I have time. But not a lot of it.

"How far out are we from that underground garage?" I ask.

"Maybe three, four minutes."

An idea comes to me. It's not a perfect idea by any stretch, but my father the beat cop, who worried about my obsessive need for perfection, used to quote Voltaire to me: "Don't let the perfect be the enemy of the good." I'm not even sure this idea would qualify as good, but it's all I got.

I still have the car window open. Now we both hear the sound of a copter.

"Shit," Philip says.

"Give me your wallet, Philip."

"You have a plan?"

"Keep heading for the underground garage. I'm going to get out there. I'll have stolen your wallet. Tell them you only had like twenty dollars. Adam should say the same. They'll put traces on your credit card, but I'll use the cash."

"Okay," he says.

"I'm going to call Semsey back on your cell phone and start making crazy demands."

"Then what?"

"We go into the underground garage while I'm talking to him. I'll get out quickly, like you didn't even stop. The only difference is, I'm going to keep your phone with me so I can keep talking to him."

Philip nods, seeing where I'm going with this. "They'll think you're still in the car."

"Right. You keep driving. The copter is above us, but they won't be able to see me get out. If I keep talking, they may still think I'm with you. Drive as far away as you can. In exactly ten minutes, I'll hang up. Find another underground area—is there another mall like this? Or some kind of office complex?"

"Why?"

"You drive through. Then you stall a few seconds. Pretend I made you stop there and that's where I ran off."

"Meanwhile you'll be here," Philip says.

"Exactly."

"Then I pull out of the underground area and signal to them that you're gone. I can't call because you took my phone."

"Right."

"So they go searching for you there, not here."

"Yes."

Philip mulls it over. "Hell, it might work."

"You think so?"

"No, not really." He glances at me. "This distraction won't last long, David."

"I know."

"Get on the first train or bus or whatever. You any good with the survivalist stuff?"

"Not really."

"The woods would be a good place to hide. They'll send dogs, but they can't be everywhere. Don't visit your father. I know you'll want to, but they'll have the place covered. Same with your ex-wife's or sister-in-law's. All relatives. You can't rely on anyone close to you. They'll be watched."

I have no one close to me anymore, but I get his point.

"I'll talk to your dad. I'll tell him I believe you—that you didn't do it."

"Do you believe that?"

Philip lets out a deep breath as he makes a right at the exit sign for the Lamy Outlet Center. "Yeah, David, I do."

"How bad is he, Philip?"

"Bad. But he'll know the truth. I promise you that."

I check behind me. Still no cop cars. Now or never. My pockets are stuffed—Adam's phone, Adam's wallet, Philip's wallet, the cash they gave me.

"One more thing," Philip says.

"What?"

138

"Leave the gun behind."

"Why?"

"You plan on using it?"

"No, but—"

"Then leave it behind. If you're armed, they'll be much more likely to not bring you in alive."

"I don't want to be brought in alive," I say. "And why would I leave the gun behind? Who's going to buy that? They'll know you were involved."

"David . . ."

But there is no time to debate this anymore. I pick up the mobile phone and call Semsey's number. He picks up immediately.

"I'm glad you called back, David. You guys okay?"

"We are both fine," I say. "For now. But I need a way out of here. Some transportation, for starters."

"Okay, David, sure." Semsey spoke with the we're-in-this-together-pal voice. He sounds calmer now, more in control. The five minutes have helped him. "We can try to arrange that."

"Not try," I snap.

We have reached the Lamy Outlet Center. Philip veers to the left. We start down toward the parking garage. I grab the car door handle and get ready.

"I want it done. No excuses."

Philip adds for Semsey's listening pleasure, "David, put down the gun. He'll do what you want."

"I need a helicopter," I tell Semsey. "Fully fueled."

Dialogue straight from an old TV show. But Semsey seems okay with it. He plays his role: "That might take a few hours, David."

"Bullshit. You have a copter in the air. You think I'm stupid?"

"That's not ours. It's probably a traffic copter. Or maybe a commuter. You can't expect us to shut down—"

"You're lying."

"Look, let's stay calm."

"I want that copter away from us. Now."

"I have a guy calling the closest airports now, David."

"And I want my own helicopter. With fuel and a pilot. And the pilot better be unarmed."

Philip nods up ahead. I'm ready.

"Okay, David, no problem. But you have to give us a little time."

Philip stops the car. I pull the handle, open the door, roll out. As soon as I hit the pavement, Philip drives off. It all happens in a matter of two, three seconds tops. I crouch down and hide behind a gray Hyundai as I say, "How much time?" to Semsey without missing a beat. "I don't want to shoot the warden."

"Nobody wants that."

"But you're forcing my hand. This is all bullshit. Maybe I'll shoot him in the leg. Just so you know I'm serious."

"No, David, look, we know you're serious. That's why we've been keeping our distance. Just be reasonable, okay? We can make this work."

I dart between cars, heading toward the entrance to the

mall. No suspicious cars have followed us in. No suspicious people are in the area. "Listen, Semsey, here is exactly what I want."

I enter the lower lobby of the mall and take the up escalator. I'm free. For now.

14

Max—FBI Special Agent Max Bernstein—paced the warden's reception area in a fury.

Max was always in constant motion. His mom used to say that he had "ants in his pants." Teachers complained that he was disruptive because he never stopped squirming in his chair. One teacher, Mrs. Matthis in fourth grade, begged the principal to let her strap him to the back of his chair. Right now, as always when he entered a new space, Max paced the room like a dog getting used to his surroundings. He blinked a lot. His eyes darted everywhere except to the eyes of another human being. He chewed his fingernails. He looked disheveled in his oversized FBI windbreaker. He was short of stature with a thick steel-wool head of hair he could never quite comb into place on the very few times a year he tried. His constant yet inconsistent jittery movements had led to him being good-naturedly dubbed Twitch by his fellow federal officers. Of course, back in the day, when he'd first come out of the closet at a time when no other federal agents were following suit, the ever-creative homophobes had switched the moniker from Twitch to—ha, ha, ha—Bitch.

Feds can be funny.

"He got away," Detective Semsey, the local cop who had unsuccessfully tried to handle this, told him.

"So we heard," Max said.

They'd set up home base in Warden Philip Mackenzie's reception area because the actual office was still a crime scene. A street map of Briggs County was hung on a wall to trace the path of the warden's car with a yellow high-lighter. Old-school idea, Max thought. He liked that. There was a laptop computer providing a feed from the helicopter's camera. Semsey and his cohorts had watched it all go down. By the time Max and his partner, Special Agent Sarah Jablon-ski, arrived, it was all over.

There were seven other people in the reception area with Max, but the only one he'd known before five minutes ago was Sarah. Sarah Jablonski had been Max's partner, his lieu-tenant, his right hand, his indispensable associate, whatever other term you need to understand that he adored her and needed her, for sixteen years. Sarah was a big redhead, a full six feet tall, broad at the shoulders, and she dwarfed Max, who was more than six inches shorter. Their size difference led to a somewhat comical appearance, something they used to their advantage.

Two of the other men in the room were federal marshals under his command. The other four were with the prison system or local police. Max sat down in front of the computer monitor. His right leg jackhammered in what would probably be diagnosed as restless legs syndrome if Max ever decided to look into it. Everyone in the room watched Max as he replayed the end of the video over and over.

"You got something, Max?" Sarah asked.

He didn't reply. Sarah didn't press it. They both understood what that meant.

Still staring at the screen, Max asked, "Who here from the prison is highest ranked?"

"I am," a meaty man who'd sweated through his short-sleeve dress shirt said. "My name is—"

Max didn't care about his name or rank. "We are going to need a few things pronto."

"Like?"

"Like a list of any visitors Burroughs had in recent days."

"Okay."

"Any close family or friends. Cellmates he might have talked to or who've been released. He's going to need to reach out to somebody for help. Let's get eyes on them."

"On it."

Max rose from the chair and began pacing again. He gnawed on the nail of his index finger, not gently or casually, but like a Rottweiler breaking in a new toy. The others exchanged glances. Sarah was used to this.

"Is the warden back yet, Sarah?"

"He just arrived, Max."

"We ready?"

"We ready," she said.

Still pacing, Max gave a big nod. He stopped in front of the laptop and hit the play button again. On the tape, Warden Philip Mackenzie was stepping out of his car and waving his hands in the air toward the helicopter filming him. Max watched. Then he watched it again. Sarah stood over his shoulder.

"You want me to bring him in now, Max?"

"One more time, Sarah."

Max started the video from the beginning. Periodically he would leap with the grace of a wounded gazelle from the computer screen to the map, trace the route with his gnawed-on index finger, go back to the computer screen. All the while Max fiddled with the dozen rubber bands—exactly a dozen, never eleven, never thirteen—he kept around his wrist.

"Semsey," Max barked.

"Right here."

"Give me the play-by-play of this ending."

"Sir?"

"When did Burroughs get out of the car?"

"In the Wilmington Tunnel. You see here?" Semsey pointed on the map. "That's where the warden's car entered the tunnel."

"You were talking to Burroughs?"

"Yes."

"As they entered the tunnel?"

"He hung up right before that."

"How long before that?"

"Uh, I'm not sure. Maybe a minute. I can check the exact time."

"Do that later," Max said, still staring at the computer screen. "How did the call end?"

"I was supposed to call him back when the copter was ready."

"That's what he said to you?"

"Yes."

Max frowned at Sarah. Sarah shrugged. "Go on."

"The rest, well, it's all on the video," Semsey said. "When the warden's car enters the tunnel, we lose sight of them."

They play that part on the computer screen.

"Burroughs knew that, right?" Max said.

"Knew . . . ?"

"He mentioned there was a copter in the air, didn't he?"

"Oh, yeah, I guess so. He made the copter, what, fifteen minutes earlier. He told us to get it away from him."

"But you didn't comply."

"No. We just moved it farther away so he couldn't see or hear it."

"Okay, so they enter the tunnel," Max prompts.

"They enter. Our copter waits on the other end because, well, we can't see into the tunnel. The ride from one end to the other shouldn't take more than a minute or two."

"But it took longer," Max says.

"The warden's car didn't emerge for over six minutes."

Max presses the fast-forward button. He hits play again when the warden's car exits the tunnel on the other end.

Almost immediately, the car pulls to the shoulder. The warden gets out on the driver's side and starts to wave furiously.

The end.

"So what do you think?" Max asked Semsey.

"About?"

"What happened with Burroughs."

"Oh. Right. Well, we know now. The warden told us. Burroughs knew the copter couldn't see him in the tunnel, so he made the warden stop in the middle of it where no one could see him. Then he carjacked another car. We have roadblocks set up."

"Is there CCTV in the tunnel?"

"No. They have like a booth in there, but it's rarely manned anymore. Budget cuts."

"Uh-huh. Sarah?"

"Yeah, Max."

"Where's the warden's son?"

"He's by the infirmary with his father."

"He okay?"

"Yeah, just procedure."

"Please send the warden and his son in. I want everyone else out of the room."

They cleared out. Five minutes later, Sarah opened the door, and Philip and Adam Mackenzie entered the room. Max did not glance in their direction. His eyes remained on the computer monitor.

"Tough day, huh, guys?"

"You can say that again," Philip Mackenzie said. The

warden stepped toward Max and stuck his hand out. Max pretended like he couldn't see it. He bounced bumper-pool-style between the television screen and the map.

"How did he get the gun?" Max asked.

Philip Mackenzie cleared his throat. "He took mine when I wasn't expecting it. You see, I had brought the inmate—"

"Inmate?"

"Yes."

"Is that what you call him?"

Philip Mackenzie opened his mouth, but Max waved him off. "Never mind. Detective Semsey filled me in on all this. How he took your gun and forced your son here to give him his uniform and then he made you take him to his car at gun-point. I got all that." Max stopped, stared at the map, frowned.

"What I meant to ask is," Max continued, "why are you lying to me?"

The silence filled the room. Philip Mackenzie stared at Max, but Max still had his back turned. He turned his furious glare toward Sarah. Sarah shrugged.

Philip Mackenzie's voice boomed. "What did you say?"

Max sighed. "Do I really have to repeat myself? Sarah, didn't I make myself clear?"

"Crystal, Max."

"Who the hell do you think you're talking to, Agent Bernstein?"

"A warden who just helped a convicted child killer escape from prison."

Philip's hands formed two fists. His face reddened. "Look at me, dammit."

"Nah."

He took a step closer. "When you call a man a liar, you better be ready to look him in the eye."

Max shook his head. "I never bought that."

"Bought what?"

"That look-me-in-the-eye stuff. Eye contact is so overrated. The best liars I know can look you straight in the eye for hours on end. It's a waste of time and energy, maintaining eye contact. Am I right, Sarah?"

"As rain, Max."

"Warden?" Max said.

"What?"

"This is going to be bad for you. Very bad. Nothing I can do about that. But for your silent son here, there may be a sliver of daylight. But if you keep lying, I'll bury you both. We've done that before, haven't we, Sarah?"

"We enjoy it, Max."

"It's kind of a turn-on," Max said.

"I sometimes tape moments like this," Sarah said, "and then I use it as foreplay."

"Feel my nipples, Sarah," Max said, jutting his chest out toward Sarah. "They're hard as pebbles."

"I don't want to get written up by HR again, Max."

"Ah, you used to be fun, Sarah."

"Maybe later, Max. When we throw the cuffs on them."

Philip Mackenzie pointed at Max, then Sarah. "You guys finished?"

"You crashed the car through the gate," Max said.

"Yes."

"I mean, you slammed your car through a half-closed gate at full speed."

Philip grinned, trying to look confident. "Is that supposed to be proof of something?"

"Why did you hit the gas with such enthusiasm?"

"Because a desperate inmate was pointing a gun in my face."

"Hear that, Sarah?"

"I'm standing right here, Max."

"Big Phil was scared."

"Who wouldn't be?" Mackenzie countered. "The inmate had a gun."

"Your gun."

"Yes."

"The one that your secretary says you never wear and never keep loaded."

"She's wrong. I keep it holstered under my jacket, so people don't see."

"So discreet," Sarah said.

"Yet," Max continued, "Burroughs managed not only to see it, but to pull it free and threaten you both with it."

"He caught us off guard," Philip said.

"You sound incompetent."

"I made a mistake. I let the inmate get too close."

Max smiled at Sarah. Sarah shrugged.

"You also keep calling him inmate," Max said.

"That's what he is."

"Yeah, but you know him, right? He's David to you, no?

You and his father are old buddies. Your son here—the so-far-silent Adam—grew up with him, am I right?"

A flash of surprise hit the warden's face, but he recovered fast. "That's true," Mackenzie said, standing up a little straighter. "I'm not denying it."

"So cooperative," Sarah said.

"Isn't he though?"

"And that's why—" Philip began.

"Wait, don't tell me. That's why Burroughs was able to get close enough to get a gun your secretary swears you never wear—"

"Or load," Sarah added.

"Or load. Thanks, Sarah. Yet somehow Burroughs was still able to reach into your jacket, unsnap your holster, and pull the loaded gun free while the two of you stood and did nothing. That pretty much it, Warden?"

Adam spoke for the first time. "That's exactly what happened."

"Whoa, it speaks, Sarah."

"Maybe he shouldn't, Max."

"Agree. Let me ask you another question, Warden, if you don't mind. Why did you visit David Burroughs's father yesterday?"

Philip Mackenzie looked stunned.

"Sarah, do you want to fill the warden in?"

"Sure, Max." She turned toward Philip. "You took the eight-fifteen flight on American Eagle to Boston yesterday morning. Flight three-oh-two, in case you're interested."

Silence.

"I can see the gears a-whirring in his head, Sarah."

"Can you, Max?"

Max nodded. "He's wondering: Should I admit I visited my old buddy Lenny Burroughs—or should I claim I was in Boston for another reason? He wants to do the latter, of course, but the problem is—and you know this, Warden— if you lie about it, you have to wonder if Sarah here will be able to track down the Uber or taxi you took from Logan to the Burroughses' house in Revere."

"Or vice versa, Max," Sarah added.

"Right, Sarah, or vice versa. The taxi you took back to the airport. And before you answer, let me just warn you: Sarah is damn good."

"Thanks, Max."

"No, Sarah, I mean it. You're the best."

"You're making me blush, Max."

"It looks good on you, Sarah." Max shrugged his shoulders and turned toward the Mackenzies. "It's a tough choice, Warden. I don't know what I'd do."

Philip cleared his throat. "I was in Boston visiting a sick friend. There's nothing wrong with that."

Max took out his wallet and smiled. "Dang, Sarah, you were right."

She put out her palm. "Five bucks."

"I only have a ten."

"I'll give you change later."

Max handed her a ten-dollar bill.

Philip Mackenzie plowed ahead. "You're right, of course. I'm close to David. And he's been acting irrationally lately. So yes, I wanted to speak to his father about it. Like you said, Lenny and I, we go way back—"

"Wait, let me guess." Max held up his hand. "You brought your son here today for that very reason. Because Adam and David were close, and David was acting so irrationally."

"As a matter of fact, yes."

Max grinned and held out his palm. Sarah frowned and handed him back the ten-dollar bill.

"Do you two think you're funny?" Philip snapped.

"We're not called the FBI Desi and Lucy for nothing, are we, Sarah?"

"Mostly we're called that because I'm a redhead, Max, not because we're funny."

Max frowned. "Seriously, Sarah? But I've been working on a modern rendition of 'Babalu.'"

There was a knock on the door. The meaty prison executive and Semsey stepped into the room. The executive said, "David Burroughs had only one visitor during his entire incarceration. His sister-in-law. Her name is Rachel Anderson. She was here yesterday and the day before."

"Wait, Burroughs's only visitor came yesterday and the day before?" Max put his hand to his chest. "Gasp. Oh. Gasp. Another coincidence, Sarah."

"The world is full of them, Max."

"It's full of something, Sarah. What say you, Warden?"

This time, Philip Mackenzie stayed quiet.

Max turned back to the meaty guy. "Do you know where the sister-in-law is staying?"

"Probably the Briggs Motor Lodge. The majority of our visitors stay there."

Max looked toward Semsey. Semsey said, "I'm on it."

Meaty Exec added, "She might also have stayed at the Hyatt by the factory outlets."

"Whoa."

Max's head spun around like someone had pulled it on a string. He did his jitterbug step back to the map. The room fell silent. Max studied the route. Then he jumped back to the computer monitor.

"Bingo, Sarah."

"What, Max?"

"Semsey?"

The detective stepped forward. "I'm right here."

"You said Burroughs was on the phone call right before they entered the tunnel, right?"

"Yes."

"And Burroughs initiated that call?"

"Yes. He asked for five minutes and called me back."

"What time was that? Exactly? Check your phone."

"Eight fifty."

"So the car would have been . . ." Max found it. "Here. On Green Street. Which would have been right before they hit the mall's underground parking lot." He turned to Philip Mackenzie. "Why did you drive through that underground garage, Warden?"

Philip glared at him. "Because the inmate told me to. At gunpoint."

Max leapt back toward the map. He pointed at the Lamy Outlet Center and traced over the nearby vicinity. "Sarah, you see what I'm seeing?"

"The train station, Max."

Max nodded. "Semsey?"

"What?"

"Stop the trains. And if any pulled out after eight fifty, I want them boarded. Let's get every cop we can over to that mall."

"Roger that."

15

At the Payne Museum of Art in Newport, Rhode Island, Gertrude Payne, the eighty-two-year-old matriarch of the New England branch of the Payne family fortune, watched her grandson Hayden take to the podium. Hayden was thirty-seven years old and while most expected him to have a genteel or patrician bearing, he looked more like his great-great-great-grandfather Randall Payne, the gritty man who founded Payne Kentucky Bourbon in 1868, thus creating the Payne family dynasty.

"On behalf of my family," Hayden began, "especially my grandmother Pixie . . ."

Gertrude was Pixie. That was the nickname given to her by her own father, though no one really understood why. Hayden turned and smiled at her. She smiled back.

Hayden continued: ". . . we are thrilled to see so many of you at our annual fundraising luncheon. All proceeds from today's event will go into the 'Paint with Payne' art development charity, which will continue to provide classes and materials for underserved youth in the Providence area. Thank you so much for your generosity."

The polite applause echoed in the marble ballroom of Payne House on Ochre Point Avenue. The mansion had been built in 1892 and overlooked the Atlantic Ocean. In 1968, not long after Gertrude had married into the family, she had spearheaded the idea of creating an art museum and selling the home to the preservation society. Payne House was indeed beautiful and majestic, but it was also drafty and cold in both the literal and figurative sense. Most believe that these mansions are donated so that others may enjoy them. That only happens when it is financially beneficial for the family. Most of the famous tourist mansions, like the Breakers or the Marble House or, as here, the Payne House, are purchased by preservation societies at a profit for the wealthy owners.

There is, Pixie knew, always an angle when you're rich.

"I know that this year holds *extra* excitement," Hayden continued, "and as promised, after we finish this delicious lunch provided by our local caterer, the divine Hans Laaspere . . ."

A smattering of applause.

". . . we will provide you, our prime benefactors, a private tour of the museum and, of course, the highlight, the reason most of you are here today, a special premiere viewing of an infamous painting not seen in public for over two decades, Johannes Vermeer's *The Girl at the Piano*."

Cue the oohs and aahs.

The Vermeer in question had been stolen nearly a quarter

century ago from Gertrude's cousins on the Lockwood side of the family and had only recently been discovered at a bizarre murder scene on the Upper West Side of Manhattan. The painting, which measured only a foot and a half high, had already been an invaluable masterpiece, but then when you add notoriety into the mix—art heist, murder, domestic terrorism—*The Girl at the Piano* was considered one of the most valuable works of art in the entire world. Now that it had finally been recovered, Gertrude's cousin Win felt that the painting should not languish in a dingy parlor at Lockwood Manor but rather travel the world and be enjoyed by thousands if not millions. The stolen Vermeer was about to start making the rounds of museums around the world with its opening one-month exhibition right here in Newport, Rhode Island.

Getting the Vermeer first had been an immense coup. The tickets for today's luncheon had started at fifty thousand dollars per person. Not that the money mattered. Not truly. The Payne family was worth billions, but philanthropy amongst the well-to-do had always been about social climbing, with perhaps a smidgeon of guilt thrown into the mix. It was an excuse to socialize and throw a party, because to be this obscenely wealthy and simply have a party would be too gauche, too tasteless, too showy—ergo you attached a charity as cover, if you will. It was all pish, Gertrude knew. The wealthy in the room could have just written a check to support the Payne charities for underserved youth. None would ever miss the money. Not only doesn't anyone "give until it hurts"—they don't even give until they feel it in the slightest. Gertrude understood that no one voluntarily shrinks or lessens their lot. Oh, sure, we may all claim to want better for those less fortunate than ourselves—we may even mean it—but we all want that without any kind of sacrifice on our part. This, Gertrude had surmised years ago, was why the rich could seem so awful.

Hayden continued: "The Payne Foundation's programs for the underserved have helped tens of thousands of needy children since our patron saint Bennett Payne created the family's first orphanage for boys in 1938."

He gestured toward the large oil portrait of Bennett Payne.

Ah, the wonderful, revered Uncle Bennett, Gertrude thought. Few knew that Uncle Bennett had been a pedophile in the days before such a word seemed to exist. "Generous" Bennett chose to work with poor youth for one simple reason—it gave him unfettered access to them. Uncle Bennett kept his predilections a secret, of course, but like most human beings, he also justified his actions. He convinced himself that in sum, he was doing good. These children, especially the extremely poor, would have died without the Paynes' intervention. Bennett fed them, clothed them, educated them—and wasn't sex an act that pleased both participants? What was the crime here? Uncle Bennett traveled the world, often with like-minded missionaries, so he could have sex—now, they correctly called it rape, didn't they?—with a wide variety of children.

For those wondering about karma, for those wondering

whether Bennett Payne, who never knew hunger or thirst or discomfort, who never worked a real job or knew anything but great wealth, eventually paid for his misdeeds, the answer, alas, is no. Uncle Bennett died of natural causes in his sleep at the ripe old age of ninety-three. He was never found out. To this day, his portrait hangs in every Payne Foundation charitable institute.

The irony here is that the Payne Foundation now does a fair amount of good. What started as a vehicle for Uncle Bennett to rape children now truly helps those less fortunate. So how do you reconcile that? Gertrude knew of so many causes that started with the best of intentions before devolving into something awful and corrupt. Eric Hoffer once said, "Every great cause begins as a movement, becomes a business, and eventually degenerates into a racket." So true. But what happens when it works the other way around?

All men, Gertrude believed, tended to have some sociopathic qualities coupled with a wonderful ability to self-justify any behavior. Yes, she was generalizing, and yes, from the back of the room, she is sure someone is yelling, "Not all men." But close to. Her father had been an alcoholic who beat her mother and demanded obedience. He justified it via biblical verses. Gertrude's own husband, George, had been a serial philanderer. He justified it via the scientific argument that monogamy was "unnatural." And Uncle Bennett, well, that had been covered up. He wasn't the only one in the family with that particular predilection. Gertrude had only one son, Hayden's father, Wade, who in her mind was the exception that proved the rule, but perhaps she'd seen her son through "Mommy glasses," as today's youth like to call it. Wade had also died at the age of thirty-one, in a private plane crash with Hayden's mother as they headed to Vail on a ski trip, perhaps before whatever sociopathy ran in his loins could reveal itself. The death had crushed her. The orphaned Hayden was only four years old at the time. It was left to Gertrude to raise Hayden, and she had done a poor job. She had not looked out for him. And he had suffered for it.

Her phone buzzed. Gertrude found modern technology fascinating. Of course, like too many things in the present day, it led to obsessions, but the idea that you could communicate with anyone at any time or see pages from all the libraries in all the world with a small device she kept in her handbag—how do people not appreciate such things?

"So once again," Hayden finished up, "I want to thank you all for supporting this wonderful cause. We will visit the stolen Vermeer in fifteen minutes. Enjoy your dessert."

As Hayden smiled and waved, Gertrude sneaked a glance at her phone. When she read the message, her heart dropped. Hayden wended his way back to her table. When he saw her face, he said, "Are you okay, Pixie?"

She put a hand on the table to steady herself. "Walk with me," she said.

"But we—"

"Take my arm, please. Now."

"Of course, Pixie."

They both kept the smiles on their faces as they made their

way out of the grand ballroom. One wall of the ballroom was mirrored. Gertrude spotted herself right before they exited and wondered who that old woman in the mirror was.

"What is it, Pixie?"

She handed Hayden the phone. His eyes widened as he read it. "Escaped?"

"So it seems."

Gertrude looked toward the door opening. Stephano, the family's longtime security head, was always in sight. He met her eye, and she gave him a head tilt that indicated they would need to talk later. Stephano nodded back and kept his distance.

"Maybe it's a sign," Hayden said.

She turned her attention back to her grandson. "A sign?"

"I don't mean strictly in a religious way, though maybe that too. More like an opportunity."

He could be so foolish. "It's not an opportunity, Hayden," she said through clenched teeth. "They'll probably catch him within a day."

"Should we help him?"

Gertrude just stared at her grandson until he turned away. Then she said, "I think we should leave now."

He gestured back toward the ballroom. "But Pixie, the patrons—"

"—only want to see the Vermeer," she said. "They don't care whether we are here or not. Where is Theo?"

"He wanted to see the painting."

She passed the two security guards and entered what

had once been the family music room, where the Vermeer now hung. A young boy stood in front of it, his back turned toward her.

"Theo," she said to the boy, "are you ready to go?"

"Yes, Pixie," Theo said. "I'm ready."

When the eight-year-old turned toward her, Gertrude's gaze couldn't help but land on the telltale port stain on the boy's cheek. She swallowed hard and stuck her hand out for him to take.

"Come along then."

PART 2

Twelve Hours Later

16

Max and Sarah took their seats at the interrogation table. Rachel Anderson sat alone across from them. They introduced themselves and asked her yet again whether she wanted counsel present. Rachel waived the right.

"Let me begin," Max said, "by thanking you for talking to us."

"Of course," Rachel said, all wide-eyed and innocent. "But can you tell me what this is about?"

Max glanced at Sarah. Sarah rolled her eyes.

They were in the FBI building in Newark, New Jersey, some five hundred miles from Briggs Penitentiary. Their BOLO— Be On the Look Out—had finally been answered by the Port Authority police when Rachel Anderson's New Jersey license plate had been picked up on camera crossing the George Washington Bridge traveling west from New York to New Jersey. After calling for backup—the BOLO had stated that

escaped convict David Burroughs was armed and dangerous—
New Jersey state troopers pulled over Rachel Anderson's white
Toyota Camry on Route 4 in Teaneck, New Jersey.

David Burroughs was not in the vehicle.

Max decided to go the direct route. "Where is your former
brother-in-law, Ms. Anderson?"

Rachel's mouth dropped open. "David?"

"Yes. David Burroughs."

"David's in prison," Rachel said. "He's serving time at Briggs
Penitentiary up in Maine."

Max and Sarah just stared at her.

Sarah sighed. "Really, Rachel?"

"What?"

"That's the route you're going to take with this?"

Max put his hand on Sarah's arm. "I realize that you've
waived your right to counsel," he said to Rachel, "but let me
offer you some reassurances."

"Reassurances?" Rachel repeated.

Max silenced Sarah's next rejoinder with a gentle squeeze.
"We will give you full immunity right now provided you tell
us the truth."

Rachel looked at Sarah, then back to Max. "I don't understand what you mean."

Sarah shook her head. "My God."

"Then let me clarify what I mean by 'full immunity.'
Suppose—shot in the dark here—you helped David Burroughs escape from prison. If you tell us where he is or what
role you played in this very serious federal crime—"

"—a crime that can put you behind bars for many, *many* years," Sarah added.

"Right," Max said, "Thank you. You won't be charged. You'll just walk."

"Wait," Rachel said, putting her hand to her chest. "David escaped?"

Sarah sat back and plucked at her own lower lip. She studied Rachel and then gestured toward her. "What do you think, Max?"

"Really fine performance, Sarah. You?"

"I don't know, Max. Don't you think maybe she's overselling her shock here?"

"Yeah, a little, I guess," Max conceded. "Her 'wait' before the 'David escaped' might have been gilding the lily."

"And the hand-to-her-chest move. It was too much. If she had pearls, she probably would have clutched them."

"Still," Max said. "I would say there has to be Oscar buzz for this performance."

"A nomination maybe," Sarah said. "But not a win."

They both offered up sarcastic golf claps in Rachel's direction. Rachel stayed quiet.

"When David Burroughs escaped," Max continued, "we sent a man over to your motel."

"Person, Max," Sarah said.

"What?"

"You said you sent a 'man' over. That's a bit sexist, don't you think?"

"I do. I apologize. Where was I?"

"Sent a law enforcement officer to her motel."

"Right." Max turned to Rachel. "You weren't there, of course. The front desk informed us that you were most likely at the Nesbitt Station Diner. I guess you'd complained about the motel's Wi-Fi."

"So?" Rachel countered. "Is it a crime to go to a diner?"

"The waitress told us that not long after the escape alarm sounded, you hurried out of the diner."

"And right before you hurried out," Sarah said, "you received a phone call."

Rachel shrugged. "I may have. So?"

"Do you remember who that call was from?" Max asked.

"I don't, no. I might not have picked up. I don't a lot of the time."

"The waitress saw you answer it."

"It was probably spam then. I get a lot of those."

"This wasn't spam," Sarah said. "It was from David Burroughs."

Rachel frowned. "David is a federal prisoner. How would he have a phone?"

"Wow," Sarah said, throwing up her hands in mock surrender.

"He stole it during his escape," Max said. Of course, Max didn't really believe that the phone Burroughs used had been genuinely stolen. He figured that both Philip and Adam Mackenzie had given David their phones as part of the escape plot, but there was no reason to offer that up now. "The caller ID would have shown the name Adam Mackenzie. Do you know who that is?"

"Sure. Adam grew up with David."

"Do you recall receiving that call from Adam's phone?"

"I don't, sorry," Rachel offered with a faux apologetic smile. "Maybe it went into voicemail. Do you want me to check?"

Max and Sarah exchanged another glance. This was not going to be easy.

"After you left the diner," Max said, "where did you go?"

"I live here in New Jersey."

"Yes, we know."

"Well, that's where I was heading. Home. I was almost there when a bunch of state troopers pulled me over with guns drawn. Scared the hell out of me. Then I was brought here."

"So you intended to drive straight home from the diner?" Max asked.

"Yes."

"But you didn't check out of the motel. Your clothes are still in your room. Your personal items."

"I planned on coming back."

"What do you mean?"

"The room is cheaper by the week," Rachel said, "so I decided to just hold on to it. I came home to run some errands, check on my place, that kind of thing. I planned on coming back up to Maine on Thursday." She sat forward. "I'm very confused, Detective."

"Special Agent," Sarah corrected. "He is Special Agent Max Bernstein of the Federal Bureau of Investigation. I'm Special Agent Sarah Jablonski."

Rachel met her eye and held it. "Special Agent. You must be very proud."

Max didn't want to get sidetracked. "After you left the diner, did you drive straight home, Ms. Anderson?"

Rachel sat back. "I may have stopped along the way."

"Eight minutes after David Burroughs called you, your Toyota Camry was picked up on CCTV near the Lamy Outlet Center."

"Right. I thought about doing some shopping." She turned to Sarah. "They have a Tory Burch store."

"Did you?" Max pressed.

"Did I what?"

"Shop."

"No."

"Why not?"

"I changed my mind."

"So you drove there and just left."

"Something like that."

"And by stunning coincidence," Sarah continued, "the Lamy Outlet Center was where David Burroughs hid after his escape."

"I don't know anything about that. Did David really escape?"

Sarah ignored the question. "We got a location tap for your iPhone from your cell provider. They pinged your phone, but guess what?"

Rachel shrugged.

"Your phone had been powered all the way down," Sarah said, "so we couldn't track it."

"Is that supposed to be incriminating?"

"It is, yes."

"Why? I turn my phone off when I'm driving sometimes. I don't like to be disturbed."

"No, Rachel, you do not do that," Sarah snapped. "According to your cell provider, your phone hasn't been powered off in the past four months. We also know that you turned it off after driving ten miles *north* of the Lamy Outlet Center, which is in the opposite direction of New Jersey."

Rachel gave another no-big-deal shrug. "I wanted to see a few sights before heading home."

"Oh, that sounds reasonable," Sarah said in pure deadpan. "Your ex-brother-in-law escapes from prison. Soon after, the phone he stole calls yours. You react by driving to the outlet center where he's hiding. Then for some reason, even though you claim you were heading home without checking out of your motel, you start driving in the opposite direction and suddenly turn off your mobile phone for the first time since updating your software four months ago. That sound about right?"

Rachel smiled at Sarah and then turned her attention to Max. "Am I under arrest, Special Agent Bernstein?"

"Not as long as you're cooperating," Max said.

"So if I choose to get up and leave?"

"Let's not do hypotheticals, Ms. Anderson, if that's okay," Max said. "We also know that you kept driving north after turning off your phone. Approximately thirty miles further up I-95, David Burroughs, using a stolen credit card, purchased survival gear of various sorts—tent, pocketknives, sleeping bag, stuff like that—from the Katahdin General Store. The store owner gave us a positive ID on him. Any comment?"

Rachel shook her head. "I don't know anything about that."

"It's all parkland and woods up in that area. Miles and miles of it. Someone could get dropped off and never be seen again. They could slowly make their way to the Canadian border."

Rachel Anderson said nothing.

Sarah decided to switch gears. Their hope was to keep her off balance and surprised by the wealth of information they'd been able to learn in just a few hours. "Why did you choose to visit David Burroughs now?"

"David was my brother-in-law. We used to be close."

"But this was your very first trip to Briggs."

"Yes."

"He'd been there, what, four, five years?"

"Something like that."

Sarah spread her hands. "So why now, Rachel?"

"I don't know. I just felt . . . I felt like it was time."

"Do you believe David Burroughs killed your nephew?"

Rachel's gaze slid to the far left. "I do, yes."

"You don't seem that sure."

"Oh, I'm sure. But I don't think he meant it. I think he had some kind of blackout or breakdown."

"So you don't blame him?" Max said.

"Not really, no."

"What did you two talk about during your visit?"

"I just asked David how he was."

"And how was he?"

"Still broken. David didn't want visitors. He just wanted to be left alone."

"Yet you came back the next day."

"Yes."

"And planned to return again."

"David and I were close. Before all this, I mean. I . . . I also confided in him."

"Do you mind telling us what about?"

"It doesn't really matter. I've had some setbacks of my own."

"And you thought, what, he'd be a sympathetic ear?"

Rachel's voice was soft. "Something like that."

"And by setbacks," Sarah said, "do you mean your recent divorce?"

"Or," Max added, "the scandal that ended your career?"

Rachel stayed very still.

Max leaned closer. No reason for subtlety anymore. "It's all unraveling, Ms. Anderson. You know that, don't you?"

She didn't take the bait.

"Look how much Sarah dug up in just a few hours. We are going to catch him. There's no question about it. If he's lucky, we will catch him alive, but David Burroughs is a convicted child killer who stole a firearm from a warden, so . . ." Max shrugged to indicate that this was out of his control. "As soon as we do catch him—probably in the next few hours—Sarah and I will turn all our efforts toward building a case against you for aiding and abetting."

"You'll serve a very long time," Sarah said.

"This is not an idle threat on our part," Max said.

"Not a threat," Sarah repeated, giving Rachel the dagger eyes again. "I can't wait to put you behind bars."

"Unless, Sarah."

"Unless what, Max?"

"Unless she cooperates. Here and now."

Sarah frowned. "I don't think we need her, Max."

"You're probably right, but maybe Ms. Anderson didn't know what she was getting involved in. Maybe she didn't understand what she was doing."

"Oh, she understood."

"But still—we agreed, Sarah. If Rachel tells us what she knows now, we give her full immunity."

"That was before, Max. Now I want her to serve time for jerking us around like this."

"You have a point, Sarah."

Rachel stayed silent.

"This is your last chance," Max said. "Your 'get out of jail free' card expires in three minutes."

"Then we arrest her, Max?"

"Then we arrest her, Sarah."

Sarah folded her hands and put them on the table. "So what do you say, Rachel?"

"I changed my mind," Rachel said. "I want my lawyer."

17

"Okay, Sarah, give me the most likely working theory," Max said.

Max and Sarah headed toward Newark Airport to catch a flight back up to Briggs Penitentiary. It had turned out that the attorney Rachel Anderson called was the notorious Hester Crimstein, who promptly got her bail and released.

"Stop chewing your nails, Max."

"Let me be, Sarah, okay?"

"It's gross."

"It helps me think."

Sarah sighed.

"So what's our working theory?"

"Burroughs escapes with the help of Philip and Adam Mackenzie," Sarah began.

"We are sure the Mackenzies are in it?"

"I think we are."

"I think we are too," Max said. "Continue."

"Burroughs gets out of the warden's car in the underground parking garage at the outlet center. He calls Rachel Anderson, who is waiting for his call at the Nesbitt Station Diner. Rachel drives over to the outlet center. With me so far, Max?"

"Yep. Keep going."

"She meets up with Burroughs. Burroughs gets in her car."

"And then?"

"They head up north. We have that last phone ping."

"Which is odd."

"How so?"

"Why turn the phone off then?" Max asked. "Why not earlier?"

"If she turns it off at the outlet center, we would know that's where she went."

Max frowned. "Yeah, I guess, maybe."

"But?"

Max shook it off. "Go on."

"They keep driving to that general store—"

"The Katahdin General Store," Max added, "in Millinocket."

"Right, where he buys the survival gear. Based on the traffic patterns and timeline I put together, I'd say she had time to drive him farther north for another half hour or so. Either way, Rachel drops Burroughs off in some heavily wooded area. We have copters and dogs covering it, but the area is black-hole vast."

"And then?"

Sarah shrugged. "And then that's it."

"So what's Burroughs's plan now?"

"I'm not sure, Max. Maybe he plans to hide in the national parks. Wait us out. Maybe he plans to sneak across the border into Canada."

Max worked the fingernail hard.

"You don't buy it," Sarah said.

"I don't buy it."

"Tell me why."

"Too many holes. Burroughs is a city kid. Does he have any survivalist experience?"

"Maybe. Or maybe he thinks, how hard could it be? Maybe he thinks he has no choice."

"It's not adding up, Sarah."

"What's not adding up, Max?"

"Let's start at the top: Was this escape planned out in advance?"

"Had to be."

"If so, wow, it's a pretty wacky plan."

"I don't know," Sarah said. "I think it was pretty ingenious."

"How so?"

"It's so simple. Burroughs just grabs the gun and walks out with Mackenzie. No tunnels to dig. No trucks to hijack or garbage cans to hide in. None of that. If that guard . . . what was his name again?"

"Weston. Ted Weston."

"Right. If Weston doesn't look out the window at just the right time—if he doesn't spot the warden and Burroughs getting into the car—they're home free. No one would have reported Burroughs missing for hours."

Max thought about it. "So let's follow that trail, shall we, Sarah?"

"We shall, Max."

"When it all went wrong—when Weston sounded the alarm—your theory is that they were then forced to improvise."

"Exactly," Sarah said.

Max considered that. "That would explain Burroughs's call to Rachel when she was at the diner. If Rachel was in on it from the get-go, he wouldn't have had to make that call. She'd have already been in place to pick him up."

"Interesting," Sarah said. "Are we now theorizing that Rachel Anderson wasn't part of the original breakout plan?"

"I don't know."

"But it isn't a coincidence. Her visiting Burroughs on the day he breaks out."

"Not a coincidence," Max agreed. He started working on a fresh hangnail. "But, Sarah?"

"What, Max?"

"We are still missing something. Something pretty big."

18

I stand on Twelfth Street in New York City and eat the most wonderful slice of pepperoni pizza ever created, from a place called Zazzy's.

I am free.

I don't think I believe it yet. Do you know that feeling when a dream gets weird—*good* weird, in this case—and suddenly, right in the middle of your nocturnal voyage, you realize that you may indeed be asleep, dreaming, and you fear you're going to wake up and so you try desperately to stay asleep, clinging tightly to the images in your head, even as they fade away? That is what I've been experiencing for the past few hours. I am terrified that soon my eyes will open, and I will be back in Briggs instead of standing on this urine-scented (a smell I welcome because you supposedly don't have scents in your dream) city street.

I stand across the street from where Harriet Winchester aka Hilde Winslow now resides.

I escaped *today*. It boggles my mind. Less than twenty-four hours ago, a prison guard at Briggs tried to murder me. Then, when it seemed that I, the victim, would be blamed for the attack, Philip and Adam broke me out. The crazy events of the day—all in this *same* day that is *still* ongoing—come hurtling toward me. I try to volley them away and focus on the task at hand.

Hilde Winslow had lied on the stand and helped convict me. The answer to why is my first step in rescuing my son.

Rescuing my son.

Every time I think about that phrase, I need to bite down and fight back the tears and remind myself of what's at stake. Before Rachel's visit, my son was dead, murdered, perhaps even by my hands. Now I believed the total opposite: Matthew is alive, and I'd been set up. Why, how—I had no idea. One step at a time.

The first step is Hilde Winslow.

After I rolled out of Philip's car at that outlet mall, I called Rachel to pick me up. She was at a diner. I explained to her where to go and when to be there. Meanwhile I headed into the employee parking lot. The stores were just opening, so most employees were beginning their shifts. That gave me time. Rachel, I knew, was from New Jersey. When the cops put an APB on her car, that's what they would be focused on—New Jersey license plates in Maine. I found a beat-up Honda Civic with screws loose enough to take off both license plates. Would the owner notice? Probably not for a while. Most people don't check to make sure their license plates are in place before they drive. But even so, even if Mr./Mrs. Beat-Up Honda noticed, it would be hours from now after their shift. We would have the head start we needed.

Rachel had wisely done as I asked—maxed out all her credit cards at ATM machines. She used three credit cards, two with an $800 maximum, one with $600. Along with the money the Mackenzies had given me, I was financially flush enough to last a little while anyway. The police would at some point figure out where Philip had really dropped me off. Philip's story, whatever he concocted, wouldn't hold water for more than a day or two.

Once Rachel arrived at the back of the outlet mall's parking lot where I was hiding, I hopped in and told her to just keep driving. Two miles later, we spotted a closed-down restaurant. I told Rachel to pull in behind it. When we were out of sight, I quickly switched out the license plates, so that her white Toyota Camry, one of the most common cars in the world, now had Maine license plates.

"What now?" Rachel asked me.

I knew the manhunt would be massive and immediate, but I also knew that law enforcement is not all-consuming or all-encompassing. The key to any plan was to have a goal. I had but one: Find my son. Period. The end. That was my sole focus.

So what did that mean in a practical sense?

Follow any lead. The biggest one I had—the only one— was Hilde Winslow. She had not only lied on the stand, but she'd changed her name and moved to New York City. So that became my plan: Get to Hilde Winslow as fast as I could. Figure out why she lied.

Once I had a destination, it became all about how to divert and obfuscate and muddy the waters. The police would soon realize that Rachel had visited me in prison and put some kind of tracker on her phone. They would also do the same with Philip's and Adam's phones, both in my possession. I'd already shut them down.

"Is your phone on?" I asked her.

"Yes. Oh shit, they can trace that, right? Should I power it down or something?"

"Wait," I tell her.

"Why?"

Once a phone was off, the cell provider wouldn't be able to track us anymore, but they'd be able to tell the police where we were when the phone was last on. I had Rachel drive in the opposite direction of my destination. Once we'd headed far enough north so that the police would conclude that we were likely heading toward the Canadian border rather than New York City, I had Rachel power down her phone. If we kept it on longer, it would be too much, I concluded—overplaying our hand. Now it would appear as though we started our escape and realized after about ten or fifteen minutes of driving that we needed to turn the phone off.

"So now what?" Rachel asked.

I was about to have her make a U-turn and start back toward New York, but I wasn't sure that the phone ping alone would do enough to divert, obfuscate, and muddy.

"Keep heading north," I said.

Twenty minutes later, we stopped at a store in Katahdin that sold survival equipment. I checked for security cameras near the pumps. None there. Not that it mattered. They'd know that I was here soon enough. Rachel filled up her car while I, shopping quickly yet not conspicuously (or so I hoped), bought survival equipment, the kind of stuff I assumed people used to hike and camp for an extended period of time. I paid for it all with the Mastercard Adam said that he would "forget" to cancel. I figured the police would still find out about the card, but it might take a little longer. If not, when the full APB hit, the old man who rang me up would remember my face.

That was okay too.

With this deed done, Rachel and I headed north for another half a mile (just in case someone asked eventually which way the car had gone) before turning around and driving south. We found a Salvation Army donation bin behind an office complex on the outskirts of Boston. I dumped the survival gear in it. According to a sign on the donation box, the next pickup was four days away. Good. If somehow the Salvation Army got suspicious of the stuff or called the police, it wouldn't matter. Even if they found us on CCTV up here, so what? We'd be long gone. I just hoped the authorities would buy that I was hiding in the woods.

We then turned around and started the long drive south. At a pharmacy near Milford, Connecticut, I stayed in the car while Rachel bought me a burner phone, clippers, shaving gear, and glasses with the lowest prescription possible. She ended up choosing sunglasses that lightened when you were inside. Perfect. At the next truck stop, I entered the bathroom wearing a baseball cap pulled down low. I rarely shave in prison, maybe once a week when it gets itchy, so my beard was somewhere between stubble and full growth. I shaved now so that only a mustache remained. Then I cut off all my hair and shaved my head and donned the glasses.

Even Rachel was impressed with my disguise. "I almost didn't let you back in the car."

When we got close to the George Washington Bridge, I had Rachel pull off on Jerome Avenue in the Bronx. We backed into a spot where I could put her New Jersey license plates back. Then I tossed the Maine ones into an outdoor trash can. If the police were fully on this now—and I suspected that they were—they'd probably pick up her New Jersey plate when she crossed the Washington Bridge. I warned her about that. We had been rehearsing what she should do when the police either pulled her over or came to her house.

"I'm making a lot of problems for you," I say.

"Don't worry about it," Rachel replies. "He's my nephew, remember?"

He's. Present tense. "You were a good aunt," I say.

"The best," she replies with a hint of a smile.

"But if it gets bad, if you get arrested—"

"I'll be fine."

"I know. But if you get backed into a corner, tell them I forced you to do this at gunpoint."

"You better go."

The Mount Eden Avenue stop on the 4 train was next door. I got on the subway and took it thirty-five minutes south to 14th Street–Union Square in Manhattan. Once there, I found a Nordstrom Rack and bought the cheapest blazer, dress shirt, and tie I could find. It may have been overkill with the shaved head and mustache and glasses, but if someone did figure out I was in New York City, they probably wouldn't look for a man in a sports blazer and tie.

From there, it was a ten-minute walk to Hilde Winslow's address on Twelfth Street. I stopped on the way for a slice of pepperoni pizza and a Pepsi. When I took the first bite, I felt woozy. I know it is beside the point, but I don't think I ever experienced anything so wonderfully mundane as that first bite of New York City pizza as a free man; it ignited something long extinguished, filling me with memory and color and texture. I was back in Revere Beach at Sal's with Adam and Eddie and TJ, the whole gang, and man, did that feel right.

Now I wait.

I wonder about Rachel, of course. She would most likely have been nabbed by law enforcement by now. Did she make it all the way home first? Did the cops pull her over? How much trouble is she in? I wonder about Philip and Adam and what the fallout for them will be. And finally, I think about Cheryl, my ex and Matthew's mother. What would she make of my escape? What would Aunt Sophie make of it? If he was able to understand, what would my dad think?

Doesn't matter. None of that matters right now.

I walk across the street. Would Hilde Winslow aka Harriet

Winchester know that I escaped? I don't know. The building doesn't have a doorman. You have to be buzzed in by an occupant. WINCHESTER, H is listed under apartment 4B. I press the button. I can hear it ringing. Once, twice, three times. On the fourth ring, a voice I still recognize from the trial comes cracking through the speaker.

"Yes?"

It takes me a second to gain my bearings. I disguise my voice by throwing a pathetically Eastern-European accent into the mix. "Package."

"Leave it in the vestibule, please."

"You need to sign for it."

I had spent the last few hours planning, and yet now, with the chance to get to her so close at hand, I am messing things up. I am not dressed like a delivery man. I don't have a package in my hand.

"Actually," I say, making it up on the fly, "if you give me the verbal okay, I can leave the package here. Do I have your permission to leave it in the vestibule?"

There is a pause that makes me wonder whether I've been made. Then Hilde Winslow says slowly, "You have my permission to leave it."

"Okay, it'll be in the corner of the foyer."

I hang up. I'm about to step away and consider what to do when I spot a man coming down the stairs toward the front door. For a moment I wonder whether Hilde has asked a neighbor to grab her package, but no, not enough time has passed. As he pushes open the door, I put the phone back to my ear and say, "Okay, I'll bring it up to your apartment now." I needn't have bothered with the subterfuge. The man passes through the door and heads outside seemingly without a care in the world.

I stop the closing door with my foot and slip inside. I let the door close behind me.

Then I head up the stairs toward apartment 4B.

———

Sarah's phone buzzed. She stared at the incoming message. "You were right, Max."

"About?"

"The license plates."

Max had found it bizarre that no one had spotted Rachel Anderson's car during the long trek from Maine back to New Jersey. The first working theory was that she'd kept off the main roads, but a quick review of traffic patterns told them that she wouldn't have made it on time if she completely stayed off toll roads.

"A guy named George Belbey noticed his license plates were missing when he finished his shift at L.L.Bean."

"I assume George Belbey is a Maine resident?"

"Yep."

"So Burroughs or Rachel switched the plates. Took off her New Jersey ones, put on the Maine ones."

"Except when the Port Authority spotted her car crossing the bridge—"

"She'd switched them back," Max finished for her. "So the question is, when did she do that? And why?"

"We know why, don't we, Max?"

"I guess we do, yeah."

Sarah's phone buzzed again. She stared at the screen and said, "Whoa."

"What?"

"We've been following up on Rachel Anderson's recent calls."

"And?"

"And after she visited Burroughs at Briggs, she reached out to an old colleague from the *Globe* for a favor."

"What kind of favor?"

"She wanted to get the murder book on Matthew Burroughs."

Max mulled that over. "Does the old colleague have that kind of juice?"

"He does not. But Rachel asked for something else specifically."

"What's that?"

"She wanted the Social Security number of a witness in the murder trial. A woman named Hilde Winslow."

"I remember that name . . ."

"Winslow testified that she saw Burroughs bury the baseball bat."

"Right. Older woman, as I recall."

"Correct, Max, but here's where it gets weird. Apparently, Hilde Winslow changed her name not long after the trial to Harriet Winchester."

They both looked at each other.

"Why would she do that?" Max asked.

"No clue. But here's the kicker: Hilde-Harriet also moved to New York City." She squinted at her phone. "One thirty-five West Twelfth Street, to be exact."

Max stopped chewing. His hand dropped to his side. "So Rachel Anderson visits David Burroughs in prison. After they meet, she asks about a key witness in the case—one Burroughs claimed lied on the stand—and finds out that she changed her name and moved." He looked up. "So where do you think Burroughs is heading?"

"To confront her?"

"Or worse." Max started for the airport exit. "Sarah?"

"What?"

"Get us a car to New York. And call our Manhattan office. I want Hilde Winslow's place swarming with cops right now."

19

I stand in front of Hilde Winslow's door.

Now what?

I could knock, of course, but since there is a buzzer downstairs and she's already naturally wary, I don't know whether that's the right move. She would ask who it is. She would use the peephole to see who knocked. Would she recognize me? Probably not. Unless she's heard the news reports on my escape. Either way, she wouldn't just open it.

So Option One, simply knocking, probably wouldn't work.

I wear a Yankees baseball cap I bought from a street vendor on Sixth Avenue, so if she ends up describing me, she won't know that my head is shaved. I plan on ditching it after I visit Hilde.

Option Two: I could try to kick the door in or, I don't know, shoot my way in. But come on. Like she wouldn't scream bloody murder. Like none of the neighbors would report the sound of gunfire. Option Two was a dumb nonstarter.

Option Three . . . I didn't really have one. Yet. But I couldn't just keep lurking in the corridor like this. Someone would spot me and wonder what I was doing. I hadn't really thought this through, had I? I'd spent all those hours today—*today!*—in a car with Rachel, and I hadn't come up with a solid plan. Now I'm paying the price.

There is a door to the fire stairs to my left. Maybe I could hide there and try to keep an eye out for her opening the door. But it's getting pretty late. Hilde/Harriet is in her eighties. Would she be going out again tonight? Probably not.

I am still debating my next move when I see the doorknob at 4B start to turn.

Someone is opening the door.

No plan, so I work on pure instinct. I don't know why the door is opening right now, though I suspect that perhaps Hilde Winslow was curious about the purported package left in her vestibule and has decided to venture out to retrieve it. Doesn't matter. I don't hesitate. As soon as the door opens a crack, I throw my shoulder against it.

The door flies open.

I worry for a moment that I've been too aggressive, that I've knocked an old woman down with a heavy door, but when I burst through, Hilde Winslow is still standing there, wide-eyed. She backs up and opens her mouth to scream. Some primitive part of my brain has taken over and so again I don't hesitate. I hurry toward her and clumsily yet firmly cover her mouth with my hand. With my foot, I kick the door closed behind me. I pull her toward me so that the back of her head presses up against my chest, my hand still covering her mouth.

"I don't want to hurt you," I whisper.

Did I really just say that? If so, I don't think my words offer much comfort. She squirms and grabs hold of my hand. She fights back. I hold on hard. I want to be kind here, rational, polite, but I don't see how that approach will help me or Matthew in any way.

With my free hand, I pull out my gun and show it to her.

"We just need to talk, okay? Once I get the truth, I'm out of here. Nod if you understand."

With the back of her skull still against my chest, she manages a nod.

"I'm going to take my hand away now. Please don't make me hurt you."

I sound like something out of an old movie, but I really don't know what else to say or how to handle this situation. I let her go and hope to hell she doesn't scream, because I'm not going to shoot her if she does. I'm not going to hit her with the butt end or any of that either. Or will I?

Hilde Winslow lied about me. She lied under oath and helped convict me of killing my own child.

So how far will I go? I hope she doesn't press me into finding out.

Hilde Winslow turns to me. "What do you want?"

"Do you know who I am?" I ask.

"You're David."

Her voice is surprisingly steady, confident. She doesn't look away. She isn't exactly defiant, but she doesn't look frightened or intimidated either.

"What are you doing here?" Hilde asks.

"You lied."

"What are you talking about?"

"At my trial. Your testimony. It was all a lie."

"No, it wasn't."

There really is no choice here. I lift the gun and press it against the old woman's forehead.

"I need you to listen to me," I say, hoping my voice doesn't crack. "I have nothing to lose. You understand that, right? If you lie to me again, if you don't tell me the truth, I'm going to kill you. I don't want to. I really don't. But right now, it is my son or you."

Her eyes start doing the rapid-blink thing.

"That's right," I continue. "My son is still alive. No, I don't think you'll believe me on that, and I don't have time to convince you. All that should matter to you right now is that *I* believe it. And because of that, I will have no qualms about killing you to find him. Do I make myself clear?"

"I don't know what to tell you—"

I hit her in the cheek with the barrel of the gun.

No, this isn't easy for me to do. And no, I didn't hit her hard. It was a tap. No more. But it's enough to both get the message across and make me feel awful. "You changed your name and moved away," I say. "You did that because you lied on the stand and needed to escape. I'm not looking for revenge or any of that. But there's a reason you lied, and that reason might lead to my son. So I'm going to either learn why or I'm going to kill you."

She stares at me. I stare back.

"You're delusional," Hilde-Harriet says.

"Could be."

"You can't possibly think your son is still alive."

"Oh, but I do."

Hilde's hand flutters up to her lips. She shakes her head and closes her eyes. I don't lower my gun. When she opens her eyes, I see a change. The defensiveness and defiance are gone. "I can't believe you're standing here, David."

I stay silent.

"Are you taping this?" she asks.

"No." I quickly pull out my phone and show it to her. Then I drop it on the table, just to emphasize the point. "This is just between us."

"If you tell anyone, I'll just deny it."

I feel my pulse quicken. "I understand."

"And if someone is taping this, I'm just telling a story to appease a crazy killer who is threatening me with a gun."

I nod encouragingly.

Hilde Winslow looks up at me and meets my eye. "I've imagined this moment for a long time," she says. "You standing in front of me, me confessing the truth."

She takes a deep breath. I hold mine, afraid that even the slightest movement on my part will break this spell.

"First off, I justified what I did because I thought my testimony wouldn't matter. You would have been convicted anyway—I was icing on the cake. That's what I told myself. I also genuinely believed you'd committed the murder. That was part of the sales pitch—I was helping put away a killer. And do you want to know the truth, David?"

I nod.

"I still think you did it. The evidence against you was overwhelming. That helps me sleep at night. The knowledge— the certainty—that you'd done it. But that doesn't really let me off the hook, does it? I was a philosophy professor at Boston U. Did you know that?"

I did know that. My attorneys dug deep into her background, looking for something that we could use on cross-examination. I knew that she'd been widowed when she was sixty, that she had three children, all married, and four grandsons.

"So I have studied all the 'ends justifying the means' type rationales. I did that here too, trying to defend my actions, but there is no way around the fact that my testimony sullied the trial. Worse, I sullied how I saw myself."

Her phone buzzes then. She looks up at me. I nod that it's okay to check it.

"No caller ID," she says.

"Don't answer it."

"Okay."

"You were saying?"

"It was my daughter-in-law. Ellen. She's a physician in Revere. An MD."

I remember this from the file. "She's married to your oldest son, Marty."

"Yes."

"What about her?"

"She had—probably still has—a gambling problem. A chronic one. I didn't know that at the time. She's a respectable ob-gyn. Delivered all my friends' grandchildren. Marty, I guess he tried everything. Gamblers Anonymous. Shrinks, therapy, controlling her access to money. But you know how it is with addictions. You'll find a way. Ellen did. She got in deep. Too deep to get out of. Hundreds of thousands. That's what they told me on the phone. Ellen was way behind in the money she owed, but she could get out from under—if I did them a small favor."

She rubs her face and closes her eyes. Again I stay still.

"You want to know why I testified against you. That's why. This man, he visits me. He is very polite. Nice manners. Big smile. But his eyes, I mean, they were black. Dead. You know the type?"

I nod.

"He also has poliosis."

"Poliosis?"

She pointed to the middle of her head. "A white forelock. Dark black hair with a white streak right in the middle."

I freeze.

"Anyway, this man, he tells me the situation with Ellen. He says I'd be doing the world a favor if I helped them. He says that you definitely did it, smashed your own child's skull with a baseball bat, but you're going to get off because your old man is a crooked cop and so the fix is in."

I swallow. The white forelock. I know the man she's talking about. "This man mentioned my father?"

"Yes. By name. Lenny Burroughs. He says that's why they need me. To help assure justice is done. If I help them with this, they'll help Ellen. He has on expensive loafers with no socks. He lays it all out for me. Do you want to know what I told him?"

I nod.

"No. I say I'm not going to do it. Let Ellen figure a way to pay it back. That's what I tell him. This little man, he says 'okay, fine.' Just like that. He doesn't argue with me. Doesn't make any threats. The next morning, the same little man calls me. He says in a polite tone, 'Mrs. Winslow? Listen.' And then . . ." She squeezes her eyes shut. "I hear this loud crack and then Marty starts to scream. Not Ellen. My Marty. The little man snapped my son's middle finger like it was a pencil."

In the distance, Hilde Winslow and I hear the sounds of the city—whooshing traffic, faint sirens, the beep of a truck backing up, a dog barking, people laughing.

"So," I say, "you agreed to help?"

"I had no choice. You understand."

"I do," I say, even though I'm not sure that's true. "Mrs. Winslow, what was the little man's name?"

"What, do you think he left a calling card? He didn't give me his name—and I didn't ask."

It doesn't matter. I know who it is. "Didn't you ask Marty or Ellen about him?"

"No. Never. I did what the man asked. Then I sold my

house and changed my name and moved here. I haven't talked to Marty or Ellen in five years. And you know what? They haven't reached out to me either. No one wants to go back there."

It is then that I hear someone out on the street start to shout.

A young woman from the sound of it. At first, I can't tell what she is saying. Hilde and I both look at one another. I move toward the window. The woman is still shouting, but now I can make out her words:

"Warning! The fucking cops are here! I repeat: The fascist pigs are here!"

Someone else joins in, yelling the same thing. Then someone else.

I glance out her window and spot squad cars double-parked in front of the building door. Four uniformed cops are running to the building's entrance. Two more squad cars come roaring down Twelfth Street.

Oh shit.

No doubt in my mind. They are here for me. I have to get out—and now. I hurry back toward Hilde Winslow's door, but when I open it I can already hear the cacophony of footsteps racing up the steps. The sound grows. I hear voices. I hear the cackle of radios.

They're getting closer.

I hurry down the corridor to the fire door and stairs. I open the door. More voices, more cackles of radios.

They're coming from both directions. I'm trapped.

Hilde is still standing in her doorway. "Come back in," she says to me. "Hurry."

I don't see how I have any choice. I rush back into her apartment. She slams the door shut. "Go to the window in my bedroom," she says. "Take the fire escape. I'll try to stall them."

No time to hesitate or even think it through. I rush toward the bedroom, toward the window, and throw it open. The breeze feels surprisingly refreshing. I wonder for a second whether the cops have the backyard covered. Not yet. At least, I think not yet. It's pretty dark below me. It is also narrow, maybe twenty feet between the back of Hilde's building and the back of one on Eleventh Street. I crawl out and close the window behind me.

Now what?

I start down the metal escape when once again I hear the cackle of cop radios followed by voices.

Someone is below me.

It's nighttime. The lighting is almost nonexistent, which perhaps works in my favor. From inside the apartment, I can hear pounding on Hilde's door, followed by shouts. Hilde yells that she's coming.

I can't go down. I can't go back inside. That only leaves one route. Up. I start climbing toward the fifth floor. I don't remember how many floors the building is. Five, six at most. I stop at the landing outside the fifth-floor window. The apartment is dark. No one home. I try to open the window. Locked. I debate breaking a pane with my elbow, but I can't see any way to do that without making too much noise. And even if I do, won't the police be on me pretty fast? I couldn't hide in another apartment indefinitely.

Keep moving.

I head up another level, hoping that the window will be unlocked there. But there's no sixth floor. I'm at the roof. I hoist myself up and onto it. My heart is pounding in my chest. Here is one cliché about a prison that is absolutely true: You exercise a lot. I do free weights in the yard when I can, but mostly, I've created my own boot camp in my cell— dips, squat thrusts, squat jumps, mountain climbers, and mostly, push-ups. I do at least five hundred push-ups a day in a variety of styles—traditional, diamond, wide hands, claps, staggered, Sphinx, flying, one-arm, handstand, finger. I am not the first to note the irony of taking people serving time often for violent crimes and putting them in an environment where the only self-improvement is making them physically stronger, but the truth is, I have never been in better shape, and it's finally paying off.

I hope.

How the hell did the cops find me so fast? Unless Rachel . . . no. She wouldn't. There are other ways. I didn't plan well enough. I am rushing, and I am missing stuff. This is all a good reminder that I'm not as clever as I think I am.

Still, here's the headline: I was able to question Hilde Winslow—and I'm not crazy. She had lied on the stand. I didn't bury the baseball bat in some fugue state.

She. Had. Lied.

And I know who made her do it.

I have a lead now.

I have to escape. If I'm caught, whatever lead is out there will dry up.

So what's my next move?

I consider hiding up on the roof. Hilde seems to be on my side for now. She might tell the cops that she hasn't seen me. She might tell them that I had come and gone. I could just stay, wait, venture down when the coast has cleared. But would she lie to the police, especially if they pressed her? Is she really on my side—or had she sent me to the fire escape because she wanted me out of her building for her own safety? Is she telling them about me right now?

Will they search the roof eventually anyway?

I have to believe the answer to that last question is yes.

The night sky over Manhattan is clear. The Empire State Building is lit up in red, but I have no idea why. Still, it is a stunning sight. Everything is. We, of course, never appreciate what we have. That's what they say. But it really isn't that. It's just conditioning. We take for granted what we become used to. Human nature. I want to revel in this for a few minutes, but alas, that's not possible. I said before that I never cared about being locked up. Matthew was gone and it was my fault, so I was content—if that's the right word—with having no life. I didn't want to feel. But now that I'm back out in the world, now that I'm tasting that city air, that electric current, that vivacity of sound and color, my head is reeling.

When the cops burst open the roof door, I am ready. I have

been eyeing the jump since I got up here. I don't know how many feet it is. I don't know if I can make it. But I am on the southeast corner of the building. I run with all my strength, my arms pumping. The wind is rushing in my ear, but I still hear the warnings:

"Stop! Police!"

I don't listen. I don't think they will shoot, but if they do, they do. I accelerate and time my steps so that I spring off my left foot just inches from the roof's northwest corner.

I am airborne.

My legs bicycle-run in the air, my arms still pumping. It is dark on the neighboring roof. I can't see if I will make it and for a moment I flash back to the cartoons of my youth, wondering whether I am going to pause running in midair like Wile E. Coyote before I drop like a stone to the ground beneath me. I feel my propulsion slow as gravity starts dragging me down.

I begin to fall. I close my eyes. When I land hard on the roof across the way, I tuck and roll.

"Stop!"

I don't. I somersault to a standing position. Then I do the same thing again. I run, I leap, I hit the next roof. Then the next. I'm not scared anymore. I don't know why. I feel exhilarated. Run, leap, run, leap. I feel as though I can do this all night, like I'm freaking Spider-Man or something.

When I find a roof that's truly dark, when I think I've put enough distance between me and the cops on the roof of Hilde Winslow's building, I stop and listen. I can still hear the cops and the commotion, but it feels as though they are somewhat distant. The back of the building is dark and really, how much longer can I play Spider-Man?

I find a fire escape and half run, half shimmy down it until I'm about ten feet off the ground. I stop again, look, listen. I'm in the clear. I let myself dangle for a moment from the bottom rung of the ladder and then I let go. I land hard, knees bent, a smile on my face.

When I straighten, I hear a voice say, "Freeze."

My heart sinks as I turn. It's a cop. He has his gun trained on me.

"Don't move."

Do I have a choice?

"Hands where I can see them. Now."

The cop is young and alone. He is pointing his gun toward me while he bends his neck to talk into one of those clipped-on microphones. Once he does, this backyard will be flooded with cops.

I have no choice.

There is no hesitation, no fake, no juke. I simply launch myself straight at him.

It has been less than a second since he told me not to move. I am hoping the suddenness of my attack will catch him off guard. It is a dangerous move obviously—he's the one pointing the gun—but the cop looks hesitant and a little scared. Maybe that will play to my advantage and maybe it won't.

But what options do I have?

If he shoots me, okay, whatever. I probably won't die. If

I do, well, that's a risk I'm willing to take. More likely, I'll be wounded and end up back in prison. If I surrender peacefully, I end up in the same situation. Back in prison.

I can't allow that.

So I lower my head and bull-rush him. He has time to start to yell "Freeze!" again, but I get there before he can complete the word. It ends up sounding more like "Free!" and because I'm hyped up and desperate, I take that as a good omen. I tackle him around the waist, jangling his utility belt and heavy vest and all the things that weigh modern cops down.

Keeping my momentum going, I follow through like a pile driver as we land hard on the concrete walk behind the townhouse. His back takes the impact hard, and I can hear the *woosh* sound as the air comes out of him.

He is struggling for air.

I don't let up.

I take no joy in this. I don't want to hurt anybody. I know that he is just doing his job and that the job is just. But it is him or Matthew and so again I have no choice.

I rear my head back and then fire my forehead toward his nose. The head butt hits the cop hard, like a cannonball hurled at a ceramic pitcher.

Something on his face cracks, gives way. I feel something sticky on my face and realize that it's blood.

His body goes slack.

I hop up. He is moving, groaning, which both scares and relieves me. I'm tempted to hit him again, but I don't think there's a need. Not if I move fast.

As I rush toward Sixth Avenue, I take off my blazer and wipe the blood off my face. I toss the blazer and my baseball hat into the shrubbery and keep moving.

When I reach the street, I try to slow my breath.

Keep moving, I tell myself again.

A crowd has formed. Most stop to watch for a few seconds. Some stand to see how it all plays out. I lower my head and let myself blend in with the onlookers. My pulse is back under control now. I start whistling as I walk east, trying so hard to look casual and inconspicuous that I feel like I stick out like a cigarette at a fitness club.

A few blocks later, I risk glancing behind me. No one is following me. No one is chasing me. I start whistling louder now, and a smile, a real live smile, comes to my face.

I'm free.

20

When Rachel finally got to her front door, bone-weary exhausted in a way she had never experienced before, her sister Cheryl was pacing on the front stoop.

"What the hell, Rachel?"

"Let me just get inside, okay?"

"You helped David escape?"

Rachel opened her mouth, closed it. "Just come inside."

"Rachel—"

"Inside."

She pulled her keys out of her purse. Rachel lived in what was generously dubbed a "garden apartment." She'd recently applied for a job with a free local paper, a job for which she was immensely overqualified—but hey, beggars can't be choosy. The editor, Kathy Corbera, one of her favorite journalism professors, had advocated for her, but in the end, the publisher knew about her past and wanted to avoid even the slightest whiff of scandal. Understandable in today's climate.

Rachel pushed open the door and headed straight for the kitchen. Cheryl was close behind her.

"Rachel?"

She didn't bother to respond. Every part of her ached and begged for numb. Rachel had never needed a drink so badly. The Woodford Reserve was in the cabinet next to the refrigerator. She grabbed the bottle.

"You want one?"

Cheryl frowned. "Uh, I'm pregnant, remember?"

"One won't hurt," she said, pulling down a glass from the cabinet. "I read that somewhere."

"Are you for real?"

"You're sure you don't want some?"

Cheryl just stared daggers. "What the actual fuck, Rachel?"

Rachel filled the glass with ice and poured. "It's not what you think."

"You call me all mysterious yesterday. You say you're visiting David, just like that, out of the blue. You say we need to talk when you get back home and now . . . ?"

Rachel sucked down a sip.

"Was this what you wanted to tell me?" Cheryl continued. "That you were going to help him escape?"

"No, of course not. I had no idea he was going to escape."

"So, what, your being up at Briggs was just a wild coincidence?"

"No."

"Talk to me, Rach."

Her sister. Her beautiful, pregnant sister. Cheryl had been through such hell. Five years ago, Matthew's murder had knocked her to her knees, and Rachel never thought that her sister would be able to get up again. To the outside world, Cheryl was moving on. New husband, pregnant, new position. But she wasn't. Not really. She was trying to build something, something new and strong, but Rachel knew that it was still flimsy and flyaway. Life is fragile at the best of times. The foundation is always shifting beneath our feet.

"Please," Cheryl said. "Tell me what's going on."

"I'm trying."

Her sister looked suddenly small and vulnerable. She was almost cringing, as though waiting for the blow that she knew was coming. Rachel tried to rehearse the words in her head, but they all came out sounding stilted and weird. You could rip this bandage off slowly or quickly, but either way, this was going to hurt.

"I want to show you something."

"Okay."

"But I don't want you to freak out."

"Seriously?"

Rachel had given the hard copy she'd printed out to David, but she had the amusement-park pic she'd snapped at Irene's house on her phone. She took one more gulp of the bourbon, closed her eyes, let it warm her. Then she grabbed her phone. She hit the Photos icon and started swiping. Cheryl had sidled up next to her. She was watching over Rachel's shoulder.

Rachel found the photo and stopped.

"I don't understand," Cheryl said. "Who's this woman and these kids?"

Then Rachel put her thumb and index finger on the boy behind them and zoomed in on his face.

21

The FBI surveillance van carrying Max and Sarah sped to a stop in front of Hilde Winslow's building. Max spotted six cruisers and an ambulance. Sarah was staring at a computer monitor and talking via her earpiece to someone on the phone. She signaled that it was important and for Max to go out on his own. Max nodded as the van's side door slid open.

An agent Max didn't know said, "Special Agent Bernstein? The suspect got away."

"I heard on the radio."

"The police are in pursuit. They're confident they'll catch him."

Max wasn't so sure. It was a big city with plenty of nooks and crannies and human beings. It was always easier to vanish when in plain sight. He and Sarah had been watching the attempted capture in the high-tech FBI van, live-streaming

four of the pursuing officers' bodycams as they ascended to
the roof.

There was something that bothered him.

"Where's Hilde Winslow?"

The agent frowned at his notebook. "She calls herself
Harriet—"

"Winchester, yeah, I know," Max said. "Where is she?"

The young agent pointed toward the ambulance. It was
open in the back. Hilde Winslow sat up, a blanket wrapped
around her like a shawl. She sipped on a juice box through a
straw. Max headed over and introduced himself. Hilde Winslow's eyes were bright and locked in on his. She looked small,
wizened, and tougher than an armor-plated armadillo.

"Are you okay?" he asked her.

"Just a little shaken up," Hilde replied. "They insisted on
taking care of me."

The paramedic, an Asian woman with a long ponytail, said,
"Just relax, Harriet."

"I'd like to go home," she said.

"You can go back up when the police say it's okay."

Hilde Winslow gave the paramedic a sweet smile and
sipped some more on her apple juice. She looked to Max
like both an old woman and a little girl at the same time.

"You said you were a special agent with the FBI," Hilde
said to him.

"Yes, ma'am. I'm in charge of recapturing David Burroughs."

"I see."

He waited for her to say more. She sipped her juice.

"Can you tell me what Mr. Burroughs said to you?"

"Nothing really."

"Nothing?"

"There was no time, you see."

"So you don't know what he wanted?"

"No idea."

"Can we back up, Mrs. Winslow?"

He'd intentionally used her old name. He waited for her to correct him. She didn't.

"What happened exactly?" Max continued.

"He knocked on my door. I opened it—"

"Did you ask who it was at first?"

She thought about that for a moment. "No, I don't think so."

"You heard a knock and just opened it?"

"Yes."

"Do you always do that? Without asking who it is?"

"You have to be buzzed in the building."

"Did you buzz him in?"

"No."

"Yet you just opened the door?"

She smiled at him. "It's a friendly building. I thought it was a neighbor."

"I see," he said.

Why, he wondered, was she lying to him?

"I'm also old. So sometimes I'm forgetful. But you're right, Special Agent Bernstein. That was a mistake on my part. I'll be more careful in the future."

He was being played. Like with Rachel Anderson. He understood Rachel's motive as a loving sister-in-law. But why would Hilde Winslow be lying to him?

"So David Burroughs knocked on the door," Max continued, "and you opened it."

"Yes."

"Did you recognize him?"

"Oh heavens no."

"What did he look like?"

"Just like, well, a man. I tried to give the police detective a description, but it all happened so fast."

"What did you say to him?"

"Nothing."

"What did he say to you?"

"There was no time for any of that. I opened the door. And suddenly there was this big commotion coming from downstairs. I guess the police were already inside and rushing up to my floor."

"I see. So what happened next?"

"I guess he got spooked."

"David Burroughs?"

"Yes."

"What did the spooked Burroughs do?"

"He jumped into my apartment and closed the door behind him."

"That must have been scary."

"Oh yes. Yes, it was." She turned to the paramedic. "Annie?"

"Yes, Mrs. Winchester?"

"Can I have another juice box?"

"Of course. Are you feeling okay?"

"I'm a little tired," Hilde Winslow said. "It's a lot of questions."

Annie the paramedic gave Max a baleful eye. Max ignored it and tried to right the teetering ship.

"So Burroughs is in your apartment with you and the door is closed now?"

"Yes."

"You'd been standing in the doorway, right? Did he push you to get in? Did you step back?"

"Hmm." Dramatic pause. "I don't remember. Does it matter?"

"I guess not. Did you scream?"

"No. I didn't want to upset him."

"Did you say anything?"

"Like what?"

"Like who are you, what are you doing here, get out of my apartment, anything?"

She thought about that. When Paramedic Annie came back over with the juice, she smiled and thanked her.

"Mrs. Winslow?"

Again calling her by the old name.

"I may have. I probably did. But it all happened so fast. He ran to my window and threw it open."

"Right to the window," Max said. "Without a word."

"Yes."

"And the window," Max said. "It was in your bedroom, right?"

"Right."

"The windows in your main room, the living room, are closer to the door, right?"

"I don't know. I never measured the distance. I guess they are."

"But they don't lead to fire escapes, do they?"

"That's right."

"Only the one in your bedroom does," Max said. He tilted his head to the right. "How do you think Burroughs knew that?"

"I don't know."

"You didn't tell him?" Max asked.

"Of course not. Maybe he got the lay of the building beforehand."

"Are you aware that David Burroughs escaped from custody just this morning?"

"One of the nice police officers told me that."

"You didn't know before?"

"No, of course not. How would I?"

"I called your phone thirty minutes ago and left a voice message."

"Oh, really? I never answer my phone. It's always some con man trying to scam an old lady. I let it go to voicemail, and truth be told? I don't even know how voicemail works."

Max stared at her. He was buying none of this.

"Why do you think Burroughs came directly to you?"

"Pardon?"

"First thing. He gets out. He drives to New York City. He comes to see you. Why do you think that is?"

"I don't know . . ." Suddenly her eyes open wide. "Oh my God."

"Mrs. Winslow?"

"Do you think . . . do you think he came here to hurt me?" Her hand fluttered to her mouth. "Is that what you think?"

"No," Max said.

"But you just said—"

"If he wanted to hurt you, I think he would have pushed you when he came in, don't you? Or hit you? Or something like that?" Then Max noticed something. "Is that a mark on your cheek?"

"It's nothing," she said too quickly.

"David Burroughs also has a gun. Did you see it?"

"A gun? Heavens no."

"Think about it a second. You're David Burroughs. You spend five years in prison. You finally escape. You head straight to see a witness you claim lied about you—"

"Special Agent Bernstein?"

"Yes."

"It's been quite an ordeal," she said sweetly. "I've told you all I know."

"I'd like to just ask you a few questions about your testimony."

"No," she said.

"No?"

"I'm not dredging this all up again, and . . ." She turned. "Annie?"

"Yes, Mrs. Winchester."

"I'm not feeling so great."

"I told you, Harriet. You need to rest."

Max was about to protest when he heard Sarah's voice call out, "Max?"

He turned. She was standing in the side opening of the FBI van waving him over urgently. He skipped the goodbye and hurried toward her. Sarah saw his face as he approached.

"What?" Sarah said.

"She's lying."

"About?"

"Everything." He hoisted up his pants. "Okay, what's so important?"

"I got the CCTV on Rachel's prison visit to Burroughs. You're going to want to see this."

———

Cheryl just stared at the photo.

"It was taken at an amusement park," Rachel said.

"I can see that," her sister snapped. "So?"

Rachel didn't bother explaining about Irene and all that. She'd zoomed in to the little boy in the background— not too much because then his face became too blurry. She'd handed her phone to her sister. Cheryl continued to stare.

"Cheryl?"

With her eyes still on the photo, Cheryl whispered, "What are you trying to do to me?"

Rachel did not reply.

Tears started to come now. "You showed this to David."

Rachel wasn't sure if it was a question or not. "Yes."

"That's why you went to Briggs."

"Yes."

Cheryl kept staring at the image and shaking her head. "Where did you get this?"

Rachel gently took the phone back and unzoomed the photograph back to the original. "This is a friend of mine. She went to Six Flags with her family. Her husband took the picture. She was showing it to me and . . ."

"And what?" Cheryl's voice was pure ice. "You saw a boy who somewhat resembles my dead son and figured you'd blow up everyone's life?"

Not your life, she thought, but Rachel figured that it was best not to voice that.

"Rachel?"

"I didn't know what to do."

"So you showed it to David?"

"Yes."

"Why?"

Rachel didn't want to get into how she wanted to protect Cheryl, so she said nothing.

Cheryl pressed on. "What did he say?"

"He was shocked."

"What did he say, Rachel?"

"He thinks it's Matthew."

Cheryl's face turned red. "Of course he does. If you throw a drowning man an anvil, he'll mistake it for a life preserver."

"If David killed Matthew," Rachel said, "you'd think he'd know it was an anvil, right?"

Cheryl just shook her head.

"It never made sense, Cheryl. David killing Matthew. Come on. You know that. Even in a fugue state or whatever. And the whole 'buried weapon' thing. Why would David have done that? He'd know better. And that witness. Hilde Winslow. She changed her name and moved away. Why would she do that?"

"My God." Cheryl stared at her sister. "You believe this nonsense?"

"I don't know. That's all I'm saying."

"How can you not know? Or maybe you're desperate too, Rachel."

"What?"

"For a story."

"Are you serious?"

"For redemption. For another chance. I mean, if my son is alive, this would be huge, right? Networks, front pages—"

"You can't—"

"And if it's not Matthew, if it's just a kid who has a passing resemblance to him, all of this—David's escaping, David finally talking to someone after all this time—well, it's still a big story."

"Cheryl."

"My murdered son could be your ticket back."

Rachel reeled back as though she'd been slapped.

"I didn't mean that," Cheryl said quickly, her voice softer now.

Rachel didn't reply.

"Listen to me," Cheryl continued. "Matthew is dead. And so is Catherine Tullo."

"This has nothing to do with her."

"It's not your fault she's dead, Rachel."

"Of course it's my fault."

Cheryl shook her head and put her hands on her sister's shoulders. "I didn't mean what I said before."

"You meant it," Rachel said.

"I didn't. I swear."

"And maybe it's true. I feel sorry for myself, for what I lost. But I pushed too hard, and now Catherine Tullo is dead. She is dead because of me. I got what I deserved."

Cheryl shook her head. "That's not true. You were just . . ."

"Just what?"

"Too close to it," Cheryl said. "You think I forgot?"

Rachel didn't know what to say.

"Halloween Night. Your freshman year."

Rachel turned away. She closed her eyes and wished the memories away.

"Rach?"

"Maybe you're right," Rachel told her sister. She stared down at the photograph. "Maybe I am seeing what I want to see. Maybe David is too. Probably, in fact. But there's a chance, right? He's got nothing. David—he's as bad as you imagine. Worse. So let him search. It can't hurt him. It can't make him worse. That's why I didn't show you the pic. If it's nothing—and yeah, sure, the odds it's nothing are pretty strong—then it goes nowhere. No harm, no foul. We end up where we began. You'd have never found out. But if it *is* Matthew—"

"It's not."

"Either way," Rachel persisted. "Let David and me see it through."

———

"Here's the footage from Rachel Anderson's first prison visit," Sarah told Max. "As I told you before, this was Burroughs's first visitor since he arrived at Briggs five years ago."

The surveillance van was a modified Ford. The back van windows appeared tinted, but they were painted black for complete privacy. Your only view of the outside world—and it was a good one—came from hidden cameras strategically placed around the van. Max and Sarah sat side by side in reclining and ergonomic seats at a workstation with three computer monitors. It was more comfortable than you'd think, what with agents spending hours at a time back here. Two agents sat in the driver's cabin. One was the tech expert, but Sarah knew her way around the system as well as anybody.

"Can you turn up the volume?"

"There is no volume, Max."

He frowned. "Why not?"

"There was a lawsuit a few years ago," Sarah said. "Something about privacy being violated."

"But privacy isn't being violated with the CCTV?"

"Once Briggs lost the right to use audio in court, they claimed the video was a matter of security and didn't infringe on privacy."

"The courts bought that?"

"They did."

Max shrugged. "So what did you want me to see?"

"Look here."

Sarah started playing the video. The camera must have been placed on the ceiling somewhere behind David Burroughs's shoulder. They had a face-on shot of Rachel, who took a seat on the other side of the plexiglass. Sarah hit the fast-forward button, and the two figures moved jerkily. When on-screen Rachel pulled out what looked like a manila envelope, Sarah stopped the fast forward and hit the play button. The speed returned to normal. Max frowned and watched. On the screen, Rachel looked down as though she were trying to muster strength. Then she took something out of the envelope and pressed it flat against the glass.

Max squinted. "Is that a photo?"

"I think so."

"What's it of?"

Even with no sound, even with mediocre quality in terms of pixels and lighting, Max could feel everything in that visitors' room change. Burroughs's body stiffened.

"I don't know yet," Sarah said.

"Maybe it's an escape plan."

"I tinkered with it before you got here."

"What could you see?"

"People," Sarah said. "One of them could be Batman."

"Pardon?"

"Maybe, I don't know. I'll need more time, Max."

"Let's also get a lip reader."

"On it. Legal says we have to apply for a warrant."

"That privacy lawsuit?"

"Yes. But I forwarded it anyway. I don't think the pixel quality will be good enough."

"Can you zoom in more?"

"This is the best I have so far." Sarah clicked a key. The image blew up. She paused so that the pixilation could catch up, but it never really became clear. Max squinted again.

"We need to ask Rachel Anderson about this."

"Her lawyer barred her from answering any questions."

"We have to try. We still have eyes on her, right?"

"Right. She's home. Her sister came over."

"Burroughs's ex?"

Sarah nodded. "She's pregnant."

"Wow," Max said. "We have taps on all the phones?"

"We do. Nothing yet."

"Rachel Anderson drove with Burroughs for hours. They planned this out. She won't be stupid enough to use her phone."

"Agreed."

"We both know her history," Max said.

"That me-too article?"

Max nodded. "Any chance that has something to do with this?"

"I can't see how, Max. Can you?"

He thought about it. He didn't. Not yet anyway. "How's the deep dive into the financials going?"

"Ongoing," Sarah said. Max knew what a slow-go it was to comb through a person's financials. It was how most white-collar criminals were able to stall for years. "But I do have something."

"On."

"Ted Weston."

"The prison guard Burroughs tried to kill?"

She nodded. "The guy is in debt, totally underwater, but there's been two recent deposits for exactly two thousand dollars each."

"From?"

"Still checking."

Max sat back. "A payoff?"

"Probably."

"It never made sense to me," Max said.

"What didn't?"

"That Burroughs would try to kill Weston." Max started gnawing at his fingernail. "This is feeling like a lot more than a prison break, Sarah."

"Could be, Max. You know how we find out for sure?"

"How?"

"We do what we do. We don't get distracted. We bring in Burroughs."

"Truer words, Sarah. Let's drag Weston's ass in before he has a chance to lawyer up."

22

Gertrude Payne stood on the cliffside of the Payne estate. The moon reflected off the churning waters of the Atlantic. She'd let her gray hair loose and closed her eyes. The wind felt good on her face. The crashing waves soothed her. She could still hear Stephano approaching, but she kept her eyes closed for another ten seconds.

When she opened them, she said, "You didn't get him."

"Ross Sumner failed us."

"And that guard, the one who told you about the sister-in-law's visit."

"He failed too."

She turned away from the ocean. Stephano was a beefy man with jet-black hair cut into Prince Valiant bangs, making him resemble an aging rocker who was trying a little too hard to hang on to his youth. Stephano's suit was custom-made but still fit his square frame like a cardboard box.

"I don't understand," Gertrude said. "How could he have escaped?"

"Does it matter?"

"Perhaps not."

"It's not as though he's a threat."

She smiled.

"What? You think he is?"

She knew the odds of David Burroughs causing any lasting damage were miniscule, but you don't reach what her husband used to nauseatingly call the Payne Pinnacle without adding the other P:

Paranoia.

But she also knew the way the world worked. You simply never know. You believe you are safe. You are certain that you considered every angle, thought about every possibility. But you didn't. Not ever. The world doesn't work that way.

No one gets it right all the time.

"Mrs. Payne?"

"We need to be prepared, Stephano."

23

I hurry-walk the streets of Manhattan.

I don't want to be conspicuous by running, but I also want to put distance between myself and that apartment on Twelfth Street. I head north. I pass the Fourteenth Street subway station and then the Twenty-Third Street one, resisting the urge to head down because if there is some kind of manhunt or dragnet, they'll probably cover all nearby subway stations.

Or not.

The truth is, I have no idea.

I have a destination, of course.

Revere, Massachusetts. My hometown.

The man who blackmailed Hilde Winslow? The one with the forelock? That's where he lives.

I know him.

I assume the FBI will have someone watching my father's house, but then again, the police can't be everywhere all at once. We get used to that viewpoint from television and movies, where every bad guy is quickly brought to justice by unlimited surveillance or a fingerprint or a DNA sample.

I also don't know what Hilde Winslow may have told the cops. She seemed to genuinely sympathize with my plight, and she had helped me escape. But it's hard to say for certain. It could have been an act. It could have been that she feared what would happen if the police broke in and I was near her. I don't know.

But I really don't have a choice. I have to risk going up to Revere.

When I arrive in Times Square half an hour later, I realize how in over my head I am. I had thought about crowded places like these—the people, the noise, the bright lights, the big screens, the neon signs—but I am ill-prepared for what I'm experiencing right now. I stop. There is too much stimulation. The swirl and onslaught of hums, of hues, of smells, of faces—of life—it all sends me reeling. I'm like a man who has spent five years in a dark room and now someone is shining a flashlight into my eyes. My head spins to the point where I have to lean against a wall or fall down.

The adrenaline that had kept me going isn't so much ebbing away as turning into smoke and vanishing into the night air. Exhaustion overtakes me. It's late. The trains and buses to the Boston area are done for the night. I need to be smart about this. I know what I need to do when I'm back in Revere, and I will need full command of my faculties to pull it off. In short, I need to sleep.

There are a lot of subway stops near here—too many for the

cops to cover—but in the end I choose to walk. The shaved head should still throw them—Hilde Winslow only saw me with the ditched baseball cap—but I also wear a surgical mask. Not many people are wearing them anymore, so I worry I may stick out with it. But it's also a great disguise. Should I keep it on? Hard call. So is deciding where to go to sleep. I think about walking north to Central Park. There are plenty of places to hide and make shelter, but again, would that be a place the police might cover? I check my burner phone. Only Rachel, who bought it for me, knows the number. I wait for her to contact me, but she hasn't yet. I'm not sure what that means, if anything. She probably still feels watched.

I make a plan. I keep the mask on, and I head up to Central Park. I take the path into the lush Ramble, the park's nature preserve, near Seventy-Ninth Street. The trees are thicker up here. I find a spot as deep and secluded as I can find. I lay out branches everywhere near me and hope like hell that if someone approaches me, I'll be able to hear and react. I lay down and listen to the babbling stream mixed in with the city sounds. Then I close my eyes and fall into a mercifully dreamless sleep.

At rush hour, when I know Penn Station will be packed, I board an Amtrak to Boston. I have the cleanly shaven head. I wear a mask. Sometime during the ride it hits me that I've now been free for twenty-four hours. I am on edge the whole time, but when I go to the bathroom and look at myself in the mirror, I realize that there is nearly zero chance anyone will recognize me. I don't know how risky taking this train is, but really, what choice do I have?

When I'm an hour outside of Boston, my burner phone finally rings. I don't recognize the incoming number. I hit the answer button, but I don't say anything. I hold the phone to my ear and wait.

"Alpaca," Rachel says.

Relief washes over me. We came up with seven code words to start every conversation. If she doesn't open with the code word, it means that it is not safe and someone is forcing her to make the call or listening in. If she reuses a password—if on the next call she says "Alpaca"—I'll again know someone, somehow, is listening in and trying to fool me.

"All okay?" I ask.

I don't have a return password or code. I didn't see a need. There is a fine line between careful and ridiculous.

"As well as we could expect."

"The cops questioned you?"

"The FBI, yes."

"They figured out where I was headed," I say.

"The FBI?"

"Yes. They almost caught me at Hilde's."

"I didn't say anything, I swear."

"I know."

"So how?"

"I'm not sure."

"But you got away?"

"For now."

"Were you able to question her?"

She means Hilde Winslow, of course. I tell her yes and fill

her in on some of what I learned. I tell her that Hilde admitted lying on the stand, but I leave out the gambling debt and the connection to Revere. If somehow someone is listening in—man, all of this can make you so damn paranoid—it's better not to give them the slightest hint of my destination.

"I'm getting as much cash together as I can. I'm going to figure a way to lose any tail that the FBI has on me, just like we talked about."

"How long will that take?"

"An hour, maybe two. Pin-drop me your location when you get where you're going. I'll come to you."

"Thanks."

"There's one other thing," Rachel says when I finish.

I wait.

"Cheryl visited me last night."

I can feel the tightness in my chest. "How did that go?"

"I showed her the photo. She thinks we are both delusional."

"Hard to argue."

"She also said that my personal issues could be interfering with my judgment."

"Those being?"

"I'm going to forward you some links, David. Read them. It's easier than trying to explain."

———

Rachel texts me links to three different articles on her proposed me-too article and the subsequent suicide of a young woman named Catherine Tullo. I settle back and read all three. I try to study the situation objectively, as though it does not involve a person I adore as much as Rachel.

But it's hard to be objective for a lot of reasons.

I have questions for Rachel, but they can keep.

I lay back and close my eyes until I hear the call for North Station in Boston. I look out the window as we pull up to the platform, fearing a huge police presence. There are scattered cops, which is normal, I guess, but they don't look particularly wary. That doesn't mean much, but it's better than seeing a hundred with guns drawn. I head out of the station and into my home city. I can't help but smile. I head down Causeway Street and hit the Boston-ubiquitous Dunkin' on the corner of Lancaster Street. I grab half a dozen donuts—two French crullers, two chocolate glazed, one toasted coconut, one old-fashioned—and a large cup of unflavored black coffee because I hate flavored coffee, especially from Dunkin'.

I head down Lancaster Avenue with the Dunkin' bag in my hand. I'm still wearing the surgical mask, but eventually I will risk that to eat the French cruller. My mouth is watering at the thought. Fifteen minutes later, I'm at the Bowdoin Street subway and on the Blue Line heading toward Revere Beach. I try to flash back to past times when I made this journey in my youth. We had a group of guys back then, all of us in the same class at Revere High. I was closest to Adam Mackenzie, but we had TJ, Billy Simpson, and the man I was on my way to visit, Eddie Grilton.

Eddie's family owned the pharmacy at Centennial Avenue

and North Shore Road, a stone's throw from Revere Beach station. His grandfather started the place. Everyone I know got their prescriptions filled there, and way back when, first Eddie's grandfather and then his father ran numbers and books for the Fisher crime family.

The small parking lot behind the pharmacy was completely isolated from the street. Back in the day, it was our main hangout. We drank beers and smoked weed. Of course, that was a long time ago. The crew was mostly gone now. TJ was a physician in Newton. Billy opened a bar in Miami. But Eddie, who had wanted out of this town more than any of us, who hated his grandfather's life and his father's life and the teen years he'd been forced to work in the pharmacy too, was still here. He'd ended up going to pharmacology school, just like his old man wanted. After he graduated, he worked that high counter until the old man, like the grandfather before him, keeled over and died of a heart attack. Now Eddie ran the place and waited his turn to keel over.

When I get off at Revere Beach station, I grow wary again, not just because of the possible police presence but because this is my old neighborhood and if anyplace will see through my disguises, it's here. I am within a thousand feet of my childhood home, the Mackenzie home, Sal's Pizzeria, Grilton Pharmacy, all of it.

Grilton Pharmacy looks slightly worse for wear, but it had been slowly deteriorating for as long as I can remember. The watered-down brick was barely red anymore. The neon sign above the store was rusting on the edges. When it was turned on, the letters spasmed illumination. I keep my head lowered and move down the alleyway toward our old hangout in the back. There was one parking space. I remember Eddie's dad always kept his Cadillac back there. It meant something to Eddie's dad, that car, and he kept it perfectly waxed at all times. Now Eddie kept his Cadillac ATS in the same spot. Things change and yet everything stays the same.

I get deep when I'm tired.

I huddle behind a garbage dumpster. The coffee is still hot. That's Dunkin' for you. I inhale a French cruller and slow down midway through the coconut. Prison has its share of abuses, but I guess I'd overlooked the inherent cruelty brought upon my taste buds. I'm giddy from the flavor or the sugar high. Or maybe it's experiencing freedom. It is so easy to shut down in prison, to make yourself numb, to not let yourself feel or experience anything remotely connected to pleasure. It helps really. It kept me alive. But now I've been forced out of that protective shell, now that I've let myself think about Matthew and the possibility of redemption, all the "feels" are rushing in.

I check the time. No one uses this back entrance. I know this from the decades we gathered here. It won't be much longer, I think, and sure enough, the back door opens and Eddie steps out, an unlit cigarette dangling from his lips. He has the lighter in his hand and the moment the glass door closes behind him, he hits the flame and puts it up to the end of the cigarette. His eyes shut on the deep inhale.

Eddie looks older. He's skinny and stooped with a paunch. His once-coarse hair is fading now, leaving him somewhere between receding and bald. He has a pencil-thin mustache and sunken eyes. I don't exactly know how to handle this, so I step into view.

"Hey, Eddie."

He goes slack-jawed when he sees me. The dangling cigarette falls from his lips, but Eddie grabs it midair. That makes me smile. Eddie had the fastest hands. He was the best ping pong player, the group pool shark, a whiz at video games or pinball or bowling or mini-golf—anything involving hand-eye coordination and little else.

"Holy shit," Eddie says.

"Do I have to ask you not to scream?"

"Fuck no, you kidding me?" He hurries over to me. "I'm so happy to see you, man."

He hugs me—that new/old sensation—and I stiffen, afraid that if I give in to this I'll collapse and never get back up. Still, the hug is welcome. Even the stench of cigarette is welcome. "Me too, Eddie."

"I saw on the news about your escape." He points to the top of my head. "You losing your hair too?"

"No, I'm in disguise."

"Clever," Eddie says. "Can we get one thing out of the way?"

"Sure."

"You didn't kill Matthew, did you?"

"I did not."

"Knew it. You got a plan? Forget it, the less I know the better. You need cash?"

"Yes."

"Okay. Business is in the crapper, but I got some money in the safe. Whatever's there, it's yours."

I try not to well up. "Thanks, Eddie."

"That why you're here?"

"No."

"Talk to me."

"You still running book?"

"Nah. That's why business is so bad. We used to do it all in the old days. I mean, my grandfather ran numbers. My dad, he took everyone's bets. The cops called them both crooks. No offense to your old man."

"None taken."

"How is he, by the way?"

"You probably know more than I do, Eddie."

"Yeah, I guess. Where was I?"

"The cops called your dad and granddad crooks."

"Right. But you know who finally put us out of business? The government. Used to be numbers were illegal. Then the government called it a lottery and gives shittier odds than we ever did and now, bam, it's legit. Gambling was illegal too, and then some online assholes paid off a bunch of politicians and now, boom, you click online and your bets are in. Marijuana too, not that my old man ever sold that."

"But you were booking five years ago?"

"That's around when it all started to tank. Why?"

"Do you remember a client named Ellen Winslow?"

He frowned. "She wasn't one of mine. Reggie on Shirley Avenue took her bets."

"But you know the name?"

"She was in deep, yeah. But I can't imagine why you'd care."

Eddie still wears the white pharmacy smock. Like he's a doctor or a cosmetics salesman at Filene's.

"So she'd have owed the Fisher Brothers?"

Eddie doesn't love where this conversation is headed. "Yeah, I guess. Davey, why are you asking me all this?"

"I need to talk to Kyle."

Silence.

"Kyle as in Skunk Kyle?"

"They still call him that?"

"He prefers it."

That had been his nickname when we were kids. I don't remember when Kyle moved to town. First grade, maybe second. He had the white forelock even then. With the white streak against the black hair and kids being kids, he immediately got the obvious nickname Skunk. Some kids would have hated that. Young Kyle seemed to revel in it.

"Let me get this straight," Eddie says. "You want to talk to Skunk Kyle about an old debt?"

"Yes."

Eddie whistled. "You remember him, right?"

"Yes."

"Remember when he pushed Lisa Millstone off that roof when we were nine?"

"I do."

"And Mrs. Bailey's cats. The ones that kept disappearing when we were like, twelve?"

240

"Yes."

"And the Pallone girl. What was her name again? Mary Anne—"

"I remember," I say.

"Skunk hasn't gotten better, Davey."

"I know. I assume he still works for the Fishers?"

Eddie gives his face a vigorous rub with his right hand. "You going to tell me what this is about?"

I see no reason not to. "I think the Fishers kidnapped my son and set me up for murder."

I give him the abridged version. Eddie doesn't tell me I'm crazy, but he thinks it. I show him the amusement-park photo. He looks at it quickly, but his eyes stay mostly on me. He drops his cigarette butt to the cracked pavement and lights another one. He doesn't interrupt.

When I finish, Eddie says, "I'm not going to try to talk you out of this. You're a big boy."

"I appreciate that. You can set it up?"

"I can make a call."

"Thank you."

"You know the old man retired, right?"

"Nicky Fisher retired?" I say.

"Yep, retired, moved someplace warm. I hear Nicky golfs every day now. Spent his life murdering, robbing, extorting, pillaging, maiming, but now he's in his eighties enjoying golf and spa massages and dinners out in Florida. Karma, right?"

"So who's the boss now?"

"His son NJ runs the show."

"Do you think NJ will talk to me?"

"I can only ask. But if it's what you think, it's not like they're going to confess."

"I'm not interested in getting anyone in trouble."

"Yeah, but it's not just that. If they really wanted to set you up for killing your own kid—and I won't go into the million reasons why that makes no sense—why wouldn't they just call the cops on you now?"

"The Fishers calling the cops?"

"It wouldn't be a good look, I admit. Of course, they might just kill you. That's more their style than this Count of Monte Cristo tale you're coming up with."

"I don't really have a choice, Eddie. This is my only lead."

Eddie nods. "Okay. Let me make a call."

24

Rachel didn't know whether she was being followed or not. Probably.

Didn't matter. She had a plan.

She walked to the train station and took the Main/Bergen line. The train wasn't crowded at this hour. She checked her surroundings, changed train cars twice. No one seemed to be following or watching her, but they could be good at their job.

She exited the train at Secaucus Junction and headed for the train into Penn Station in New York City. Pretty much everyone else on the train did the same. Again, she tried to keep an eye out, but no one seemed to be watching her.

Didn't matter. She had a plan.

She walked the streets of Manhattan for the next forty-five minutes, winding her way through various midtown locations until she reached a high-rise on Park Avenue and Forty-Sixth Street where Hester Crimstein, her attorney, had told her to go. A young man was waiting for her. The young man didn't ask Rachel her name. He just smiled and said, "Right this way." The elevator door was already open. They went up to the fourth floor in silence. When the doors opened, the young man said, "It's down the hall on the left." He waited for her to exit and then led the way. She opened the door and went in. Another man stood by a sink.

"Have a seat," the other man said.

She sat with her back to the sink. The man worked fast. He cut her hair short and dyed it a subtle red. No words were exchanged during the whole process. When he was done, the first man, the younger man, came back. He led Rachel back to the elevator. He pressed the button for G3, which, she assumed, was the third floor of the garage. In the elevator he handed her a car key and an envelope. The envelope had cash, a driver's ID in the name of Rachel Anderson (her maiden name), two credit cards, a phone. The phone was some kind of clone. She could get normal calls or texts, but the FBI wouldn't be able to track where she was. At least, that was how the young man explained it to her.

When they reached G3, the elevator doors slid open. "Parking spot forty-seven," the young man said. "Drive safely."

The car was a Honda Accord. It wasn't stolen or a rental, and Hester had assured her that there was no way it could be traced to either of them. She checked the phone as she slid behind the wheel. David had just sent the pin drop.

Whoa.

She was surprised to see he was in Revere, not far from his old home. She wondered about that. Going home had not been part of the plan. In fact, David had been careful to stress the dangers in going anywhere familiar.

That meant something Hilde Winslow had told him brought him back to Revere.

Rachel didn't get why, but she didn't have to yet. She started up the car and drove north.

———

When Eddie gets off the phone, he tells me it's going to be a few hours before the meet.

"You want to stay in my back room until then?" Eddie asks.

I shake my head and give him the number of my burner phone. "Can you call me when you know a time?"

"Sure."

I thank him and start across the street. I know this neighborhood like the proverbial back of my hand. Things may change, but in places like this, not much. By the water, sure. There are new high-rises overlooking Revere Beach. But here, where I grew up, the row houses may have fresh paint jobs or aluminum siding or the occasional addition, but it's all pretty much the same. A big part of my childhood was about cutting through every yard to save a step or avoid being seen or maybe it was just about adventure.

I am so close now to my father.

I realize the danger here. There is, I'm sure, a fairly massive manhunt for me. That may mean that they are watching my childhood home, where my father and aunt still reside. It makes sense. But as I noted before, the cops can't be every-where. They know that last night I was in New York City. Do they think I would come up to Revere from there? It would depend, I guess, on what Hilde Winslow has told them, but I would highly doubt she would confess to committing per-jury during my trial.

I check all the angles as I duck into the backyards of my youth. I realize that surveillance doesn't require a van parked in front of the house, but I see nothing indicating danger. I wonder whether it's safe. I wonder whether this even makes sense. Taking a step back for a moment: What's the point in seeing Dad and Aunt Sophie after all this time? Won't my visit just upset them?

But I'm drawn to my old home. I am an escaped convict with a few hours to kill, and I want to see the people I love the most. Is that so strange? No. But my motive and focus remain locked on finding Matthew.

I feel safe as I hit the backyards between Thornton and Highland. The homes, mostly multi-dwellings, were stacked close together so that you never really knew where your prop-erty ended and the next one started. That had led to some interesting battles over the years. When I was fourteen, the Siegelmans claimed that Mr. Crestin's garden went over the property line, and so they wanted some of Crestin's award-winning tomatoes. I pass by that disputed border right now and reach Mrs. Bordio's place. Mrs. Bordio lived there with her son Pat, who had what we used to call a lazy eye. They moved out in the early 2000s, and the place looks well cared for by the new owners. Mr. Bordio, Pat's father, died before my time, in Vietnam, and the yard was always overgrown. My old man finally set up a rotating schedule where the men in the neighborhood took turns mowing her lawn. Mrs. Bordio repaid the men with her homemade peanut brittle. Mr. Ruskin—I'm walking past his place now—had spent an entire summer building an enormous pizza oven out of brick and concrete. It's still there, of course, even though the Ruskins moved out in 2007. If a tornado ever took out this neighborhood, that oven would be the only thing left standing.

Up ahead I can see the back of my childhood home.

The shrubbery is thicker here. One of my earliest memories—I must have been three or four—is my dad and Uncle Philip building a swing set in the yard. Adam and I watched our dads in awe. It was a hot day and mostly I remember the way my dad would pick up a bottle of Bud and bring it to his lips. He'd take a deep sip, lower it, notice me watching, wink.

And of course, I remember my high school girlfriend Cheryl.

As I make my way closer to my home, my strongest memory is a sacrilegious one involving the tent that Mr. Diamond put up every year to celebrate Sukkot. A sukkah tent, if you will, is normally a hut-like structure made out of twigs and branches with no roof. You keep it outside. That's a must. I don't remember all the religious details anymore. The guys in prison are oddly the most religious I've ever met. I do not fit into that camp.

Anyway, the Diamonds' sukkah was a step above everyone else's in the neighborhood. It was a large tent with rich color and Hebrew lettering, and when Cheryl and I were seventeen years old, late on a cool October evening, we sneaked into the Diamonds' sukkah tent and lost our virginities.

Yep. Just like that.

I can't help but smile and wince at the memory.

Man, I loved Cheryl.

I'd had a crush on her since her family moved onto Shirley Avenue when we were in eighth grade, but it wasn't until right before junior prom that Cheryl reciprocated at all, and even then, we'd end up going to the prom as "friends." You know the deal. We were in similar friend groups and neither of us had anyone to go with. We ended up making out that night, in her case more out of boredom than anything else.

That's when we became a couple.

I lean against the tree in the Diamonds' old backyard. Cheryl and I had been good for so long. We had a brief breakup in college. That was more my doing than hers. Everyone told us that we were too young to settle down and never experiment with anyone else. We gave it a try, but for me no one else measured up. We got engaged our senior year of college, but we promised ourselves no marriage until Cheryl finished med school. We stuck to that plan. Then we got married and she got the residency of her dreams and then, following on this smooth, predictable, happy streak, we decided to have kids.

This is where things went wrong for us.

Cheryl—or should I say we?—couldn't get pregnant.

If you've had fertility issues, you know the stress and strain. Cheryl and I both wanted kids. Badly. It had been a given. We wanted four. That was our plan. We had agreed to that. But we tried for months and months and nothing happened. When you want to get pregnant, it seems as though everyone else in the world—the worst people, the most undeserving people, the people who don't even want children—are all getting pregnant. Everyone is getting pregnant but you.

We visited a specialist who ran tests and more tests and discovered the culprit was me. Yes, we all know that it's "no one's fault," that you're in this together, that it doesn't make you less of a man yada yada yada, but discovering that my sperm count was too low to have children messed with my head in an awful way. I know better now, I guess. I know about toxic masculinity and all that, but when you grow up the way I did, in a place like this, a man has certain jobs and responsibilities and if he can't even get his own wife pregnant, well, what kind of man is that?

I felt shame. Dumb, I know. But your feelings don't know from dumb.

Cheryl and I tried and failed at IVF three times. The strain between us grew. Every conversation was about having a baby or worse, when we tried not to let it consume us—we'd been told that sometimes if you just relax, it magically happens—it became the figurative elephant not only in the room but in the bed. That elephant never left us.

Cheryl was great about it.

Or so I thought.

She never blamed me, but being an idiot with self-esteem issues, I let my imagination run wild. She is looking at me differently, I thought. She is looking at me and finding me wanting. She is looking at other men—virile, fertile men—and wondering how she ended up with such a dud.

It almost destroyed us.

Then we got some good news. One of my dad's old Revere buddies was a general practitioner in New Hampshire. Dr. Schenker told me that he'd had the same issue and got cured with varicocele surgery. I don't want to go into the details and you don't want me to, but in short, you remove swollen veins inside the scrotum. Long story short: It worked. Suddenly my sperm count soared past normal.

Four months later, Cheryl was pregnant with Matthew.

It was all good again.

Except it wasn't.

The years of infertility hell had played havoc with us and our relationship, but once Matthew was born, I thought that it would be behind us. And it was. Until I found out that while saying all the right things to me, Cheryl had gone behind my back and visited another fertility clinic to look into donor sperm. She hadn't gone through with it. That's what she kept reminding me. She explained it so clearly—she had been desperate not just to have a baby but to put us both out of this purgatory and so for a moment, a brief stupid moment, she considered getting donor sperm, something she knew that I would never agree to, and not telling me.

It was, she admitted, an awful thing to even consider. She

apologized profusely. But I didn't accept the apology. Not at first anyway. I was hurt. Her actions played into all my stupid insecurities and so then I lashed out. She had broken my trust—and I compounded the issue by handling it badly.

Through the back window of my family home, I see movement. I move behind a shrub, and when I see my aunt Sophie enter and sit down alone at the kitchen table, my heart bursts. She wears a blue formless housedress. Her back is hunched. Her hair is in bobby pins but some wisps have escaped and dangle in her face. A potpourri of emotions course through me. Aunt Sophie. My wondrous, generous, kind, fierce aunt who raised me from the time my mom died of cancer. She looks weary, spent, old before her time. Life had sucked away that vitality. Or had it been my father's illness?

Or me?

Aunt Sophie always believed in me. Others caved. But never, ever Sophie.

I am not sure how to handle this, but I find myself tentatively approaching the back window. She has the radio on. Sophie always loved playing music in the kitchen. Classic rock. Of course, it might not be a radio anymore. It might be an Alexa or some other kind of speaker device. I can hear Pat Benatar belt out that we are young, heartache to heartache. Sophie had loved Pat Benatar and Stevie Nicks and Chrissie Hynde and Joan Jett. I creep up the back porch steps and without thinking about it, I lightly rap my knuckles on the window.

Sophie looks up and sees me.

I expect her to be startled or confused or—at the very least—thrown off by my sudden appearance. I expect some kind of understandable hesitancy, even for a moment or two, but with Aunt Sophie, there is none of that. She has always meant unconditional and ferocious love, and that's all I'm seeing here. She jumps up and beelines straight for the back door. Her face is already a sun shower—bright smile, wet tears on her cheeks. She flings open the door, looks left and right in a protective way that tweaks my heart, and says, "Get in here."

I listen. Of course. I flash back to the days my dad would come home late from a night shift and wonder where I was, and Aunt Sophie would make up an excuse and sneak me in through this back door so he wouldn't know. I step inside and close the door. She hugs me. She feels smaller now, frailer. I'm afraid at first to squeeze too tight, but she'll have none of that.

I want to hold back, stay upright and focused, to not give in to the emotion of the moment, but I don't stand a chance. Not with Aunt Sophie. Not with an Aunt Sophie hug. I feel my knees buckle and maybe I let out a small cry, but this frail woman of towering strength holds me up.

"It's going to be okay," she tells me.

And I believe her.

25

Briggs Correctional Officer Ted Weston told Max and Sarah his story once, twice, thrice. Max and Sarah stayed quiet for most of it. Max nodded encouragingly. Sarah stood leaning against a corner of the prison office they were using as an interrogation room, arms folded. When Ted finished his tale for a third time, proudly winding down with how he spotted the warden and the prisoner getting into the warden's car, Max kept nodding and then he turned to Sarah and said, "I like that last part best. Don't you, Sarah?"

"The part about spotting the warden's car, Max?"

"Yes."

"Yeah, me too."

Max started plucking his lip with his index finger and thumb. He did this to stop himself from biting his nails. "Do you want to know why Sarah and I like that part best, Ted? I can call you Ted, right?"

Ted Weston's smile was uneasy. "Sure."

"Thanks, Ted. So do you want to know why?"

Weston gave a half-hearted shrug. "Sure, I guess."

"Because it's true. I mean it. That part of the story—the way you looked out the window and spotted the car and did kind of a 'whoa hold up a moment' thing—when you tell that story, your face beams with honesty."

"It really does," Sarah added.

"Like you're using a high-end moisturizer. The rest of the time—like when you're telling us about how you took poor sick David Burroughs to the infirmary late at night—"

"—in a way that defies all protocol," Sarah added.

"—Or how he turned on you suddenly—"

"—with no motivation."

"You're right-handed, aren't you, Ted?"

"What?"

"You are. I've been watching you. Not a big deal except whenever you're telling us about getting Burroughs from his cell and taking him to the infirmary, your eyes look up and to the right."

"That's a sign you're lying, Ted," Sarah said.

"It's not foolproof, but it's accurate more often than not. If you are really trying to access a memory, a right-handed person—"

"—eighty-five percent of us anyway—"

"—looks upwards and to the left."

"And the darting eyes, Max."

"Right, thanks, Sarah. This is kind of fascinating, Ted. I think you'll like this. Your eyes dart around a lot when you lie. Not just you. That's most people. Do you want to know why?"

Ted said nothing. Max continued.

"It's a throwback, Ted. It's a throwback to an era when humans felt trapped, maybe by another human, maybe by an animal or something, and so their eyes would dart around looking for an escape route."

"Do you really buy that origin story, Max?" Sarah asked.

"I don't know. I mean, no doubt about it—darting eyes usually indicates a lie. But if that's the origin, I don't know, but it's a compelling story."

"It is," Sarah agreed.

"Darting eyes," Ted Weston repeated, trying to look confident. "I don't need to take this."

Max looked back at Sarah.

Sarah nodded "Very manly, Ted."

Weston stood. "You don't have any proof I'm lying."

"Sure we do," Max said. "Do you really think we'd just rely on that eye thing?"

"He doesn't know us, Max."

"He doesn't indeed, Sarah. Show him."

Sarah slid the bank statement across the table. Ted Weston was still standing. He looked down at it. His face lost color.

"Sarah was kind enough to highlight the important part for us, Ted. Do you see that?"

"You should have asked for cash, Max," Sarah said.

"Yeah, but then where would he have put it? It's nice they kept the amounts under ten grand. Figured no one would notice."

"We did."

"No *we*, Sarah. *You*. You noticed. How was Ted here to know you're the best?"

"I'm going to blush, Max."

Sarah's phone buzzed. She stepped aside. Ted Weston collapsed back into his seat.

"Do you want to tell me what really happened," Max asked him in a stage whisper, "or do you want to get thrown into general population and see how the other half lives?"

Ted kept staring at the bank statement.

"Max?"

It was Sarah. "What's up?"

"Facial recognition may have gotten a hit on our boy."

"Where?"

"Getting off a train in Revere Beach."

———

"You can't stay," Aunt Sophie tells me. "The FBI was here this morning. They'll be back."

I nod. "Can I talk to him?"

She tilts her head to the side and looks sad. "He's asleep. The morphine. You can see him, but I don't think he'll know you're there. I'll take you up."

We pass the piano, the one with the lace top and all the old photographs on it. I notice that Cheryl and my wedding picture is still front and center. I don't know what to make of that. Most of my friends in this neighborhood have at least two or three siblings, often a lot more. I was an only child.

I never asked why, but I suspect that whatever caused my issue may have been hereditary, the worst kind of "like father like son," which could have led, of course, to no son at all. But that's speculation on my part.

I take the chair next to his bed—Dad's old desk chair—look down at him. He's sleeping, but his face is twisted up in a grimace. Aunt Sophie stands behind me. I love my father. He was the best father in the world. But I also don't really know him. He didn't believe in sharing his feelings. I have no idea what his hopes and dreams were. Maybe that's best, I don't know. We get a lot of grief nowadays about that, about men bottling up their feelings, about toxic masculinity. I don't know if that was it or not. My dad fought in Vietnam. His dad fought in World War Two. My grandmother told me that the two men who came home were not the same as the ones who left. That's obvious, of course, but my grandmother also said that it wasn't that they had changed, but that whatever they had seen over there, whatever they had done and experienced, these men felt the need to keep it locked away. Not for their sake, but because they didn't want to expose those they loved to those horrors. These men weren't cruel or distant or even damaged. They were sentinels who wanted to protect those they loved, no matter what the cost to themselves. When Matthew was born, I tried to remember every single thing my father had done with me. I wanted to be that kind of dad. I wanted to make him feel safe and loved and strong. I wondered how my dad did it, like a child watching a master magician. I wanted to know his secrets so I could perform them for Matthew.

I love my dad. He would come home exhausted, change into a white T-shirt, and go outside to throw a ball with me. He took me to Kelly's for a roast beef sandwich and a shake on Saturdays for lunch. He'd let me tag along to the dog track and explain about the favorites and the odds. I cheered him on when he pitched for the Revere Police softball team, especially when they had their annual game against the firefighters. He taught me how to tie a tie. He let me pretend-shave with him when I was seven, lathering up my face and giving me a razor with no blade in it. He took me to Fenway Park twice a year to watch the Red Sox. We would sit in the bleachers and I'd get a hot dog and Coke and he'd get a hot dog and beer and he'd buy me a pennant of the opposing team so I'd remember the game. We watched the Celtics over at Uncle Philip's house—he had the big-screen TV. My dad never made me feel like a nuisance or burden. He valued his time with me, and I valued my time with him.

But all that said, I don't know my father's hopes and dreams, his worries and concerns, how he felt about my mother dying or if he wanted more or less from this life.

I sit now and wait for him to open his eyes and recognize me. I expect the miracle, of course—that my coming home would somehow cure him, that my very presence would make him rise from the bed, or at least, he'd have a moment or two of clarity and a final word of wisdom for his only child.

None of that happened. He slept.

After a while, Aunt Sophie said, "It's not safe, David. You should go."

I nod.

"Your cousin Dougie is away for the month on a shark expedition. I have the key to his place. You can use that for as long as you need."

"Thank you."

We rise. I study my father's limp hand for a moment. There used to be such power in that hand. It's gone now. The knotty muscles on his forearm as he would work a screwdriver or wrench are gone too now, replaced with spongy tissue. I kiss my father's forehead. I wait one more second for his eyes to open. They don't.

"Do you think I did it?" I ask Aunt Sophie.

"No."

I look at her. "Did you ever—?"

"No. Not for a second."

We leave him then. I realize that I will probably never see my father again, but there is no time or need to process that. My phone buzzes. I check the message.

"Everything okay?"

I tell Aunt Sophie that it's Rachel. She's half an hour out. I text her Dougie's address and tell her to come in through the back entrance.

"Rachel's helping you?" my aunt says.

"Yes."

She nods. "I always liked her. Shame what happened. You'll be safe at Dougie's. Both of you. Contact me if you need anything, okay?"

I hug her then. I close my eyes and hold on. Then I ask something stupid, something that has been annoying me like a sore tooth I keep probing with my tongue: "Did Dad think I did it?"

And because Aunt Sophie can't lie: "Not at first."

I don't move. "But then?"

"He's an evidence man, David. You know that. The black-outs. The fights with Cheryl. The way you used to walk in your sleep as a teenager . . ."

"So he . . . ?"

"Not on purpose, no."

"But he thought I killed Matthew?"

Aunt Sophie lets go of me. "He didn't know, David. Can we leave it at that?"

———

With the bob cut, I barely recognize Rachel.

"What do you think?" she asks, trying to keep the mood light.

"Looks good."

And it does. The Anderson sisters have always been considered beautiful, albeit in different ways. Cheryl, my ex, was a little more traffic-stopping. You noticed her. It hit you right away. Rachel's beauty came at you slower and grew with time. She had what Aunt Sophie called—and she meant this in the best of ways—an interesting face. I got that now. What society would call imperfections made it more like a painting where you keep discovering new things every time you look at it and it changed depending on the time of day or light in the room or angle at which you stood. The bob suited her, I guess. It accentuated the cheekbones or something, I don't know.

I fill Rachel in on what's happened with Hilde and Eddie and the Fisher family. As I do, the phone chirps with a text from Eddie:

Don't come back here. Cops were here looking for you.

I write back that they seem to know I'm around. He replies:

Revere's crawling with them. Meet is at Pop's Garage. 280 Hunting Street in Malden. 3PM. Can you get there?

I tell him I can.

Pull into the bay on the left. Come alone. That's what they told me to tell you.

Rachel is reading over my shoulder. Dougie is a fifty-four-year-old bachelor, and the place is done up as if to prove that. The walls are all dark wood paneling like a dive bar. He has a dart board, and a huge-screen TV takes up an entire wall. The carpet is green shag. The chairs are faux leather recliners with metal poking through the footrests. There's an old oak bar with oversized neon beer signs—one for Michelob Light, one for Blue Moon Belgian White hanging over the bar. The place was dark when I came in except for those neon signs.

I didn't turn any lights on or off, so right now they provide the only illumination.

"I'll drive you," Rachel says.

"You saw the 'come alone' part?"

"I still don't get it," she says. "The Fishers are all about extortion and drugs and prostitution, stuff like that. Why would they be involved in Matthew's . . ." She stopped. "I don't even know what to call it."

"Let's call it kidnapping," I say.

"Okay. Why would they be involved in that?"

"I don't know."

"And you expect them to just tell you?"

"We don't have any other leads."

"But maybe we do," Rachel says, opening up her laptop. She clicks on a file, and photographs start downloading. "I started going through various image searches in line with what we know about Irene's photo from Six Flags. We know the location. We know the date. I started with that. I looked up on Instagram, for example, any photo that was tagged for Six Flags on that day. I spread it out three days forward to start because I figured some people wouldn't get to posting right away. Then I did image searches of Irene and her family, hoping that maybe they'd be in photographs someone else posted, all hoping maybe we'd get another glimpse of Matthew."

"And?"

"And the search came up with six hundred eighty-five photos and videos from across social media—Instagram,

Facebook, Twitter, TikTok, whatever. We have a little time. I figure we could go through them."

They are organized in time sequence—time posted, not time taken—and then further subdivided by social media outlet. I see couples and families on rides, getting on rides, coming off rides, waving from the Ferris wheel or the merry-go-round or hanging upside down on roller coasters. I see posed shots, candid shots, distance shots of the rides. I love rides. I was always the adult who would readily volunteer to take cousins, nephews, nieces—anyone—on the harshest coasters there were. My dad loved rides too, even when he got older. I think about that now. I took Matthew a few times. He was obviously too young for any of the major roller coasters, but he loved the little train, that airplane ride, the slow boats. Matthew looked like my dad. That's what everyone said, and once again, after my visit to my dad, I can only think about what passes down, from my grandfather to my father to me to Matthew. It's all there in the echoes.

Some of the photos are of people driving to the park. Some are with animals from the park's drive-thru safari. Some are with ice cream or burgers or waiting on long lines. Some feature dressed-up characters like Batman or Bugs Bunny or Porky Pig. Some are of arcade prizes like a stuffed turtle or blue dog or assorted Pokémon characters.

Amusement parks are diverse melting pots. There is every creed, religion, what have you. I see boys in yarmulkes and girls with head coverings. Everyone is smiling.

There are a surprising number of group shots with ten,

twenty, or even thirty people. We stop here and zoom on every face. The children I understand. We are trying to find Matthew, of course. As for the adults, we are both looking for anyone we recognize in any way, anyone who might be—I don't know—suspicious.

We find Tom and Irene Longley and their two boys in a group photo with sixteen other people. We take our time with that one, but we get nothing.

I check my watch. We may not have time to get through them all before I need to head to my meeting at Pop's Garage in Malden. We start picking up the pace, realizing we can go through them later, when we pass another photograph of the Longley family with actors dressed up as yellow Minions from the *Despicable Me* movie.

Rachel hits the button to continue, but I say, "Wait."

"What?"

"Go back."

She clicks back.

"One more."

She does. It's the Longleys. Just the Longleys. No one else in the photo. But that isn't what catches my eye.

"What are they standing in front of?" I ask.

"Looks like one of those screens for corporate events."

It is one of the backdrop banners people use to advertise the movie being premiered or the company holding an event, normally decorated with a repeat logo. But that wasn't the case here. There are various logos.

"I think Irene said they were at a corporate event," Rachel

said. "I told you that her husband works for Merton Pharmaceuticals. That's their logo over there."

There are others. I see one for a common over-the-counter pain medication. I see one for a popular line of skin care products.

"It's a huge conglomerate," Rachel says. "They own food brands, pharmaceuticals, chain restaurants, hospitals."

"Do you think they rented out the whole park?"

"I don't know. I can ask Irene. Why, what's up?"

"There are other photos like this, right? In front of the banner?"

"Yeah, a bunch, I think. We're just getting to them now. Usually, you take a picture like this when you come in, but I guess they wanted to wait to the end of the day."

"Keep clicking," I say.

I see it on the third click. When I do, I feel my entire body freeze.

"Stop."

"What?" she asks.

I point to a logo on the bottom right. I'd been able to see part of it with the Longley family, enough to make me pause, but now I can see it clearly. Rachel follows my finger. She sees it too.

It's a stork carrying three words in what looks like a sling:

Berg Reproductive Institute

Rachel stares another second before turning to me.

My mouth feels dry. "That's where she went," I say. "Cheryl, I mean."

"Yeah, so?"

I say nothing.

"What does that have to do with anything, David? I mean, this company also owns pizzerias. You've been to those."

I frown. "My marriage didn't fall apart because of a visit to a pizzeria."

"I don't understand what you're trying to say here."

"Your sister went to that"—I make quote marks with my fingers—"'institute' behind my back."

"I know," she says in a voice so soft and gentle it almost feels like a caress. "But it led to nothing. You know that too."

"Except it didn't."

"What do you mean?"

"I stopped trusting her."

"You didn't have to, David. Cheryl was in pain. You could have understood that. She didn't go through with it."

I see no reason to argue and perhaps she's right. I stare at the logo and shake my head. "This isn't a coincidence."

"Of course it is. I just wish you could have understood."

"Oh, I understood," I say, my voice surprisingly matter-of-fact. "I was shooting blanks. It was putting a strain on our marriage. Cheryl figured maybe she could get pregnant with a donor and claim the baby was mine. I'm surprised she just didn't fuck another guy and cut out the middleman."

"That's not fair, David."

"Who's she married to now, Rachel?" I counter. "You didn't tell me that part."

"It doesn't matter."

"It's Ronald, isn't it?"

She says nothing. I feel my heart crack again. "Just a friend. That's what she kept saying."

"That's all he was."

I shake my head. "Don't be naïve."

"I'm not saying Ronald didn't hope for—"

"It doesn't matter," I say because it's true and I can't listen to another word of this. "The only thing I care about now is finding Matthew."

"And you think this"—she points at the stupid stork logo—"is the answer?"

"Yeah, I do."

"How?"

But I don't have the answer, so we sit in silence for a while.

After some time passes, Rachel says, "Are you still going to meet with that Skunk guy?"

"Yes."

"You better go then."

"Yes." I look at her. "What aren't you telling me?"

"Nothing," she says.

I keep looking at her.

"It's just a coincidence," Rachel says. "Nothing more."

And I don't know if she's trying to convince me or herself.

26

"Pixie?"

Gertrude turned away from the window with the magnificent view and toward the little boy. This Payne house, completed only four years ago, was altogether different from the museum-quality Payne House of yesteryear. Yes, the property was expansive. There was a tennis court and swimming pool and horse trails and all that. But instead of the old mammoth tomb-like marble, this estate was light, airy, postmodern modern, a complex of white cubes and wall-to-ceiling windows. It surprised guests, but Gertrude loved it.

"Yes, Theo?"

"Where's Dad?"

She smiled at him. Theo was pure light despite all the darkness. He was a good boy, kind, intelligent, thoughtful. He spoke not only English but French and German as well, because he had spent most of his life at a boarding school in St. Gallen. The Swiss school had fewer than three hundred students, horse stables, mountain climbing, sailing, and cost nearly $200,000 per year. Hayden, not wanting to be an absentee father, spent a lot of time in the area. This had been the boys' (that was how she thought of them) first journey back to the United States in a long while. They'd been staying at the Payne estate with her now for three months. Gertrude had been in favor of the trip. She was getting older and wanted to spend time with them.

But it had been a mistake.

From behind the boy, Hayden entered the room. "I'm right here, buddy."

Hayden put his hands on the boy's shoulders. The boy blinked. This had been his issue from the start. He was a wonderful boy, truly, and after the initial transition stage, he seemed to be in a decent place. But there was a skittishness to Theo, a wince and a cringe almost as though he expected to be struck. He wouldn't be. He hadn't been. But sometimes, even though the boy didn't know the truth, it was as if something inside of him, something primordial, did and involuntarily threw up safeguards.

Hayden gave Gertrude a tight smile, and she could see immediately that something was wrong. She summoned Stephano, who would lead Theo outside to play. Stephano closed the door behind them, giving grandmother and grandson some privacy, though Stephano was privy to all the family skullduggeries.

"What is it, Hayden?" she asked.

"He assaulted a police officer."

She had not yet checked the news. While Gertrude understood technology and the completely connected world, she believed that the secret to longevity was a mix of routine and new experiences. Her mornings, though, always started the same way. Seven a.m. wake up. Twenty minutes of stretching. Twenty minutes of meditation. Coffee and a novel for an hour if time permitted. Then, and only then, did she bother with the news. As she aged, she realized that the news became more about entertainment—stressful entertainment at that—than enlightenment.

"I assume they captured him?"

"No. Not yet."

That surprised her. David Burroughs was more resourceful than she'd imagined. "You can't stay. You know that."

"Do you think David knows something?"

Something? Yes. But there was no way he could know enough. "This assault," she said. "Where did it take place?"

"New York City."

Gertrude didn't understand. "Do they know why he was there?"

"The rumors are he was seeking revenge on a witness."

"Any idea which one?"

"Almost all the witnesses were local experts."

"Except one," Gertrude said. "That woman who lied about seeing him with the baseball bat."

Hayden nodded slowly. "Could be."

That had puzzled her, of course. They'd known the woman was lying. They had no idea why.

"I'm tired of hiding him, Pixie."

"I know, Hayden."

"He has Payne blood coursing through his veins."

"I know that too."

"We even ran the tests. He's my son. Your great-grandson. He's a Payne man, after all."

She almost smiled at that. A Payne man. Like that was a good thing. The damage those men had done. Surprise pregnancies, blackmail, extortion, even murder—all covered up with the mighty dollar. Back in the day, Gertrude hadn't been surprised in the least by the Kennedy Chappaquiddick incident—she had only been surprised that it hadn't been covered up before word leaked out. That sort of thing happened a lot. The rich pay off the family. That's the carrot. But the rich use the stick too. Sure, you could try to stand up for the loved one who'd been knocked up or injured or killed, but it will only make it all much worse in the end. You'll never get justice. The rich will deny and obfuscate and bribe and pressure and bankrupt and sue and threaten and if none of that works—and that almost always works—you'll be made to disappear. Or maybe you have other children who will suffer. Something. Anything.

So when you wonder how a family can seemingly take money in exchange for something like the death of a daughter, it isn't because they are greedy or immoral.

It is because they have no choice.

"I know, Hayden," she told him.

"There has to be another way."

Gertrude did not respond.

"Maybe," Hayden said, "the truth should come out."

"No," she said.

"I mean, even if they somehow find Theo—"

"Hayden?"

"—what can they prove?"

"Hayden, stop."

Her tone silenced him more than her words.

"We will make arrangements for you both to leave this afternoon," she said, ending the conversation. "In the meantime, I don't want that boy to leave the estate."

PART 3

27

Had David seen the lie on her face?

Rachel almost told him the truth. Maybe she should have, who knew? But right now, she needed David to trust her absolutely. If he understood the truth about Cheryl's visit to that fertility clinic, the full truth, he might push her away. They couldn't afford that. So for now, right or wrong, Rachel would have to go with deceit. Remaining his ally was more important than honesty.

After David left for Pop's Garage, Rachel combed through the photographs yet again—this time with a new goal in mind. She was looking for a familiar face, one David wouldn't really know. To her relief, she didn't find it. There was still a chance that David was wrong—that the Berg Reproductive Institute being one of the sponsors at the amusement park that day was a coincidence—but the more Rachel thought about it, the more she realized that there had to be something to it.

But how did the fertility clinic fit into all this?

She stared now at her phone. She had put off making the call for long enough. She needed answers, and he might have them. She dialed the number. He answered on the second ring.

"Rachel?"

There was a lilt in his voice. It made her smile.

"Hey."

"Oh my God, it's been so long."

"I know, I'm sorry about that."

"No need. How are you?"

"I'm okay," she said.

"I called you, you know."

"I know."

"When the whole thing went down with that article and our alma mater—"

"I know," she said again. "I should have replied to you. I owed you that."

"You don't."

"I do. I'm sorry. I was just . . . It was a lot."

Silence. Then: "There a reason you called?"

"I need a favor," Rachel said.

"I'm always here for you. You know that."

She knew. She cleared her throat. "Did you read about my brother-in-law escaping prison? I don't know if the news would reach—"

"I saw that, yes."

"I'm hoping you can help with something."

He hesitated. "Look, Rachel, where are you?"

"What do you mean?"

"Are you home?"

"No, I'm . . ." Should she say? "I'm near Boston."

"Good."

"Why?"

"Can you get to Toro restaurant on Washington Street? In, say, an hour?"

"Wait, you're back?"

"It's better we talk in person, don't you think?"

She did.

"And it will be so good to see you, Rachel."

"It will be good to see you too," she said.

"Toro," he said again. "One hour."

"I'll see you there."

———

I don't like the setup at Pop's Garage.

I don't like it at all.

I am driving the purportedly untraceable car Rachel drove up to Revere. I grabbed one of Dougie's baseball caps and a pair of his Ray-Bans, and while I'm not totally disguised, I don't think the police will set up a roadblock between Revere and Malden. If they know I'm here, I am assuming they somehow tracked me coming in on the train. They are not going to suspect that I was able to secure a vehicle. Or maybe they would. Either way, I have to take risks, but this one seems pretty calculated.

Hunting Street is a bizarre blend of residential homes and car mechanics on the border of the town center. Pop's Garage is jammed between Al's Auto Center and Garcia Auto Repair and across the street from Malden's Body Work and Repair. I am, of course, on the lookout for cops or vans or anything suspicious. But there is nothing and no one on this normally congested thoroughfare—and that is what is making me suspicious.

Al's appears closed. So are Garcia's and Malden's. They aren't just quiet. They are shut down, shades pulled, lights out, no movement.

I don't like that.

Only one person is visible. A man in a blue work coverall with a name I can't make out stenciled in script on the chest waves at me. He motions toward the one open garage bay like one of those guys at the airport who direct the pilot in and out of the gate. I make the turn off Hunting Street into Pop's. The opening looks wide, dark, cavernous, as though it may swallow me whole.

I hesitate, staring into the garage's mouth, when Skunk emerges from the darkness like some horror film ghost rising from the grave.

He is pale. The hair is slicked back and oily. The forelock seems more pronounced than ever. Skunk smiles at me, and I feel the chill run down my spine. He hasn't aged much if at all. His suit is too shiny and glistens in the morning sun. He steps to the side and beckons me to enter.

Do I have a choice?

I pull in with Skunk leading the way. He is signaling me

to keep coming forward. At some point he gestures for me to slow down and then brake. I do. I am inside the garage now, the door sliding closed behind me.

There are just the two of us.

I step out of the car.

Skunk comes up to me with a big smile.

"Davey!"

He embraces me, the third person to do that today and in the past five years. This embrace offers no comfort or warmth, just hard edges; it's like being hugged by a coffee table. He reeks of cheap European cologne. I have smelled some awful things in the prison, but this nearly makes me gag.

"Davey," he says again, pulling back. "You look well."

"You too, Kyle."

"I'm sorry about this," he says.

And then he punches me hard in the stomach.

It is a total sucker punch, but I saw it coming. One of the great lessons of prison: You learn to always be on guard. That lesson gets honed every single day. In Briggs, you revert to primitive man, always wary, always prepared. When I was in high school, I played attack on the lacrosse team. My coach would consistently scream out, "Head on a swivel!" which means keep looking for someone blindsiding you. That becomes your life in prison.

I shift a little and tighten my abdomen. The blow still lands but not where it does me much damage. His knuckles graze my hip bone, and I bet that hurts him more than me. I react on instinct, even as some other part of me is saying to back off, that I can't seriously hurt him, that I need him to get the information on Hilde Winslow.

But the hell with that.

Skunk isn't going to tell me anything. I should have known that. My best chance at learning the truth?

Beating it out of him.

Before Skunk's blow has fully landed, I start to swing my right arm around, using the big muscles near the shoulder, shifting my weight down and to the left, I am able to both neutralize his punch and gain momentum for my counter. I tuck my thumb in the palm and lead with the inner edge of my hand.

The strike lands hard against the side of Skunk's skull.

I feel a vibration in my hand, something akin to a tuning fork for the hand bones, but there is no time to worry about that. I know that Skunk is ferocious and vicious in a thousand different ways. If I let up, he will kill me. That is true in every fight. Fights should never be something casual. That's something most people don't get. Every fight you see—drunks at a bar, idiots at a football game—there is the potential for ending up maimed or dead.

Skunk staggers from the shot to the side of his head. I stick out my foot and spin hard. My instep connects with his lower leg. It doesn't knock Skunk down, but it keeps him off balance. He tries to stumble back, hoping to put some distance between him and me.

I don't let him.

I step in and then I jump tackle him. He hits the ground hard, me on top of him.

I flip him onto his back and mount his chest. I make two fists and get ready to start throwing lefts and rights at his face. Soften him up, I figure, before I ask him about Hilde Winslow.

But when I cock my right fist, the doors burst open.

I hear someone shout, "Freeze! Police!"

I turn to see a cop pointing a gun at me. My stomach plummets. Then another cop enters the garage. He is pointing a gun at me too. Then another.

I am debating what to do when a small voice in my head reminds me that I've turned my attention away from Skunk.

Doesn't matter.

Something hard—gun butt, tire iron, I don't know—whacks me in the side of the head.

My eyes roll back. Someone—one of the cops, I think—delivers a body blow. I slide off Skunk. Another cop jumps on top of me. I try to raise my hands, try to fight back, but I have nothing left.

I'm on my stomach now. Someone pulls my arms back. I hear more than feel the handcuffs.

Another blow lands on the side of my head. Blackness swims in. I take one last gasp.

And then there is nothing.

———

Rachel had texted David that she had an errand to run.

She didn't tell him where or why.

She took the train because David had her car and this phone

didn't have a ride-share app. She checked the time. Again. David had been gone almost an hour. There had been no word. She feared the worst—you always fear the worst in situations like this, she thought, as though situations like this were commonplace in her life—but she also knew that she had to compartmentalize and move forward. If this Skunk guy had done something to David, there was nothing she could do about it. If the police had found and arrested David, well, same thing.

Move forward.

When Rachel arrived at Toro, she thought about something frivolous: Her hair. The styling she'd gotten in New York City this morning had been intentionally designed to disguise her. It had been a long time since she'd seen him in person.

Would he recognize her?

That question was quickly answered. As soon as she entered the restaurant, he rose from his table and gave her the warmest smile. She returned it and for the briefest of moments, she fell through some kind of time portal and forgot why she was really here. Suddenly, this seemed like a reunion of sorts, a deep-dive one, nothing superficial when you bond in tragedy. She wondered how they'd let their friendship drift apart. That was life though, wasn't it? You graduate from college, you move away, you take other jobs, you meet new people, partners, create families, divorce, whatever. Sure, you stay in touch, check social media, exchange the occasional text, promise you'll get together, and meanwhile the years fly by and now here you are, in need of a favor, and suddenly you're back together.

They both hesitated for a moment, not sure how to greet the other, but then she hugged him, and he hugged her right back. The years melted away. When you've been through a lot together—when your bond is formed in tragedies like theirs—you never really let go.

"It's so good to see you, Rachel," he said.

She held on to him another moment. "You too, Hayden."

28

When I wake up, I'm wearing handcuffs.

I'm also seated on a small airplane.

It's over.

Skunk or the Fishers had sold me out to the cops. I'm an idiot. Truly. What had I expected? They'd set me up to take the fall for the murder of my own son—why would I be dumb enough to think they wouldn't sell me out to put me back behind bars?

I try to crane my neck to look behind me. It's hard because I'm also cuffed to an armrest. Two goons—plainclothes cops or federal agents or marshals, I don't know which—sit in the back and fiddle with their smartphones. Both are bald with black tees and blue jeans.

"When do we land?" I ask.

Without glancing up from his phone, the one sitting in the aisle says, "Shut the fuck up."

I decide not to antagonize. No point. We land half an hour

later. When the plane comes to the proverbial full stop, the two goons unbuckle their seat belts and come toward me. Without warning, one goon throws a black bag over my head while the other snaps off the arm rail restraint.

"What's with the blindfold?" I ask.

"Shut the fuck up," Goon One says again.

The plane door opens. I rise. Someone pushes me forward, and I know something is very wrong—even before we reach the tarmac, even with the bag totally blacking out my vision.

We are not at Briggs.

I'm immediately perspiring. It's hot. It's humid. I may not be able to see the tropics, but I can smell, taste, and almost touch them. The sun is strong too, slicing through the black bag.

This isn't Maine.

"Where the hell are we?" I ask.

No answer, so I say, "Aren't you supposed to tell me to shut the fuck up?"

The two goons push me into the back of a vehicle with the air-conditioning cranked up. The drive is maybe ten minutes, but it is hard to figure out time when you have no watch and are blindfolded and think you may be headed back to prison for the rest of your life. Still, the ride doesn't feel long. When the vehicle—I'm up high so it must be some kind of SUV—stops, the goons push me out. There is pavement beneath my feet, and it's so hot I feel the heat coming up through my shoes. Music is playing. Awful music. Some kind of instrumental country-rock mix, like something a Carnival cruise band would play during the poolside "hairiest chest" contest.

I know I seem glib right now. Oddly enough, that is how I feel. Part of me is crushed, of course, because I failed my son again. Part of me is depressed because I seem headed back to prison or worse. Part of me is scared-yet-curious because I don't know what the hell I'm doing in the tropics.

But part of me, maybe the biggest part, is—just for this moment—letting it all go.

I hopped on this crazy ride when I broke out of prison, and the ride is going to take me where it takes me. Right now, I don't control it and I'm accepting that.

I wouldn't say I'm not concerned. I am just doing a major mental suppression. Maybe it's a survival instinct. The two goons—well, I assume it's the same two goons, I'm still blindfolded—take my arms and drag-escort me indoors. They throw me onto a chair. Like the vehicle, this room also mercifully has the air-conditioning set on Hi Frost. I almost ask for a sweatshirt.

Someone grabs my wrist. I feel the pinch before the handcuffs slide off me.

"Don't fucking move," Goon One says.

I don't. As I sit in this non-cushioned chair, I try to plan my next move, but the options before me are so grim my brain won't let me see the obvious. I'm doomed. I can hear people moving around, at least three or four from the sound of it. I still hear the awful music in the background. It sounds like it's coming over a loudspeaker.

Then, again without warning, the black bag is pulled off my head. I blink through the sudden onslaught of light and look up. Standing directly in front of me, mere inches from my face, is a wizened old man who looks to be in his eighties. He wears a straw hat and a yellow-green Hawaiian shirt blanked with jumping marlins. Behind him I see the shaved-head goons from the plane. Both have their arms folded across their chests and now wear aviator sunglasses.

The wizened man offers me his liver-spotted hand. "Come on, David," he says in a voice that sounds like threadbare tires on a gravel road. "Let's go for a walk."

He doesn't introduce himself, but I know who he is, and he knows I know. In most of the photographs I have seen of him over the years, he's a robust man, usually in the center of groups of men, looking more like an explosive device than a human. Even now, with the years shrinking him down, he still has that incendiary air about him.

His name is Nicky Fisher. In another era, he'd have been called a godfather or don or something like that. When I was in school, his name was whispered in the same way a later generation of children would whisper "Voldemort." Nicky Fisher ran the crime syndicate in the Revere-Chelsea-Everett area from the days before my father joined the force.

He is—was?—Skunk's boss.

When we step outside, I blink into the sun. I look left and right, and I frown.

Where the hell am I?

These are indeed the tropics, but it looks like Disney-Epcot built a retirement community after a few too many mojitos. I see a housing development and a cul-de-sac, but it all has a round, cartoonish feel, like where the Flintstones live. The homes are all one-level and handicap accessible and built out of some kind of too-clean adobe brick. The cul-de-sac has one of those giant choreographed fountains, forcing the water to dance to the awful music that I guess plays nonstop.

"I retired," Nicky Fisher told me. "Did you hear?"

"I've been sort of out of the loop," I say, trying to keep the sarcasm out of my voice.

"Right, of course. Prison. It's why I brought you down."

"What did you do to my son, Mr. Fisher?"

Nicky Fisher stops walking. He turns toward me, craning his neck so that his eyes, those cold ice-blue eyes that ended up being the last thing dozens or even hundreds of people had seen before meeting their demise, bore into mine. "I didn't do anything to your son. That's not how we do things. We don't hurt children."

I try not to make a face. I despise that mob-code bullshit. *We don't hurt children, we give to the church, we look out for our neighbors*, all of that sociopathic babble to justify being criminals.

"This is Daytona," Nicky Fisher says to me. "Florida. You ever been?"

"Not before now, no."

"So anyway, I retired here."

We circle the fountain. The dancing water splashes onto the faux marble, gently spraying us. The spray feels good. The two men are following us at a discreet distance. There are other old people milling about, seemingly directionless. They nod at us. We nod back.

"Did you see the big sign on the way in?" he asks me.

"I was blindfolded."

"Right, of course," Nicky says again. "Not my orders, by the way. My guys, they always go for the drama, you know what I'm saying? And I'm sorry about Skunk too. You know how he is. He was just supposed to put you on my plane. I told him not to damage the package, but did he listen?" Nicky puts his hand on my arm. I try not to pull away. "You okay, David?"

"I'm fine."

"And having the cops grab you—that was stupid, though you gotta admire Skunk's flair on that one. He wanted to make you think you were going back to jail. Funny, right?"

"Hilarious."

"It was overkill, but that's Skunk. I'll talk to him, okay?"

I don't know what to say so I just nod.

"Anyway, the sign out front says 'Boardwalks.' That's it. That's the name of this village. Boardwalks. It's kind of a dumb name. I was against it. Lacks imagination. I wanted something fancy, you know, with words like 'mews' or 'vista' or 'preserve.' Like that. But the whole community voted, so . . ." Nicky shrugged a what-can-you-do and kept walking. "Do you know what retirement village is right down the street?"

I tell him I don't.

"Margaritaville. Like the song. You know it?"

"The song? Yes."

"Wasting away again in Margaritaville. Or wasted away. I don't know. But right, that's the name of the place. Ridiculous, right? Jimmy Buffett has his own goddamn retirement community. Communities, I should say. They got three Margaritavilles now. This one, another in South Carolina, and I forget where the third is. Maybe Georgia. It's like someone took one of those crappy chain restaurants and made it into a place to live. Who'd want that?"

I don't reply because that's exactly what this place looks like to me.

"Anyway, it gave me an idea. I mean, I don't know from getting wasted on Margaritas and hanging out on the beach. That's not my fantasy place, if you know what I mean. So we did something different here at Boardwalks. Follow me, I want to show you something."

We are on a sidewalk lined with palm trees. There is a sign with bright arrows pointing in various directions. One says POOL. One says FINE DINING. The one pointing left says BOARDWALK. We follow it. Nicky Fisher grows quiet. I can feel his eyes on me. When we break into the clearing, I can see why. He wants to gauge my reaction.

There, spanning as far as I can see in both directions, is a giant boardwalk.

The boardwalk is expansive. It's also trying hard to feel vintage, but it's far too neat and clean. Another Disney-like reproduction that may look nice but feels like something out of an old *Twilight Zone* episode. There are rides and arcades and soda fountains and chintzy shops and a merry-go-round.

The rides are moving, but no one is on any of them, adding to the place's unreal ghostlike feel. A man sporting a bow tie and handlebar mustache is selling cotton candy. Someone is dressed up like Mr. Peanut from the Planters peanut commercials. A sign advertises SKEEBALL-PINBALL-MINIGOLF.

"Boardwalks," Nicky Fisher says to me. "With an S. We mostly based this place on the Revere Beach one, but we got stuff from Coney Island, Atlantic City, even Venice Beach out in California. And the rides, well, you can see we got coasters and Ferris wheels, but they're a little gentler than in the old days for our older bones." Nicky hits my arm, friendly-like, and smiles. "It's fantastic, right? It's like living on vacation every single day—and why the hell not? We earned it."

He looks at me for affirmation, I guess. I try to nod through it, but I'm not sure he's getting enough enthusiasm from me.

"Oh, and let me show you the main draw, David. Right over here. Man, I wish I could bring your old man down here and see it. I know, I know. We were enemies all our lives, Lenny and me, but come on—tell me your old man wouldn't love this."

He gestures to a white booth with a sign reading PIZZERIA NAPOLITANA on top. There are three men behind the counter wearing white aprons. Underneath them, another sign reads "Specializing In Italian Food" and some drink called "C.B. Coate's Tonic."

I look a question at him.

"It's the old Revere Beach pizza stand that became Sal's Pizzeria!" he exclaims. "Can you believe it? It's an exact reproduction of what it looked like in 1940. Sit. I ordered us a couple of pies. You like pizza, right?" Nicky Fisher winks at me then, and it's as creepy as you can imagine. "If you don't like Sal's pizza, I'm going to have Joey here put a bullet in your brain just to take you out of your misery."

Nicky Fisher laughs at his own joke and slaps me on the back.

We sit under an umbrella. Two fans spit cold air at us. One of the aproned men brings each of us a personal-size pizza. We are then left alone.

"How's your old man?" Nicky Fisher asks me.

"He's dying."

"Yeah, I heard that. Sorry."

"Why am I here, Mr. Fisher?"

"Call me Nicky. Uncle Nicky."

I don't reply, but I'm not going to call him uncle.

"You're here," he continues, "because you and I need to have a little chat."

Nicky Fisher talks like a movie gangster. I know a lot of tough guys now. None really talk like this. A hit man serving life at Briggs told me that real-life gangsters started talking like the gangsters in movies after those movies became popular, not the other way around. Life imitated art.

"I'm listening," I say.

He leans forward and turns his eyes up at me. We are getting to it now. It is quiet. Even the piped-in music has stopped. "Your father and me, we have some bad history."

"He was a cop," I say. "You ran a crime syndicate."

"A crime syndicate," Nicky replies with a small chuckle.

"Fancy words. Your father wasn't pure either. You know that, right?"

I choose not to reply. He stares at me some more, and even in this humid hellhole, I feel a chill.

"You love your old man?" he asks me.

"Very much."

"He was a good father?"

"The best," I say. Then: "With all due respect, uh Nicky, why am I here?"

"Because I have sons too." There is a small snarl in his voice now. "Do you know that?"

I do—and now I'm pretty sure I'm not going to like where we are going.

"Three of them. Or I had three. You know about my Mikey?"

Again, I do. Mikey Fisher died twenty years ago in prison. My father had put him there.

Nicky Fisher makes sure I'm looking him in the eyes when he says, "Is it starting to make sense to you now, son?"

And oddly enough, I fear it does. "My father put your son in prison," I say. "So you returned the favor."

"Close," he says.

I wait.

"Your father, like I said, he wasn't clean. He and his partner Mackenzie arrested Mikey for killing Lucky Craver. Mikey was just supposed to hurt Lucky, but my boy, he often went too far. Did you know Lucky?"

"No."

"They called him that because he never ever had a moment

of luck in his life. Including at the end there obviously. But anyway, your old man arrests Mikey for it. You know the deal. But the problem is, your old man and Lenny couldn't make the case. I mean, everyone knew Mikey did it. But you gotta prove it in a court of law, am I right?"

I stay quiet.

"Your dad had done some solid work on the case. No question. Located some key witnesses. Got Lucky's ex to testify. But see, the cops have to follow the rules. Me? I don't. So I sent some of my guys out to talk to the witnesses. Guys like your old pal Skunk. Suddenly, the witnesses' memories got real hazy. You know what I'm saying?"

"I do."

"Lucky's ex was a little more stubborn, but we took care of that too. There was some evidence in the police locker. Angel dust. A claw-back hammer. They vanished. Poof. So you see, it became hard for your old man to make a case. Must have been real frustrating for him."

I don't move. I barely breathe.

"So that's when your father and Mackenzie, they crossed the line. Suddenly they come up with new evidence. No reason to go into details on the how. They don't matter. But the phony evidence that put my son away? Your old man and Mackenzie planted it."

Nicky Fisher takes a bite, savors it, tilts back in his chair. "You're not eating?"

"I'm listening."

"Can't do both?" He still chews. "I get it. You want to hear the rest, but I think you see it now. My Mikey goes down for the crime, but really, it wasn't that big a deal. I had it worked out so that the conviction would be overturned by a judge friend. So I told Mikey to just lay low in the joint for a few weeks. But he couldn't manage that. My Mikey, he was a sweet boy, but what a hothead. Thought he was a tough guy because his father was the boss. So in the yard he got into a beef with two big guys. Gang members from Dorchester. One of them held Mikey's arms. The other stabbed Mikey in the heart with a shiv. You know about that, right?"

"Yes. I mean, I heard."

Nicky Fisher starts to lift the pizza to his mouth, but it's as though the memories are making it too heavy for him to do that. He lowers his gaze. His eyes glisten. When he speaks again, I can hear the sadness, the anger, the raw. "Those two big guys. You don't want to know what I did to them. It wasn't quick. I'll tell you that."

I wait for him to say more. When he doesn't, I ask, "Did you hurt my son?"

"No. I told you. I don't do that. I didn't even blame your father. Not right then and there. But then, you know, years pass. Then I read about how you killed your son—"

"I didn't—"

"Shh, David, just listen. The problem with you kids today. No one listens. Do you want to hear the rest or not?"

I tell him that I do.

"So like I said, your dad wasn't above bending the law when it suited him. Like with Mikey. We both know a lot of cops push it. They drop the dime bag on the floor of the car. They got the throw-down piece in case they need a reason to blow you away. You know the deal. So after your son—what was his name again?"

"Matthew," I say, and I swallow.

"Right, sorry. So after Matthew was murdered, a cop found that baseball bat in your basement."

I make a face. "The bat wasn't found in my basement."

"Yeah, it was."

I am shaking my head.

"You hid it down there. In some vent or pipe or something."

I am still shaking my head, but again I think I see where he is going with this. I think I've seen from the moment we sat down.

"So where was I? Oh, right. The baseball bat. So a cop found it in your basement. New guy on the force. Named Rogers, I think. Why I remember his name, I don't know. But I do. So Rogers, he wanted to make friends with your old man. Thin blue line, all that. So he told your father about the bat. Your dad, he knows this bat cooks your goose. You're a dead man walking if the DA finds out about that bat. Your old man can't have that. He has to protect his boy. But he also can't get totally rid of the bat. That would be going too far."

Nicky Fisher grins at me. There is tomato sauce on his lower lip. "You can guess what your dad decided to do, right? Come on, David. Tell me."

"You think he planted the bat in the woods."

"I don't *think*. I *know*."

I don't bother contradicting him.

"It was smart. See, if *you* were the killer, the bat would still be in the basement. Hidden. In the vent or whatever. But if someone else was the killer, he would have run away. Dumped or buried the bat somewhere nearby."

I shake my head. "That's not what happened," I say.

"Sure, it is. You, David, killed your son. Then you hid the weapon, figured you'd get rid of it when you had the chance." He leans across the table and flashes that smile again. His teeth are thin and pointy. "Fathers and sons. We are all the same. I would have done anything to keep Mikey out of prison, even though I knew he was guilty. Your father was the same."

I shake my head again, but his words have the stench of truth in them. My father, the man I loved like no other, believed that I had killed my own son. The thought pierces my heart.

"The DA had a problem now," Nicky Fisher continues. "It'd rained that night. There was a ton of mud and dirt in those woods. Forensics, they checked all your shoes and clothes. No dirt. No mud. So once your old man planted that bat— once it was found in the woods—it helped keep you free. That didn't sit well with me, you know what I'm saying?"

I nod because I see it clearly now. "So you got Hilde Winslow to testify that she saw me bury the bat."

"Bingo."

"You set that up."

"I did, yeah."

"Because you wanted vengeance for Mikey?"

Nicky Fisher points at me. "You say my boy's name again and I'll pull out your tongue and eat it with this pizza."

I say nothing.

"And for crying out loud, have you been listening to a word I've said?" he snaps, pounding the table with both fists. The two goons look over, but they make no move. "This had nothing to do with vengeance. I did it because it was the right thing to do."

"I'm not following."

"I did it," he said through clenched teeth, and now there is real menace in his voice, "because you murdered your own son, you sick crazy son of a bitch."

I can't believe what I'm hearing.

"Your old man knew it. I knew it. Oh, maybe you had some kind of blackout or amnesia thing going on, I don't know. Who gives a shit? But the DA had you dead to rights. Then your father, the decorated cop who used false evidence to put *my* son away, fixed it so you'd get off. You ever see a statue of Lady Justice? Your old man put his finger on the scale, so what I did is, I put my finger on the other scale to balance it out. You get it now?"

I don't even know what to say.

"Justice was served. You were doing time like you were supposed to do. There was, I don't know, cosmic balance or some such shit. But here's my problem: My son, my Mikey, is still dead. And here you are, David, living and breathing and enjoying a fucking pizza."

Silence. Dead silence. It's like the entire boardwalk is trying to stand still.

His voice is low now, but it slices through the humidity like a reaper's scythe. "So now I have a choice. Do I put you back in prison—I figured a life sentence is as good as death—or do I kill you and have my boys here feed you to the gators?"

He starts to wipe his hands on the napkin as though this is over.

"You're wrong," I say.

"About?"

"What you did. It wasn't the same as with my dad."

"What wasn't the same?"

And then I risk saying the name again. "Mikey did the crime. You said so yourself."

Nicky Fisher scoffs. "Oh, and you're going to tell me you're innocent?"

He gestured to the goons with his right hand. They start toward us. I debate bolting. Maybe I have a chance of getting away here at the community. They won't just shoot me, will they? But I don't think running will work, so I try another route.

"I'm more than innocent," I tell him. And I stare directly back into those soulless ice-blue eyes. "My son is alive."

Then I tell him.

I tell him everything. I make my case and speak with a passion and urgency that surprises me. He sends the two goons back to their posts. I keep talking. Nicky Fisher shows me nothing. He is good at that.

When I finish, Nicky Fisher picks up a napkin again. He studies it for a moment. He takes his time with it, folding it into halves, then quarters, then placing it neatly back on the table.

"That's some crazy story," he says.

"It's the truth."

"My son is still dead, you know?"

"I can't do anything about that."

"No, you can't." He shakes his head. "You really believe it."

I don't know whether he is asking a question or stating a fact. Either way, I nod my head and say: "I do."

"I don't," he says. His mouth starts twitching a little. "I think it's crap."

My heart sinks. He sits back, rubs his face, blinks. He looks off, toward the narrow waterway that pathetically doubles as an ocean. Then he says, "But some things aren't adding up for me."

"Like?"

"Like Philip Mackenzie," he says.

"What about him?"

"He helped you break out of the prison. I know that part is true. So I ask myself: Why? He wouldn't do that just to help your old man. And why now? And then that makes me wonder about more stuff." His fingers start drumming the table. "Like once you were out, you could have gone underground, tried to make a new life for yourself, whatever. But you didn't do that. Like a stupid lunatic, you ran straight to our phony witness. Why? And then after you see her, you're stupid enough—check that, you're *suicidal* enough—to come at my people in Revere. Skunk, of all people."

I don't interrupt. I let him keep going.

"So here's my problem, David: If you're telling the truth, then I helped put you in prison for a crime you didn't commit. Not that I'm above that. I mean, we've had people take the fall before. But not—I mean, not for something like this. Bad enough to lose a child. To be put in jail for killing him? I don't know. Right now, that doesn't sit right with me. See, I thought I was balancing the scales. I wanted justice for myself, my Mikey—and, I don't know, the world. You know what I'm saying?"

He hesitates, waiting for a response. I nod slowly.

"I was sure you did it. But if you didn't, and if somehow your boy is maybe still alive . . ."

Nicky Fisher shakes his head. Then he stands. He looks off toward that ocean-cum-lagoon again. His eyes still glisten, and I know he's thinking of his Mikey.

"You're free to go," he says to me. "My guys will fly you wherever you want."

He doesn't look at me when he says this. I don't risk saying anything back.

"I'm an old man. Made a lot of mistakes. I'll probably make a few more before I'm done. I'm not trying to make it right with the man upstairs. Too late for that. I think . . . this place. It's not just about nostalgia for me. It sometimes feels more like a do-over. You know what I'm saying?"

I don't. Not really.

"If your old man feels better, I'd like to fly him down here. As my guest. I want to sit right here and have a pizza with him. I think we'd both like that, don't you?"

I don't, no, but again I keep that to myself.

And then Nicky Fisher leaves me.

29

"I took the liberty of letting the owner order for us," Hayden said. "This place has the best tapas."

Rachel nodded, trying not to seem too distracted. She left the phone on vibrate and willed it to sound. David had been gone for far too long. The fear that he'd been captured—or worse—hardened in her chest. She pushed it away and looked into Hayden's green eyes. He wore the idle-rich uniform of khaki pants and blue blazer with some kind of crest on the chest. His hair had thinned and was now plastered against his skull. He was still handsome, still boyish, but there was more softness now. His jowls sagged a bit. His complexion had grown ruddier. Hayden was, she thought, transforming into one of those old family portraits they kept at the Payne Museum.

They exchanged pleasantries. Hayden commented on her new hairstyle. He claimed to like it, but that didn't feel like the truth. She'd told him about her divorce in an email, so they didn't have to cover that. Hayden had discovered a few years ago that he had a son via a B-movie Italian actress he dated a few years back—a boy named Theo—and was now helping to raise and support him. Hayden had spent most of the last decade overseas, purportedly watching over the family's European interests, but mostly Rachel figured that he was skiing in St. Moritz and partying on the French Riviera.

Maybe that wasn't fair.

When they moved on to the story that destroyed her journalism career, Hayden said, "Going after your old enemy."

"I pushed too hard."

"Understandable."

"I know I should have told you . . ."

He waved it away. Hayden had been there, all those years ago, the night of the Halloween party at Lemhall University during their freshman year. They had, in fact, met that night by the beer keg. They flirted a bit. She knew who Hayden Payne was—everyone on campus knew the scions of wealthy families—and so it had been fun. Hayden had been charming and sweet, but for Rachel, no sparks commenced.

She dressed as Morticia Addams, and she probably drank too much. But that wasn't the issue. She'd been roofied, she'd later learn, and somewhere, maybe two hours after she met Hayden, her night derailed like a runaway train. She felt stupid, even now, falling for not watching her drink closely after all the warnings.

There was a young humanities professor named Evan Tyler, whose mother was on the board of trustees. He was the one who slipped the drug into her drink. The rest of the night was a blur. She had vague recollections, visions that she saw through internal gauze—her clothes being torn off, his curly hair, his mouth on hers. She could feel the weight of Evan Tyler on top of her, crushing her, suffocating her. Rachel had tried to say no, tried to scream for help, tried to push him away.

That was the image that ended up seared into her brain. Evan Tyler. On top of her. Grinning with maniacal glee. The image still visited her in her sleep, of course, but it popped up when she was awake too, an awful jack-in-the-box, startling her whenever she felt relaxed and at ease. Even now. Even after all the years, that image—that maniacal grin—was always with her, walking a few steps behind her, taunting her, sometimes tapping her on the shoulder when she felt any confidence. It followed Rachel day and night for days, months, years, fueling her anger, urging her to work harder and harder, to do the story, to seek justice, to smother that awful maniacal grin, to pressure everyone and anyone, including Catherine Tullo . . .

But right then, on this horrible Halloween Night, when she couldn't breathe, when it might have ended up even worse for her—or maybe, who knows, she would have passed out and forgotten it all—Evan Tyler suddenly vanished from atop her.

The weight was gone from her chest. Just like that. Poof, gone.

Someone had tackled him.

Rachel tried to sit up, but the brain impulses still couldn't reach the muscles. She just lay there, her head lolling to the side, where she heard Hayden let out a primal scream. Then Hayden punched Tyler and then punched him again and then again. His fists just flew, spraying blood across the room. There was no tiring, no letup, and Rachel was sure that Evan Tyler would have been killed if two other guys hadn't heard the commotion, burst into the room, and pulled a bloodied Hayden off him.

Evan Tyler was comatose for the next two weeks.

Rachel still wanted to press charges, especially after she heard that she had not been Tyler's first victim, but the school wanted it swept under the rug. Tyler was in a coma, after all, with facial fractures that would take months to heal. Hadn't he suffered enough? His mother was an important woman. Did Rachel really also want to drag the school through the dirt? What was the point in that?

Rachel didn't care about any of that.

She did, however, care about Hayden.

That was the issue. The beating had gone well beyond the act of stopping a crime, and while the Payne fortune would certainly assure a soft landing, Hayden's family wanted it kept quiet for all the obvious reasons. So that was how it went. Deals were made. Money might have exchanged hands.

Swept away for the greater good. Over. Onward.

Except for those images of Evan Tyler, who would later become president of the college, seared into her brain.

As for Rachel and Hayden, they became close friends.

That, she realized, happened often when you are bonded in either tragedy or a secret—or in their case, both.

When David and Cheryl met Hayden during a visit to Lemhall University, David pulled Rachel aside and said, "That guy's in love with you."

"No, he's not."

"He may be settling for the Friend Zone," David said. "But you know better."

She did, but that seemed to be the origin story of ninety percent of boy-girl friendships on campus in those days. The guy likes you, wants to sleep with you, doesn't get to, settles on being a friend, the tension goes away. Either way, she and Hayden became close confidantes—the kind of close confidantes where you could never really date after all you knew, even if you wanted to.

The waiter came over with a plate. He placed it between them. "Lobster paella," he said.

Hayden smiled at him. "Thank you, Ken."

It smelled wonderful.

He picked up his fork. "Wait until you taste this."

"I didn't call you about Lemhall or that story," she said.

"Oh?"

"Do you know if there was a Payne Industries event on May twenty-seventh at Six Flags amusement park?"

He frowned. Hayden still wore the Lemhall University ring, a tacky thing with a purple stone and the school crest, and she never understood why. He was, in fact, fiddling with it now, turning it around his finger like it was some sort of stress reliever. Perhaps it was. Still, the ring seemed too much to her. She wanted to forget the place. She guessed that for some reason he needed to remember.

"May twenty-seventh?" he repeated. "I really don't know. Why?"

She took out her phone, swiped, showed him a photo of a family standing in front of the backdrop with logos. Hayden took the phone from her hand and studied it.

"I guess there was," Hayden said. He handed her back the phone. "Why do you ask?"

"It would have been, what, a corporate event?"

"Probably. We buy a bunch of tickets to a theater or a ballpark or an amusement park. It's a perk for employees and clients. Is this for a story you're doing?"

She pressed on. "You'd have had photographers on hand, right?"

"I assume so."

"I mean, like this photo in front of that backdrop. A photographer you guys hired probably took pics like this?"

"Again: I assume so. What the hell is this about, Rachel?"

"Can you get me all the photos?"

Hayden's eyes flared for a millisecond. "Pardon?"

"I need to go through them."

"Corporate events like this," he began, "we sometimes rent half the park. There could have been, I don't know, five, ten thousand people at it. What are you looking for?"

"You won't believe me if I told you."

"Tell me anyway." Then Hayden added, "I assume this has something to do with your brother-in-law escaping prison."

"It does."

"You can't still have a crush on him, Rachel."

"What, I never had a crush on David."

"You talked about him nonstop."

"You almost sound jealous, Hayden."

He smiled. "Perhaps I was."

This was a minefield she didn't want to wander into. "Do you trust me?" she asked him.

"You know I do."

"Can you get me the pics?"

He picked up the water glass, took a sip. "Yes."

"Thank you."

"So what else?" he asked.

She knew him well. "This favor is trickier."

The waiter came over with a second dish. "Jamon Iberico with caviar."

Hayden smiled at him. "Thank you, Ken."

"Enjoy."

"You're going to love these," Hayden said. He scooped some of the paella onto her plate. It smelled fantastic, but Rachel ignored it for the moment. Hayden took a bite, closed his eyes as though savoring. When he opened them again, he said, "So what's the favor?"

"One of the logos on that backdrop," Rachel said, "is for the Berg Reproductive Institute."

"Makes sense," Hayden says. "It's one of our holdings. You know that."

"I do."

"So?"

"So ten years ago, I made an appointment at one."

Hayden stopped midbite. "Pardon?"

"I called Barb." Barb Matteson was the institute's manager at the time. "You introduced us."

"I remember. At the family holiday party."

"Right."

"I don't understand." Hayden put the fork down. "Why did you make an appointment?"

"I told her I wanted to look into getting pregnant via donor sperm."

"Are you serious?"

"About making the appointment? Yes. About going through with it? No."

"I'm not following, Rachel."

"I made the appointment for Cheryl."

"Okay," he said slowly. Then: "I'm still not following."

"She didn't want David to know."

"Ah."

"Right."

"So Cheryl made the appointment in your name so her husband wouldn't find out?"

"Exactly."

Hayden tilted his head. "You realize that's probably against the law."

"It's not, but I know it's an ethical breach. Anyway, Rachel checked in under my name. She used my ID. We look enough alike. The bills came to my house."

"Okay," he said slowly.

"I even made the appointment for Cheryl at your satellite office in Lowell—in case Barb was around at the Boston one."

"All to protect your sister from telling her husband?"

"Yes."

"Interesting," he said.

"She was going through some stuff. I thought it would be harmless."

"Doesn't sound harmless," Hayden said. "Did David ever find out?"

"Yes."

"He must have been furious with you."

"He doesn't know about my part in it."

"But he knows Cheryl went to look into donor sperm."

"Yes."

"And you never told him your role in this—shall I use the word 'deception'?"

"I never told him," Rachel said softly.

The waiter came by and poured some wine. When he left, Hayden asked, "So what do you want now?"

"David doesn't think it's a coincidence."

"Doesn't think what's a coincidence?"

"You're going to think this is insane."

"We're past that, Rachel."

"He thinks . . . that is, *we* think . . ." It sounded so ridiculous that for a moment, Rachel couldn't finish the thought. Then: "We think Matthew was at the amusement park with your group."

Hayden rapid-blinked as though he'd been smacked across the face. Then he cleared his throat and asked, "Who is Matthew?"

"My nephew," she said. "David's son."

More blinking. "The one he murdered?"

"That's the point. We don't think he's dead at all."

Rachel handed Hayden the phone again, this time with the photograph of Maybe-Matthew. "The boy in the background. The one holding the hand."

Hayden took the phone and held it in front of his face. He used his fingers to try to blow up the image. She waited. He squinted. "It's so blurry."

"I know."

"You can't really think—"

"I'm not sure."

He frowned. "Rachel."

"I know. It's crazy. It's all crazy."

Hayden shook his head. He handed the phone back to her as though it were on fire. "I don't know what you want me to do here."

"Can you send me all the pics from Six Flags?"

"Why?"

"So we can scour through them."

"And what would you be looking for?"

"Any other photos of this boy."

He shook his head. "This blurry boy who looks like a million other boys?"

"I don't expect you to understand."

"You're right about that."

"But for my sake, Hayden. Please? Will you help?"

Hayden sighed. Then he said, "Yes, of course."

30

Like most decent interrogators, Max employed a variety of tactics on his perps. Currently his most effective method involved disruption. He teamed up with Sarah to keep suspects off balance with a constantly evolving rotation of accusations, humor, disgust, hope, friendship, threats, alliances, skepticism. He and Sarah played good cop and bad cop and switched roles in the middle and then sometimes both were good and sometimes both were bad.

Chaos, baby. Create chaos.

They peppered suspects with a barrage of questions—and then they let them linger in long silences. Like the best of major league pitchers—and baseball being the only sport Max even mildly understood—they kept changing it up: fastballs, changeups, curveballs, sliders, you name it.

But right now, as he sat across from Warden Philip Mackenzie in the corner booth at McDermott's pub, Max threw all of that away. Sarah was not with him. She didn't even know he was here. She wouldn't approve—Sarah was very by-the-book—and moreover, he was (to keep within his piss-poor metaphor) throwing a scuffed-up spitball, clearly illegal, and if someone was going to get thrown out of the game, it might as well be him and him alone.

Mackenzie had ordered an Irish whiskey called Writers' Tears. Max was going with a club soda. He didn't handle spirits well.

"So what can I do for you, Special Agent Bernstein?" Mackenzie asked.

Max had chosen to meet Mackenzie at the warden's favorite watering hole because this wasn't about intimidation or pressing an advantage. Just the opposite, in fact.

"I need your help finding David."

"Of course," Mackenzie said to him, sitting a little straighter. "I want that too. He was my prisoner."

"And your godson."

"Well, yes. All the more reason to want him back safe and sound."

"I can't believe nobody picked up on that before now."

"Picked up on what?"

"On your relationship with him. But I also don't care. Look, we both know you helped break him out."

Mackenzie smiled, took a deep sip of his drink. "You heard my attorney. The CCTV backs up my story. Burroughs was seen holding a gun—"

"Look, this is just us talking. I'm not recording this. It isn't a cute trap."

Max placed his phone on the grossly sticky table in front of them.

"Oh my," Mackenzie said, his voice thick with sarcasm. "Your phone is on the table. Now there is no way you can possibly be recording this."

"I'm not. I think you know that. But for the sake of anyone maybe listening, we are having a hypothetical discussion. That's all."

Mackenzie frowned. "Seriously?"

"Look, Phil, I want this to be nice. I don't want to add threats. Okay? You know I'm going to nail you for aiding and abetting. You'll go down. Your son will go down. You'll both go to prison or if I really mess up, you'll just lose your jobs and pensions. It's going to be bad, and if I'm angry—forget me, if *Sarah* is angry—you're going to be toast. She will crawl up your sphincter and make a home there."

"Colorfully put."

"But today I don't care about any of that. Today I want to know why you did it. Why now. Hypothetically."

Mackenzie took a swig. "Sounds like you have a theory, Special Agent Bernstein."

"I do. Would you like to hear it?"

"Sure."

"David Burroughs gets no visitors for years. Suddenly his sister-in-law shows up. I've checked. There were no letters exchanged before her visit, no phone calls, nothing. I've also seen the video of her first visit. He didn't know she was coming. With me so far?"

"Sure."

"She showed him a photo. I can't make out what it is. That's the thing. But when Burroughs sees it, everything changes. You can feel it right through the CCTV. When the visit is over, he contacts you—again, from what I can see, for the first time. Do you want to help me here and tell me what he wanted?"

"I already said—"

"Okay, you're not going to help, fine. Let me go on then. You respond to his visit by going to see your old police partner, who happens to be Burroughs's father. As soon as you come back, you help break Burroughs out. I'm not sure how the fight with Ross Sumner fits in. I'm also not sure about the correctional officer Ted Weston. He's one of your men. You know him better than I do. Anyway, Weston lawyered up after we found out someone was bribing him. Did you know about that?"

"No."

"Surprised?"

"That he took a bribe?"

"Yes."

Mackenzie took another sip, shrugged.

"Okay, don't answer. But here's why it's important. I don't think Burroughs attacked Weston. I think it was the other way around. Weston went after him. So that's weird to me. And one last thing: When Burroughs does escape, the first person he goes to is a key witness from his trial. An old woman who changed her name and moved away right after the trial ended. And that old woman? I talked to her. She's lying about what

Burroughs said to her during his visit. I think for some reason she's protecting him."

Max spread his hands. "So I add this all up, Phil, and you know what I come up with?"

"What's that?"

"Burroughs's sister-in-law, who used to be a very good investigative journalist, found something that could free him. She brings it to him. Shows it to him through that plexiglass. Burroughs goes to you. Tells you what Rachel Anderson has. You agree to help. Thing is, you're too good to have rushed an escape like that, leaving so many things to chance. So my guess is, the Sumner or Weston attack—or both—forced your hand."

"This is some story, Special Agent Bernstein."

"Call me Max. I don't have it exactly. I'm missing parts. But we both know I'm close. Here's the thing. We have to bring David in. You get that. And I don't know why this evidence couldn't just be given to his attorney or something. I assume there is a good reason for that."

Mackenzie still gave him nothing.

"And Sarah? She is strictly by the book. If Burroughs was set up, if he didn't do it, I'm not like that guy in *The Fugitive*—remember that movie?"

Mackenzie nodded. "I even remember the TV series."

"Before my time. But there's the great scene when Harrison Ford tells Tommy Lee Jones—Tommy plays the federal agent trying to capture him—'I'm innocent,' and do you remember what Tommy Lee Jones says?"

He nodded. "He says, 'I don't care.'"

"Right. That's Sarah. She doesn't care. We have a job to do. Bring Burroughs in. Period, the end. It's why you and I are meeting alone in this bar. I'm vulnerable now. You could tell them what I said. But unlike Tommy Lee Jones, I do care. If Burroughs didn't do it, I want to help him."

The warden picked up his drink and held it up to the light. "Suppose," he said, "I told you that you're mostly right."

Max felt his pulse quicken.

"But suppose," Mackenzie continued, "I also told you that the real story is stranger than what you've concocted."

"Stranger how?"

"Suppose I told you that the *real* reason David escaped was because a child may be in grave danger."

Max looked confused. "You mean another child?"

"Not exactly."

"You mind explaining?"

Philip Mackenzie smiled, but there was no joy in it. "Tell you what," he said, draining his whiskey and sliding out of the booth. "You draw up papers giving my son full immunity, we can finish this chat."

"What about immunity for you?"

"I don't deserve immunity," Mackenzie said. "At least, not yet."

———

The same two goons escort me back to the plane. No handcuffs, no blindfold, no rough stuff. When we arrive at the tarmac, I speak for the first time.

"I need my phone back."

The "Shut the Fuck Up" Guy reaches into his pocket and tosses it to me. "Charged it for you."

"Thank you."

"Heard you beat up a cop."

"No."

"In New York City. Said so on the news. He's in the hospital."

"I was just trying to escape."

"Still, my man. Props to you."

"Yeah," the other goon says, speaking for the first time. "Props."

"Thank you" doesn't seem the appropriate response, so I say nothing. We board the same plane and take the same seats. I check the incoming texts, all from Rachel, of course, getting progressively more panicky.

I text back: *I'm fine. Sorry. Waylaid.*

The dots start dancing. Learn anything important?

To Rachel's credit, she hadn't wasted time asking for a full recap or even where I'd been. Still focused.

I text: *Hilde Winslow won't lead us to Matthew.*
Dead end?
More or less, yeah.

I wait for the plane to take off and get high enough for the Wi-Fi to kick in. I look behind me. My escorts are both wearing headphones and watching their phones. I call Rachel.

"What's all that noise?" Rachel asks. "I can barely hear you."

"I'm on a plane."

"Wait, what?"

There is no way to continue without giving her some details, so I give her the nonthreatening sketch recap of what happened since I left her in Revere.

"How about you?" I ask when I'm done. "Anything new on your end?"

Silence—and for a moment I think that the call has dropped.

"I may have a lead," she says. "You remember my old friend Hayden Payne?"

It takes me a few moments to place the name. "The rich guy who had the big crush on you?" And then I see it: "Oh wait. His family is involved in those corporations, right?"

"Owns them. All part of the Payne group."

I think about that. "Another can't-be-a-coincidence."

"What do you mean?"

But I don't want to derail her. "What about Hayden?"

"They had a corporate event at Six Flags. That's where that photo was taken. I asked him to get me all the photos taken that day."

"Can we also get a list of attendees?"

"I guess I can ask, but he said it would be in the thousands."

"It's a place to start."

"It might be, yeah. Also the company didn't rent out the whole park. Matthew could have been with someone else."

"Still worth a try."

"I know."

"What else?" I ask her.

"Are you flying back to Boston?"

Answering a question by asking a question. "No."

"Then where?"

"I'm heading to New Jersey."

"What's there?"

"Cheryl," I say. "I need to talk to her face to face."

31

"Please tell me you're joking," she said.

Max tried to stare her down. He wasn't good with eye contact. Never had been. Like he said before, he felt it was overrated. Still, he persevered. Her name was Lauren Ford, and she ran the Criminal Investigations Unit for the Boston area. Right now, Lauren was the one giving off the much more fiery glare.

"I'm not good with jokes," Max said.

"So let me make sure I got this straight." Lauren stood behind her desk and started pacing. "You want me to authorize my lab to run another DNA test to make sure the murder victim was really Matthew Burroughs?"

"Precisely."

"A case that's, what, five years old?"

"More like six."

"And where we already arrested and convicted someone."

"That's correct."

"And where said perpetrator recently escaped from federal prison."

"Again: Correct."

"And where it's your job, as far as I know, to apprehend him and put him where he belongs, not retry him."

Max did not reply.

"So," she asked, hands spread, "why do you need a DNA test on a long-deceased victim to find an escaped convict?"

"Did you run one the first time?"

Lauren sighed. "Did you hear me say 'another DNA test'?"

"I did."

"Does that imply we already ran one?"

"It does," Max agreed.

"And let me explain that's not protocol. We already had a positive ID, despite the body's condition. People watch too much *CSI*. In reality, we rarely do DNA tests on murder victims. No law enforcement in the land does. We don't do fingerprint tests either. It is only done when there is doubt about the victim's identity. There was none here. We knew who the victim was."

"But you still did one?"

"Yep. Because like I said before, every jury member watches too much TV. If you don't have all the forensics and DNA, they figure you don't know what you're doing. So it was overkill, but we did it."

"How?"

"What do you mean?"

"Did you compare the victim's DNA to the mother's DNA or the father's or . . . ?"

324

"Who remembers? You realize, of course, this was a high-profile case for us?"

"I realize that, yes."

"We didn't make any mistakes."

"I'm not saying you did. Look, you still have the victim's blood on file, right?"

"Sure. I mean, it's stored in the warehouse, but yes, we have it."

"And we have David Burroughs's DNA in the system."

That was a routine matter now, Max knew. Every prisoner's DNA is automatically added into the databank when they are convicted.

"Doing another test, opening this door in any way," Lauren Ford said, "it's a big deal."

"Then keep it quiet," Max said. "This is just between you and me."

"Do I look like a lab tech?"

"You, me, a lab tech. You can keep it down-low."

She frowned. "Did you really just use the term 'down-low'?"

Max waited.

"I could just tell you to get the hell out of my office," she said.

"You could."

"It was a righteous bust. It was done by the book. A cop's son—a *popular* cop's son—was the perp, and we still made sure no one played favorites."

"Admirable," Max said.

She leaned back, started gnawing on a fingernail Max-style.

"I'm going to tell you something in confidence. Because any way you look at it, this was a righteous conviction."

"I'm listening."

"The DNA lab back then."

"What about it?"

"They made a few mistakes."

"What kind of mistakes?"

"The kind where you suddenly quit your job when an internal investigation starts and move overseas."

Silence.

"Shit," Lauren said. "Are you telling me it's not the kid?"

"I'm telling you," Max said, "to run the test. And while you're at it? Run the DNA through all the missing person databases. If the dead boy wasn't Matthew Burroughs, we have to find out who he is."

———

Rachel's car is allowed on the tarmac, one of the perks, I guess, of flying private. After we deplane, the two goons shake my hands with much gusto.

"Bygones?" the STFU guy asks me.

"Bygones," I say.

I get in Rachel's car. She looks at the plane and says, "The perks of criminality."

"Yep."

We start driving.

"You wanting to see Cheryl," Rachel says to me. "Is this about that fertility clinic?"

"It's not a coincidence, Rachel."

"You keep saying that." Her grip on the wheel tightens. "I need to clear the air about something."

"About what?"

"It's old news. It shouldn't matter anymore."

But her tone says that it matters a lot. I turn to her. Her eyes are too focused on the road in front of her.

"Go on," I say.

"I helped Cheryl make the appointment at that fertility clinic."

I am not sure I understand what she means. "When you say 'helped'—"

"I met the manager of Berg Reproductive through Hayden Payne," she said. "So I called her and made the appointment."

"Instead of Cheryl?"

"Yes."

"That hardly seems like a big deal," I say. "I mean, I wish you'd told me about it—"

"I said the appointment was for me." Rachel swallows, her eyes still on the road. "When Cheryl went, she used my ID instead of her own."

I take in her profile. My voice is oddly calm. "Why would you do that?"

"Why do you think, David?"

But the answer is obvious. "To hide it from me."

"Yes."

I feel tears push their way into my eyes, but I don't even know why. "I don't really give a shit anymore, Rachel."

"It isn't what you think."

"I think Cheryl wanted to explore getting donor sperm and for me to never know about it. I think you conspired to help her. Am I wrong?"

Rachel kept both hands on the wheel.

"You learn in prison," I said. "Nobody's on nobody's side."

"I'm on your side."

I say nothing.

"She's my sister. You get that, right?"

"So you went along with it?"

"I told her it was a bad idea."

"But you still went along with it."

Rachel carefully hits the turn signal, checks her rearview mirrors, changes lanes. Even after not seeing her for five years, I still know her so well.

"Rachel?"

She doesn't reply.

"What are you leaving out?" I ask.

"I didn't agree with what she was doing. I thought she should tell you."

I wait for the proverbial shoe to drop.

"And once Cheryl didn't go through with it, I thought . . ."

"Thought what?"

Rachel shook away my question. "How did you find out Cheryl went to Berg?"

"Someone at the clinic left a message on the home answering machine."

"Think about it," Rachel said. "Why would they do that if her patient records were all in my name?"

I stop. It takes me more time than it should. "You?"

She keeps her eyes on the road.

"You left that message?"

"It was over. She didn't go through with it. I hadn't liked being dragged into it, and no matter how I try to justify it, I betrayed you. That didn't sit right with me. So one night, I had too much to drink, and I thought shit, Cheryl should tell him. For her sake. For his sake. Hell, for my sake. So we wouldn't all be living with this awful lie hanging over our heads for the rest of our lives. You two were starting a family of your own."

I sit there. Just when I think nothing can stun me again, there it is.

"I've learned the hard way," Rachel said. "Lies like that, they stay in the room. They never leave. They rot you slowly from the inside. You and Cheryl couldn't build a family on a secret like that. And yeah, okay, it wasn't my secret to tell. But Cheryl made me part of the deception. That secret was poisoning our relationship now too. Yours and mine."

"So you decided to end the secret," I say.

Rachel nods. I turn away.

"David?"

"Doesn't matter," I say. "Like you said, it was a long time ago."

"I'm sorry."

Something else in me breaks; I need to get off this subject. "Does Cheryl know I'm coming?"

Rachel shakes her head. "You told me not to tell her."

"So she thinks—"

"She thinks it's only going to be me. We're supposed to meet in her office."

"How much longer?"

"Half an hour," Rachel says, and we fall into silence.

32

Rachel parks in the visitor lot at St. Barnabas Medical Center in Livingston, New Jersey. We both don surgical masks. Since Covid, no one thinks twice about seeing someone with a mask, especially near a hospital. Again, it's a pretty effective disguise.

We start toward the front entrance.

"How long has Cheryl been working here?" I ask.

"Three years. They have a good kidney transplant program."

"But Cheryl loved working at Boston General."

"She did," Rachel agrees. "But staying became untenable after your conviction. The hospital called her a"—Rachel made quote marks with her fingers—"distraction."

I stare up into the sky.

"One more thing," Rachel says. "She goes by Dr. Cheryl Dreason now."

Another pang. "She took Ronald's name too?"

"It gave her more anonymity."

"That was really clever of her," I say.

"Seriously?"

I make a face.

"She lost everything too."

New husband, fresh pregnancy, still doing the transplant surgery she loves—Rachel's words don't seem quite accurate, but it feels ungenerous to say so.

We move inside. Rachel heads to the desk and grabs us visitors passes. We take the elevator to the fourth floor and follow the signs reading RENAL AND PANCREAS TRANSPLANT. Rachel pulls down the mask and waves to the receptionist.

"Hey, Betsy."

"Hey, Rachel. She's waiting for you in her office."

Rachel smiles one more time and then pulls the mask back up. I keep walking by her side, as though this is routine and I know where I'm going. My pulse starts picking up speed. My breath shallows.

I am mere yards away from Cheryl—my ex-wife, the mother of my child, the only woman I ever loved.

I feel myself start to well up. It is one thing to think or imagine this moment. But now that it's here . . .

Rachel stops short. "Shit."

Cops, I figure in the millisecond before I see that no, she isn't talking about anyone in law enforcement. She's talking about Ronald Dreason, Cheryl's new husband. I know Ronald, of course. He was an administrator at Boston General who was always "looking out" for Cheryl. You know what I mean. He just wanted to be her "friend" and it was obvious to me and everyone else, including Ronald's wife—who, to be somewhat fair, he was separated from at the time—that was bullshit. Naturally I wasn't happy with the constant "work" texts because, again, obvious. Cheryl laughed them off.

"Okay, yeah, Ronald probably does have a little crush on me," Cheryl would say. "But it's harmless."

Harmless, I scoff now, almost saying it out loud.

Ronald looks at Cheryl first. He starts to smile. Cheryl and Rachel are close, so I am sure that Rachel visits here often enough. This encounter is probably, if not familiar, nothing particularly surprising or new. I lower my head and veer a little to my right. I have the mask pulled up. I slow down and turn behind me, as though I'm not with Rachel. Rachel doesn't miss a step. She keeps walking toward Ronald, takes hold of his arm, and says a little too merrily, "Hey, Ronald."

Ronald kisses her cheek.

The kiss is stiff, but then again, so is everything about Ronald. I stop right there, not taking that thought any further. I start walking back toward them, staying close to the wall, my face turned toward it. I don't break stride. I don't risk a glance in his direction.

I close my eyes and move past him.

Safe.

Rachel is trying to escort him away from us, but he stops her.

"I didn't expect to see you here," Ronald says to her. "Did you hear about David's escape?"

I hurry-walk away. There are three unmarked doors in front of me. One is where my wife—ex-wife, sorry—will be. Time is ticking. I take hold of the knob on the first door, turn it, step inside.

And there she is.

I had interrupted Cheryl typing on some kind of tablet. She looks up. I still have the surgical mask on and my head is shaved, but that doesn't matter. She recognizes me right away. For a second, neither one of us moves. We just stare. I am not sure what I feel or, more apropos, what I don't feel. I feel it all and then some. Every emotion surges through my worn-out veins. It is overwhelming.

For her too.

Cheryl and I fell in love in high school. We dated, got engaged, married, and had the sweetest little boy together.

A weird thought pops into my brain: Ronald might come back. Or a nurse or colleague might come in. I turn and lock the knob. That's it. That's the first move I make after seeing Cheryl. I turn back to her, not sure what I will get, what sort of reaction, but Cheryl is already on her feet and running around the desk, and when she gets to me there is no pause, not the slightest hesitation, and as she throws her arms around me and pulls me toward her, I half collapse and she, I swear, holds me up.

"David," Cheryl says softly, with a tenderness that tears my heart out of my chest and rips it into little pieces.

I hold her. She cries. I cry. I can't. I just can't. I have a million questions, but there is a reason I'm here, and it's not this. With perhaps a little too much edge, I take hold of her arms and pull her off me.

There is no time for a preamble.

"Our son may still be alive," I say.

She closes her eyes. "David."

"Please listen to me."

Her eyes are still squeezed shut. "No one wants that to be true more than I do."

"You saw the pic?"

"It's not Matthew, David."

"How can you be so sure?"

Tears start flowing down her cheeks. She lifts both hands and takes hold of my face. For a moment, I fear I may collapse again and never get up. "Because Matthew is dead," she says almost too softly. "We buried our little boy. You and I. We stood together and held hands and we watched them put that tiny white coffin into the ground."

I shake my head. "I didn't kill him, Cheryl."

"I wish so much that was true."

The words sting more than I would have imagined. She looks down. Pain etches its way onto her face. I don't want to go there, not now, not ever, but I can't help myself.

"Why did you give up on me, Cheryl?"

I hear the pathetic whine in my voice and hate myself for it.

"I didn't," she says. "Not ever."

"How could you think I did it?"

"I never blamed you. Not really."

I open my mouth to ask again why she stopped believing in me, but I make myself stop. Again: Now is not the time to go down that road. Stay focused.

"He's alive," I say a little more firmly, and then: "It doesn't matter if you believe me or not. I need to ask you something. Then I'll leave you be."

The pity on her face is so cruel. "What is it, David? What do you need from me?"

"Your visit to Berg Reproductive," I say.

The pity turns to confusion. "What are you talking about?"

"That clinic, the one you visited."

"What about it?"

"It has something to do with what happened to Matthew." She takes a step back. "What . . . no, it doesn't."

"That picture Rachel showed you? It was taken at a company event. For Berg Reproductive. It's connected."

Cheryl shakes her head. "No."

I say nothing.

"How can you think that?"

"Just tell me, Cheryl."

"You know everything."

"You didn't tell me you pretended to be Rachel."

"She told you that?"

No need for me to reply.

"I don't understand." Again, Cheryl's eyes squeeze shut, as though she's wishing it all away. "What does that matter now?" Her voice is more a plea than a question. The pain is growing, consuming her. I want to offer some kind of comfort, even now, even after all this, but there isn't a chance I'm going to do that. "I should have never gone to that clinic."

I say nothing.

"It's all my fault," she says.

I don't like the timbre in her voice; it drops the room temperature ten degrees.

"What do you mean?" I ask.

"I went there behind your back. I'm so sorry."

"I know. That doesn't matter anymore."

"I shouldn't have done that to you."

I almost wince. "Cheryl."

"We were falling apart. Why, David?" She tilts her head the way she used to and for a second we are back in our yard with our coffees and books and the morning sun is making the yard glow a golden yellow and she's tilting her head to ask me a question. "We weren't the first couple to experience the strain of infertility."

"We weren't, no."

"So why did we fall apart?"

"I don't know," I say.

"Maybe the cracks were always there."

"Maybe." I don't want to hear any of this. "It doesn't matter anymore."

"But it was a terrible betrayal."

I don't say anything because I don't think I can speak.

"And because of that"—there is a hitch in her voice now—"because of what I did to you, our son . . ."

Then Cheryl bursts into tears.

I have, of course, known my ex-wife a long time. I have seen her go through pretty much every emotion. I have seen her cry. But never like this. Not even when Matthew died. Cheryl was never one to let go. Not fully. Even when she made love or held our son, there was a part of her that maintained control. You felt a coolness, a detachment, which sounds like a criticism, but it is not. She just never lost complete control.

Until this very moment.

I want to do something. I want to hold her or at least offer her a shoulder. But I also feel a sudden chill blowing through my heart.

"What is it, Cheryl?"

She continues to sob.

"Cheryl?"

"I went through with it."

Just like that. I freeze. I know what she means, but I ask it anyway: "Went through with what?"

She doesn't answer. "You knew."

I shake my head.

"You knew," she said again. "The anger, the resentment, the stress."

I still shake my head.

"You started sleepwalking again."

"No."

"You did, David. Because of what I did. You got angry. You started to unravel. I should have seen it. It was my fault. And then one day, I don't know, you had too much to drink maybe. Or the strain got too much."

I keep shaking my head. "No."

"David, listen to me."

"You think I killed our son?"

"No," she says. "I think I killed him. Because of what I did to you."

I can barely breathe.

"I was sure the procedure didn't take, that Matthew was yours, but that didn't matter. Going through with it. My betrayal. It changed you."

I fight through it, try again to stay on message, swim through the emotional battering. "You tried to get pregnant with donor sperm."

"Yes."

"You told me you didn't."

"I know. I lied."

I don't know what to say here. "And you thought . . . ?"

I see it now—how she thinks it all played: I found out she'd used donor sperm, and I lost my mind. I thought Matthew wasn't mine. *"The anger, the resentment, the stress."*

Plus the sleepwalking. In her mind, I didn't do it intentionally, but somehow my hidden rage manifested itself and I had too much to drink or a bad mix of antidepressants and alcohol, or whatever past trauma rushed back into my damaged psyche, and unconsciously I rose from my sleep and grabbed a baseball bat and walked into Matthew's room and . . .

So much of what happened makes sense now. Cheryl blames herself. All this time. She hasn't only lost her son. She believes I did it—and worse, she believes that she is responsible.

"Cheryl, listen to me."

She bursts into tears again. Her knees give way. I can't let that happen. Whatever, I can't let her fall like that. I hurry over, and she grabs onto my shirt and sobs. "I'm so sorry, David."

I don't need to hear this. I don't want to hear this. *Focus on the goal*, I tell myself. "None of that matters anymore."

"David . . ."

"Please," I say. "Please look at the picture."

"I can't," she says.

"Cheryl."

"I can't give myself that kind of hope. If I do, I'll break."

I don't know what to say to that.

"I want so badly to believe, David, but if I let myself go there . . ." She stops, shakes her head. "I'm pregnant again."

"I know," I say.

And that is when I hear a key jangle the lock on the door. A second later, it swings open.

It's Ronald.

It takes him a few seconds to recognize me. When he does, his eyes go wide.

"What the hell is going on here?"

I don't have time for this. I look back toward Cheryl.

"Go," Cheryl says to me, wiping her eyes. "He won't say anything."

I hurry toward the door. For a moment I think Ronald is going to block my path. He doesn't. He steps aside. I want to say something like "You better be good to her" or even "I'm happy for you guys" but I'm not that selfless and I've had enough melodrama for one afternoon.

I give him the slightest nod and am on my way.

33

Max saw the call was from Lauren Ford's office. He glanced around the room to make sure he was alone before he answered it. Sarah wouldn't like it. As Lauren had pointed out, their job was to apprehend David Burroughs, not help clear him. Sarah would not approve.

"Hello?"

"I got something," Lauren said.

"Is Burroughs the father?"

"That one I don't know yet. Believe it or not, it took a while to get into the prisoner databank. But I did run the victim's DNA through the missing kid database."

"And?"

"And he doesn't pop up."

"It was a long shot, I guess."

"No, Max—may I call you Max?"

"Sure."

"No, Max, it's not a long shot. The missing child databases

are pretty complete. When a kid goes missing, the DNA is collected in some way the large majority of time. Not always. But most of the time. And that's not all."

"What's not all?"

"I ran a description through every missing kid database. Not just DNA sites. All the missing kid sites. Put in the age, size, whatever. And to make sure I didn't miss anything, I made the search federal. The entire United States. Got my best people on it. Because, well, if the victim isn't Matthew Burroughs—Christ, it sounds crazy just to say that—but if Matthew isn't the victim, then some other little boy was brutally murdered that night."

"Agreed," Max said. "And?"

"And nothing. No matches. Zero. No one even close."

Max started twitching.

"You hear what I'm saying, Max?"

"I do."

"There's no one else. It has to be Matthew Burroughs who was in that bed."

He gnawed on a fingernail. "You got anything else?"

"What do you mean, do I have anything else? Are you listening to me?"

"Yes."

"Shit," Lauren said. "You still want me to run the paternity test."

"I do."

"I don't have to," Lauren said.

"I know."

"Shit. Fine. And then we put this to bed. Deal?"

"Deal."

"I should have the result soon."

Lauren hung up.

From behind him, Sarah asked, "Who was that, Max?"

"Another case," he mumbled. "What's up?"

"What other case?"

Max knew that she wouldn't let this go. "It was a guy, okay?"

"A guy?"

"I met him on a dating app. It's new. I didn't want to say anything."

"I'm happy for you," Sarah said.

"Thank you."

"I'm also not buying it. But we can deal with that later. Let's go."

"Why, what's up?"

"Burroughs just left St. Barnabas Hospital in New Jersey. That's where his ex-wife works."

———

"I just wanted to have a normal day," Hayden said. "Is that too much to ask? And you should have seen him, Pixie. Just a boy at an amusement park. I don't think I've ever seen Theo so happy. It was all so wonderfully"—Hayden looked up at the ceiling as though searching for the right word before settling on—"normal."

Normal, Gertrude thought. Nothing about this family or

their lives was normal. No one wanted normal. Not really. She remembered when she brought Hayden's father and his siblings to Disneyland a million years ago. She paid the park a ton of money, and so the park opened early for them. The Payne family spent two hours alone, the park closed to the "normal," and then, when the park opened for real, a senior vice president took them around the grounds and moved them to the front of any line.

No one who waited two hours to go on Space Mountain wanted to be "normal" on that day.

"I wish you had told me you planned to take him."

"You would have stopped me," Hayden replied.

"And now you know why."

"I was so careful. I wore a baseball cap and sunglasses. I didn't tell anyone I was coming. I kept him away from all the company photographers. And come on, Pixie, what are the odds? He was a little boy when I rescued him. Even if you were looking dead straight at him, there is no way you'd know. And it's not as though he's a missing boy. The world believes he's dead."

Gertrude flashed back to that night five years ago. Hayden hadn't consulted with her first. He hadn't warned her either, because he'd known she would never allow it. It was almost morning when he'd brought the little boy here to the Payne estate.

"Pixie, I have to tell you something . . ."

It is startling what the human mind can justify. We all live via self-justification and self-rationalization. Pixie was hardly immune. Morality is subjective. She could have done the "right" thing that night, but we only do the right thing when it doesn't cost us. It reminded her of the old chicken-extinction question. There is an argument that if we didn't eat chickens, they'd go extinct, ergo it would be bad for chickens to stop eating them. A vegan friend of hers had told Gertrude that this was nonsense, but that wasn't the point. Certainly, millions of chickens get to be born and live, however briefly and brutally, because they will eventually be eaten. Is that life better than none at all? Is it better for the chicken to have a life of, say, six weeks than never exist? Who are you to decide that for the chicken? Is it better to stop eating chicken altogether and let the chickens go extinct? Are we actually doing a good thing by eating chicken? On and on, like that.

The point isn't that one side is right or wrong. The point is, if you want to eat chicken, you'll use this argument, even if you don't care in the slightest about chickens or their survival as a species. Because, well, you want to eat chicken.

Apply that tenfold to the family. Family matters. Your family, that is. Rich, poor, ancient times, modern days—that's a constant. We all know this. Those who deny it are either delusional or lying. We pay lip service to a vague greater good, but only when it serves our interest. We don't really care about others, except when convenient. Don't believe it? Ask yourself this: How many lives would you trade to save your child or grandchild from being killed?

One person? Five? Ten?

A million?

Be honest with that answer and perhaps you'll understand what Gertrude did that day.

She chose Hayden. She chose her family. We all know the saying that you have to break a few eggs to make an omelet. That was true, of course, but in most cases, as in this one, the eggs were already broken, so the question becomes, Do you make an omelet or a mess?

"And yet," Pixie said, spreading her arms, "here we are. It's time for you to go, Hayden. Both of you."

Hayden was looking off. "The red stain," he said in a soft voice.

Gertrude closed her eyes. She didn't want to hear this again.

"There was a reason God gave him that on his face."

"It's a birthmark, Hayden."

"It's how they spotted him. There's a reason."

She knew that wasn't so. It wasn't fate or God's will or any of that. You see a street crossing. Millions of people cross that street every year. Nothing happens. Then one day, a combination of things—ice on the road maybe, a driver texting, too much drink, whatever—and a pedestrian gets hit and killed. It's a one-in-ten-million thing, but it isn't a coincidence. It happens. If it doesn't, there is no story.

That photograph was their one in ten million.

Or perhaps Hayden was right. Perhaps a higher entity wanted it to happen.

"Either way," Gertrude said, "it's time for you both to leave."

"It will look suspicious," Hayden said. "Rachel asks me for the amusement-park photos, and I suddenly end up out of the country?"

"Pixie, I have to tell you something . . ."

He'd sounded like such a little boy that night, but that's what men always sounded like when they were in trouble and needed to be saved. So she saved him. She saved her family. She saved them all. Again.

And had she saved Theo?

It didn't matter. She would keep this secret. Again.

She had also created a fresh secret, one about the boy, one that no one, not even Hayden, knew.

That didn't matter now. None of it did. Once again, Gertrude Payne was left to save the family. And so, no matter the cost to others, she would.

———

Max and Sarah were entering St. Barnabas Medical Center to question Cheryl Burroughs when Max's phone buzzed. He saw the incoming call was from Lauren.

"Give me a second," he said to Sarah.

He moved away from her so she couldn't hear. Sarah still eyed him. He put the phone to his ear and said, "What's up?"

"I got the paternity result," Lauren said.

She gave it to him. Then she said, "Do you want to tell me what the hell is going on?"

"Maybe nothing. Give me an hour."

He hung up the phone and came back to Sarah.

"Who was that?" she asked.

"Uh, my new guy."

"Again? He's kind of needy."

"Sarah—"

"Did you two meet at summer camp? Does he live in Canada?"

"Huh?"

"Who called, Max?"

"You'll see in a minute."

"What's that supposed to mean?"

"Where's Burroughs's ex-wife?"

"She's in her office."

"Let's go."

"Her new husband is here too," Sarah said. "Ronald Dreason."

Max thought about that. "Should we divide and conquer?"

"No, Max. I think we should stay together on this. I have him cooling off in another room."

He didn't protest. They moved down the corridor and into Cheryl Burroughs's office. Cheryl Burroughs greeted them professionally, as if they were there as patients. She sat behind her desk. They sat in the two chairs in front of it. The office was sparse. Max looked for the diplomas on the wall and saw none.

Sarah let Max take the lead. Max dove straight in.

"What did your ex-husband say to you?"

"Nothing."

Like with Hilde Winslow. Max shifted in the chair. "He came here to see you, no?"

"I don't know why he came here," she said.

"You didn't talk?"

"He ran out before he could say much."

Sarah and Max exchanged a look. Sarah sighed and took that one. "We have the security footage, Dr. Burroughs."

"It's Dreason now," she said.

Sarah was in a mood. "Yeah, whatever. Your ex-husband, the escaped convict who murdered your son, was in this very office for eight minutes before your husband entered. Are you telling us he didn't say anything in all that time?"

Cheryl took her time. She turned toward the office window and now Max could see the red in her eyes. She'd been crying, no question about it. "I'm not compelled to speak to you, am I?"

Sarah looked at Max. Max looked at Sarah.

"Why wouldn't you want to speak with us?" Sarah asked.

"I have patients. I would like you to leave."

Max figured that it was time to drop the bomb.

"Your ex-husband," he said. "He's not Matthew's father, is he?"

Both women stared at him stunned.

"What are you talking about?" Cheryl asked.

Sarah's face was asking the same question.

Cheryl said, "Of course David is Matthew's father."

"Are you sure?"

"What are you getting at, Agent Bernstein?"

Sarah was looking at him as though to say, I'd like to hear the answer too.

"When Matthew was murdered," Max continued, "you already knew your current husband, Ronald Dreason. Isn't that correct?"

"We were colleagues."

"You weren't sleeping together?"

Cheryl didn't rise to the bait. In an even tone she said, "We were not."

"You're sure?"

"Very," Cheryl said. "What are you getting at, Special Agent? Get to it, please."

"I visited the district attorney's office who handled your son's murder case. They still have Matthew's DNA on file."

Something in Cheryl's face was changing. He could see it.

"Your ex-husband's DNA is on file too. All convicted inmates have to submit a sample. So I had them do a paternity test."

Cheryl Dreason started to shake her head no.

"According to the test, David Burroughs, the man convicted of murdering Matthew Burroughs, is not the father of the boy found in the crib."

Sarah's eyes widened in surprise. "Max?"

Cheryl's voice was barely a whisper. "Oh my God . . ."

Max kept his eyes on Cheryl. "Dr. Dreason?"

She just kept shaking her head. "David was Matthew's father."

"The DA's results are conclusive."

"Oh my God." Tears sprang to her eyes. "Then David is right."

"About?"

"Matthew is still alive."

34

I have finally managed to access my old email account when Rachel turns into a parking lot at a PGA golf store off the Garden State Parkway. I am looking for an email from eight years ago. The search engine helps me find it. I read it just to make sure. Then I read it again.

"David?"

The PGA store parking lot is huge, much too large for the store, and I wonder what else is going to be built here. There is a car parked alone in the distant corner near the woods, a Toyota Highlander. I can see a golf course through a strip of trees. Convenient location, I guess.

"What happened with Cheryl?" Rachel asks.

"She went through with the sperm donation."

Silence.

"Did you know?" I ask.

"No." Her voice is soft. "David, I'm sorry."

"It doesn't change anything."

She doesn't reply to that.

"Even if I'm not the biological father, he's still my son," I say.

"I know."

"And he is mine. Not that it matters. But I know it."

"I know it too," Rachel says as she parks next to the Toyota Highlander.

A man in a Yankees cap gets out of the Highlander.

Rachel says to me, "Let's go."

She leaves the keys, and we head for the Highlander. The man in the Yankees cap says, "Drive out in the lane hugging the tree line. The CCTV doesn't cover that area."

We switch cars. Simple as that. Rachel's attorney arranged it. We both realized as soon as we left the hospital that we couldn't trust that Ronald wouldn't make a call or that somehow our covers weren't blown.

Rachel pulls back onto the highway. The man with the Yankees cap left us new burner phones on the car seat. We set them up so that any communications to our old burners will be forwarded to us. There is also a hammer inside one of those reusable grocery store bags. At a Burger King up the highway, I jump out with our old burners and the hammer. Once inside the bathroom, I close myself into a stall, obliterate the burners with the hammer, dump the remains in a garbage bin.

Rachel picked up food at the drive-thru. I always hated fast-food restaurants. Now a Whopper with fries feels like a religious experience. I scarf it down.

"What's our next move?" she asks.

"Only two leads left," I say, between bites. "The amusement park and the fertility clinic."

"I asked Hayden to get us all the pictures from the company photographers." We hit a red light. Rachel checks her phone. "In fact . . ."

"What?"

"Hayden came through."

"He sent the photos?"

The traffic light turns green, so Rachel says, "Let me pull over and take a look."

She veers onto the ramp for a Starbucks and parks. Rachel fiddles with the burner. "They're in some kind of cloud we have to access. The files are too big to download."

"Can we do that on a burner?"

"I think we're going to need a laptop or something. I have mine, but they might be able to track it."

"I think we need to take the chance."

"I have a VPN. That might be enough."

Rachel reaches into her bag and takes out a superthin laptop. She turns it on and gets to the relevant page. We don't want to stay on too long, so we fly through the photos. They are all taken in front of that corporate banner/backdrop.

"How long should we sit here and go through this?" she asks.

"I don't know. Maybe you should drive? A moving target might be harder to locate."

"I doubt it, but okay."

I keep going through the photographs. I speed through a bunch, but this feels like a waste of time. If you're going to an amusement park with a kidnapped boy, you don't pose in front of the welcoming screen. Or do you? It's been five years. He's grown. Everyone believes he's dead. No one is doubting it. So maybe you do. Maybe you figure enough time has passed. No one is going to spot a boy they believe is dead. And even if it is somewhat risky, what else can you do? Keep the boy locked up in a cage forever?

I skip around, but it all feels futile. I start blowing up photographs, trying to look in the deep background, because that, I figure, is where the gold lay. The files are so large that I can magnify and see pretty much every detail in every shot. At one point, I spot a little boy who might have been about the same age as Matthew, but when I zoom in, the similarities are only on the surface.

I hear a phone buzz. It is coming from Rachel's burner. She checks the number and picks it up. She signals for me to move closer so I can listen.

"Hello?"

"Can you talk?"

"Yes, Hester."

Hester Crimstein, I know, is Rachel's attorney.

"You're alone?" Hester asks. "Just say yes or no. Don't say any names."

She means my name, of course. In case someone is listening in.

"I'm not alone," Rachel says. "But it's safe to talk. What's up?"

"So the FBI just paid me a visit," Hester says. "Guess who is now considered a 'person of interest'?"

Rachel looks over at me.

"You, Rachel," Hester says. "You."

"Yeah, I kind of guessed that."

"They have you on video from your sister's hospital walking with an alleged escaped convict, so your cute new hair? It isn't a good disguise anymore. I told the FBI it's not you on the video. I also told them it's a photoshop. I also told them if it is you, you're clearly under duress. I told them some other stuff too, but I don't remember it all now."

"Any of that help?"

"Not a bit. They've issued an APB on you. A photo featuring your new do will be on the news any minute now. Fame awaits."

"Terrific," Rachel says. "Thanks for letting me know."

"One last word to the wise," Hester says. "To the world at large, your brother-in-law is an escaped murderer. The worst kind. A child killer. He stole a gun from a prison warden. He assaulted a police officer who remains hospitalized. Do you understand what I'm telling you?"

"I think so."

"So let me make it clear then. David Burroughs is considered armed and extremely dangerous. That's how he'll be treated. If he's found by law enforcement, they won't hesitate to shoot. You're my client, Rachel. I don't want any of my clients caught in a crossfire. Dead clients don't pay their legal bills."

Hester hangs up. I stare down at the computer screen at a picture of three men in their early thirties on a Ferris wheel. The men are all smiling. Their faces are red, and I wonder whether it's from sun or drink.

"You should let me do this on my own," I tell her.

Rachel says, "Shh."

I smile. She won't listen and I'm not going to push it hard anyway because I need her. My fingers are still fiddling with the screen, zooming in close, and then a thought comes to me.

"The picture of Matthew," I say.

"What about it?"

"You said your friend Irene showed you a bunch of photos?"

"Yes."

"How many?"

"I don't know. She probably blew up ten, fifteen of them."

"I assume after you saw Matthew, you looked through them all?"

"I did, yeah."

"How did she take them?"

"What do you mean?"

"Film, digital, phone—"

"Oh, right. Her husband Tom is a photo buff. But I don't know. I asked Irene about other photos, but she said that's it."

I turn toward her. "Can we reach Pretty-Funny Irene?"

"I tried right before I visited you, but they were in Aspen for a wedding. I think they came back last night. Why?"

"Maybe she or Tom can blow the picture up. Or other photos. Like we can do here. Get a better look. Or whoever brought Matthew there, I don't know but it seems they kept him away from the professional photographers. The only person we know who got a shot of him is Tom."

"So maybe we can find some other clue in his photos."

"Right."

Rachel mulls that over. "I can't just call Irene."

"Why not?"

"If I'm on the news as a person of interest and Irene sees that . . ."

"She may call it in," I finish for her.

"I would say it's likely. She's certainly not going to welcome me with open arms."

"She might not be here at all."

"We can't take that chance, David."

She's right. "Where do the Longleys live?" I ask.

"Stamford."

"That's only about an hour from here."

"So what's our plan, David? We just drive up and I ring her doorbell and say I want to look at the photos?"

"Sure."

"She might call the police then too."

"If she heard the reports, you'll see it on her face and we can run."

Rachel frowns. "Risky."

"I think it's a chance we have to take. Let's head up that way and then we can decide."

———

The orphanage in the tiny Balkan nation called the baby Milo.

Milo had been left for dead in a public bathroom. No one knew who his parents were, so he was brought to the orphanage. He looked healthy, but he cried all the time. He was in pain. A doctor diagnosed him with Melaine syndrome, a rare but fatal inherited condition caused by a faulty gene. A child rarely survives past the age of five.

Under most circumstances, a boy like Milo would be dead within weeks. Reaching the age of five and living in any kind of comfort would require a massive amount of money, and even this orphanage, one of many funded by a generous American family, wouldn't use that much of its limited resources on a child who had no chance. One would have to use extreme measures at great cost to prolong a life that would be miserable and painful in any event.

Better, most would agree, to arrange for a peaceful, even merciful, death.

Except that wasn't what happened.

Hayden Payne, a member of the generous American family, heard about this boy's plight. Why a scion of the Payne fortune would hear about this particular case or take such a strong interest no one was certain. People gossiped, of course, but unbeknownst to most working there, Hayden had put in a request that if a boy matching this general size and physical description was located, he should be notified. When Hayden heard the boy was also in ill health, his interest became more acute. Why such a man would care to find a boy fitting this specific profile was a question no one at the orphanage dared to ask.

Why? Simple. Because the Paynes funded the orphanage.

Whatever their shortcomings, the facts were the facts: No Paynes, no orphanage, no saved children, no jobs.

To everyone who witnessed Hayden with the little boy, however—and that wasn't a great number of people—Hayden Payne was a godsend. He did all he could for Milo. This was so important to Hayden. He did all in his power to make certain that the little boy's short life would be rich with pleasure. No expense was spared. Nearly every day, Hayden took the boy on exciting adventures. Milo was a fireman for a day and got to ride on a big truck. He was a policeman on another and loved pressing the siren button as they drove. Hayden took the boy to football matches where he got to suit up with the players and watch from the field. Hayden took Milo to horse races and car races and town fairs and zoos and aquariums.

Hayden made Milo's short life as great as it could be.

He didn't have to, of course, but this became important to Hayden. The truth was, if Hayden hadn't intervened, Milo would have died long ago and in pain. Thanks to Hayden— thanks to Hayden's generosity—the boy's limited days were happy and fun-filled. In Hayden's mind, he should be commended for what he did. He didn't have to do it this way. He could have been more pragmatic about it. He could have taken a healthy child that no one would miss. That would have been easier for Hayden. It would have worked far better because then Hayden could have done the deed faster and with less risk. But no, Hayden bided his time instead. He did the right thing. The moral thing. He found a life that would have been lost anyway, made it special and sparkly. All of us have a limited time here on Earth. We understand that. Milo's time was both extended and tremendously enhanced because of Hayden Payne.

And then one day, when the time was right, when the boy was exactly the right size and weight, when the plan was laid out perfectly and, even with the medicine, little Milo was starting to suffer again, Hayden flew him on a private jet to the United States. He drove him to a home in Massachusetts. He gave the boy a small sedative, one that wouldn't show up in the bloodstream, just enough so he wouldn't feel anything. He took him upstairs to the other boy's bedroom. He gave the other boy the same sedative and brought him to the car. He had already made sure the whiskey, the father's favorite, contained a slightly stronger sedative.

Then Hayden put Milo in the other boy's Marvel-themed pajamas.

Milo was asleep in bed when Hayden raised the baseball bat above his head. He closed his eyes and thought about Professor Tyler and that bully in eighth grade and that girl who wouldn't stop screaming, all the times he had lashed out before, always with good reason. He channeled that rage and opened his eyes.

Hayden hoped and believed that the first blow killed Milo.

Then he raised the bat again. And again. And again. And again.

When he arrived with the boy at the Payne estate, when he finally could feel safe, that, oddly enough, was when Hayden Payne started to panic.

"Pixie, I have to tell you something . . ."

What had he done? After all the planning, all the years waiting to make this wrong finally right, why was he suddenly

consumed with doubt? Suppose, he voiced to his grandmother, he had made a terrible mistake. Suppose the boy
wasn't really his. Could he somehow go back in time and
make it all okay?

Was it too late?

But as always, Pixie had been the prudent, calm, rational
one. She sent Stephano to make sure Hayden had made
no mistakes, left no clues that could lead them to Payne.
Then just to quiet any doubts, she had Hayden do a paternity test. It took a full day for the results to come back—a
day that felt like an eternity to Hayden—but in the end, Pixie
proudly announced that the test confirmed that Hayden had
done the right thing.

Theo—once known as Matthew—was his son.

Pixie's voice knocked him back to the present. "Hayden?"

He cleared his throat. "Yes, Pixie."

"You sent her the photographs," Gertrude said.

"From two of the four photographers," Hayden said. "They
were nowhere near where we were. I also looked through
them myself."

"Either way, I think you and Theo should go now."

"We'll leave in the morning," Hayden said.

35

We pull up to Irene and Tom Longley's three-bedroom ranch on Barclay Drive in North Stamford. I looked up the house on Zillow while we drove. It sits on a one-acre corner lot and is valued at $826,000. There are two and a half bathrooms and an in-ground pool in the back.

I lay in the backseat, a blanket over me so I stay out of sight. Barclay Drive is a cookie-cutter suburban street. A man sitting alone in a car will draw attention.

"You okay?" Rachel asks.

"Peachy."

Rachel has her burner. She calls mine. I answer. We do a quick test where she speaks and I listen. Now I'll be able to hear her conversation with Irene or Tom or whoever answers the door, if indeed someone is home. Primitive but hopefully effective.

"I left the keys in the car," she says. "If something goes wrong, just take off."

"Got it. I have the gun too. If you're caught, just tell the cops I forced you."

She frowns at me. "Yeah no."

I burrow back down and wait. We don't have headphones of any kind, so I press the phone against my ear. It feels weird hiding in the backseat of a car, but that's the least of my issues.

Through the phone, I hear Rachel's footsteps and then the faint echo of the doorbell.

A few seconds pass. Then I hear Rachel say softly, "Someone's coming."

The door opens and I hear a woman's voice say, "Rachel?"

"Hey, Irene."

"What are you doing here?"

I don't like that tone. No doubt in my mind: She knows about the APB. I wonder how Rachel is going to play it.

"Do you know those pictures you showed me from the amusement park?"

Irene is confused: "What?"

"Were they digital?"

"Yes. Wait, that's why you're here?"

"I took a photo of one with my camera."

"I saw that."

"I'm wondering whether I could see the others again. Or the files."

Silence. It's not a silence I like.

"Listen," Irene says, "can you just wait here and give me a second?"

I know what I'm about to do is stupid, but I'm working off

363

instinct again. Instinct is overrated. Going with your gut is the lazy man's way. It's an excuse to not think or consider or do the heavy lifting needed in good decision-making.

But I have no time for that.

When I roll out of the car, the gun is already in my hand.

I sprint toward the front door. Even from this distance I can see Irene's eyes go wide in surprise. She freezes. That's good for me. My worry is that she will step back into the house and close the door. But I have the gun raised.

Rachel says, "David?" but she doesn't have time for the "what the hell are you doing?" before I reach Irene and say in a half yell/half whisper, "Don't move."

"Oh my God, please don't hurt me!"

Rachel shoots me a look. I shoot her one back saying I had no choice.

"Look, Irene," I say. "I just don't want you to call the police. I won't hurt you."

But her hands are up and her eyes are growing wider.

"We just need to see the photos," I say to her. I lower the gun and take out the photograph in my pocket. "Do you see that boy? The one in the background."

She is too terrified to take her eyes off me.

"Look," I say a little too loudly. "Please?"

Rachel says, "Let's move this inside, okay?"

We do. Irene only has eyes for the gun. I feel bad about this. No matter how this turns out, she will never be the same. She will know fear. She will lose sleep. She lost something today, and I took it from her the moment I took out the gun. That's

what any kind of threat or violence does to a person. It stays
with them. For good.

"I'm not going to hurt you," I say, but I'm babbling now.
"I've spent the last five years in jail for killing my son. I didn't
do it. That's him in the picture. That's why I escaped. That's
why Rachel and I are here. We are trying to find my boy.
Please help us."

She doesn't believe me. Or maybe she doesn't care. Instinct
is working here for her too. The most primal instinct—survival.

"He's telling the truth," Rachel adds.

Again I don't think it matters.

"What do you want from me?" Irene asks in a panicked voice.

"Just the pictures," I say. "That's all."

Three minutes later, we are in Irene's kitchen. There are
dozens of photos stuck to the refrigerator of Irene and Tom
and the two boys. She sits at the kitchen block and with a
shaking hand, she opens her laptop. I notice the way she
keeps glancing at the refrigerator. I don't know if she's finding strength in her family or reminding me that she has one.

"It's going to be fine," I tell Irene. "I promise."

That doesn't seem like much of a comfort to her. I feel the
pang again, not for myself, but for what I'm doing to her. She's
an innocent in all this. I try to find some consolation in the
fact that when I'm vindicated, whatever hint of PTSD that
I'm leaving her with today may vanish.

"What do you want me to do?" Irene asks.

Rachel tries to put a comforting hand on her shoulder.
Irene shrugs it off.

"Just bring up the photographs from that day, please," I say.

Irene mistypes, probably due to nerves. I have tucked the gun away so that she can't see it anymore, but it remains the proverbial elephant in the room. Eventually she clicks on a folder and a bunch of thumbnails start crisscrossing the screen.

She stands up from the stool and gestures for one of us to take over. Rachel sits and clicks on the first photograph. It's of one of the boys grinning and pointing at a huge green roller coaster behind him.

"Can I go now?" Irene asks. Her voice is shaky.

"I'm sorry," I say as gently as I can. "You'll call the police."

"I won't. I promise."

"Just stay with us another minute, okay?"

What choice does she have? I'm the guy with the gun. We start clicking through the photographs. There are more shots involving roller coasters mixed in with shots of costumed characters and some kind of water-dolphin show, that kind of thing. We scour through the background of every photograph.

Eventually we land on the photograph that launched all this. I point to it and ask Irene, "The boy in the background. Do you remember him at all?"

She looks at me as though my face will hold the correct answer.

"I don't. I'm sorry."

"He has a port-stain birthmark on his face. Does that help?"

"No, I'm sorry. I don't . . . he's just in the background. I don't remember him. I'm sorry."

Rachel zooms in and right away I feel my heart race. The

online quality of the photograph is excellent, especially against the version I saw in that visitors' room, where Rachel snapped a photo of the photo and then had it printed out. I don't know how many pixels this file has, but as she gets closer to the boy's face, pressing the plus key to slowly zoom in, I feel my entire body well up. I risk a quick glance at Rachel. She is seeing it too. The blur is gone. Soon the boy's face takes up the entire screen.

We look at each other. No doubt about it anymore.

It's Matthew.

Or again, is that just a projection on our part? Want becoming reality. I don't know. I don't care. But as I start to wonder whether this is a dead end, Rachel starts to hit the right arrow key. The image slowly moves off the boy's face.

"What are you doing?" I ask.

Rachel doesn't respond. She hits the right arrow key some more. We are traveling up Matthew's little arm toward his hand. And when we do, when we reach his hand, I hear Rachel gasp out loud.

"Rachel."

"Oh my God."

"What?"

She points to the man's hand gripping my son's. "That ring," she says.

I can see the purple stone and school crest. I squint and try to get a better look. "Looks like a graduation ring."

"It is," she says. Then she turns to me. "It's from Lemhall University."

36

"Do you want to tell me what the hell is going on, Max?"

Sarah was driving. Max was in the passenger seat. Her eyes were on the road, but it felt like her gaze was boring through his skin.

"I'm not sure Burroughs did it."

"Did what?"

"Killed his kid."

"You're a defense attorney now?"

"No," Max said. "I'm a law enforcement officer."

"Who is assigned to capture an escaped convict," Sarah said. "If he didn't do it, there are courts and laws and an entire legal system that can remedy that. It's not your job. It's not my job. Our job is to bring him in."

"Our job is about justice."

"He broke out of prison."

"That's up for debate."

"What?"

"He had help. We both know that."

"You're talking about the warden."

"Yes. I spoke to him."

Max filled her in. Sarah's face reddened.

"My God," Sarah said. "We need to arrest Mackenzie."

"Sarah—"

"Are you listening to yourself, Max? You're being played."

"The DNA test—"

"—shows he's not the father. Big whoop. If anything, this hurts his case."

"How so?" Max asked.

"The wife. The one we just visited. She's not telling us everything. You can see that, right?"

"Right."

"It's pretty simple, Max. She had an affair. Or a boyfriend. Heck, probably with her current husband. Maybe Matthew is his son, that Dreason guy's, and David Burroughs found that out."

"So Burroughs killed the little boy?"

"Sure, why not? You think he's the first cuckold to kill an offspring? But either way—and I need you to listen to this, Max—we have a legal system to remedy these things. A perfect system? No. In your free time, you can go through all the prisons and find innocent people who have been incarcerated and help free them. Do it. I'll admire it. But don't break them out of prison, Max. Don't give them guns. Don't let them destroy whatever is left of our tattered, flawed system.

We need to capture Burroughs. That's it. He's an armed and dangerous felon. We need to treat him like one. You got that?"

"I want to know if he did it or not."

"Then I'm calling this in," Sarah said.

"What do you mean?"

"I'm getting you removed from this case, Max. You don't belong on it."

"You'd do that to me?"

"I love you," Sarah said. "I also love our oaths and our legal system. You're not seeing straight."

Her phone buzzed. She answered it. "Jablonski."

"Burroughs just broke into a home in Connecticut. He held a woman hostage at gunpoint."

———

What else could I do?

I couldn't shoot Irene Longley. I couldn't tie her up. That all looks good on television, but the practicality of it made no sense. I guess if we had more time, we could have taken her phone and locked her in a closet, but she was trying to get us out of the house fast because her boys would be home and so they'd find her and again did I want to leave this poor woman with any more mental scars, not to mention what finding their mother locked in a closet would do to two young boys?

So we begged her not to call the police. We explained as best we could that we were trying to rescue my son. She nodded, but as I've now mentioned several times, she was only doing this to placate me. She wasn't listening. And so we drove fast and hoped for the best.

What else could we do?

The police would find us. It was only a question of time. We debated changing license plates with a car in a lot again or trying to get Hester Crimstein to send us another vehicle or even just taking an Uber. We concluded that any of that would just slow us down.

In the end, the drive from Irene's house to the Payne estate would be a little over two hours. The police had no idea where we were going. It was best, Rachel and I decided, to go for it.

We were now at the end game. There was no reason to run anymore.

Rachel has given me the wheel now. I am driving over the speed limit but not fast enough for us to get stopped. It is odd to be driving a car after five years. It isn't like I forgot or anything. The old line about never forgetting how to ride a bike applies to cars too, I guess. But the experience, after spending the last five years in a cage, is strangely invigorating. I am focused solely on finding my son, on rescuing him, on learning the truth about what happened on that horrible night. That was the only reason I wanted to escape. I didn't care about freedom for myself. But now that I'm out, now that I am tasting what life used to be like, I can't help but want to be free. I am not saying it was something I took for granted. It just didn't matter with Matthew gone.

"I don't understand this," Rachel says to me. "Why would Matthew be with Hayden Payne?"

I have some theories, but I don't want to voice them yet.

"Should I call him?" she asks.

"Hayden?"

"Yes."

"And say what?"

She considers this. "I don't know."

"We have to drive up there."

"And then what, David? They have a gate. They have security."

"I'll hide in the back again."

"Seriously?"

"We can't tip him off, Rachel."

"I get that, but I also can't just show up out of the blue. We don't even know if Hayden is home."

In a sense, it doesn't matter. There is only one direction for us now. The Payne estate in Newport on Easton Bay. If Hayden Payne isn't there, we park somewhere nearby and hide and wait.

He has my son.

"Maybe we should call the police," Rachel says.

"And tell them what?"

"That Matthew is alive and we believe Hayden Payne has him."

"And what do you think the police will do with that information? Issue a warrant on one of the country's wealthiest families off . . . off what? That photograph?"

She doesn't reply.

"And if that boy becomes a threat to the Payne dynasty, do

you think they'll produce him—or do you think they'll get rid of the evidence?"

I drive, spending too much time looking in my rearview mirror, convinced that any moment I'll see the flashing lights of a squad car. We are making good time.

"Look at my phone," I tell Rachel.

"What?"

"I took a screenshot of an old email. Look at it."

She does. When she puts the phone back down, she asks, "Do you want to talk about it?"

"No time now. We need to focus on this first."

Rachel and I come up with a plan of sorts as we hit RI-102 South. She picks up her mobile and calls Hayden.

I can hear the phone ringing. My heart is in my throat.

"Rachel?"

His voice. Hayden Payne's. I hear it and I know. He has my son. He took him from me. I think I even get why now, but none of that matters.

Rachel clears her throat. "Hey, Hayden."

"Are you all right?"

"I'm fine."

"Did you get the photographs I sent you?"

"I did, thank you. That's why I'm calling. Can I come see you?"

"When?"

"Like, in ten minutes."

"I'm at the Payne estate."

"Yeah, I'm just driving into Newport. Can I come by?"

There is a long pause. Rachel looks over to me. I try to keep my breathing even. Another second passes. Rachel can't take it.

"I want to talk to you about a few of the photos."

"Do you think you see this mystery boy in any of them?" he asks.

"No, I think you were right about that, Hayden."

"Oh?"

"I don't think Matthew is in any of the pictures. I think my nephew died five years ago. But I think someone is trying to set David up."

"Set him up how?"

"I need your help in identifying some of the people in the photos."

"Rachel, thousands of our employees were at the event. I've been overseas. I don't really know—"

"But you can still help, right? I just need to show you the people I mean and maybe you can ask around? I'm almost at your gate. Can you just help me with this?"

"Is David with you?"

"What? No."

"The police think you're involved in his escape. It's on the news."

"He's not with me," she says.

"Do you know where he is?"

And now Rachel sees her opening. "Not on the phone, Hayden. I'll be there in five minutes."

She hangs up. We find a quiet spot to pull over and move

fast. I open the back hatch door and squeeze in. There is a black plastic top to hide whatever you might store in there. I fold myself down and drop it on top of myself. I'm hidden. We call each other so I can hear all. Rachel takes the wheel.

I lay in darkness. Five minutes later, Rachel says, "I'm pulling up to the guardhouse."

I hear muffled conversation and then I hear Rachel say her name. I don't know what's going on, of course. I'm in a dark hatch. I try to stay perfectly still.

Rachel says in a faux cheery voice, "Thank you!" and we start moving again.

"David, can you hear me?"

I take the phone off mute. "I'm here."

"In about fifteen seconds I'm going to pull around the curve I told you about. You ready?"

"Yes."

We had discussed this. The road up to the estate is lined with emerald evergreens. There is something of a blind curve, Rachel told me, where I can hop out and duck behind the trees and perhaps—*perhaps*—not be seen.

"Now," she says.

The car stops. I ease out of the back, hit the ground, shut the back hatch. It takes me no more than three seconds. I keep low and roll behind an evergreen. She continues to drive. I move to the other side of the shrub. When I stand up, the view laid out before me is beyond awe-inspiring. The Payne estate is built on a cliff. In the distance, over an expanse of green, I can see the waves of the Atlantic Ocean. The lawn has gardens that must be manicured by the gods. There are shrubs shaped as animals, as people, as skyscrapers even. The fountain in the middle is a large-scale sculpture, modern, a giant head seemingly made of mirrors with water spouting from the mouth. It reminded me of the *Metalmorphosis* by David Cerny down in North Carolina. The mansion is up to the right. You'd expect an old opulent masterpiece, but the Paynes had gone with something white and cubist. Still, despite the modernity, I can see climbing vines and ivy along the side. To the left is what appears to be a golf course. I can only see two holes, but this is private grounds along the prime real estate of Easton Bay, so how many holes would make sense? There are two waterfalls and what looks like an infinity pool blended into the ocean.

There is no one outside. It is silent other than distant echoes of the crashing waves.

So what now?

Our plan, which we admit is piss-poor, is for me to skulk around the property and see whether I can spot . . . anything really. Ideally, Matthew. I know, I know, but what other plan is there? Rachel is going to talk to Hayden. Confront him even. And if none of that worked, if we couldn't find Matthew or any clues . . .

I still have the gun.

I feel oddly safe. I assume, of course, that Pretty-Funny Irene has called the police. At some point, they will find traffic cameras or whatever and may be able to trace us into Newport, but we still have time. Or at least I think that we do.

I make my way up the drive, sticking close to the ever-greens. When I'm close enough to see the front door, I duck down and watch. Rachel heads for the door. I'm probably fifty or sixty yards away. The estate, no surprise, is massive.

When Rachel approaches the front door, it opens.

Hayden Payne steps out.

37

Gertrude Payne finished her laps in the indoor pool. She had been doing forty-five minutes of pool laps every day for the past thirty years. She mostly stayed here in Newport, but her mansion in Palm Beach and the ranch in Jackson Hole also had both indoor and outdoor pools. They were important to her. The exercise was great, of course. She swam slower than she used to, which was hardly a surprise at her age. When she was young, she had wanted to be a competitive swimmer, but she'd been maddeningly caught up in a time when her father still believed "girls' sports" were a waste of time. Still, she loved the water, the quiet of it, the utter stillness in your head where the dominant sound was the steady rhythm of your own breathing.

One of her great-grandsons called it "Pixie's little mental health break."

He wasn't wrong.

As she slipped out of the water, Stephano was holding a towel for her.

"What's wrong?"

"Rachel Anderson has just arrived."

He filled her in on Hayden's call with his old college chum. They'd been monitoring Hayden's calls since Burroughs had broken out of prison. Hayden could be irrational and child-like. He worked off emotion and could vacillate with the best of them.

When he finished, Pixie said, "What should we do?"

"This is spinning out of control," Stephano said.

"You don't buy that she wants his help identifying someone in the photograph?"

Stephano frowned. "Do you?"

"No. Do you have a plan?"

"According to the news reports, Rachel Anderson is aiding and abetting a convicted child killer with his escape from a federal penitentiary," Stephano began in his customary matter-of-fact way. He never raised or lowered his voice. He was always calm, always in control, never flustered or ruffled, no matter how dire the situation. "I will put this coldly. We should grab her when she is here. We find out where David Burroughs is hiding. She has to know. We find him. We make them both vanish. For good. I get one of my people to drive her car out so if the police find out she was here, we have evidence she drove out. If asked, we say she asked to see some photographs."

"So they just . . . vanish?" Gertrude said.

"Yes."

"The police will think, what, that they escaped?"

"Probably. They will continue their search, of course."

"But they will never find them."

"Never," Stephano said.

"Suppose they told someone already."

Stephano smiled. "No one would believe it. And even if they did, between your attorneys and my work, we would shut it down hard."

Gertrude thought about it. In a way, this was not unique. The best way to get rid of any problem is to get *rid* of the problem.

"There really is no other way, is there?"

Stephano did not reply. There was no need.

"So when does Rachel arrive?"

"She's just pulled in," Stephano said. "I'm just waiting for your approval."

"You have it."

————

Hayden stepped outside and hugged Rachel. She let him, doing her best not to squirm away or even cringe. But now she knew. There was no question about it. She could feel it in him now—the lies, the deception, the evil. He had hinted at it to her so often over the years. His propensity for violence. The times his family had covered it up. She had accepted it, embraced it even, because it had benefited her. He had saved her that night. She knew that. And so her vision of him became skewed. Part of her knew that. Part of her could feel something wrong in him, but she'd allowed herself to be deceived. He had helped her. He was also rich and powerful and in truth, being around that was fun and exciting.

"It's good to have you here again," Hayden said, still holding her against him. "It's been too long since you've been to Payne."

When he backed away and looked at her face, she tried to smile through it.

"What's wrong?" Hayden asked.

"Can we just take a walk through the gardens?"

"Of course. I thought you had photographs you wanted to show me."

"I'll show you in a bit. I want to talk first, if that's okay."

Hayden nodded. "That would be nice."

They walked in silence toward the side yard. Up ahead, Rachel could see the mirrored-head fountain and hear the ocean in the background.

"Beautiful, isn't it?" he said.

"Yes."

"You are seeing it the same as I am, aren't you?"

"I'm not sure what you mean, Hayden."

"We both see this beauty. We both experience the same thing. We have employees here. We have people who work inside the house and outside the house. They have eyes, just like mine, and see the same view I do. We experience it the same. There's no special platform here just for the rich. So why are they so envious? We see the same thing. We can experience the same pleasure."

Hayden liked to do this, she knew—justify his wealth in various ways. This was not a rabbit hole she wanted to go down right now. She scanned down the row of hedges looking for David, but he was either well hidden or not there.

"Hayden?"

"Yes?"

"I know."

"Know what?"

"You have Matthew."

"Pardon?"

"Can we just skip the denials? I know, okay? You made up the Italian actress. You moved overseas so no one would see the boy. Your family is uber rich, but you're not gossip fodder, so it isn't as though paparazzi are dying to take pictures of this son you're supposedly raising."

Hayden walked with his hands behind his back. He looked up at the sky and squinted.

"I was able to get the digital file of that photograph and blow it up," she continued. "The boy in the picture is holding a man's hand. The hand is yours, Hayden."

"And you can tell that how?"

"Your ring."

"Do you think I'm the only one with a graduation ring?"

"Were you at the amusement park? Yes or no?"

"And if I say no?"

"I won't believe you," Rachel said. "Whose body was in Matthew's bed?"

"You sound crazy, Rachel."

"I wish I was. I really do. David came up with a theory."

"David Burroughs," Hayden said, forcing up a chuckle. "The escaped convict you're abetting."

"Yes."

"Oh, I'm dying to hear it."

"He thinks you were in love with me."

"Does he now?"

"I saw it somewhat. I mean, that you had a crush on me in college. I figured it was because we bonded over something so awful."

"By 'so awful,'" Hayden said, with just a hint of steel in his voice, "do you mean when I saved you from being raped?"

"Yes, Hayden, that's exactly what I mean."

"You should be grateful."

"I was. I am. But we handled it wrong. We should have reported it. Let the chips fall where they may."

"I would have ended up expelled or worse."

"Then maybe that's what should be."

"For saving you?"

"Yeah, well, if that's the case, then the powers that be would have understood. But we will never know. Instead, we kept it a secret. And that's what always happens with the Paynes, isn't it, Hayden? Your family uses its resources to bury what they don't want to see."

"Oh yes," Hayden said. "The rich are bad. What an intriguing insight."

"It isn't a question of good or bad. There is no accountability."

"Do you believe in God, Rachel?"

383

"What difference does that make?"

"I do. I believe in God. And look what He gave me." He spread his arms and circled. "Look, Rachel. Look at what God gave the Payne family. Do you think that was just happenstance?"

"Actually, I do."

"Nonsense. Do you know why the rich feel special? Because they are. You either believe in a just God that rewarded us— or you believe the world is chaos and random luck. Which do you believe?"

"Chaos and random luck," Rachel said. "Where's Matthew, Hayden?"

"No, no, I want to hear David's theory. You were saying that he felt I was in love with you. So go on from there."

"You were, weren't you?"

He stopped, turned toward her, spread his arms. "Who's to say I'm not right now?"

"And when I asked Barb Matteson to make an appointment for Cheryl at the fertility clinic, she told you, didn't she?"

"And if she did?"

"You would have been upset. You wanted me for yourself. Now suddenly I'm going to have a baby with donor sperm. That made no sense to you, did it?"

Hayden grinned. "Do you have your phone on you?"

"I do."

"Let me have it."

"Why?"

"I want to make sure you're not recording this."

She hesitated. He was still grinning like a crazy man. She glanced around again, trying with as much subtlety as she could to see David. No sign of him.

"Give me your phone, Rachel."

His voice had an edge now. No choice. She reached into her pocket, hoping to find the red hang-up button so she could disconnect the call before he saw it, but he grabbed her hand to stop her.

"Ow! What the hell, Hayden?"

He reached into her pocket, took the phone from it, looked at the screen.

"What kind of phone is this?"

"It's a burner."

He stared down at it. "I want to hear the rest of your theory, Rachel."

"How did you feel when you heard I was getting donor sperm?" she asked.

"The same way I felt whenever you got some contemptuous, pathetic new boyfriend. What a waste."

"It should have been you," Rachel said.

"It should have been me. I rescued you, Rachel. You should have been mine."

"Your family owned the fertility clinic."

"Go on."

"So it would have been easy to set up. Did you threaten someone or pay them off?"

"I rarely see a need to threaten. Money and NDAs are usually enough."

"You made sure that they used *your* sperm for the donation."

Hayden closed his eyes and smiled and lifted his face toward the sky. *me*

"It's only you and I here, Hayden. Might as well come clean."

"I wish you hadn't done this."

"Done what?"

He shook his head, the smile gone now.

"What did you think would happen, Hayden?"

"I thought that you'd have my son. That I'd tell you about it later."

"And that would make me fall in love with you?"

"Perhaps. Either way, we would be a family, wouldn't we? At worst, you'd push me away and raise my child. But chances are, you'd let me in your life. You're not immune to my family's influence. Remember that spring break when we took the family plane to that mansion in Antigua? Your face, Rachel. You loved it. You loved the parties. You loved the power. It's part of why we became close. So yes, my plan was to impregnate you. Why would you want some anonymous donor sperm when you can have mine?"

"Someone special in the eyes of God," she added.

"Exactly. Great genes. Someone who cares about you. It made perfect sense."

"Except, of course, I never went to the clinic."

"Yes. Your charade fooled everyone at Berg. It's ironic when you think about it. Here you are, talking about how destructive my family was with burying secrets—"

"—when my sister and I were doing the exact same thing."

"Yes, Rachel."

"When did you figure out it was Cheryl and not me?"

"When you never got pregnant—and Cheryl did. So I went to the Berg clinic you supposedly visited. I showed the doctor your photograph. She didn't recognize you. Then I showed her Cheryl's photo . . ."

He shrugged.

"And then?"

"Then I waited. I planned. I watched. David was falling apart anyway. You know that, don't you? The marriage wasn't going to last. What Cheryl did. That lie ate him up. I think he always knew the boy wasn't his. So I kept an eye on them. I remained patient."

"You killed another child."

"No, Rachel."

"Someone was murdered that night."

"That was part of the delay. I waited. I gave that child a spectacular life."

"What does that even mean?"

"It's not important."

"It is to me."

"No, Rachel, all that concerns you is the little boy whom I rescued that night. My son."

"You set David up for the murder."

"Not really. When that old woman testified at the trial about seeing him with the baseball bat, I confess that I was shocked. Do you know what I thought?"

"Tell me."

"That he started to believe he had done it, so he buried the bat himself. Later I learned there was some grudge against his father. But no, I didn't intend to send David to prison for life. None of this was his fault. He had done his best in raising my son. I didn't want to hurt him more than necessary."

"Why such extreme measures?"

"What else could I do, Rachel? I couldn't admit I had made my clinic use my sample." He held up his hand. "And before you get all high and mighty, let's remember who started all this. You and your sister. Your lies."

There was, Rachel knew, some truth to that. "So who knows?"

"Pixie, of course. Stephano. That's about it. I brought my son here when I made the switch. I confess I was in a panic. I worried I had made a terrible mistake. Pixie ran a paternity test. It came back that the boy was mine. We stayed at the Payne estate for almost six months. I never left the property. The boy was upset at first. He cried a lot. He didn't sleep. He missed his mother and . . . and David. But kids adapt. We named him Theo. We came up with the cover story about the Italian actress. Eventually I took him overseas. I put him in the most exclusive boarding school in Switzerland. And I waited for that damn birthmark to fade away. The doctor said it would. But it didn't. It stayed there, stubbornly. And yes, no one was looking for Matthew. He was dead, not missing. But the resemblance between him now and the boy taken . . ."

"Hayden?"

"What?"

"We can still make this work."

"How?"

"Give Matthew back."

"Just like that?"

"No one has to know where he was or who had him."

"Oh, come on. Of course they will. And you can't prove any of this, Rachel. You know that. You'll never get your hands on the boy, and if you do, do you really think you'll be able to compel a Payne to take a DNA test? Besides, the DNA test will show what? That I'm the father and Cheryl is the mother. I'll say Cheryl and I had an affair."

It was then that David stepped out from behind the shrub. The two men just stared at one another.

Then David said, "Where's my son?"

38

"Where's my son?" I say.

I stare at this man who destroyed my life. My whole body is quaking.

Rachel says, "David."

"Call the police, Rachel."

"She can't," Hayden says. "I have her phone. It wouldn't matter anyway. The police wouldn't be allowed on this property without a warrant." He steps toward me. "But David, I think we can make this work."

I glance at Rachel, then back at him. "Where is Matthew?"

"There is no Matthew. You killed him. If you mean Theo—"

I don't need to hear this. I start toward the house. I'll tear it apart if I have to. I don't care anymore. I'm going to see my son again.

They both follow me. "Don't you want to hear my proposal?" Hayden asks.

I make a fist. He's too far away for me to hit him with it. "No."

"He's not your son. I'm sure you know that by now. But you were wronged. I always felt bad about that—about you taking the fall, about you ending up in prison. So let me help. Listen to me, David. The Paynes have means. We can get you out of the country, set you up with a new identity—"

"You're a lunatic."

"No, listen to me."

And that's it. We are about twenty yards from the front door now. I turn and rush him and grab him by the throat with one hand.

I hear Rachel again say, "David."

But I don't care. I am about to throw Hayden Payne to the ground when I hear another voice, a man's, calmly say, "Okay, that's enough."

The man is heavyset with dark hair. He wears a black suit.

He also has a gun in his hand.

"Let him go, David," the man says.

The man speaks casually, softly even, but there is something in the tone that makes you pull up and listen closely. His eyes are cold and dead in a way I've seen too often in prison.

And right there and then, I have an epiphany.

I don't know if that's the right word, but it's close enough. It all happens in less than a second. I know men like him. I know the situation. I know that he is armed and on a private residence. I know that he is here to kill me. I know in the end I have to protect Rachel and Matthew and that for me, there are no consequences.

With all that in mind, I move very fast.

I still have my hand around Hayden's throat. I pull him in front of me, using him for the briefest of moments as a shield.

With my free hand, I pull out my gun.

This isn't the first time I've handled a gun. My father was a police officer. He was big on gun safety. He and Uncle Philip used to take Adam and me to the range with them In Everett on Saturday afternoons. I became a pretty good shot, not so much with stationary targets, but the simulation exercises where cardboard cutouts pop up at random times. Sometimes it would be a bad guy. Sometimes it would be an innocent civilian. I wasn't the best at differentiating the two, but I remember what my father taught me.

No head shots. No aiming for the legs or trying to wound. Aim for the center mass of the torso and leave yourself the most room for error.

The man quickly sees what I am doing.

He raises his weapon. But my boldness, the suddenness of my actions, plus using Hayden Payne as a temporary shield, gives me the advantage.

I fire three times.

And the man goes down.

Hayden screams and runs toward the front door. I turn to follow him, but then I spot another man pulling out a gun.

No hesitation.

I fire three more times.

This guy goes down too.

I don't know whether the two men are dead or injured. I don't care. Hayden is inside the door.

I run toward the first fallen man. His eyes are closed, but I think he's still breathing. I don't have time to check. I bend down and pry the gun from his hand. Then I turn back toward Rachel.

"Come on!" I shout.

Rachel does. We hurry toward the front door. I worry that it may be locked, but it's not. Who needs to lock a front door when you live in a place like this? We enter the foyer. I close the door behind me and hand her one of the guns.

"David?"

"For protection. In case anyone tries to get in."

"Where are you going?"

But she knows. I'm already heading up the stairs where I hear running footsteps. I don't know how many armed men they have. I have already shot two men. I don't care how many more I'll need to shoot. I just worry about the bullet count.

The home is pure white, sterile, almost institutional. There are very few splashes of color. Not that I see any of that. Sound echoes. I follow it.

"Theo!"

Hayden's voice.

I tighten my grip on the gun and continue down the corridor. An old woman steps out into it and says, "Hayden? What's going on?"

"Pixie, look out!"

When the old woman turns, our eyes meet. Hers widen in recognition. She knows who I am. I hurry down the corridor where I heard Hayden's voice. The old woman doesn't move. She stands and stares in defiance. I'm not ready to bowl over an old woman, though I will if I have to, but I don't think there is a need. I rush past her on the side and keep running,

"Pixie?"

It's Hayden again. He's right up ahead, in the bedroom on the left. I rush into the room and raise my gun because he's going to tell me where my son is or . . .

And there's Matthew.

I freeze. The gun is in my hand. My son is staring up at me. Our eyes meet and the eyes are still my boy's. In Times Square I felt a sensory overload. Here I experience something similar, but it is all internal, in my blood and veins, a thrum that rushes through every part of me with no outlet, no way to escape. I may be shaking. I'm not sure.

Then I notice the hands on his shoulders.

"Theo," Hayden says, trying hard to keep his tone even, "this is my friend David. We're playing a game with the guns, aren't we, David?"

My first thought is a strange one: Matthew is eight years old, not four. He's not falling for that line. I can see it in his face. Part of me just wants to end this now, to raise my gun and blow this motherfucker away and deal with the aftermath. But my son is here. Like it or not, this is the man he sees as a father. My son is not scared of him. I can see that. He is, heartbreaking as it sounds, scared of me.

I can't shoot Hayden in front of Matthew.

"David, this is my son Theo."

I feel my finger on the trigger. Then again, I've already shot two people. What is one more?

In the distance I hear a noise. The room, like the rest of the house, is modern, with floor-to-ceiling windows. I move toward them and look out. A helicopter comes into view, landing on the open lawn.

The old woman he'd called Pixie comes in and stands next to me. "Come on, Theo. It's time to go."

"He's not going anywhere," I say.

Pixie meets my eyes and there is the smallest smile on her face. "What's your plan here, David? We've called the local police. Freddy—that's the chief of police here—is on his way with probably half the force. They know you're armed and dangerous and that you've already shot two men. I think Stephano is dead. Freddy loves Stephano. They play poker once a week. If you're lucky—if you put the gun down and now stand on the lawn with your arms high in the air—you may, *may* not get shot."

"I know what you both did," I say.

"But you'll never be able to prove it. What evidence do you have?"

I look over at Theo. He doesn't seem particularly scared anymore. He looks more puzzled and engaged, an expression that's a heartbreaking echo of his mother's.

"You think, what?" Pixie continues. "They'll run a DNA test on the boy? Not a chance. You need a court order. You need to convince a judge that there is compelling reason, and we know every judge in the land. We have the best attorneys. We work hand in hand with every politician. Theo will be back overseas by the time you're back rotting up in Briggs."

"Besides," Hayden adds, "it's like I told Rachel—what do you think a test would show?" He grinned. "You want to raise a boy with the Payne blood coursing through his veins? He's my son."

I glance at the old woman and see something cross her face.

Then I say, "No, Hayden, he's not."

Hayden looks puzzled. He looks toward the woman he calls Pixie. Her eyes are on the floor.

"I never believed my wife when she said she didn't go through with it," I say. "It was, I think, the final straw in our marriage. We tried with Matthew, but I'm not sure as a couple we would have survived."

Hayden looks at Pixie. "What's he talking about?"

I take out my phone. "I was able to get into my old email address. Here. These emails are eight years old. When I found out Cheryl went to a fertility clinic, I took a paternity test. Two, in fact. Just to be sure. It confirms that I'm Matthew's father."

His eyes almost bulge out of their sockets. "That's impossible," he says. "Pixie?"

She ignores him. "Come along, Theo."

"Don't," I say.

"You won't shoot me," she says.

"But I will."

It's Rachel. She steps into the room with gun in hand. "Hayden?"

He's shaking his head no.

"Let me guess," Rachel says. "You brought Matthew back here. You were in a panic. You wondered whether you'd done the right thing. That's what you told me, right?"

He still shakes his head. I hear the sirens approaching.

"If the paternity test came back that you weren't the father, what would you have done? Told the truth probably. Confessed." Rachel looks over toward Pixie. "She couldn't have that. She lied, Hayden. You aren't the father. It shouldn't matter. A father isn't about biology. But he's David's son. David and Cheryl's."

Hayden's voice is that of a little boy. "Pixie?"

I hear sirens. For a moment I figure she's going to deny it, but there doesn't seem to be that fight in her. "You'd have given him back," she says. "Or worse. Either way, you'd have destroyed the family. So yes, I told you what you wanted—needed—to hear."

Squad cars, at least ten of them, race up the drive and set up in formation outside the house.

"It doesn't matter, Hayden," Pixie says. "You two need to go to the helicopter."

"No."

It's my son speaking now.

"I want to know what's going on here," Matthew says.

"This is all part of the game, Theo," Pixie says.

"How stupid do you think I am?" He looks at me. "You're my father."

I can't tell if it's a question or a statement. The cops are in the house now, running up the stairs, shouting about coming out with my hands up and all that. But I barely hear it. I ignore it all. I only see my son.

My son.

I am tempted to get down on one knee, but in truth, Matthew is an eight-year-old boy, not a toddler. I meet his eye and say, "Yes. I'm your father. He kidnapped you when you were three."

My son is looking at me. Our eyes meet. He doesn't turn away. He doesn't blink. Neither do I. It is the purest moment of my life. My son and I. Together. And I know he gets it. I know he understands.

And as that realization washes over me, the first bullet hits my body.

Eight Months Later

I stand to the left of my aunt Sophie as my father's casket, a plain pine box, is lowered into the ground. Philip and Adam Mackenzie are both pallbearers. Cops young, old, and retired have come out in big numbers. My father had a lot of friends. He hadn't been in their lives in a long time, but they've come out to say a final goodbye.

I can feel Uncle Philip's eyes on me. He gives me the smallest of nods, but it says a lot. He was there. He'll be there.

I was shot three times at the Payne estate.

It would have been more. That's what I was told. But Matthew ran over to me. When the cops saw that, they stopped firing. I wasn't conscious for any of that.

From my right side, I feel a small hand slip into mine. It's comforting. I turn and smile down at Matthew. I look past my son to Rachel, who holds Matthew's other hand. She gives me a small smile, and my chest fills. I meet her eye and let her know I'm doing okay.

My father had been sick for a long time. He was more than ready to go. I think he held on long enough to see me exonerated—and to see his grandson again.

I can't tell you how grateful I am for that.

We all lower our head for the Kaddish. I am first in line to throw ceremonial dirt on my father's grave. Aunt Sophie goes next. I hold her arm as she does it, more for my balance than hers. I spent two months in the hospital and went through six operations. I'm told that it is unlikely I will ever walk without a cane again, but I'm going to work my ass off in physical therapy.

I like trying to defy the odds. I'm good at that, I guess.

After the funeral we head back to the old house in Revere to sit shiva. The ghosts are there, of course, but they seem respectfully quiet today. None of us are religious, but we find solace in the ritual. Friends have sent us enough food to fill Fenway Park. I sit in the low chair, as is the custom, and listen to stories of my dad. It is a comfort.

Aunt Sophie will live here alone now.

"This neighborhood," she told me. "It's all I know."

I understand, of course.

When there is a break in the line of mourners, Aunt Sophie nudges my arm and gestures toward Rachel. Rachel is helping set out yet another plate of sloppy joe sandwiches.

"So you and Rachel . . . ?" she asks.

"Early days," I say.

Aunt Sophie smiles. She will have none of that. "Not so early. I'm very happy about it. Your father was too."

I swallow and stare at this woman I love. "She makes me happy," I tell my aunt. And I'm not sure I've ever meant something so much in my life.

Special Agent Max Bernstein is at the end of the mourners' line with his partner Sarah Jablonski. They both shake my hand and offer their condolences. Bernstein's eyes dart all over the room.

"I don't know if this is the right time," Bernstein says to me.

"For?"

"For giving you an update."

I look at his partner, then back to him. "It's the right time," I say.

Jablonski takes that one. "We may have a lead on . . . on the victim's identity."

The little boy in Matthew's bed. I look toward Bernstein.

"There's an overseas orphanage the Payne family runs," he says. "That's all we know right now."

"But we'll learn more," Jablonski adds.

I believe them. But I don't think it will be enough.

It took three months for me to be freed. Philip and Adam both lost their jobs. There is still talk about prosecuting them and even Rachel for aiding and abetting. They also make noise about the two "security guards" I shot at the Payne estate. But our attorney Hester Crimstein seems to think nothing will come of any of that. I hope she's right.

I need to stretch my legs, especially the one that took the bullet, so I stand. I am about to head toward the kitchen when I stop.

Nicky Fisher stands in the corner with his arms folded. He is watching me.

The night before, Nicky flew up from his Florida compound and came right to the house in Revere. He asked me to step outside, so we could talk in private on the front porch. My two goon friends were on the walkway, standing by a black SUV. They waved to me. I waved back.

Nicky Fisher stared up into the starless black sky and said, "I'm sorry about your old man."

"Thank you."

"Tell me everything, David. Leave nothing out."

So I did.

You, like Nicky Fisher, will probably want to hear how both Gertrude and Hayden Payne are now serving long prison sentences. They are not. After I was shot, Max showed up at the estate. Uncle Philip had confided in him, and so he understood a lot of it. That helped. Still, when I was stable, I was taken back to the Briggs infirmary. The wheels of justice churn slowly. There was, as the Paynes had pointed out to me, not much evidence of any crime committed by Hayden or his grandmother. No clue Hayden had been involved in any murder or kidnapping other than, well, having Matthew. No clue Gertrude Payne knew anything other than that Hayden had told her that this boy was his son. How did Hayden end up with the boy? Hayden told a story about an Italian actress being the mother. Yes, these were lies. Some were obvious. But when you have a team of powerful lawyers, judges, and politicians who can gaslight with the best of them, those wheels grind to a halt.

Money greases the wheels. Money can also stop them.

I explained all this to Nicky Fisher on the front porch last night. Nicky Fisher listened without interrupting. When I finished, Nicky said, "That can't stand."

"What can't stand?"

"Them getting away with it."

Then Nicky Fisher walked off the front porch, and the SUV drove him away.

Now he's back. Our eyes lock, the old man's and mine, and he too nods at me. But this nod is different from Uncle Philip's. This one sends a cold finger down my spine, but a cold finger that could be good or bad.

I'm going to go with good for me, bad for the Paynes.

I make my way through the mourners, nodding, smiling, shaking hands. When I reach the kitchen, I see Ronald Dreason, Cheryl's husband, looking out the back window into my old yard. I stand next to him.

"You doing okay?" Ronald asks me.

I nod. "Thanks for being here."

"Of course," he says.

We stand side by side looking out that kitchen window. Cheryl is there. She is holding her four-month-old daughter, Ellie, in her arms. I sneak a glance at Ronald, the proud father, and see him smile at them. He loves Cheryl. I'm happy about that too.

"Your daughter is beautiful," I say to him.

"Yeah." Ronald is practically bursting. "Yeah, she is."

And there, standing in my old backyard with his mother, is Matthew.

It is new, all of this, but for now Cheryl and I are sharing custody of our son. He spends one week with Cheryl and Ronald. Then he spends one week with Rachel and me. So far, it seems to be working.

And how is Matthew?

He has nightmares, but fewer than you'd think. Children are resilient, him especially so. Will there be long-term adverse effects? Everyone says that's likely, but I'm more optimistic. Eight years is a curious age. He's old enough to understand most of it. You can't lie about what happened or try to sugarcoat it. Hayden treated Matthew well, thank God, but the boy had spent most of his life parentless in a ritzy Swiss boarding school. He seems to miss his friends and teachers more than the man he once believed was his father. But he has nice memories of Hayden. He asks me about that, about how a man who could have done such evil could also be kind. I try to explain to him that human beings are more complex than we know, but of course, I don't really have an answer.

I watch now as Rachel hands little Ellie to her brother.

Matthew loves his sister. He holds her gently, carefully, like she's made of glass, but his face beams. As I stare out at him, at my beautiful son, I feel Rachel's arm snake around me. She stands there and watches too. We all do, all of us struggling to make a life together, and maybe somewhere my father is watching too.

Acknowledgments

The author (who every once in a while likes to refer to himself in the third person) would like to thank the following in no particular order: Ben Sevier, Michael Pietsch, Wes Miller, Kirsiah Depp, Beth de Guzman, Karen Kosztolnyik, Lauren Bello, Jonathan Valuckas, Matthew Ballast, Brian McLendon, Staci Burt, Andrew Duncan, Alexis Gilbert, Janine Perez, Joseph Benincase, Albert Tang, Liz Connor, Rena Kornbluh, Mari Okuda, Rick Ball, Selina Walker, Charlotte Bush, Becke Parker, Sarah Ridley, Glenn O'Neill, Mat Watterson, Richard Rowlands, Fred Friedman, Diane Discepolo, Charlotte Coben, Anne Armstrong-Coben, Lisa Erbach Vance, Cole Galvin, and Robby Hull.

This is the part where we authors usually note that all mistakes are ours, but really, these people are the experts. Why should I take all the heat?

I'd also like to give a quick shout-out to George Belbey, Kathy Cobrera, Tom Florio, Lauren Ford, Hans Laaspere,

Barb Matteson, and Wayne Semsey. These people (or their loved ones) made generous contributions to charities of my choosing in return for having their name appear in this novel. If you'd like to participate in the future, email giving@harlancoben.com.

About the Author

Harlan Coben is a #1 *New York Times* bestselling author and one of the world's leading storytellers. His suspense novels are published in forty-six languages and have been number one bestsellers in more than a dozen countries, with eighty million books in print worldwide. His Myron Bolitar series has earned the Edgar, Shamus and Anthony Awards, and five of his books have been developed into Netflix original series, including *The Stranger*, *The Innocent*, *Gone for Good*, *The Woods*, *Stay Close* and *Hold Tight*, as well as the upcoming Amazon Prime series adaptation of *Shelter*. He lives in New Jersey.

For more information you can visit:

HarlanCoben.com
Twitter: @HarlanCoben
Facebook.com/HarlanCobenBooks
Netflix.com/HarlanCoben

WITHDRÁWN

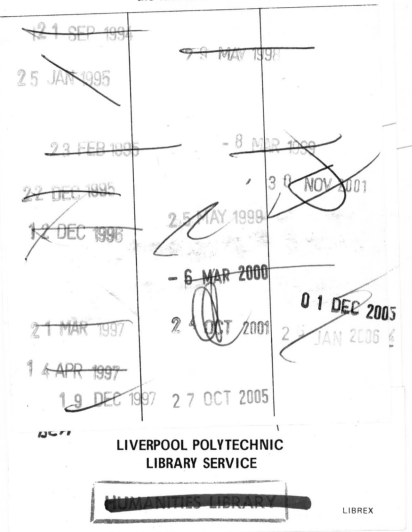

This book is to be returned on or before

Books are to be returned on or before
the last date below.

2 1 SEP 1994

25 JAN 1995

2 3 FEB 1995

2 2 DEC 1995

1 2 DEC 1996

9 9 MAY 1998

- 8 MAR 1999

3 0 NOV 2001

2 5 MAY 1999

- 6 MAR 2000

0 1 DEC 2005

2 1 MAR 1997

2 4 OCT 2001

2 JAN 2006

1 4 APR 1997

1 9 DEC 1997   2 7 OCT 2005

**LIVERPOOL POLYTECHNIC
LIBRARY SERVICE**

HUMANITIES LIBRARY

LIBREX